ROYAL INSTITUTE OF MAGIC

THE SILVER DWARF

VICTOR KLOSS

ALSO BY VICTOR KLOSS

The Royal Institute of Magic Series

Elizabeth's Legacy

The Shadowseeker

The Protectors

The Silver Dwarf

The Last Guardian

The High Council

Vinci Books

vinci-books.com
Published by Vinci Books Ltd in 2026

1

This work is a work of fiction. Names, characters, places and incidents are the product of the author's imagination or are used fictitiously. Any resemblance to actual persons, living or dead, places and incidents is entirely coincidental.

A CIP catalogue record for this book is available from the British Library.
Paperback ISBN: 9781036707033
The EU GPSR authorised representative is Logos Europe, 9 rue Nicolas Poussion, 17000 La Rochelle, France contact@logoseurope.eu

CHAPTER I
DANGEROUS DECISIONS

Date: *24th August 1614*

Michael Greenwood glanced back, and saw a flash of the red and gold – the royal guard; lots of them. Another glance. How many? Ten? Twenty? It was hard to tell as they had spread out among the many alleys and lanes. Their intention was obvious – they were blocking any chance of escape.

The royal guards weren't after him, but only because they weren't aware he was back in town. However, the bounty for the man they were after was almost as big.

Angus Breeze, Guardian of Elizabeth's Breastplate.

Michael increased his pace, darting through

narrow passages and stepping over foul-smelling puddles that soaked the muddy ground. The weather was grim, matching his mood. Dark clouds blocked the summer sun and a brisk breeze whipped through the alleyways. It was noisy here, with people flogging their wares and complaining about the weather. Their chatter would cease the moment they spotted the royal guards.

Michael came to a crossroads and he paused. His heart jumped as he spotted guards in both directions, and he quickly concealed his features underneath his hood. For a moment he thought they might have spotted him, but his concern eased when the subsequent charging and screaming failed to materialise.

The road started to gently incline. At the top of the hill was his intended destination. Five minutes away, no more, which meant the royal guards would be there in less than ten, assuming they knew exactly where to go. Michael broke into a jog, his eyes fixed on an unassuming wooden house in the distance. He gave a little smile as he approached. Angus could have lived anywhere with the salary the Institute paid him as the Director of Diplomacy, but he had always preferred mediocrity over extravagance. Such anonymity was the sole reason Angus was the last remaining director with a house in London that hadn't been destroyed. But that honour was going to last only another ten minutes.

The front door was a little cleaner than its neighbours, and there were colourful flowerpots by the entrance, but nothing else gave any clue as to the type of individual who lived inside.

Michael rapped the handle three times. He gave several furtive glances about while waiting for a reply.

A friendly, perfectly round face appeared, and gave a smile the moment he recognised the visitor.

"Ah, Director Greenwood, what a pleasant surprise," Angus said, opening the door to let Michael in.

Michael stepped inside and shut the door quickly. He turned to Angus, who appeared so relaxed that he was clearly oblivious to the threat that was about to enter his house. He was short and chubby, reminding Michael of a snowman, with a beach ball stomach matching his balding head. He had big, friendly, brown eyes, which in most circumstances could calm the most bad-tempered argument – hence the role of Director of Diplomacy.

"They're coming," Michael said, walking past Angus and into his small living space. "You need to pack up essentials and get out of here."

Michael turned, and saw Angus giving him a good-natured smile.

"I know they're coming," Angus said, ambling

forwards leisurely. "I've been expecting them actually."

Michael frowned. "Then why are you still here?"

"I'm going to talk to them," Angus said, plucking a piece of fruit from a bowl on the table.

"Angus, no," Michael said, his voice suddenly urgent. "Nobody knows more than me how good you are with your voice, but the royal guards might as well be deaf. You've got more chance of getting a pig to stop eating."

"You are right," Angus said with a shrug of his wide shoulders. "But it would be deeply hypocritical of me not to try. How can I possibly encourage people to resolve conflicts by communication if I don't do it myself?"

"In most circumstances, I would agree with you," Michael said. "But they have Captain Moorlock with them."

Michael said the name with an undertone of gravity and resentment, but, to his surprise, Angus appeared unflustered.

"I know he is with them, and I also know my chances of persuading someone as zealous as Moorlock are virtually non-existent."

"Then why try?"

"Because I must," Angus said. He smiled, but Michael could detect a hint of sadness in those eyes. "Even Captain Moorlock has some humanity to him."

"I would argue that point," Michael said.

The sound of faint footsteps interrupted their conversation. Michael hurried to the window and peered down the hill.

"They're almost here."

Angus nodded. "Good." His relaxed expression became grave. "Now, you must go, Michael. They do not know you are here, and it would put your family and friends in danger were they to see that you are back in London. I will be fine by myself."

Michael ran a hand through his hair. His eyes went to Angus's ample hips; there was no spell-shooter, nor any sign of a weapon.

"I'm not going anywhere," Michael said, touching his own spellshooter. "You will need me, once diplomacy fails. They are armed, and they will not be gentle."

Angus walked with frustrating leisure over to the table and picked up a broom leaning against it. He unscrewed the brush at the end.

"Now I am armed," Angus said with a smile.

"I'm not sure how well a stick will fare against the swords of the royal guard," Michael said.

Michael made a move to stand beside him, but Angus raised a hand. "In ordinary circumstances, a quarterstaff would not be sufficient. But I have something else to add a little punch."

Angus lifted his jumper. Underneath was a

gleaming silver breastplate, fitted snugly against Angus's round stomach.

Michael's eyes widened, and his heart skipped a beat. "You have the Queen's Breastplate here? Angus, that's madness. We were instructed to hide each piece to the very best of our ability, not keep it at home as a curiosity."

Angus nodded, looking suitably guilty. "You are right, but I have an explanation for keeping Her Majesty's Breastplate here. However, I fear it will have to wait, as we have guests."

The sound of the footsteps grew, and Michael saw a flash of colour beyond the window. He turned quickly back to Angus.

"The breastplate – do you know what powers it holds?"

Angus nodded. "Yes, I can feel it. Trust me, I will be okay. You need to go before they arrive."

Michael smiled. "I'm not going anywhere. But I will disappear."

He lifted his spellshooter, pointed it to his chest, and fired. A small white pellet exploded into his shirt, and the world shimmered. He positioned himself at the corner of the room. He might have been invisible, but he wasn't a ghost, and if the royal guard accidentally crashed into him, they would immediately suspect an intruder.

"Good luck. You're going to need it," Michael said.

A heavy rapping on the door drowned out Angus's reply.

"Open up in the name of the prince!" a commanding voice said. Michael recognised Captain Moorlock's nasal tone immediately.

"Certainly," Angus said, and ambled forwards to open the door.

As soon as it was ajar, Captain Moorlock pushed the door violently, sending Angus stumbling backwards. Moorlock strode right past him, and waved his soldiers in.

"I want six upstairs and six down here," Moorlock said briskly. "I want no stone unturned. If I come up there and find even the smallest closet that hasn't been thoroughly searched, you will all be fined a day's pay."

The royal guards filed in, and immediately got to work. Chairs were upturned, dishes were broken and Angus's possessions were strewn carelessly across the floor.

Angus watched calmly as his house was destroyed. Michael toyed with his spellshooter, but as if reading Michael's mind, Angus raised a hand and gave a subtle shake of the head.

Captain Moorlock turned to face Angus. He was

tall but skinny. The cruel smile on his thin lips were, Michael suspected, part of his default expression. His neck protruded forwards, like a vulture, and his long, pointed nose seemed perfectly suited for poking into other people's business.

"You are under arrest, Breeze," Moorlock said, spitting out the words with relish. "If you tell us where the breastplate is, I may be able to have a word with the judge and convince him to order a painless death."

"Most kind of you," Angus said. His hands were placed behind his back, which gave the effect of his ample stomach being thrust out even further than normal. "On what charge, may I ask?"

"Treason," Moorlock said, stamping the point of his sword into the floorboards for emphasis. "Colluding with the Royal Institute of Magic and hiding a piece of Elizabeth's Armour, keeping it from the prince, its rightful owner. Spying on the king's allies, selling information to the French and seeking to supply them with magical weapons. Need I go on?"

Michael watched Angus as Moorlock delivered his damning indictment.

"I do find some of those accusations slightly difficult to believe," Angus said, now tapping the broomstick against his hand. "First of all, technically, the prince is commander of the Institute, so I'm unsure how colluding with them would constitute treason. Secondly, I have several documents, witnessed by some of the highest lawmakers in the country, testifying to the transference of ownership of the late queen's armour. Finally, the French and I are not on good terms, since they kidnapped and tortured my cousin."

Michael saw a look of regret cross a couple of nearby royal guards' faces. Angus's soft, honest voice had a way of changing ordinary people's minds. But Moorlock was not an ordinary person, and Angus's clear rationale seemed only to infuriate Moorlock further. He went red, and then a funny shade of purple. But before he could speak, Angus continued.

"No sane man would call me a traitor. And to prove it, I will happily submit myself before a court of justice. All I ask for is to be treated as innocent until proven guilty."

Angus's offer clearly resonated with some of the royal guards – one or two even relaxed a little. But Moorlock shook his head, and gave a nasty smile.

"Nice try, silver tongue," Moorlock said. "But your honeyed voice doesn't fool me. Innocent until proven guilty? Madness."

Most people would have missed it, but Michael spotted the subtle change in Angus's expression. The faint hope there had been of some productive dialogue disappeared. He still looked calm, serene even, but Michael could see Angus's grip on the broomstick tighten. Angus might have acted as a successful peace negotiator between some of the most powerful Unseen Kingdoms, but at the end of the day, it was difficult to reason with an insane man.

Moorlock drew his sword and stepped forwards, thrusting it right under Angus's chin, and turned to one of his guards, who was busy de-feathering Angus's couch.

"Lucas, have you found the breastplate yet? I was reliably informed that Angus was keeping it here. It's a breastplate, not a needle – it can't be that hard to find. Don't make me punish your soldiers for failing to find it."

Lucas cringed. "Sorry, Captain. We have looked everywhere, but it is nowhere to be found."

"Have you tried beneath the floorboards? Start ripping them out."

Angus gave a polite cough. "You won't find it there, I'm afraid."

Moorlock wheeled back to Angus, daggers in his eyes. "This is your last chance, Moorlock. Tell us where you are hiding the breastplate or face a slow, agonising death. We have torturers who can make you scream until your vocal cords give out."

"Well, here's the thing," Angus said with a little smile. "You failed to look in the most obvious place."

"What are you talking about?" Moorlock spat.

Angus lifted his jumper, revealing the breastplate underneath.

Moorlock's eyes turned into saucers, and he almost dropped his sword in astonishment.

"You dare wear the prince's armour?" Moorlock asked, his voice a whisper. He appeared momentarily lost for words.

Michael couldn't tell if he was just stunned into silence or lost in the beauty of the breastplate.

Moorlock shook himself out of his stupor. "Guards! Remove the breastplate from Angus's body."

The guards quickly surrounded Angus, swords drawn. Michael frowned, and readied his spell-shooter. Angus was resting an arm on the broom-stick, but made no move to defend himself. The royal guards hesitated, their eyes anxious.

"What are you waiting for?" Moorlock shouted. Michael noted that Moorlock himself was standing outside the circle. "It's one small, overweight man against a dozen of you. Attack!"

Michael knew exactly why they were waiting. Angus was wearing Elizabeth's Breastplate. There were many rumours of its power, most of them false.

In a fit of courage, the guard directly in front of Angus raised his sword and charged, a manic gleam in his eye. With two quick steps he was upon Angus, and he swung his sword in a vicious arc into Angus's midriff. The sword hit the armour and promptly shattered, as if it were made of glass. The guard stepped back in astonishment.

"Let's get this over with, shall we?" Angus said, lifting his makeshift quarterstaff.

Three of the braver guards charged, encouraged by Moorlock, who was pointing his sword and screaming at the consequences of their cowardice. Michael trained his spellshooter on the attackers, but he needn't have bothered. Angus swung his quarter-staff, ignoring the sword thrusts that penetrated his limited defence, and moments later three royal guards were rolling on the ground in pain.

"Get that breastplate off him!" Moorlock screamed.

The rest of the guards attacked, trying to crush him with the weight of numbers. But Angus charged forwards, and broke free of the circle. His quarterstaff was a blur, and Michael winced as it cracked against limbs. A couple of the guards had the sense to strike Angus's exposed areas, and Michael grimaced as a sword grazed Angus's cheek, drawing blood. But to his amazement, the wound healed within moments, leaving only the faintest scar.

The fight took less than three minutes. Moorlock stared in horror at his fallen guards. He lifted a trembling sword at Angus.

"Don't hurt me," he said, his lips quivering. "I can offer you a pardon. I can offer you freedom."

Michael almost choked in disgust, but Angus kept a level head.

"No, you won't. As soon as you leave, you will run back to the palace and get reinforcements." He sighed. "Get your men, and leave. Some of them require medical attention."

Michael knew Moorlock wanted to leave without his guards, but he wasn't about to disobey the man who had taken down his entire unit with nothing more than a broomstick. So he dragged each man out, until Angus and Michael were once again alone.

Michael fired another spell into his chest, removing the invisibility that shrouded him.

"That was impressive. I don't remember you being that handy with a quarterstaff. Was that the breastplate?"

"In part," Angus said. "Amongst other things, it increases my reaction time and strengthens my muscles. You probably noticed that it also helps me heal."

Michael smiled. "Yes, I noticed." His smile faded as he looked around the ruined house. "Why did you let them search the place? You could have stopped them."

"It doesn't matter," Angus said. "I'm leaving."

Michael relaxed. "About time. You should have

moved to the Unseen Kingdoms the moment Elizabeth passed away. I know some really nice houses on the west side of Taecia, not far from my place."

"I'm not moving house," Angus said. He fixed the broomstick back onto the brush and idly started sweeping. It was a lost cause – the place was a wreck – but Angus had always been a bit of a neat freak.

"I don't follow," Michael said, frowning. "Do you intend to be a beggar?"

"I plan on travelling," Angus said. "I need somewhere to hide the breastplate. Somewhere secure, somewhere nobody would think of looking, with natural defences that are almost impossible to breach."

"You have a place in mind?" Michael asked.

"I have an idea," Angus said. "It is based on a whisper of a rumour, and I need to go there to confirm whether it might work. It is deep within the Unseen Kingdoms, and there are some very unfriendly, dangerous people there." Angus stopped sweeping for a moment, and gave Michael a long look. "I may not make it back."

"Surely there is somewhere less dangerous to hide the breastplate? Somewhere without people who might kill you?" Michael asked.

Angus gave a little smile. "Those are the very people I plan to use to help me guard the armour."

Michael couldn't contain his surprise. "How are

you going to manage that? Even if you could convince them, could they be trusted with the breastplate?"

"If they are the people I believe they are, then yes," Angus said. "I have seen first-hand how desperate the prince has become. And the breastplate..." Angus paused, considering his words. "Let's just say the breastplate, more than any of the other pieces, would not be good for him. It would be very, very dangerous for the prince to get his hands on it."

Having seen Angus wearing it, Michael believed him.

"I'm guessing you want to keep your proposed destination a secret?"

Angus nodded. "We all keep our hiding places a secret. But if my plan comes off, the prince will never get his hands on the breastplate."

"And if you don't?"

Angus looked right into Michael's eyes. "Then you may have to come and find me."

Michael stared long and hard at his old companion, and placed a hand on his shoulder. Of all the directors, Angus was his closest friend, closer even than Charlotte. They both came from humble beginnings, and they both had to face adversity from outside the Institute and within to get to the top. The thought of losing him made his stomach churn. He desperately wanted to change Angus's mind, but knew it would be fruitless. Angus was a stubborn man.

"Good luck," Michael said.

He couldn't shake the feeling that, somehow, he would never see Angus again.

He was right.

CHAPTER 2

CHASING THE KEY

Date: *Present Day*

Ben pumped his arms as he ran, his eyes focused on a tiny gleaming sparkle in the distance. The key – their one possible clue to the next piece of Elizabeth's Armour – was getting away from them. It cut through the air, like a hawk on a mission.

"I'm losing it!" Ben said with increasing panic.

Natalie ran – or rather, glided – beside him, her feet flying over the grass.

"I can still see it," she said, sounding more like she was taking a pleasant walk, rather than sprinting over the hillside.

Ben filed in behind her as they cut between small

valleys and up gentle hills. Had he not been so focused on following the key, Ben might have admired the lush green countryside and the flowers that sprinkled the hills. There was a stiff breeze, which helped cool him down as he tried to keep up with Natalie.

"There it is!" Natalie said, pointing.

They stopped at the base of a hill so steep it was almost vertical.

"Well done, Nat," Ben said, as he took several deep breaths to recover.

The key was half-buried into the grass on the hill, and only the ornate hilt could be seen.

Ben heard heavy footsteps and the sound of laboured breathing, and he turned. Charlie's face was a bright tomato, but beneath the anguish of running was a look of triumph.

"I must be getting fitter," Charlie said, when he got his breath back. "I managed to run almost five minutes without collapsing. What do you reckon?"

"Oh, absolutely," Ben and Natalie chimed in.

Charlie nodded happily, unaware of the sarcasm, and they turned to the key embedded in the hill.

"What's so special about this hill?" Natalie wondered out loud.

Ben went up to the key and grabbed its handle. He gave it a shake.

"It's stuck in a keyhole," Ben said with suppressed excitement.

Charlie and Natalie stepped up to take a closer look.

"Can you turn it?" Charlie asked.

Ben applied pressure, and the key turned easily, giving a loud click. He pulled it open, using the key as a handle. A small door, covered in grass and mud, swung open. The bright sun revealed a narrow, dark passageway that descended downwards.

"Oh my word," Charlie said, stepping back, and wafting his hand in front of his nose. "What is that smell?"

"It smells of..." Natalie's voice faded, and her eyes widened.

"It smells of death," Ben said.

They stared into the passageway with growing alarm. The smell was faint, but unmistakable.

"Are there any alternatives to going in?" Charlie asked.

"I can't think of any," Natalie said, glancing at Ben for confirmation.

Natalie was right. They had been given the key by Nigel Winkleforth, one of three Protectors responsible for safeguarding Elizabeth's Helm. It made sense that Winkleforth might also have some connection to another piece of the armour. Or so Ben kept telling himself.

"This is our only lead," Ben said.

Charlie frowned. "Doesn't it seem like a rather large coincidence that the key happens to fly off and end up here? What were the chances of us being near this hill in the first place?"

"You're right. Perhaps we got lucky or maybe there is another reason. But it doesn't matter – this is where the key led us, and it's our only lead."

Charlie loosened his spellshooter with a sigh, but the mystery the key presented eased his anxiety.

Ben took a deep breath, and stepped into the passageway. He was immediately plunged into near darkness. He fired a simple light spell, and a flare ignited from the tip of his barrel, illuminating the path.

The passage was wide enough only for single file, so he led, and Charlie brought up the rear, with Natalie in the middle. The passage was created as if the builders had been trying to make as much progress as possible without much attention to structure. The ceiling was uneven and only at the very centre could they stand up straight. Occasionally the passage would widen to fit two abreast, but then it would narrow so dramatically that they would have to sidestep to keep going.

They walked in silence for what seemed like an eternity, the only sound coming from their footsteps on the rough stone floor. The path wound left and right, but always maintained its gradual descent.

The smell started to get stronger. At first, it was faint enough to almost ignore, but gradually it became worse, until it seemed to clog the passage and seep into their pores.

"Is anyone else getting a bad feeling about this?" Charlie asked, breaking the silence. "I don't want to alarm you, but this smell of decay is most likely going to come from dead bodies and, by the smell of it, lots of them."

"Dead bodies can't hurt you," Natalie said.

"No, but what if there are some still living?" Charlie said.

Ben was about to reply when he noticed a faint glow in the distance. He stopped instinctively, and Natalie bumped into him.

"Looks like we're about to get to wherever we're going," Ben said. "Make sure you have your spell-shooters handy."

He continued forwards slowly, his spellshooter held in front of him. Now more than ever silence was required, but it was difficult with the smell, which was so overwhelming he had to stop himself gagging on several occasions. He took deep, calming breaths, but he could do nothing about his beating heart, which sounded like a bass drum, reverberating off the walls.

He stopped just before the end of the passageway, wiped his sweaty hands on his shirt, and stepped through, into the dim light.

Ben stared in horror at the sight.

Below them, dead bodies littered the floor of what looked like a great underground hall. Dwarves and dark elves lay sprawled everywhere, caked in blood, with weapons criss-crossing their bodies. There was barely room to walk between them all. The smell was clearly coming from the bodies, but unlike humans, there was almost no sign of decay, making it impossible to date the incident.

Ben wasn't sure how long he stared at the carnage before he finally had the sense to scan the rest of the hall for danger.

Nothing moved. He cast his eye upwards to the vaulted ceiling, from which a dull light shone, illuminating the horrific scene below. Ben saw no movement there either. The place was a graveyard.

A gagging noise made Ben turn, and he saw Charlie vomiting on the floor, hands on knees. Natalie was coping marginally better, though her face had turned pale and she also looked ready to be sick.

"I can't go down there," Charlie said, pulling out a handkerchief and wiping his mouth.

For once, Ben had no witty, tongue-in-cheek

response. He too had no stomach for trawling through piles of dead bodies. Instead, they remained where they were, until the initial shock and horror started to wear off.

"What happened here?" Natalie asked, her voice a whisper.

"Looks like the dark elves attacked the dwarves," Ben said.

Eventually they made their way down to the great hall, via a steep staircase, and they were soon walking among the bodies. Ben felt his stomach heave more than once, and tried averting his eyes from the carnage. Behind him, he heard Charlie attempt to empty his stomach again. Both he and Natalie looked ready to faint.

"You think this was the dwarves' home, then?" Natalie asked.

Ben nodded. "I think so. We know dwarves are far more likely to live underground. The dark elves must have attacked them."

"But why would they want to do that?"

"A more appropriate question might be – when?" Charlie said, finding his voice.

Ben forced himself to look at the dead bodies. They were pale and lifeless, the blood dry. Even close up there was no sign of decay, though it stank to high heaven.

"Can't be more than a week or two, would be my guess," Ben said.

"Who won the fight, do you think?" Natalie asked.

"The dark elves," Ben said. "Those who survived must have left already. The dwarves wouldn't have left their dead colleagues to rot."

"Are you sure all the dark elves have gone?" Natalie asked, looking around furtively. There were several passageways leading out from the hall, but nobody felt inclined to search them.

"I think we'd know if any were left," Ben said. "No, what I want to know is why did the dark elves come in the first place? And why did the key lead us here?"

"What's that?"

Charlie's voice echoed loudly in the hall, in sharp contrast to their hushed whispers and ruining their efforts at keeping a low profile. He was pointing and looking intently at the far corner of the room.

Ben couldn't believe he hadn't noticed it before. A small energy dome surrounded a dwarf sitting cross-legged on the floor. His eyes were closed, but he was clearly still alive.

They picked their way through the bodies. Charlie accidentally stepped on several heads and other dead body parts, but he barely noticed, so intent was he on their target. Nevertheless, Ben picked the path of fewest dead people, and it took them several minutes to reach the dwarf.

He was most definitely still living and looked completely unharmed. Ben extended his hand out, but, as he expected, it came up against the shimmering barrier protecting the dwarf.

"Fascinating," Charlie said. All anxiety had gone from him now, replaced with interest and curiosity.

This dwarf was clearly not like the others. He wore no armour and was dressed all in red, with a hood that partially covered his bright ginger hair. On his lap was a small staff with a glowing orb at its tip. The dwarf was frowning, and making occasional twitches of his lips, as if he were involved in a bad dream.

"Hello?" Ben said, waving his hand in front of the dwarf.

"He's not going to hear you," Charlie said softly, staring intently at the dwarf.

"How about if I go louder?" Ben suggested.

"It wouldn't make a difference if you brought a full symphony orchestra down here," Charlie said.

"Why not? Do you think he's in some sort of trance?"

"Not quite," Charlie said. He turned to Ben. "If I'm reading all the signs correctly, I think he's gone into the void."

Ben felt his stomach do funny things at the

mention of the void. It was a strange other-worldly place that, from what he'd read, sounded like a version of hell. While there in spirit, your body could not be harmed in the physical world. His parents had used it to protect themselves from the dark elf king, and it seemed the dwarf was doing the same.

"I bet his only way to stay alive was to flee into the void," Charlie said.

"But why hasn't he come back?" Natalie asked. "I would have thought he'd want to return as soon as it was safe."

"I don't know," Charlie admitted. "Perhaps he doesn't know it's safe here, or perhaps he can't return. I've read that it can be difficult to get back."

"Why didn't the dark elves follow him in?" Ben said. Glancing around, there was clearly no sign of anyone else having entered the void nearby.

"Oh, that's obvious," Charlie said, waving a hand. "The demons recognise the dark elves as a true threat to their domain, and always wipe out that enter. It's not that the dark elves couldn't hold their own, but it would take a concerted effort, and I think they'd rather focus on conquering the Unseen Kingdoms."

The three of them studied the dwarf from every angle, and tried poking at the dome at numerous different places, but to no avail. It was only when they finally stepped back to get a broader view that they noticed what they had been missing.

In a small crevice next to the dwarf, hidden from plain sight, was a symbol etched in blood on the wall and drawn so that it must have been at least two feet high. To Ben, who knew little of symbols, it looked like some sort of complicated ancient character.

"That is dark elf lettering," Natalie said, frowning. "I don't know what it says, but I recognise the style."

Ben ran a finger over the symbol. The blood was dry, and now firmly part of the rock. Eventually he stepped back, hands on hips, feeling a little frustrated.

"So, what do we have to go on? A dwarf mage in the void and a strange dark elf symbol etched in blood. I'll be honest – I was hoping for a little more."

To Ben's surprise, Charlie was smiling.

"Don't tell me you can understand this?"

"Of course not," Charlie said, waving his hand. "But don't you see? This symbol is a clue! Up to now, we had nothing, even with the dwarf, as interesting as he was. But the symbol gives us something to go on."

"It may not be easy deciphering a dark elf symbol," Natalie said, still frowning at the wall.

"I bet we can work it out," Charlie said. "I've seen several dark elf dictionaries in the Institute library."

Ben felt his optimism returning. He turned and took another sweeping look at the hall, cringing once more at the sight of the dead bodies. "So, what do we make of this?"

Charlie was tapping his cheeks thoughtfully. "This is what I think – and correct me if you think I'm horribly wrong. For some reason, the dark elves decided to attack these dwarves. We have no idea why, but, from history, the dark elves don't really need a reason to cause mayhem. The dwarves were outnumbered, but, by the number of dead dark elves, gave a good account of themselves. The sole survivor was this dwarf mage, who saved himself by fleeing into the void."

"And the symbol on the wall?" Natalie asked.

"I'm not totally sure," Charlie admitted. "Perhaps the dark elves wanted to leave a message to those who came after or perhaps it's some sort of signature."

"I agree," Ben said. "There's not much more we can learn until we research this symbol."

"What about the key?" Natalie asked. "Why do you think it led us down here? Do you think it was to speak to one of these dwarves, or could it be something else?"

Ben looked around the place again, rubbing his arms. He had been so engrossed in their discoveries that he hadn't realised how cold and stale the air felt.

"That's a good point," he said. "We should search

this place thoroughly to see if there is anything more we can learn."

"What, even those dark, unpleasant-looking tunnels over there?" Charlie asked, losing some of his enthusiasm.

"It won't take long," Ben said, "and we'll do it together."

They spent the better part of an hour searching the many tunnels that spiralled off from the main tunnel. Many of them led back to the surface, but they found nothing but the occasional dead body within them. Even Charlie began to relax when it became obvious that this once thriving underground dwelling was truly deserted.

When they finally returned to the main hall, even Ben was eager to get going.

"So, I guess the symbol is our only real clue, then," Natalie said, looking slightly downhearted. "I don't know why, but I can't imagine the key leading us here just for that."

"I know what you mean," Ben said, looking wistfully at the dwarf mage. "I get the feeling we were supposed to find something else."

"No," Charlie said firmly.

"No, what?" Natalie asked, turning to Charlie in surprise.

He was staring at Ben with a frown. "No, the void," Charlie said.

It was Natalie's turn to frown. "What do you mean? Go into the void? Don't be ridiculous, Charlie; not even Ben would think of something that ridiculous – would you, Ben?"

Ben gave her an offhand smile. "No, of course not. That would be madness. Come on, let's get out of this place. I need some air."

CHAPTER 3
SPELLSTRIKE TRAINING

Despite the discovery of the dwarf mage and the strange dark elf symbol, life at the Institute resumed some semblance of normality – or as normal as could be expected given the growing threat of the dark elves and their recent attacks on English towns.

To Ben's relief, Abigail passed the initiation test and had settled in wonderfully. She loved every single department and, to his surprise, excelled in Diplomacy. She was fascinated by the different Unseens, and her sweet demeanour seemed to help with the diplomatic scenarios. Ben checked in on her daily, but after a while, it was clear he didn't have too much to worry about. As a Guardian, she would in time need to learn how to master the helm, but there was much she needed to experience first.

However, Abigail wasn't Ben's primary concern right now, nor were the dark elves or even Elizabeth's Armour. There was something far more pressing going on, and his reputation was riding on it: the spellstrike game against Aaron's team.

"You realise we're going to get hammered, right?" William said.

"No, but thank you for your words of support. I appreciate the optimism," Ben said.

There were eight of them, sitting round a table in a small meeting room. Ben stood at the end, leaning on the table.

William shrugged, his entire body seeming to ripple with muscle. "Just stating the obvious, Ben. But you're not dumb – I'm sure you know this already."

"On the face of it, yes, we are at a slight disadvantage—"

A sizeable hand thumped the table. "Slight – ha! There's more chance of Ross County winning the Scottish Championship."

Ben turned to Lydia, maintaining a calm expression. It didn't do to get angry at Lydia; she might crush you. To say she was big would be understating things, and Ben had concerns about the chair she was sitting on. She had a mass of curly, brown hair and fiery eyes that looked ready to explode. But she was an excellent spellstrike player, and that's all Ben cared about. William had recruited her, and Ben suspected she might have a crush on the muscular third-grader, as one of the few people who might be able to deal with her.

When it was clear Lydia was finished, Ben continued.

"Yes, I'm not sure if anyone in this room knows who Ross County are, but thank you. So, Will, where are we at?"

"I managed to persuade Taecia's youth team to share their timeslot on the Taecia battleground with us," William said. "So every day at 6pm we get a couple of hours to train, as long as we don't get in their way."

"Aaron's team are training three hours a day, at his own world-class battleground," Simon said.

Ben turned to Simon, who was slouched in his chair like a kid, playing with a pen by clicking it on and off.

"More good news, thanks," Ben said with false cheer. "Can anyone tell me something positive?"

"Afraid not," Lisa said. She had come on board out of sympathy for their plight, and Ben immediately recognised her as a natural athlete. She was wiry and strong, with bright blue eyes and a fresh face. "I do have some news to report, though. You asked Simon and me to spy on Aaron's team. We watched them for a good hour last night, and it was impressive. I think their plan is to humiliate us by going with a five-pronged attack right at the start. If their scouts can locate our flag, they've got a good chance of making this the shortest game in history."

Ben nodded. It was getting increasingly difficult to remain upbeat. "Well, at least we know what they're planning, so we can counter that, right, Will?"

He turned to his captain with an almost pleading look.

Will seemed to sense his desperation and, to Ben's immense relief, he gave a nod.

"Yes, we can tailor our own tactics around that," Will said. "I have a few ideas for traps we can set, which will punish them."

Ben thumped a clenched fist on the table. "Great. And remember, we can all practise by ourselves during our free time in the evenings. Even if it's just taking a jog to increase our stamina, it all helps. Alright, does anyone have anything else to add before Will takes the floor?"

"Nothing that you'll want to hear," Lydia muttered.

"Okay, then," Ben said. "Over to you, Will."

William eased himself up, towering over them. He emptied a small box of contents onto the table. They looked like chess pieces, except none of them were recognisable.

"This is a brief introduction to spellstrike, mainly

for Ben and Charlie's sake, though going over the basics can't harm."

He threw eight red pieces down the other end, and kept the blues himself.

"It's eight against eight, with both teams having two reserves, which we don't have. The object is to capture their flag. Unlike traditional capture-the-flag games, you win the moment you have caught it – you don't need to return to your own base. Got it?"

Will looked at Ben and Charlie, who both nodded with differing levels of enthusiasm. Ben had tried reading textbooks on the game, but they just made his head spin, so it was nice to have it simply explained.

"There are a few basic positions in the game," William said. He dragged a piece shaped like a bird to the back of the table.

"The first is the owl. He or she is usually stationed as high as possible, with a panoramic view of the battleground. Their job is to watch and report. The owl can use her spellshooter like a walkie-talkie, and communicate to the other players on her team. They can reply, but cannot communicate with anyone except the owl." William stopped and turned to Natalie. "Ben has told me about your exceptional eyesight. You will be our owl."

Natalie nodded, as if she had expected it.

"The field is then broken down to those whose

job it is to defend the flag and those who seek out the enemy flag. Our defenders will be myself, Damien, Lydia and Lisa."

He laid out four pieces that looked like shields across the table, just in front of the owl piece.

"Is that enough?" Charlie asked anxiously. "Aren't they going to go all-out attack?"

"We will be able to deal with it – for a while," Will said. He gave a sudden smile. "To be honest, I'd be more worried about yourself, Charlie boy. Because you and Ben will be our only attackers, responsible for capturing the enemy flag."

William threw out two pieces carved out as swords up towards the centre of the table.

Charlie tried to talk, choked, and then tried again. "Are you serious? You want me as an attacker? I know I'm not an expert at spellstrike, but that sounds like a horrible idea. Don't you have to be fit and good at spellshooting?"

"Yep," William said, now grinning.

Charlie shook his head slowly, incomprehensibly. "I'm sorry, I must be missing something. I seem like the least likely person to retrieve the enemy's flag."

"On the face of it, yes," William said. He thrust a finger in the air. "But – Ben will need someone with him; he hasn't a chance by himself. You never start an attacker alone. And you have a relationship with Ben that is something we couldn't forge with any of the others in just two weeks."

Charlie appeared lost for words, and looked about for support.

"Plus, if we're going to waste someone attacking their flag, it might as well be you," Lisa said, grinning.

Charlie nodded. "Ah, that makes more sense. Thanks."

"That leaves one last position – the hyena."

Will chucked a hyena piece casually onto the table.

"The hyena's job is to basically cause mayhem, and has a licence to go anywhere and do anything. That position will be filled by Simon, who has a lot of experience playing the hyena with his local team. Simon, I don't normally say this, but I want you to cause absolute havoc."

Simon straightened himself in the chair and grinned impishly. "That's what I do best, Captain."

"I've heard good things about you from your coach," William said. "So I'm expecting you to take at least a couple of Aaron's team down."

"Easy," Simon said, waving his hand.

"Good. Lastly, each team gets a darzel to ride," William said. He placed a figure of something resembling a winged crocodile next to the four defenders.

Lisa will ride the darzel and give us some air support when needed. Any questions?"

Charlie immediately raised his hand.

"Sorry, yes. What happens if – as I envision – they all come charging at us straight away? Aren't we going to be pinned down and subsequently shot to pieces?"

"No," Will said immediately. "Our starting positions are sufficiently far enough apart from our opponent that it would take them at least ninety seconds of sprinting to reach our area. You and Ben will have that time to get out of their firing range and find your own way into their territory, without getting shot."

Charlie seemed to pale. "This game just gets worse and worse."

There were several more questions fielded at Will, who answered each of them well, even those thrown in anger from Lydia. Damien, who had sat silently the whole time up until now, asked a couple himself, and Ben was surprised how intelligent they were.

After half an hour of what seemed like hard work, with Ben trying to absorb everything, they called it a day.

"See you all at 6pm, at the Taecia battleground," Ben said, as they filed out the room.

Ben, Charlie and Natalie were last to leave.

"I thought that went quite well," Ben said cheerfully.

"William seems like he knows what he's talking about," Natalie agreed. "I'm just worried about lack of practice. Spellstrike is a real team game, and we've done hardly anything; whereas Aaron's team train every day at world-class facilities."

Ben put an arm round Charlie and Natalie. "Well, that will change. William is going to knock us into shape."

~

THAT EVENING, they left the Institute and headed on foot towards the Taecia spellstrike stadium. The air was cool and refreshing, and there were plenty of people about, either travelling home from work or perhaps heading towards their local tavern. There was a pleasant atmosphere, which was becoming increasingly rare with the threat of the dark elves. Even in Taecia, home to the Royal Institute of Magic, people didn't feel truly safe, though Ben knew it highly unlikely they would ever get a direct attack – he had heard the place was better magically protected than most royal households.

Their journey took them away from the town centre, where things became increasingly sparse. They found themselves on a well-worn path, lined with occasional houses and surrounded by farmland.

"I'm going to be worn out just getting there," Charlie said.

"Maybe we should have hired a few darzels for transport," Natalie agreed.

"We'll know for next time. We're almost there now – look," Ben said, pointing directly ahead.

A large archway spanned across the path, draped with a colourful banner, which said "Taecia Spell-strike Stadium". Beyond the banner, a large oval stadium came into view. Even in the fading light, it looked an impressive feat of construction, built of concrete and sand. Ben estimated the size to be similar to an average football stadium, but, unlike a football stadium, he could see giant trees sticking out from within.

Ben, Charlie and Natalie walked through the main entrance into the stadium, trying to take everything in at once.

"I can just tell this is going to be death," Charlie said, as they entered the battleground.

It looked similar to the one on Aaron's estate, only smaller. The playing field looked like a crazy obstacle course, combined with a gigantic treehouse. There were man-made hills, houses in which to hide, mini castles and thick bushes. Then there were the huge trees, linked with roped bridges and platforms. At either end of the battleground was a really tall tree, with a lookout platform near the top.

"Ah – our final team members have arrived," a friendly voice said.

William, Damien, Lydia, Lisa and Simon were gathered near the centre. William was waving them over.

"This place is great," Ben said.

"It's small," Lydia grunted, giving the place a resentful look.

"It's fine for what we need," William said. "We're not trying to become professional spellstrike players – we're just trying to develop some team relationship."

Ben longed to climb the trees and walk the roped bridges, but he forced his attention back to William.

"So, what's the plan?" Ben asked.

"Spellstrike relies heavily on fit players – players with stamina who can run, jump and sprint," William said.

Charlie groaned. "I don't like where this is going."

William cracked his knuckles, and gave them all a grin that even Ben didn't like the look of.

For the next half an hour, William made them run, climb trees, and squeeze through tunnels again and again. Natalie excelled; Ben found that he, Simon and Lisa were at a similar level; and then lagging behind came Damien, Lydia and Charlie. By the end, they all lay on the grass, breathing heavily, their bodies caked in sweat.

"I can't go on," Charlie said. His arms and legs were sprawled in a star shape, his face flushed bright red and his stomach gently heaving up and down.

"We've just started," William said with a grin. "Grab your spellshooters – it's time for target practice."

William poked a series of targets on stakes into the grass, and then handed them each a dozen pellets. "An important part of shooting in groups is to make sure you aren't all shooting at the same person. You each need to focus on someone different, to maximise damage and to bring down the enemy as quickly as possible."

Over the next hour, they turned from a coordinated mess to something resembling cohesion, as they shot down target after target. Ben was so engrossed in the exercises he completely lost track of time, so it came as a great surprise when William gave a little blow of his whistle.

"That's all for today, team," William said. "Same time tomorrow."

Ben swallowed his disappointment and, to his surprise, saw Charlie do the same, as they packed up and slowly left for home. Ben saw several darzels slither down the trees, and slink their way to his team mates. Within moments, they had hopped on the winged crocodiles and were flying out of the stadium, leaving Ben, Charlie, Natalie and William alone. William was also on a darzel, but instead of shooting off, he joined them.

"I thought that went well," Ben said.

William, who was already imposing, looked even more so standing on the darzel.

"It's a start, yes," William said. "We have potential. If we had three months, I could turn us into a good team."

"But we don't have three months," Charlie pointed out. "We've got two weeks."

"Have you seen Aaron's team play?" Ben asked.

"Yes. They are good. Right now they'd flatten us in less than fifteen minutes, which in spellstrike terms is a mauling."

Ben could just imagine Aaron's face should that happen. He would be outwardly gracious in victory of course, but he would make comments, disguised as harmless jokes, intended to squash Ben still further.

"We have two weeks. We'll get better," Ben said, staring into the distance with a grim expression.

CHAPTER 4

DELAYING TACTICS

During the next week, they improved dramatically, slowly turning from a bunch of individuals into a team that looked as though they might have played the game before.

As the time to the spellstrike game drew near, the pressure started to build. In the lunch rooms and the corridors, talk of the game started to become more common than the dark elves. Ben hadn't realised how many people were into spellstrike. It seemed even more popular than football, and Ben heard all sorts of strategy talk, much of it over his head. One thing was abundantly clear, though – there weren't many people backing them to win.

"I think Aaron's side will destroy them inside fifteen minutes..."

"...my guess is they'll just rush and overwhelm Ben's team."

"William is a good captain, though; I bet he'll set them up to hold out as long as possible."

"...Ben and Simon are hotshots, so they could spring a surprise."

"Charlie, I've got twenty pounds on you being the first player to get shot. Don't let me down."

Charlie's face flushed and he quickened his pace.

"Don't let it affect you," Ben said, as they headed up to the Diplomacy simulation room.

"Easy for you to say," Charlie said. "You don't get hounded every day."

"Sure I do," Ben said. "At least once a day someone tells me we're going to get crushed. It's become part of my daily routine. But as long as we keep practising and getting better, I think we'll surprise a few people."

But their practice sessions hit a hitch on the final week before the spellstrike game. The eight of them had taken to travelling to the battleground together – team bonding, William claimed – riding on darzels to get there. As they approached the stadium, Ben noticed a light coming from within.

"That's not normal, is it?" Ben said.

William was frowning. "No, it's not. The Taecia youth team gave us use of the battleground from 6pm to 8pm. There shouldn't be anyone in there."

Ben had a bad feeling even before they passed through the entrance and into the stadium.

"Another lap – go!"

Ben felt a stab of anger the moment he clocked the voice.

Aaron turned as they entered the battleground, a smile plastered over his sickeningly flawless face.

"Ah, Ben, William – there you are. I was told to expect you," Aaron said.

Ben quickened his pace, eager to impart some of his anger on Aaron, but William beat him to it.

"What's going on? We have the battleground booked for this time," William said, squaring up to Aaron. They were a similar height, but William had the advantage of countless hours at the gym, and it showed.

"You're quite right," Aaron said, seemingly unfazed. "However, this week we booked it in. I felt my team needed to train in a different battle-ground. This one might be small, but it gives us a different set of challenges to work with, don't you agree?"

"Whether I agree or not is irrelevant," William said. "We had this battleground booked. I spent several hours convincing the Taecia management team to give us this time. So I need you to leave – *now*."

Ben enjoyed the way William emphasised that

last word. But still, Aaron remained unconcerned. He raised a finger.

"You *had* an agreement," Aaron said. "But that agreement has changed."

Aaron turned and called a name. A bald-headed, suited man stepped out of the shadows, looking slightly flustered.

"Mr. Ackney," Will said with surprise. "What's going on here?"

"Ah, William, my boy, I'm sorry," Mr. Ackney said. He sounded anxious, and his eyes were lined with worry. "I received word this morning from the Taecia spellstrike board – the deputy chairman no less. He instructed me to give Aaron's spellstrike team this slotted time, effective immediately."

William frowned. It was a look that would have scared a braver man than Mr. Ackney, who flinched, and took a step back.

"I am sorry, William; there was nothing I could do," Mr. Ackney said.

William maintained his stony stare. "You could have told them you had already made an agreement and you weren't willing to break your word."

Mr. Ackney went red, and thrust out his chest, anger fuelling his courage. "Do not insult my integrity, William. It was only down to me that your misfit team got to train here in the first place. You should be grateful."

"Oh, I am grateful," William said, raising a fist. "Do you want to see how grateful I am?"

Ben saw the danger and stepped in, just as Aaron did the same, pulling the two apart.

"Let's all take a deep breath," Aaron said. "Will, think about it – we're not training at my battleground anymore. It's free, and I would be more than happy to let you guys use it. Remember, that's where we're going to be playing, so it would be ideal for you to get a feel of the battleground."

From the corner of his eye, Ben saw the rest of his team perk up. William, though, wasn't totally convinced.

"You would let us do that?" William asked, doubting the offer.

Aaron spread both his arms. "Of course. This isn't a world cup final. It's a friendly school game, and it's only fair that we both get the same training set-up, right?"

William gave Aaron a long, hard look. Aaron stared back, all open honesty in those big, brown eyes.

"How long will it take us to get there?"

"From the Taecia Dragonway you can be there in less than ninety minutes," Aaron said. "If you go now, there will still be time to get a good hour or two of training in. I'll send word that you're expected."

After what seemed like an age, William gave a subtle nod. Without a word of thanks, he turned, and headed for the exit.

"Come on, team; we're leaving."

They stepped onto their darzels and were soon speeding back to Taecia, skimming along the pathway.

Ben rode at the head of the group, alongside William, who was staring impassively ahead.

"I was kind of hoping you'd hit him," Ben said.

"I considered it," William admitted. "But it wouldn't help us right now. Maybe later, after this is all done."

"Well, let me know before you do, because I want to be there," Ben said with a smile.

"I'm glad we're training at the D'Gayle battle-ground," Simon said. He was flying in a zigzag pattern alongside Ben. "That Taecia ground was rubbish. Now we can try out some real moves." He grinned. "I have a few that I made up last night that I want to try out. They're mental."

Talk was limited during their journey on the Dragonway to Alexia Bay, a small island off the coast of Ireland, home of the D'Gayle family estate. By the time the dragon pulled up at the station, it was getting dark, and Ben guessed it to be past eight o'clock. The platform was as extravagant as he remembered it – all glass, marble and open spaces everywhere. Even at this time of the evening, there were white-gloved porters standing to attention, ready to deal with luggage or any other needs. They went straight to the taxi station outside. Waiting patiently were at least a dozen pristine silver carriages of various sizes, pulled by white Pegasus. They split up into two carriages, and gave the drivers the address. Moments later they were in the air, relishing the sea breeze, as they sailed up and over the bay, before turning inland, towards the hills. Extravagant houses lit up the top of those hills, and they flew towards the brightest of them all.

Less than ten minutes later, the carriages landed them on a familiar cobbled road, just outside the main gated entrance. They disembarked, paid the taxis, and were soon standing alone, in the fading light, in front of the vast mansion.

William and Ben promptly walked up to the gate. Immediately an elf, dressed in an impeccably tailored white suit, appeared on the other side.

"Ah, the Greenwood spellstrike team, I assume?" the elf said, with a perfectly clipped English accent.

"That's us," Ben said with a small sigh of relief. He had half-expected Aaron to be lying when he said he'd send word.

"Very good. I have been given specific instructions that under no circumstances are you to enter the D'Gayle estate."

There was a moment of shocked silence, before all eight team members spoke at once. Lydia grabbed the gate and started shaking it violently.

"That lying, scheming backstabber!" she cried. "You let us in so we can tear up the place!"

Ben's own fury lasted less than the others. Deep down he wasn't surprised, and looking at William's impassive face, he guessed Will wasn't either.

The elf stood calmly, hands behind his back, watching the scene in front of him without the slightest care in the world.

"Alright, that's enough," William said. "Put your spellshooter away, Lydia. Blowing their house up won't help us."

"It will help me," Lydia said, holstering her spell-shooter with reluctance.

"I, too, would like to see Lydia shoot at the house," Charlie said.

"No. We'd just end up with a bill that none of us could pay, and the Institute would have to fork out the money," Will said. "We will meet up at the Institute tomorrow morning, and decide what to do."

They fired a taxi-hailing spell into the sky, and waited. A sullen silence soon replaced their fury. Will turned unexpectedly to Ben with a grim smile.

"You said you wanted to be there when I beat the life out of Aaron, right?" Will said.

"Absolutely."

Will cracked his fingers. "You might want to stick by me tomorrow morning, then."

CHAPTER 5

DESPERATE MEASURES

Aaron managed to avoid them that following morning, and it wasn't until they were all in the lunch hall, munching down a chicken and mushroom pie, when he finally showed up.

Aaron, Joshua, and another chap who looked almost as big as William entered the hall. To Ben's surprise, Aaron headed right over to their table. Even more surprising was the huge grin on his face. Ben's gaze flickered to Will, who had just pushed his pie away. Would he start a fight in such a public place?

Aaron spread his arms as he approached, as if he was expecting a hug, not a thump to the face.

"So, how was it?" he asked with a smile. His voice was unusually loud – was he trying to be overheard? "It blows that Taecia battleground away, doesn't it? I'm almost regretting letting you guys train there."

William frowned at him. "We didn't train there. Your elf wouldn't let us past the front gate."

Aaron's jaw dropped quite spectacularly. "What? Are you serious? I sent a message to him the moment you guys left."

Aaron was a good actor. He was really good. Those around listening were left in no doubt that Aaron was genuinely shocked. Ben even suspected one or two of his own team members believed him, though William wasn't among them. But Ben could see Will was in a spot. If he challenged Aaron now, it would look all wrong. Will hesitated, unsure how to respond, and Aaron pressed on.

"I'm going to personally make sure the front gate is open tonight," he said. His eyes narrowed, as if he were genuinely angry, and he clenched his fist. "Don't worry about that elf – he won't be there."

Aaron was right. That night, when they travelled again to the D'Gayle mansion, the elf was nowhere to be seen and the front gate was unlocked.

"We're in!" Simon said, licking his lips and rubbing his hands.

As they walked round the side of the building, Ben spotted several golf buggies, similar to the one the elf had driven them in the last time. Charlie, whose memory and sense of direction equated to an inbuilt satnav, directed them through the formal landscape and into the gentle rolling hills. Eventually the winding path opened up into a large valley, and Ben saw an arch ahead, engraved with the words "*D'Gayle Stadium*". The buggies passed through the arch, and then came to a stop.

The stadium was just as Ben remembered it – huge, imposing, and dug deep into the valley, with sloped seating running all around the battleground.

There was just one problem.

"I can't hardly see a thing," Charlie said, squinting. "Shouldn't there be some magic lights or something?"

"Yes, there should," William said.

They walked down the centre aisle until they reached the battleground. Without any natural light, Ben could make out only shadows. He walked forwards and nearly fell into a tunnel that was concealed in the grass.

"Should we go back to the house and tell them to fire up the lighting system?" Natalie asked.

"No," William said. "That would take too long, and they would just ignore us."

"Why?" Natalie asked. "How can they expect us to train here without light?"

"They don't," William said. Ben couldn't see his face clearly, but he could guess as to the expression.

It slowly dawned on the rest of the group what was going on.

"He's done it again, hasn't he," Natalie said. "Tricked us."

"Not only that," Lisa added. "He's wasting our time. We didn't train yesterday, and now we can't train again today."

Ben heard a clap – possibly William slapping his fist into his hand.

"Yes, we can," William said firmly. "We train here."

"What, in the near darkness?" Lisa asked. "That's a bit dangerous, isn't it?"

"We have no choice," William said. He raised his voice. "Form a line, now!"

They tried valiantly to train for half an hour, using their spellshooters for lights, but it was difficult. After several awkward falls – Charlie falling down a tunnel and Lydia running headlong into a tree – William finally called it a day.

They headed back home bruised and more than a little deflated.

~

"I don't believe it!"

Aaron slammed a hand on the table, during lunch

the following morning. He had made the same play – coming in late and walking straight over to their table, making sure everyone was watching. If anything, he looked more put out than before, and that was saying something. He planted a hand on his forehead.

"You know what? That's entirely my fault. The elf I dismissed was responsible for firing the lighting spells in our battleground."

"How unfortunate," William said, his voice cold.

"So you guys missed training again?" Aaron said, putting his hands on hips. "Tough break. Time is running out now. There's only a few days left."

"Actually, we did train," Natalie said. Her green eyes flashed, and Ben was surprised to see how angry she looked.

"Really, in the dark?" Aaron gave a chuckle. "I guess that explains the cuts and bruises I see. Let me guess – trees and tunnels get in the way?"

There was a burst of laughter from the surrounding tables. Ben couldn't believe how many people Aaron had managed to get listening.

"I'm sorry, it's not funny," Aaron said, wiping a tear he had somehow managed to generate from his eyes. Ben had to admire how good he was at fake laughing. "Look, I have to go home early tonight; my parents are hosting some important people – royalty actually – and they want me there. I will absolutely make sure everything is set up for you tonight, no fail."

Ben couldn't believe Aaron's nerve – trying to fool them again. William, however, just gave Aaron a little smile.

"You know what? We've found an alternative solution, but thanks anyway."

For the first time, Ben saw a flash of concern cross Aaron's face. "An alternative solution? On such short notice?"

"Yep, so we're good," William said. He made a simple waving motion at Aaron. "Bye bye."

Aaron, realising he was the subject of much attention, recovered quickly, and bid them farewell with a slightly flustered wave.

"We've found somewhere else?" Lisa said, arching an eyebrow at William.

"Course we haven't," Simon said. "He was just lying. It takes a liar to spot one, and I'm a great liar."

William resumed his eating. "Actually, I do have somewhere in mind, but let's just say it's not your conventional battleground."

At five o'clock they met at the Institute entrance, and William led them off, down the hill. Ben noted the natural formation they took. Damien often walked with Lydia; Charlie and Natalie walked together; and he walked with William and Lisa. Simon walked alone, though he didn't appear to care.

William led them away from the busy town district and into a leafy, residential zone that ran on the edge of a small forest. They walked among houses, before turning into the forest. Tall trees stared down at them, spread out to allow a pleasant walking experience, with plenty of light filtering through. The forest floor was alive with moss and thick grass.

"You're kidding, right?" Simon said, as soon as they entered the forest.

William smiled. "You know where we're going?"

"Yes, but I hope I'm wrong," Simon said. "Come on, Will, we're supposed to be training properly, not like kids."

"Ooh, I like this place!" Lisa said. "I used to train here when I was really young."

"That's my point: it's for kids," Simon said.

"I'm lost," Charlie said. "Are we training in this forest?"

"Ignore them," William said. "We're not there yet."

They continued into the forest for another ten minutes, before they entered a large clearing.

Ben grinned. "Oh, that's cool."

"Yeah, if you're a ten year old," Simon muttered.

The clearing was clearly deliberately cleared. There was evidence of several stumps of varying sizes still left in the ground. A handful of trees had been left in the middle, with branches aplenty, making them great for climbing. Then there were the wooden constructions – sheds, houses, and even a small castle right in the middle. It reminded Ben of a paintball shooting arena.

"There have been several professionals who started their spellstrike days training here," William said.

"Yeah, but they were ten years old," Simon said. He had his hands in his pockets and was staring sullenly at the clearing.

"I think it's great," Ben said, clapping his hands. "At least we can practise here without Aaron interfering."

"We hope," Charlie said. "Until tomorrow, when it turns out that his family has bought this entire forest and we're kicked out."

William rubbed his hands. "Alright, if everyone is done complaining, line up in front of me. I'm going to show you the meaning of exhaustion."

"Can't wait," Charlie said miserably, as they formed a line.

For the next three days, William worked them to the brink of mental and physical exhaustion. The first half of every session was the worst. It was filled with quick sprints, followed by jumping and climbing exercises. By the end of the three days, even Charlie could scramble up a tree like a monkey. The second half of the session was all about the game of spell-strike itself – tactics; rules; common plays. Ben had no idea there was so much to learn. He and Charlie started way behind, but they both took large text-books home with them every night, and read into the small hours of the morning.

Ben was so focused on the spellstrike game that weekend that he barely had time to focus on his apprenticeship. Even Elizabeth's Armour, which he normally thought about every day, was temporarily cast aside. When in the library, he read his spellstrike textbooks. Other than the Spellsword Department, he wasn't sure he passed a single practical point on his checklist.

"You think you can convince a tribe of ice trolls to breakfast with you by staring at them?"

Ben blinked. In front of him were half a dozen frost-coated trolls, with large ears and warty noses, all armed with clubs.

"You're dead, Ben," Marie said. "I can't even be bothered to play the simulation out. You cannot stare at ice trolls, it infuriates them. I am certain you have read this, but perhaps not."

He had been thinking about different diversion tactics and had completely forgotten that he was in the Diplomacy simulation room, trying to deal with some ice trolls.

"I'm sorry. Can we try that again?"

"No time," Marie said. "Others are waiting."

Ben gathered his stuff and started to leave.

"Ben Greenwood."

Ben turned back towards Marie, who was giving him a stern look.

"From next week, I expect more concentration, yes?"

Ben nodded furiously. "Absolutely. I'm really sorry."

"Don't apologise – it's your future at the Institute that is at stake," Marie said. "Your second-grade exam is coming up, and you are starting to fall behind."

Ben cursed as he left the room. Great, another thing to worry about. Marie hadn't been the first person this week to comment on his poor performance. As soon as this spellstrike game was over, he would focus on the apprenticeship.

On Friday, the day before the game, Ben didn't even bother trying to work on the apprenticeship. His instructors didn't seem to miss him, and he suspected they realised it would be a thankless task to get him to concentrate.

Will ordered them to hang out together as much as possible, but most of the time they just lounged around in the common room, drinking tea, and occasionally talking about the game. They got plenty of encouragement from fellow apprentices, but just as many digging jokes from others, though there would have been more had William not been around.

"Put that book away, Charlie," William ordered.

Charlie shut the book, reluctantly. "There's so much more to know. This book goes over the top ten most famous games in detail."

William calmly sipped his tea. "There's nothing we can learn now that will change anything. We have decided on our strategy. We can only execute it to the best of our ability. So stop worrying about it."

"Well, I think we've become a pretty good outfit," Ben said.

He got a few eager nods, a few impassive stares, and a few scornful laughs from the other apprentices in the room.

"We're going to get slaughtered," Simon said.

"Come on, Simon," Natalie said. "That's not helpful."

"The odds are against us," William said. "But I think we'll give them a game."

Ben watched Will closely. Though he kept his expression neutral, it was obvious to him how William thought the game would end.

"Well, it's only a game, right?" Natalie said.

"Please don't say that," Simon said, covering his eyes with his hand.

Charlie put down a bun he had been tucking into. "Natalie's right. It's not as if the fate of the

Unseen Kingdoms rests on this game. I don't think the dark elves are watching, thinking, *We're going to declare war* unless *Ben's team wins tomorrow*."

That got a few laughs, even from Simon, and the group lightened up a little.

Ben sipped his tea, deep in thought. How important was the game? It had all come about because of Aaron's misguided belief in thinking that Ben was the one apprentice who could rival him for future leadership at the Institute. The truth was, Ben hadn't given one moment's thought to leadership. He had years to think about that and couldn't believe Aaron was scheming already. The problem was, though he didn't care, he certainly wasn't going to become one of Aaron's lackeys, which was what Aaron had proposed. *"You are either with me or against me."* And so began Aaron's plan of destroying Ben's reputation, starting by humiliating him at spellstrike. Ben knew he could, and perhaps should, have just declined the game. But Aaron had managed to get under his skin, with his suave charisma, dishonesty and arrogance. He was infinitely more irritating than Joshua, who was at least up front with his feelings.

And so, he had fallen right into Aaron's trap. At best, they would lose honourably; at worst, they would get humiliated. Either way, Aaron would work out how to use the result to highlight his own importance, while squashing Ben's.

"I want you all to get a good night's rest," William said. He turned to Simon. "That means no Xbox until 3am." Then to Lydia. "I don't want you reading your romance novels until the early hours."

Ben saw Lydia blush for perhaps the first and, almost definitely, the last time.

"Sleep is important, especially for a morning game. Have a good breakfast, and we will meet at the front of D'Gayle's mansion at ten o'clock. That will give us two full hours before the game starts."

CHAPTER 6
THE BIG BUILD-UP

It took Ben an eternity to get to sleep, but thankfully he had planned for that eventuality and went to bed extra early, so that when he woke the following morning he felt fully refreshed. He had a proper breakfast, attempted a couple of polite words with his grandma, and then headed out the door.

He met Charlie outside Croydon headquarters, and they headed down to the Dragonway together.

"I think I might have overdone it on the breakfast front," Charlie said, patting his stomach. "Three eggs, four pieces of bacon, beans, two hash browns, two slices of toast with jam and a cup of tea."

"No sausages?"

"Oops, forgot them. Four sausages. They were the skinny kind, though."

"Which makes it okay, of course," Ben said with a smile.

"I think I was owed a big breakfast after that week Will put us through," Charlie said. "I've gotten so fit that I'm going to have to buy some new trousers this weekend."

Charlie certainly did look trimmer. He walked with a certain confidence, and his breathing seemed more relaxed than usual. Whatever happened today, the training had certainly done Charlie a world of good.

They tried talking about other topics, even branching off to Elizabeth's Armour briefly, but it was difficult not to come back to the spellstrike game, and for the entire journey they talked for the hundredth time about the various strategies they might take once the game started.

When they pulled up at Alexia Bay station, Ben noticed just how many other apprentices had turned up to watch, as well as a fair few Institute members. He felt like a celebrity as they stepped off the Dragonway.

"It's a popular game," Charlie said, as they made a beeline for a taxi. "I bet the Institute members just want to get away from the constant pressure of the dark elves for a few hours."

It was slightly unnerving, as they hadn't expected anyone to be watching. Ben, however, was used to a bit of a crowd from playing football. They were glad to get into the air, away from the stares, and enjoyed the short journey over the bay and inland towards the D'Gayle mansion.

The others had already arrived, and they were loosely surrounded by other apprentices wanting to wish them well. The taxi landed them expertly, despite the foot traffic on the path.

"Over here, guys," William said with a wave.

The greetings were short, and Ben sensed the tension on each of his team members' faces. Only Simon seemed truly at ease. He had probably decided they were going to lose and didn't really care, as long as he had fun.

The front gates were open, and plenty of people were walking in and out. Will led them round the house. To their surprise, two buggies had been reserved for them. Ben had imagined Aaron wanting to tire them out by making them walk.

They drove through the estate until they came upon the battleground. Despite having seen it before in full light, the battleground seemed even more impressive, with much of the lower tier now filled with people.

"Game faces, guys," William said, as he led them down the stairs.

Ben's heart was pounding as he followed William down the stairs. Near the bottom was a security guard, who let them through, right onto the battleground.

There must have been several hundred people watching. From the centre of the battleground, it was hard to make out faces, and Ben stopped trying to pick out individuals. Aaron's team had yet to arrive and, for the moment, they were on the battleground alone. Ben took it in once more, but this time with a critical eye. He had studied exact layouts of the D'Gayle battleground on paper, but seeing it first-hand was something else. In the distance, he could just make out the enemy's owl tree, looking over the battleground like an air traffic tower. The middle of the battleground was where it got interesting. You could either try to go overground, using the trees and their bridges, or you could risk the tunnels, though Ben knew many of them would be booby trapped. Alternatively, you could stay at ground level, using the many small houses and beautifully crafted wooden statues to run and hide behind.

"Team Greenwood," a firm voice called out.

Ben turned. A referee, dressed all in black, was waving at them to approach the centre circle. The D'Gayle team had arrived, and were standing just behind the referee in a line. They were dressed in matching dark green outfits, with the word "D'Gayle" written across their chests. Ben had to admit, they looked impressive, especially when compared to their own gear, which ranged from jeans to tracksuit bottoms.

"Camouflage," Charlie said. "Why didn't we think of that?"

"It's overrated, that's why," Will said.

"Line up facing the D'Gayle team," the referee said. "Captains in the middle."

Ben was pleased to note the brisk, no-nonsense tone in the referee's voice. He was a bald, ageing man with a perfectly groomed moustache and hawk-like eyes. A whistle dangled around his neck. Hopefully he'd be able to weed out any devious tricks Aaron might have up his sleeve.

"I'm going to make this quick, because we are due to start in seven minutes," the referee said, tapping his watch. "This might be a friendly school game, but that does not in any way negate the rules. There is absolutely no physical combat, no fire breath from the darzels, and no communicating with anyone outside the game. Furthermore, anyone found using spells they were not issued with will be automatically disqualified. Any questions?"

Charlie raised a tentative hand. "What spells are we issued with?"

"I'm just coming to that," the referee said a little tersely. "Standard issue for the game is thirty freeze spells, twenty blast spells, and twenty freedom spells."

Ben had to mentally recall what each spell did. The blast spells eliminated the player straight away; whereas the freeze spells did exactly that – froze them in place, where they could be unfrozen if shot with a freedom spell.

"There will be six neutral players in today's game," the referee continued.

Neutral players. Ben remembered them well, as Will had been eager to know just how many would be playing today. They were on neither side, and would shoot anyone on sight. Fortunately, they couldn't move from their designated positions, and could be shot, just like any other player.

The referee pointed to a series of large plastic balls, set on wooden poles. Each one had a label on.

"Load up your spellshooters," the referee ordered.

Ben went over to the ball with his name on. There were seventy pellets inside, each a different shade of grey. He watched as the others twisted the middle of the ball, and the top half came off. Ben did the same, and spent several minutes loading up his spell-shooter until there was a multitude of pellets floating around his orb.

The referee gave a blow of his whistle. "Into your positions!"

The crowd cheered, and Ben felt his heart jump up a gear. He glanced at Charlie, who had suddenly gone extremely pale.

"Back to the owl tree," William said. Ben noted the red flag he was carrying in his hand.

He set a quick jog, and they followed. It wasn't long before they were standing under the tall, skinny trunk of the owl tree. Joining them was a darzel, lying casually in the grass.

William turned to them, his face serious, but calm.

"Natalie, get into position," he said, giving her the red flag. Natalie nodded and immediately started climbing the tree.

"Simon, do your thing," William said.

Simon gave a mock salute, and darted away, heading right into enemy territory.

"Defenders, get into your positions. Lisa, mount the darzel."

Ben watched as Lisa, Damien and Lydia quickly spread out in a rough diamond formation. Finally, William turned to Ben and Charlie.

"You guys know what to do, right?"

Ben nodded, and pointed at a nearby tree. "We'll climb that one. It's fairly straightforward, and has good links to the main trees."

"Good choice," Will said, nodding. "Now, listen, there is a chance that you will run into some of the neutral players in the trees – that is often where they are stationed. Normally I say don't waste your pellets on neutrals, but if they see you and are blocking your way, you may have to take them down."

"Got it," Ben and Charlie said.

"And remember, if you see the enemy below, don't shoot at them. That will only alert them to your presence. The whole point is we want you to get into their territory unseen. I know it will be difficult, but just let them pass. We will deal with them here."

William placed a large hand on each of their shoulders. "Good luck, guys."

A loud, piercing whistle cut through the forest, and Ben heard the crowd cheer again.

"Go!" William said.

CHAPTER 7
SPELLSTRIKE

Fuelled by an almost overwhelming surge of adrenaline, Ben darted for the tree, Charlie right behind him. His eyes were fixed on the lowest hanging branches, and he stuttered only a fraction as he prepared to jump, before launching himself and grabbing a branch with both hands. He scrambled up like a monkey. Though he knew the enemy wouldn't be anywhere near yet, he wanted to get above ground level as quickly as possible. He climbed steadily until he reached the rope bridge, which spanned a good twenty yards to the next tree. Twenty yards of unprotected walkway, with nowhere to hide, should they be spotted.

Ben glanced at Charlie, who was right behind him. He was shaking a little, but gave Ben a reassuring nod.

They crossed the ladder and reached the next tree without incident. Ben was now counting the seconds, knowing it wouldn't take the D'Gayle team more than a few minutes to show up. He was looking down so intently that he almost missed the branch he was aiming for.

"How about you look ahead, and I'll look down," Charlie said.

"Good idea," Ben said. He led them onwards, through the trees, searching out ladders and roped bridges, taking them ever closer to enemy territory.

A cackle of laughter and several loud spellshooter blasts almost shook Ben from the tree.

"Down there!" Charlie hissed, pointing.

Ben had to adjust his position to get a direct look at the forest floor. There he saw Simon's unmistakable ginger hair, hiding and ducking behind a tree. Every so often he would peek round, and fire a series of remarkably accurate shots at the green-uniformed D'Gayle team. Ben counted five of them. One was frozen in place, and another was down permanently.

"Simon is good, isn't he," Charlie said.

Ben grinned. "Yes, he is."

At that moment, Simon made a crazy dash to a large fallen trunk. Spells flew everywhere, but Simon somehow managed to make it to the cover, and hit the ground. Slowly, he crawled forwards, until he was at the trunk's end. He stuck his spellshooter out, and returned fire. Ben couldn't believe how accurate his no-look shots were.

"Would someone please down that little pain in the backside?" a familiar voice cried.

Ben was delighted to hear the frustration in Aaron's suave voice. There he was – hiding safely behind a large tree. If Ben shifted his position, he might be able to get an angle on him.

"No," Charlie said, the moment he saw what Ben intended. "Remember what Will said: we are not to give away our position, under any circumstance."

Ben grit his teeth. "There are five of them here – we could take them out and practically win the game."

"Wrong. You shoot, and they'll probably just run. That will completely ruin Will's plan."

Ben took a deep breath. "You're right. What a shame – I was really looking forward to showing Aaron what's what. It would have been such fun."

They took one last look at Simon's plight, which was starting to look a little desperate as the D'Gayle team slowly started to close in on him, before they continued on their way.

They had passed six opponents, including Aaron, which meant there were just two left to encounter.

"I bet they're defenders, protecting the flag somewhere," Charlie said.

"So if we find them, we'll probably find the flag," Ben said.

"Unless they're playing some sort of diversion tactic and are actually nowhere near the flag," Charlie pointed out.

They continued through the trees and across the bridges, but it was slow going, though they went with less caution now that they had passed the attackers.

Ben was making good progress over a particularly long bridge, when a familiar voice came out from nowhere.

"Ben? Can you talk?"

It was Natalie.

"Your spellshooter," Charlie said.

Ben lifted the bottom of the handle to his face. "Nat, is that you?"

"Yeah." Natalie's voice sounded breathless. "The enemy has just arrived. There are five of them. Simon managed to hold them up for a while, but he was able to remove only one from the game. That means there are two left for you to deal with, protecting their flag."

"Doesn't that include the owl, who can't even fight?"

"I don't think they bothered having an owl," Natalie said.

Ben lowered his spellshooter and promptly started climbing down the tree.

"What are you doing?" Charlie said, following suit.

"The enemy has reached our defenders," Ben said. "We need to speed up and get to their flag before they get to ours."

Their pace increased dramatically once on the forest floor. Ben was just starting to pick up some real pace, when a spell smashed into the ground next to him, spraying dirt. Another hit, and another, peppering the ground all around him.

"Get behind that car!" Charlie shouted.

An old Jaguar lay upended on two wheels, right in the middle of the battleground. Ben and Charlie dived for cover, and sat, with their backs to the car, panting.

"The defenders?" Ben said.

Charlie shook his head. "No, it's the neutrals. I saw two of them, but I think there could be more. The spells were coming from all angles."

Ben cursed, picturing his own team battling the D'Gayle attackers. "We were making such good progress."

"Yeah, I was starting to think we'd be able to stroll up to their camp, and politely pluck the flag out of their hiding place," Charlie said. "So now what?"

"On three, we turn and fire," Ben said. "You ready?"

"No."

"Good. One, two – three!"

Ben spun one way, Charlie the other. The neutrals had the advantage of knowing exactly where they were, and immediately Ben was almost hit, but he was able to get a sighting of one neutral, and even fire a few wild spells back, before retreating.

"I saw one in the trees," Ben said.

Charlie wiped his forehead with the back of his hand. "I saw two others. They have us pinned down. Should we retreat and try something else – maybe come from a different angle?"

"No time," Ben said. "Let's fire again."

This time, Ben was able to roll and fire with an accuracy that had the neutral ducking for cover. Again and again they fired and hid, until Ben managed to finally knock one of them off.

"Nice shot!" Charlie said. "I think I also actually scared my guy that time."

Their temporary elation was cut off suddenly by the sound of Natalie's voice.

"Guys? You still alive?"

"Yeah, but we're pinned down by a couple of neutrals," Ben said.

"Oh – okay," Natalie said. "No pressure of course,

but if you could speed up, that would be great. I'm not sure how much longer this fight is going to last."

"What's happening?" Charlie asked.

"Lydia is down, Damien is frozen and I think our team are out of freedom spells. Aaron is still alive, and he is with two others who are really good. I don't know how much longer Will and Lisa will survive. So, yeah – hurry up, please."

"Of course – no problem," Ben said, rolling his eyes at Charlie.

As soon as Natalie had finished talking, Ben and Charlie launched another attack.

"Got him!" Charlie said, sitting back down with a huge grin on his flushed face.

They did a little fist pump, and went again, trying to eliminate the final neutral player, but it was clear he was far more skilled than the other two, and despite being numerically disadvantaged, the neutral was able to dodge their spells and launch his own with unerring accuracy. Several more times they tried, but without success. Ben became increasingly frustrated.

"We can't do this anymore; we don't have time," Ben said.

"What do you suggest? Hoisting a white flag and asking him politely if he'll let us past?"

"Not quite. I'm sick of ducking back all the time. It's time for plan B."

Ben explained his idea, and Charlie immediately started shaking his head.

"It's stupidly risky," he said. "We could both get hit."

"It's better than our current plan, which isn't working," Ben said. He was in no mood to argue. "Are you ready?"

"No," Charlie said.

"Good – let's go!"

Ben leapt up and over the car. He brought his spellshooter up and started firing. Instead of a quick burst and a retreat behind the car, he started walking forwards and kept shooting, angling himself to get a better shot at the neutral. He was getting closer, his spells were missing by mere inches. The neutral had the perfect position, nestled on a treetop, giving them little to aim at. But Ben was in the zone, and he launched three spells in quick succession, bang on the mark. The neutral managed to spot the first two, but the third hit him right in the forehead.

"Boom! Got him," Ben said, thrusting a hand in the air.

The expected celebration from Charlie never materialised. Ben turned, and saw his friend frozen mid-stride, his face wide with shock.

Ben fired a freedom spell into Charlie's chest, and he immediately became unstuck.

"Thanks," Charlie said. "That was weird. I could

still see and hear everything, but I couldn't move a muscle. I saw your shot, though – very nice."

"Yeah, it was a good one. Now, we'd better move," Ben said. "The D'Gayle team could capture our flag any moment."

Ben set a good pace. He ran right down the centre of the battleground, taking the quickest possible path, not bothering with concealment. They no longer had time to dodge and weave in the interests of self-preservation. The whole game could be over in a matter of minutes, and Ben would kick himself if they didn't win because he didn't run fast enough. But he kept a keen eye out for trouble and, more importantly, any sign of the blue flag they were searching for. It wasn't long before Ben could make out the owl tree straight ahead. The forest started to thin and, suddenly, they found themselves running in open land, with absolutely nowhere to hide if trouble started brewing.

"Dead ahead!" Charlie shouted.

Ben came to a grinding halt. At the base of a tall, slender tree was one of the D'Gayle defenders, standing with his spellshooter at the ready. The moment he spotted them, he raised his spellshooter and fired.

"Zigzag and shoot!" Ben ordered.

The defender fired like a maniac, mostly at Ben,

and he was almost hit twice. He kept his own spell-shooter trained on the defender, and returned fire with equal zest. The defender took one hit, but, to Ben's surprise, kept firing. It took three more hits before the defender finally went down. Ben and Charlie made it to the base of the owl tree, and stared down at the unconscious defender.

"Did you see that? It took several shots to knock him out."

"Yes, that was interesting," Charlie said. He looked around, his face anxious. "Now what? I don't see any sign of the flag, nor the final defender. Are we in the wrong place?"

Ben had been thinking the same thing. "Let's climb the tree, and see if it's up there. If it isn't, hopefully we'll be able to see it from the top."

The owl tree wasn't an easy climb, especially when compared to the other trees near the middle of the battleground, and progress was slow, with some branches spread far apart. Ben was concentrating so hard on reaching the next branch that he failed to register the screech that pierced the air.

"What was that?" Charlie asked.

Ben looked up, branch forgotten. He knew that sound.

"Darzel!" Charlie screamed, pointing. "Darzel coming right at us!"

Riding the darzel was Joshua, standing with supreme confidence as the beast shot towards them, his spellshooter armed and ready.

Ben scrambled into position, trying to use the main trunk as protection, while grappling for his spellshooter. As soon as he picked it up, he sensed that his orb was almost empty. Rapid firing was no longer an option.

“Incoming!” Charlie said, his face scrunched, awaiting impact. He hadn’t been able to get his spell-shooter out, and was instead hugging the trunk, trying to minimise target area.

Ben watched with growing dread, as Joshua pulled the trigger, and the spells went flying right at them. Ben plastered his body against the trunk, and felt the spells smash against the tree. As soon as the onslaught stopped and Joshua zoomed by, Ben turned and fired three shots at the darzel’s back. But Joshua seemed to sense the spells, and banked grace-fully. Ben cursed, and felt his orb. How many spells did he have left? Six? No more.

“Better climb, before he swings around,” Charlie said from behind. “You go as quickly as you can; I’ll see if I can distract him.”

Ben didn’t argue, and started scrambling upwards as fast as possible, ignoring the scratches his haste brought, as he grasped on to improbable footholds. Another screech from the darzel nearly threw him off, and he paused, watching Joshua come right at them again.

"Keep climbing!"

Charlie's voice echoed from below.

Spells started streaking towards the darzel, and Joshua had to swerve and divert his course. Ben grinned. Charlie clearly had no shortage of spells. Ben continued scrambling upwards. He could now see the platform at the top, where the owl could view everything. On top of it was a small basket – the perfect lookout spot. Could the flag be in there? If not, he was in trouble.

"Ben, if you're still alive, you need to get moving!"

Natalie's voice came through loud and clear.

Ben grabbed his spellshooter and spoke through the handle. "I'm still alive. What's happening?"

"Will is the last man standing, and he's up against Aaron and one other guy. You've got minutes before they take down Will and start climbing. Our flag is in my lookout nest, and there's nothing I can do to stop them."

Ben didn't even bother replying, but renewed his climb. He got only a few steps before the darzel's screech alerted him to Joshua's renewed attack. Charlie launched another blistering strike, but Joshua returned fire and, all of a sudden, Charlie's attack stopped. Ben glanced down and could just make out Charlie, slumped over one of the branches.Ben tore his eyes away and climbed a few more steps, before Joshua diverted his darzel, and started flying right at him. Ben could see the steely determination in Joshua's deep blue eyes, as he honed in on Ben with frightening speed.

Joshua fired. Ben hung on for dear life. Joshua turned, almost lazily, and came round for another go, at a slightly different angle. Ben only just managed to adjust his position, to keep the tree trunk between himself and a direct attack, before Joshua fired again. The tree was peppered with spells, but Ben managed to avoid them. Again and again Joshua fired, with the margin for error getting ever smaller. Each time, Ben was able to make only tiny inroads up the tree, before scrambling back into a defensive position. The lack of pace was infuriating. Was Joshua simply toying with him? Had he guessed that Ben was almost out of spells? More importantly, did he know what was going on at the other end of the battleground? Without having an owl, surely he was clueless or else he would have finished Ben off by now.

"Ben!" Natalie came through as a frantic squeal. "Will is down! They're climbing the tree! They'll be here in less than a minute."

Ben cursed. He was pinned down, and couldn't move more than a few feet at a time. He glanced up.

He still had a good twenty feet to go. He wasn't going to make it. It was time to change tactics. Ben drew his spellshooter out, and got into position – no longer cowering behind the tree, but with a full view to track and shoot any oncoming target. He watched as Joshua came right at him, noting the slight frown as he clocked Ben's change in position. Ben waited as Joshua flew ever closer. To his surprise, Joshua didn't open fire from a distance like normal – was he too running out of pellets? Ben waited until he could see the green of the darzel's eyes and the saliva trailing from his sharp, white teeth before pulling the trigger. Joshua fired at exactly the same time. A flurry of spells crossed mid-air, some even colliding in an explosion of sparks. Joshua was almost upon the tree when Ben's last remaining spell clipped the darzel's wing. The creature screeched and went into a nose dive. Joshua reacted instantly, and flung himself onto the tree, grabbing hold of a branch, and grunting as he slammed into the trunk. For a split second, Ben had a clear shot. Joshua was busy rubbing his head, unaware of the danger. Ben pointed his spellshooter and fired.

Nothing happened. He was out of spells.

Ben cursed. He almost threw the spellshooter down at Joshua, hoping to dislodge him, but remembered that might be against the rules. Instead, he started climbing. As he approached the nest, Ben had to think about how to climb round the sides to get inside.

"Ben!" Natalie's voice was a screech. "They're here! They're about to climb into the nest!"

Ben accelerated, all thought of self-preservation forgotten. He practically flew up to the nest, and grabbed hold of the base. Groaning with effort, he managed to find a branch so he could keep climbing up and around the nest. Just one final spurt and he'd be inside.

A spell smashed into the nest, making the whole construction shake so violently that Ben almost lost his grip. He glanced down, and saw Joshua slowly climbing up, spellshooter in hand, the tip glowing. Ben braced himself, as another spell collided into the nest, this one more violent than before.

Ben knew he had to move. He could practically envision Aaron climbing inside his team's nest right now. The thought spurred him on and, with a cry of defiance, he leapt up, and over the nest, falling into the small basket, head-first. He righted himself, and looked about frantically.

The blue flag stared innocently back at him, planted firmly into the basket. His heart almost exploded with exhalation and relief.

"Ben!" Natalie shouted. "It's too late, they're—"

Ben's hand swept up the blue flag.

A loud horn sounded from somewhere far off.

Not one horn, but two, each a slightly different pitch, Ben realised.

"What's that noise?" Ben asked, speaking into the spellshooter.

"Oh my goodness!" Natalie said. Her frantic, almost fever-pitch tone had gone, replaced with relief and unexpected joy. "You must have picked up the flag at exactly the same time as Aaron. Both horns have gone off. It's a draw!"

Ben wasn't sure how long it took him and Charlie (who came back to life as the game ended) to stumble down the tree and make their way back to the centre of the battleground. Neither felt in a hurry and both revelled in the fact that they could just walk without fear of being shot at. It was most liberating.

The reaction of the two teams to the result of the game was vastly different. The moment Ben and Charlie made it back, they were mugged by their team. To a man, they were grinning ear to ear, even Damien and Lydia. Ben was pleased to hear the crowd giving them a thunderous welcome, and delighted to see the D'Gayle team looking sullenly on. The sour expression on Aaron's face was priceless.

"I can't believe you guys did it!" Natalie said, giving them both effusive hugs before the rest of the team could get in.

"It was Ben, mainly," Charlie said, his face going red. "I just came along for the ride."

"Complete rubbish," Ben said. "How did you guys do?"

"We held them off as long as possible," William said. "As expected, they were really well trained as an attacking group, and ran all sorts of different strategies, many I'd not even seen before."

"Will was incredible," Lisa said. "We only held out that long because of him."

The others nodded in approval, and Ben realised again how lucky he had been that Will had decided to join his team.

His thoughts were interrupted by footsteps, and he turned around to see Aaron approaching. The sour expression had gone, replaced with a gracious smile.

"I just came to congratulate you guys on a great game," Aaron said, extending his hand.

A few of Ben's team looked at Will, to see how he would respond. William didn't hesitate in stepping forwards and accepting the handshake, leading the rest of the team to do the same.

Aaron stepped back, hands on hips. "I don't think I've ever played in a tie game before. It was definitely a surprise for both myself and the crowd. I think they were expecting a winner."

"It was a surprise," William said. "Not that

surprises are bad – quite the opposite actually, they often make a nice change."

"I agree with you completely," Aaron said. He gave an awkward smile and pointed a thumb back at his team. "I have to confess, my team were hoping for a replay. A few of them even heard the crowd demanding one. They're not used to seeing a draw, you see, and I think they're a bit unsatisfied."

"They look fine to me," Ben said.

Aaron gave one of his great patronising smiles. "Of course, now that you're here, they're putting up a front. But underneath, it's a different story. Trust me." Aaron extended his arms. "So what do you say, do we have a replay?"

The team looked to William, and William turned straight to Ben. His initial reaction was to say yes. With more training, he was certain now he could beat the D'Gayle team. On top of which, it was fun as heck, and got the adrenaline going like all great games did. He looked at his team to see if he could read their thoughts. It was fairly obvious that Lydia, Damien, Simon and Lisa were up for another game, and a chance to get one over on Aaron's team. William's expression was completely neutral and impossible to read. Both Charlie and Natalie, however, were a different story. They both looked anxious. It took Ben a moment to realise why.

Elizabeth's Armour. Tracing down the meaning

of the dark elf symbol. The second grade of the apprenticeship. These were the things that mattered, and he'd put almost no attention on them while focusing on the spellstrike game. Another game would surely continue to distract him from what he should be doing. It was a soul-crushing decision, but he knew what he had to do.

Ben looked Aaron right in the eye. "Thanks for the offer, but we're going to have to pass."

Aaron was caught by surprise, and Ben could see from the corner of his eye the surprise and disappointment from some of his team.

"Fair enough," Aaron said, recovering quickly. "It's your choice, of course. Some people aren't going to be best pleased, but I'll see what I can do to handle them."

"Why'd you say no?" Simon asked, as soon as Aaron was out of earshot. "We could take him down next time, I'm sure of it."

A few of the others voiced similar thoughts, until William raised his hand.

"It's Ben's choice, and we have to respect that. Personally I'm sick of dealing with Aaron, so I'm happy with Ben's decision. Let's face it, none of us – except Ben – thought we had a chance of winning, so let's be satisfied with what we achieved, and move on."

Ben smiled his thanks at William's support. He

felt a huge weight lift from his shoulders, knowing the spellstrike ordeal was finally over, and without losing face against Aaron.

Now it was back to the simple matter of completing the second-grade apprenticeship and continuing their search for Elizabeth's Armour before the dark elves took over the world.

CHAPTER 8

BACK TO THE APPRENTICESHIP

The following Monday, Ben arrived at the Institute raring to dive into the apprenticeship. What he wasn't expecting was the mixed looks he got from fellow apprentices. Many congratulated him on the spellstrike game, but others gave him disappointed, even annoyed stares.

"Ignore them," Natalie said. "Aaron has been at it again, explaining that the reason we're not getting the replay is because you didn't want one. There is even a silly rumour going round that you were too scared for it."

"Morons," Charlie muttered.

"I really don't care," Ben said with a shrug. "I'm done with Aaron's games. I just want to get on with the apprenticeship and forget about him."

They lined up for morning muster and were early

for once. Ben watched as the apprentices wandered in, and the room slowly filled up.

Dagmar, Master of Apprentices, walked in, with one minute to spare. Not for the first time, she reminded Ben of a miniature army general, with her impossibly straight back, crisp clothing and baton held behind her back. The effect was ruined slightly by her comically large shoes and her long eyelashes that softened her otherwise rock-hard face.

"Good morning, apprentices," Dagmar said, after she had rattled off muster. "I have a couple of announcements to make – the first applies to everyone; the second to a select few."

Like everyone else, Ben's interest was piqued. Dagmar didn't often make announcements, but when she did, they were usually interesting.

"The first announcement concerns the dark elves. I have made it known to all the directors that I want as little disruption as possible, but Draven, the Head Warden, is in desperate need of resources in the War Room, so don't be surprised if you are requisitioned at some point. There are various duties the other directors have requested, but I will attempt to tie them in with your apprenticeship, so you are not wasting time. Is that clear?"

Simon's hand shot up. "What is this War Room? It sounds awesome."

"You will find out, should you be called to work

there. Any other, less ridiculous questions? No? Good. My next announcement is only for Ben, Charlie, Amy, Georgia, Frederick and Aaron. The rest of you are dismissed."

The apprentices filed out, many of them giving Ben and those remaining a curious stare. Ben noticed they were all second-graders, by the two stars floating above their right shoulders. He didn't know Amy, Georgia or Frederick that well, but they had hung out a bit recently and he found he enjoyed their company. When they were alone, Dagmar called them forwards, and they lined up behind her desk.

"You six are here because I have booked you in for the second-grade exam in exactly four weeks from today," Dagmar said.

Ben saw the colour drain from his fellow apprentices' faces – except for Aaron, who looked perfectly calm.

"Needless to say, you all have work to do to catch up in various departments. Now that the spellstrike game is over, I expect your full commitment and attention to finishing the handbook checklist and readying yourself for the second-grade exam. I don't need to remind you that failure constitutes elimination from the apprenticeship. Any questions?"

None were raised – partly, Ben suspected, because nearly everyone was in shock.

"I will attempt to exempt you from dark elf duties

for as long as possible, but I suspect, as all of you are competent apprentices, that you will be drawn in sooner rather than later. However, they have assured me it will not occupy more than an hour per day, until you have finished your exam. I have managed to temporarily excuse you from Barrington School, so you can come straight here in the morning. Any further questions? No? Good. Dismissed."

Ben and Charlie headed straight to their lockers, pulled out their handbooks, and went to the common room.

"Over here, guys!" Natalie said, waving. She had saved them a nice table in the corner, surrounded by low, squishy chairs. They plonked themselves down, and opened their textbooks on their laps.

"Exam in four weeks," Charlie said, meeting Natalie's enquiring stare.

"Oh my goodness," Natalie said. "You guys are going to be swamped." She lowered her voice to a whisper. "I guess that means we won't be able to research that dark elf symbol we found in the dwarf hall. I'm really curious as to what it might be."

"So am I," Ben said, his head buried in his checklist. "But as much as I hate to say it, it's going to have to wait. As usual, I'm behind in Diplomacy and Scholar. I'm just about on target in Trade, and I'm ahead in the Warden and Spellsword departments."

"Basically the opposite to me, then," Charlie

replied. "I'm well ahead in Scholar and Diplomacy. I'm a little behind in Trade, and well behind in Warden and Spellsword."

Ben glanced up at Natalie, and made sure nobody was watching them. "I really can't see Charlie or myself getting even a minute free for the next four weeks. If you get any time, could you do some research into the dark elf symbol?"

"I'm sure I can," Natalie said. "I've already got a few ideas of where to look. How about we meet up at Cherzo's for dinner at six o'clock each night for a catch up?"

"Sounds good," Ben said, standing up. He glanced at Charlie, who rose with him. "So, what do we tackle first?"

"I saw how horribly behind you are in the Scholar Department," Charlie said with a severe frown. "So let's hit the library. We need to get you up to speed."

Ben groaned, his enthusiasm suddenly dulled. "I thought you might say that. I really don't get how you enjoy it so much."

"I'll attempt to show you. Come on."

While the Department of Scholar was never going to be as fun as the Spellsword or Warden departments, Charlie certainly made it more bearable. He knew where all the good books were and managed to limit the monotonous reading. To Ben's surprise, he found that there were talking books that read to you and responded to your questions. Then there were diagrams, illustrations, and real-life examples of things they were studying – maps; historical documents; real bits of armour from past battles – all located in areas of the library Ben didn't know existed. With Charlie's help, it wasn't long before Ben was starting to catch up in the Scholar Department.

Then the tables turned. With Ben now up to speed, it was his turn to help Charlie, who was horribly behind in the Warden Department.

"I hate real-life exercises," Charlie muttered.

Ben and Charlie were hurrying down the hill, towards the Dragonway.

"Why? Simulations are okay, but you can't beat the real thing," Ben said.

Charlie had been given an assignment from Heidi, the Warden responsible for tracking low-level Unseens. A pixie was rumoured to be attempting to travel to London without a proper visa, and it was Charlie's job to make sure that didn't happen. He had with him his spellshooter, armed with a number of basic spells, and a small wooden box to capture the pixie if necessary.

"I just hope the pixie listens to reason, because I really don't want to try to catch the thing in this," Charlie said, holding up the box miserably.

"You'll be fine," Ben said with a grin. "Remember,

the objective is to stop the pixie getting on the Dragonway – it doesn't really matter how you do it."

Ben and Charlie headed straight for the Dragonway entrance, and stopped at the archway in front of the stairs that led to the platforms. Ben didn't have his spellshooter, nor did he plan on helping Charlie with the capture, as that would violate the objective requirements. Charlie was supposed to do this by himself; Ben was just here for moral support.

"Look relaxed," Ben said. "You look too obvious, like you are clearly here on duty."

"Well, I have the stars floating over my shoulder, don't I?" Charlie said irritably. "It's hard to avoid being seen as an Institute apprentice like this."

"Doesn't matter," Ben said. "If you look relaxed, you're less likely to be suspected, which will make stopping the pixie easier – trust me."

Charlie attempted to relax, and even tucked into an apple, which helped. Ben spotted several pixies enter the Dragonway, but it wasn't for another twenty minutes before Charlie's eyes widened.

"There he is!" he said, pointing.

"Put your finger down. You're calling attention to yourself."

Charlie's brow was starting to perspire and he wiped it with his hand.

"Stay relaxed," Ben said. "He's coming this way,

and he clearly hasn't noticed you yet. Just ease yourself into position."

The pixie was clearly troubled. He flew just above the crowd, occasionally knocking his legs into a lumbering giant or a hulking troll. The pixie's nerves could help Charlie or they could make things complicated, depending on how Charlie handled it.

"Here he comes," Charlie said. He looked just as nervous as the pixie, but, to his credit, the moment they locked eyes on each other, Charlie put on a passable show of authority.

"Excuse me, Mr. Alendor?" Charlie said, stepping forwards, into the path of the pixie.

The pixie gave a little start, as he finally clocked Charlie, just feet from his face.

"Yes," the pixie said, in a typically high-pitched voice. "What is it?"

"My name is Charlie Hornberger, and I work for the Institute," Charlie said, pointing to the stars above his shoulder. He pulled out a letter. "I have been led to believe that you plan a trip to London without holding the necessary paperwork. Is that correct?"

"Yes. No – possibly," the pixie said. There was a growing alarm in his voice, and he made several furtive gestures with his wings that Ben was fairly sure Charlie hadn't noticed.

Stay calm, Charlie, Ben wanted to say. The trick was to let the pixie know they were on the same side.

Charlie produced a small bracelet from his pocket. "If you agree to wear this tracking bracelet and calmly return home, I will be happy to forget the matter."

Too early! Ben thought. *You haven't won him over yet.*

The pixie looked at Charlie, and then over his head, at the stairs leading up to the Dragonway platforms.

Ben tensed himself. Charlie, on the other hand, had his arm halfway extended with the bracelet to the pixie, a hopeful smile on his face.

The pixie bolted, flying right over Charlie's head, zooming up the stairs.

Charlie whipped round in astonishment. "Blast! I thought I had him."

"Not quite," Ben said urgently. "Let's go, you have to get him before he makes it onto the Dragonway."

To Charlie's credit, he responded immediately, reaching for the wooden box, and flying up the staircase. Ben followed just behind. Charlie did a decent job of avoiding fellow passengers, mainly by screaming "Sorry, excuse me, coming by, Institute business!" at the top of his voice. Ben could just make out the wings of the pixie as it sped along the bridge that overlooked the platforms. As it approached platform seven, it took a shortcut, and flew over the bridge, directly towards the platform, avoiding the need for stairs.

"Oh no you don't," Charlie said. He ran right up to the edge of the bridge, stuck his spellshooter through the rails, and trained it on the pixie. Before Ben had time to ask what he was attempting, Charlie fired a couple of white spell blasts. The first skimmed by the pixie, but the second hit him right in the back. The pixie's wings immediately stopped flapping, and the pixie fell the remaining few feet onto the platform. He got up straight away and started running towards the dragon.

Charlie darted down the platform stairs, with Ben just behind. To Ben's amazement, Charlie managed to close the gap on the wounded pixie with some determined running.

"Got you!" Charlie cried, and leapt onto the pixie. They both hit the floor. Ben hung back, ready to help, but there was no need. The pixie squirmed and fought, but it was no match for Charlie's superior strength. Ignoring the scratches and bruises from the pixie's sharp nails, Charlie stuffed the squealing pixie into the wooden box, and slammed it shut.

Charlie sat, legs sprawled, on the platform floor, huffing and puffing, but with a large smile plastered across his face.

"That was impressive," Ben said, hauling Charlie

to his feet. "I mean it. The shot under pressure was fantastic, and the way you chased him down was epic. A few weeks ago you'd never have been able to do that."

Charlie was beaming from ear to ear. "Let's get this thing back to Heidi, before it tears a hole in the box. Then I think we both deserve some serious lunch."

Over the next couple of weeks, Ben and Charlie continued helping each other in their weaker areas, while working to finish up the checklist in their strong fields. It was a harmonious relationship that worked wonderfully, except for the odd occasion when they both got stuck, such as the time they failed to convince a family of dwarves to sell them a set of cooking bowls for their target price. Or when neither of them could work out how to resolve a petty squabble between two neighbouring pubs. Diplomacy and Trade continued to be a pain at times.

"Other than those two hiccups, we're doing okay, though," Charlie said.

"That's great," Natalie said. "You guys will definitely be ready in two weeks' time."

The three of them were back in the common room, catching a well-earned break, before another intense session in the combat room for Spellsword training.

"You guys are still on the checklist, then?"

Aaron's voice floated across the room. He was sitting on a table with the other grade-two exam candidates.

"Yes, we are," Ben said coolly.

Aaron shrugged. "I see. I thought you'd be done by now, Ben. I'm finished, and now just spending time revising. I highly recommend it if you want to score high grades in the exam."

"Are the rest of you guys finished?" Ben asked.

They all shook their heads, and Ben felt a little better.

"I've still got to finish up the Warden and Trade checklists," Frederick said. "Trade is a nightmare."

"We've got a little bit to do on each of the departments," Amy said, referring to herself and Georgia. "But I definitely want to take Aaron's advice and get some revision in before the exam. I bet it will help."

She gave Aaron a smile, and was delighted when he returned it.

"It will be interesting to see what scores we all get," Aaron said. "Personally, my family are expecting me to maintain my record of straight As. I don't want to disappoint them. How about you, Ben? What are your expectations?"

Ben shrugged. "I just want to pass, and make it to the third grade."

"Oh, I'm sure you'll do that," Aaron said. "However, you'll need a really good score if you want to—"

Aaron's sentence was cut short, as his eyes shot past them to someone who had entered the common room.

Ben turned. It was Dagmar, and she was marching right up to them.

"Ben, Charlie, come with me," Dagmar said.

Without waiting for a reply, she turned, and immediately left.

Ben and Charlie exchanged confused glances, and then followed Dagmar out of the common room.

CHAPTER 9
THE WAR ROOM

"Where are we going?" Ben asked.

Dagmar was marching upstairs, her large feet clacking on the marble staircase.

"The War Room," Dagmar replied, upon reaching the gallery on the Warden floor. She looked even stonier than normal as she led them through the double doors, and along the corridor. Ben immediately spotted Wardens hurrying along at breakneck pace, many of them lost in conversation, so that Ben had to sidestep to avoid being knocked over. Dagmar didn't move a jot, and several Wardens almost crashed into her, until they spotted who she was, and promptly moved aside. Dagmar eventually stopped by the aforementioned War Room. Ben could hear lots of voices beyond.

"Stay by me or you'll get flattened," Dagmar instructed.

Without further explanation, she opened the door, and they stepped inside.

Sticking with Dagmar was harder than Ben had anticipated. His first reaction was to stop and stare. The room was huge, and absolutely packed. There must have been at least fifty members in the room, almost all of them talking, or shouting, creating a scene of mayhem. Taking up most of the right side of the room was a huge table, on which a giant map of England lay, dotted with tiny, coloured flags, reminding Ben of various war games he'd played. Surrounding the table must have been at least two dozen Wardens, plus several apprentices, busily placing more flags or shuffling existing ones to different positions.

"Ben! Charlie!"

Dagmar's sharp voice called them from the other side of the room.

"This is Lorena," Dagmar said, introducing the two of them to a small, shapely Warden with three red diamonds floating above her shoulder. "You will be under her. I have told her specifically that you are not to work more than an hour a day."

Dagmar said no more, and promptly left them in the hands of Lorena.

"I am extremely busy, so I will be brief," Lorena

said in an appealing, but hurried voice. “See this table? We call that our incoming table.”

The table in question wasn’t as big as the one across the room, but it looked just as interesting. There were dozens of large bowls that were being filled with spells from Wardens. Each bowl was marked by county – Sussex; Surrey; London; Middlesex; and so forth.

“Each spell has been fired at an Unseen. Unlike most spells, these ones do not explode on impact, but return to the spellshooter with information that we can use to track the Unseen. Make sense so far?”

“I think so,” Charlie said. “The spells in the bowls contain data on Unseens we’re tracking in various parts of England.”

“Good. Now, look what happens to each spell.”

They watched as an apprentice took one of the spells, and squashed it onto an empty flag. Immediately the flag turned red and started vibrating. The apprentice did this at least a dozen more times with other flags, and then headed over to the large table on the other side of the room, dodging and weaving his way through all the members, most of whom didn’t notice his presence.

“The apprentice will run over, and stick all the flags in their correct places. The flags will vibrate until placed in the correct position.”

"What are the colour codes?" Ben said, already suspecting he knew the answer.

"They represent the different races. Red is goblin; green is troll; purple is dark elf; and so forth. There are more than a dozen different colours." Lorena clapped her hands. "Right, I need to get going. Charlie, you take South London. Ben, I want you on West Sussex. Dagmar informs me that you've got only an hour, so you'd better get going. Your bowls are getting full. Come and see me before you leave."

Ben and Charlie exchanged looks, and sat down in front of their respective bowls. There were already a dozen other apprentices on the table, working furiously, dipping their hands into the bowls and squashing the spells against the flags with frightening pace.

"Oh, hello Ben, I didn't expect to see you here."

"Abigail!" Ben said with a smile. "I didn't expect to see you here either. How are you?"

Ben hadn't had much time to check up on her progress since he had gone all-out on the apprenticeship, but was delighted to see how much she appeared to be enjoying herself. Her delicate features and long lashes made many of the younger apprentices give her a second glance.

"I'm doing fine, though they have me working here quite a lot at the moment. I don't mind; the buzz is nice and you get to hear things."

"What things do you hear?" Ben asked.

Abigail gave a gentle shrug. "Oh, you know – things. Mainly about the dark elves. They're always talking about which towns they might have taken over. I even recognise some of them."

Ben wanted to query her further, but Abigail seemed to recognise a passing Warden, and quickly got back to work.

"You'd better get going," Abigail said. "The supervisor doesn't like it when the spells in the bowls start to overflow. Just grab a spell, and squish it. You don't need to be too delicate about it."

"Thanks," Ben said. He promptly got to work. Abigail was right: it was pretty straightforward. He would grab a spell, squash it into a flag, and watch in fascination as the flag coloured and began to vibrate. Ben knocked out twelve of them, and carried them over to the large map. He had to wiggle himself some room to get to the table, and then placed the first flag down in the centre of West Sussex. Immediately the flag started vibrating violently, and it took several minutes to locate the exact spot where the flag was happy.

"You'll get faster," Abigail said. She was putting up her flags on Surrey, and had placed three of hers in the time it took Ben to do his first one. "Looks like you have lots of trolls in Sussex. I hear they like the hillside."

Ben noted the green flags he was placing. Yes, green was for trolls, he remembered. Ben wanted to get a better look at what else went where, but as soon as his eyes started wandering, he got a slap on the back.

"No slacking!" a passing supervisor said. "Lay those flags down and go get some more."

Slowly Ben started to get the hang of it and, after half an hour, he was almost as proficient as Abigail. No longer having to give all his attention to the job at hand, Ben took the opportunity to look around the room. It was mainly filled with Wardens, but there was also a smattering of other departments, most noticeably Spellswords. The higher-ranking ones could often be seen huddled in a corner, talking in hushed voices, pointing at various sections of the map. Ben looked for Draven, but to Ben's relief the Director of Wardens was absent.

"Ooh, look at that," Abigail said.

She was staring down at the flags Ben had processed. He had been so busy looking about that he hadn't noticed the similarity between them all.

They were all purple. All twelve of them. Twelve dark elves.

Ben's heart skipped a beat. He checked to see if anyone had noticed; not yet. He picked up the dozen flags, and walked over to the map to position them. The first flag stopped vibrating over a small town called Plompton. The second flag ended up just inches away from the first. To Ben's increasing amazement, all dozen flags were located right next each other, forming a perfect little circle.

Ben stared at the sight, his mind working furiously. He wasn't even aware of the supervisor who had stopped behind him, until the man gave a cry of alarm.

"A dozen dark elves here, sir! Town of Plompton, West Sussex."

Immediately a trio of Wardens made their way round the table. Ben quickly removed himself from the space, but not before he had taken one final look at the scene for himself.

Plompton.

Could that small town in West Sussex have been taken over by dark elves? If not, it could still be extremely useful. They needed information on the dark elf symbol. Who better to ask than a dark elf?

CHAPTER 10

SECOND-GRADE EXAM

With one week to go until the second-grade exam, Ben started getting a little nervous, though it was insignificant compared to the others. Only Aaron remained calm, cheerful even, whenever they met in the common room or in class.

"It's just about being thorough, that's all," Aaron would say, whenever he had an opportunity. "Make sure you have all departments fully covered, as I have heard the second-grade exam requires use of all of them."

Amy and Georgia gave nervous smiles of thanks whenever he offered out titbits of advice, but Ben was pleased to see that Frederick, at least, was getting sick of it.

Dagmar had managed to get Ben and Charlie off

War Room duty, enabling them to focus on the exam exclusively for the final few days. They spent every available moment finishing up the checklist and cramming as much information as they could into their heads.

With just a day remaining, Ben was feeling thoroughly frazzled. He and Charlie had gone back to the library, with books splayed in front of them.

"I can't do this anymore," Ben said, pushing away the tomes, and slouching back in the chair.

"Come on, Ben, this is our last day," Charlie said. He was diligently poring over a book titled *Tracking the Big Unseens*.

"I don't care anymore. I'm done," Ben announced. "Either I'm going to pass this thing or I'm not. I can't take any more studying or practicals."

"Easy for you to say," Charlie said, looking up for a moment. "You'll just wing the whole thing and somehow end up with straight As. Some of us actually have to work to pass."

Ben almost laughed. "You were always the exam genius at school, not me, remember?"

"That was school," Charlie said, as if that explained everything. "Give me books and theory and I'll be fine. But I bet the exam will have us tracking and shooting stuff as part of the Warden and Spellsword sections. Not exactly my strong suit."

On Charlie's insistence, they worked late that

evening, and it was only Natalie who managed to drag them out of the Institute at a reasonable hour, so they could get a proper dinner.

Ben went home that night going over each department, wondering what he would need for tomorrow's exam. By eight o'clock his head was spinning and it was only a good game of FIFA on the Xbox that managed to finally switch him off and eventually get him to sleep.

Ben's stomach felt more than a little funny the following morning, but he forced down some eggs and bacon, before setting off to the Institute. He met Charlie on the Dragonway platform, his head buried deep in a book titled *Last-Minute Second-Grade Exam Revisions.*

"Why aren't you reading?" Charlie asked, by way of introduction, as they boarded the Dragonway. "We've still got almost two hours of cramming we can get in."

Ben shrugged. "If I read another book, I'm fairly sure I'll vomit."

The journey to the Institute was one of the least pleasant in Ben's memory. By the time they arrived in Taecia and started climbing the hill to the Institute, Ben's stomach was making peculiar noises with each passing step. He wasn't one to sweat, but every time he checked his forehead, he noticed it was damp, despite the brisk morning weather.

Natalie waited for them at the door with a nervous smile, and they headed into muster together.

"Any last words of advice?" Ben said. "You did the second-grade exam not too long ago, right?"

"Yes, and you know I'm not allowed to say anything," Natalie said with a gentle, but firm frown. "Just remember – the exam tests all departments. It's up to you how to use them all. If you leave one out, you may fail that department."

"Good, no pressure, then," Ben said, who had secretly been wondering if he could ditch Diplomacy entirely.

Muster was rattled off quickly. To Ben's surprise, he noticed that even Aaron had a crease of anxiety on his normally ice-cool face. Dagmar dismissed the apprentices in double-quick time, and then beckoned the six of them forwards. Natalie gave them a thumbs up before leaving with the rest.

"Follow me," Dagmar said.

She led them out of muster and along the hallway, stopping at a series of doors Ben rarely paid much attention to. They were labelled "Exam Room #1", "Exam Room #2", and so on. Dagmar stopped in between rooms five and six. From her pocket she pulled out six small, purple envelopes. Each one had a name written on it.

"Do not open these until you are inside the exam room," she said, handing them each an envelope.

"This is not your first exam, but the rules bear repeating. There are no questions; no right or wrong answers. You will be given a task, and it is up to you how you complete it. The more you can display what you have learnt in each department, the better your marks will be. You have until four o'clock to complete the exam, though the quicker you finish, the higher you will score. Your final grade will be comprised of individual marks for each department. Failure to complete the exam, or complete it with a score too low, and you will not be invited to continue to the next grade of the apprenticeship. Your performance will be closely monitored by an Institute examiner, though you will not see them, and they will not intervene unless it is a matter of life or death. Any questions?"

Ben knew he'd have some the moment he entered the exam room, but his mind had gone temporarily blank. Charlie looked incapable of speech. Even Aaron had gone slightly pale.

"Very well. You may start the exam." She gave them a nod, and said, "Good luck." That was all the encouragement they were going to get from her.

Dagmar walked away, leaving the six of them to their envelopes.

Aaron stepped into his room immediately. Ben exchanged glances with the rest of the group.

"Good luck, guys," he said.

The others mumbled returned sentiments, with various levels of anxiety. With the envelope firmly in hand, Ben entered door number five.

It was very similar to last time. The room was bare except for a long table, covered with an expensive-looking tablecloth. On it was an array of items. There was a file, with several sheets of paper inside. Next to the file was a silver collar attached to a rope. It looked like some sort of dog collar, with a latch for opening. There appeared nothing else remarkable about it, except its obvious value in the metal. The only other item was money – two hundred pounds in used notes. Ben searched the room to make sure he had missed nothing, checking underneath the table. Once satisfied he opened the letter Dagmar had given him, and started reading.

"EXAM: *Second-Grade Apprenticeship, Ben Greenwood*

MISSION GOAL: *Locate and remove the German kobold haunting the neighbourhood of Igloor, Taecia.*

MISSION DETAILS:

A rare German kobold has been sighted in the neighbourhood of Igloor, causing unrest amongst citizens. Noted as the strongest of the kobold family, these creatures are notoriously difficult to capture and not to be underestimated. It is your job to locate the kobold, and take any means necessary to get it back to Germany."

Ben re-read the mission several times, making

sure he grasped its entire significance. The good news was that he didn't have to leave Taecia, which also meant that discretion wasn't as important as in the previous exam, where tracking a goblin in the streets of Sussex had been a nightmare.

The bad news was the German kobold and getting it back to Germany. Ben felt his stomach drop to his knees. He had run a few magic simulations against kobolds, and to say they were a pain in the backside would be an understatement. They made the goblin he had faced in the first exam look like a walk in the park. Ben hadn't even heard of the German variety, but if the exam description was anything to go by, it might end up being really difficult.

Ben opened the file and read a very brief description of what a German kobold was and what it could do. It was a pitifully small read, and told him little more than what he already knew. It wasn't going to be enough to get the job done. In times gone past, Ben might have tried winging it, but he knew better now. Grabbing the contents of the table, Ben stuffed everything in his pocket and left the room. Immediately he noticed the two diamonds on his shoulder flashing, an indication that he was now officially in exam and should not be interrupted.

Ben took the stairs to the library, trying to gather his thoughts, which were already starting to scramble. It was ten o'clock; he had until four to complete the task. Plenty of time for a bit of research, providing he found what he needed in due course. This might be his only opportunity to display his Scholarly knowledge, and he didn't want to blow it.

He found an empty table, and sat down. Now what? Books. Books on kobolds, ideally of the German variety. Silently thanking Charlie for his continued orientation on the library, it wasn't long before he had a stack of books that could be useful. The German kobold, as it turned out, was as elusive in textbooks as it was in the real world, and it took Ben some time before he came upon a passage of use.

"While the common kobold is generally considered less dangerous and intelligent than the goblin, the German variety is a noted exception. Similar in appearance to their goblin cousins, they are tricky, devious and take apparent pleasure in causing mischief. The German kobolds are particularly adept at this. They are noted for their ability to turn almost invisible for extensive periods of time and can climb like monkeys. Unlike goblins, they have little intention of mingling among humankind. Their only redeeming feature is that they are not truly evil. The German kobolds are magic-resistant, but are vulnerable to fire and silver."

It was the best Ben could find, but he needed more. How do you find these German kobolds if they are so elusive? And once found, how do you convince them to stop causing mayhem? Ben decided to give himself until lunchtime to solve these mysteries. But by twelve o'clock, he still didn't have the answers, and was left staring at the textbooks with growing frustration, unable to discover anything further that might help. What he really needed now was Charlie.

Ben slapped his hands down on the table. He couldn't afford to waste any more time. He ran up to the dining hall, grabbed a sandwich, and then headed out of the Institute, munching on a chicken baguette and making a beeline for the local spell market. Stuffed in his pocket was the collar and lead, along with the money he had to spend.

An hour later, Ben felt he had fully worked off the chicken baguette he had eaten, negotiating with some of the toughest traders to get the most out of his two hundred pounds for spells he might just need against the German kobold. Hopefully that took care of the Scholar and Trade departments. It was now two o'clock, which gave him a couple of hours to track down the kobold. Ben picked up the pace.

Ben knew the neighbourhood of Igloor fairly well, having passed through it regularly to get to one of his favourite restaurant districts. It was an uninspiring area, known primarily for housing people who couldn't afford to live in other areas of Taecia. Its only redeeming feature was a quaint bridge that ran over a bubbling stream and led to a pleasant green area.

Next to it was a small woodland, famous for its apple trees, according to Charlie.

But on this occasion, the aromas coming from the restaurants could be a problem. Ben had read that the German kobold emitted a very specific smell from the household it chose to domesticate, and the smell of food from the nearby restaurants would only complicate matters. Ben was still debating the issue when he came upon Igloor Street. He stopped, hands on hips, examining the houses and the small stream that ran alongside them, already testing his sense of smell to see what he could detect.

"Ben?"

A familiar voice made him turn. To his great surprise, he saw Aaron strolling down the street towards him. He was looking at each of the houses with great interest.

"Well, that's good timing," Aaron said, with one of his easy smiles. "The question is – are we here to look for the same thing? Because if so, one of us is going to be disappointed and, frankly, I'd rather that wasn't me."

Ben didn't take the bait. "What are you looking for?"

Aaron gave a soft laugh. "Come on, Ben, don't be ridiculous. I'm not going to tell you that. We're not on the same team, remember?"

"So you keep reminding me," Ben said. "What do you want to do? I'm not leaving this street."

Aaron clearly wasn't happy about that, but Ben couldn't care less. He couldn't imagine the Institute having them look for the same creature, for it would mean one of them would have to fail. But Aaron looked worried, and Ben wasn't about to reassure him.

"If you won't do me the honour of leaving," Aaron said eventually, "I guess we'll both wander down this street, until one of us finds something."

Ben smiled, enjoying Aaron's displeasure. "Yes, let's do that."

Aaron set a purposefully slow pace, which Ben matched. It was an odd moment, both of them examining each passing house. Was Aaron looking for the same signs? One thing was for certain: Ben wasn't going to give his game away with Aaron around.

A sudden cry from nowhere disrupted Ben's thoughts and made him jump.

"What was that?" Ben asked, taking his attention off the houses.

He saw the problem immediately, on the open field across from the stream. There was a mother pushing a buggy with a young boy in tow. It was she who had made the cry, and was staring into the small woodland with a look of pure horror.

A huge wolf emerged, stepping out from the woods onto the field. It wasn't a wolf, Ben realised, but a Ferral Dog. It had a huge grizzled body, spiky ears, and long fang-like teeth. It gave an excited growl, and started forwards towards the mother and her children.

"Uh oh – you see that?" Ben asked, turning to Aaron.

Aaron was watching the scene keenly, his hand on his spellshooter. "I see it. Come on, let's go help."

Ben didn't need asking twice. He dashed across the bridge, over the stream, and onto the field. Heart thumping, he sprinted towards the mother and her children, his only thought to get there before the Ferral Dog. He made it just in time. The Ferral Dog had spotted him and slowed its advance, taking in its new adversary. But its surprise wouldn't last long, especially when it realised Ben didn't pose much of a threat.

"Oh, thank you!" the mother said, scrambling to get herself and her boy behind Ben. Her initial reaction at Ben's obvious youth was dismissed the moment she saw the spellshooter in his hand, and the flashing diamonds over his shoulder.

"No problem," Ben said, throwing the mother a reassuring smile. He turned to Aaron. "What sort of spell do you—?"

Ben stopped.

Aaron wasn't with him. To his astonishment, he spotted Aaron across the stream, still on Igloor Street. He hadn't moved a jot.

"What's your friend doing?" the mother asked. "Is he going to get more help?"

Ben shook his head. "I don't think so."

He dismissed Aaron's treachery from his mind and drew his spellshooter. He had only a limited number of spells, and they were meant for the German kobold.

"Are you going to shoot the bad doggy?"

Ben turned, and saw the little boy looking with remarkable lack of fear at the Ferral Dog.

"I'm still thinking about it," Ben admitted, pulling the little boy back, out of harm's way and into the arms of his mother. What had Natalie said about Ferral Dogs? They don't eat young ones, but that didn't stop them playing with them. What sort of spells could he use against these things? Now Ben wished he had paid more attention to the section on freakishly large pets during his studies.

"Where do you live?" Ben asked, keeping his voice light, while watching the dog.

"Across the bridge, on Igloor Street," the woman replied. Despite the danger, she was doing a remarkably good job of remaining calm in front of her kid.

"Okay." Ben took a deep breath. "As soon as I fire, I want you to start walking to the bridge. Don't run, as it might attract the dog's attention. Got it?"

The mother nodded nervously.

Ben set himself and readied his spellshooter. He mentally sifted through the spells in his orb. There wasn't really any he could spare, but he had to use something.

"Get ready!"

Ben fired a small fireball right into the Ferral Dog's nose.

The dog roared. The mother grabbed her buggy and child, and headed for the bridge. Ben stood fast, placing himself between the dog and the fleeing family.

The Ferral Dog was rattled, and shook its ragged fur furiously. Ben hoped it would retreat back into the small woodlands. But it didn't. Instead, it shook itself down and gave Ben a rather unpleasant look, green eyes shining with malevolence.

Ben couldn't afford to waste any more spells, unless he wanted to sacrifice any chance of capturing the German kobold.

The Ferral Dog hunched down, ready to strike.

With a curse of frustration, Ben holstered his spellshooter, and raised his arms, tensing himself.

"You want to fight?" Ben growled. "Let's do this."

Before the dog could move a muscle, Ben leapt right at him, diving into the dog's broad shoulders with everything he had. It was only surprise that gave Ben any sort of chance, for it was clear the Ferral Dog was not used to being attacked by a human.

They both went down in a heap – Ben punching and scrapping; the Ferral Dog trying to get its mighty claws and jaws to bear. Ben managed to avoid them for a few valuable seconds, but eventually he cried out in pain, as the dog dug his teeth into Ben's arm. A solid knee into the dog's underbelly quickly released the jaws. Ben felt dizzy, blood seeping along his shirt, but the Ferral Dog's appetite for combat was also starting to wane. Summoning the last of his strength, Ben thumped the dog squarely in the jaw, like a prize fighter going for the killer blow. The Ferral Dog had had enough. With a yelp, it tore away from Ben, and fled back into the woodland.

Ben lay flat on his back in the grass, panting, pain raking through his body. He seemed to be stinging everywhere, and his skin was a mass of red welts. Elation at victory temporarily revived him, and he stood up; but another look at his injured body promptly had him sitting down again. He tenderly wiped away the blood as best he could, and stumbled to his feet. From across the bridge, he could see the mother staring at him. He gave her a reassuring wave, but it took a little time to hobble along the field and over the bridge to re-join her.

"Oh my goodness, are you okay?" she asked, the moment she saw his state. She extracted a bunch of baby wipes from her nappy bag and started dabbing onto his exposed scratches.

"Ow! I'm fine, thanks," Ben said. "Just a little scratched. Nothing that won't heal."

"I cannot thank you enough," the mother said, reluctantly putting the baby wipes away. "I shall be reporting your bravery to the Institute – it is exemplary. You know, I've walked along here for years now and never encountered any Ferral Dogs before." She lowered her voice in a conspiratorial manner. "Do you think it has anything to do with any of the dark elf rumours? I've heard they are causing all sorts of trouble."

Ben shrugged. "Possibly. I wouldn't worry about it too much, but it might be wise to walk somewhere else in future, just in case."

"Oh, don't worry about that." She gave Ben one more look of gratitude. "Are you sure there's nothing I can do for you?"

Ben turned and glanced down the neighbourhood. "You didn't see my friend, did you?"

"No – he left as soon as I came across the bridge, which was a shame because I wanted to have a few words with him."

Ben smiled. “I would have liked to have seen that.”

Had Aaron found what he was looking for or had he moved on? It didn’t much matter now.

“You said you live around here, right?” Ben asked.

“Yes – why?”

Ben ran a hand through his hair. “I know it’s a long shot, but I’m on duty for the Institute, trying to track down an Unseen that shouldn’t be here. They aren’t easy to find, but they do have one distinctive giveaway, and that’s their smell.”

The mother brightened immediately. “Tomato ketchup?”

Ben grinned. “That’s it! Have you smelled anything like that around here recently?”

In a way of acknowledgement, the mother started pushing the buggy down the street. As they approached the corner, Ben got his first whiff – it was faint, but unmistakable.

“These three houses have all complained of the smell in the last forty-eight hours,” the lady said. “I’ve also heard rumours that they’ve been complaining about their basements.”

Ben’s heart quickened. “What sort of complaining?”

“Noises, mainly,” the lady said. “Things being moved. Smells. I don’t think any of them have had the courage to investigate. Your timing might be perfect."

"Let's hope so," Ben said. "Thank you very much, that's very helpful."

"It's the very least I can do," the mother said. With one last effusive thank you, she left at a pace that suggested she was eager to get off the street, and Ben didn't blame her.

He turned his attention to the three houses, hands on hips. Helping the mother had proved to be a stroke of good fortune. Instead of a whole neighbourhood to search, he was already down to three houses. Ben glanced at his watch – 2:45pm, which gave him just over an hour to try to locate and capture the German kobold. Ignoring the urge to hurry, he began circling each of the houses, focusing his attention on the foundations and concentrating on the smell. It took a dozen passes, but the subtle scratches and crumble of cement on the corner house left Ben in little doubt that he had his most likely candidate. To top it off, the smell of ketchup was definitely stronger.

Ben attempted to tidy himself up, momentarily regretting not allowing the mother to indulge him in a few more of those baby wipes. He did as best he could, making sure there was no blood showing and grimacing while he scraped off the last little bits of red on his arms. There wasn't much he could do about the raw scratches, except cover them up as best he could.

Ben climbed the little stairs to the front door and gave a confident rap. For a moment, he thought nobody was in, but after a minute waiting impatiently, a chubby lady with rosy red cheeks opened the door.

CHAPTER 11

THE GERMAN KOBOLD

"Hello?" she said in a crisp voice that was perhaps a little more defensive than Ben might have expected.

Ben put on his most relaxed smile. "Hi there. My name is Ben Greenwood – I work at the Institute. I understand you've been having some problems with an Unseen in your basement? I'm here to help."

It was a long shot, but Ben went direct. He didn't have time to come up with an alternative plan. Fortunately, the lady's suspicious glance quickly gave way to an agreeing nod.

"Aye, I have," she said. "Just these last two days."

She beckoned him in. Ben waited politely in the hallway while the woman shut and then, to his surprise, bolted the door.

"This way," she said, directing him straight to a narrow flight of stairs that went both up and down. Now that they were safely inside the house, the lady gave him a more thorough look, noting the two flashing diamonds over his shoulder.

"You are an apprentice?" she asked.

"I am."

Ben was expecting some disgruntlement, but instead she just shrugged. "Better than nothing. The Institute is so busy these days that I never thought I'd get any help at all. Do you know what you're doing? I don't want my house destroyed."

Confidence, that was key. The lady needed reassuring, and he didn't blame her. Ben, after all, was a barely sixteen-year-old apprentice, who probably looked a little worse for wear.

"I believe you have a German kobold in your basement," Ben said, placing his hands authoritatively behind his back. "They can be troublesome and are best removed as quickly as possible, before they decide to domesticate the place."

The lady paled. "I had a feeling from the smell that it was a kobold. How bad are German ones?"

"They can be dangerous, if not dealt with properly," Ben said diplomatically. "However, I have everything at hand, and should have the matter wrapped up in less than an hour."

"Are you sure?" the lady said, looking at him doubtfully.

No, I'm completely winging it, Ben wanted to say. *I've never tackled a German kobold before, and I'm exhausted from fighting that Ferral Dog*. Instead, he smiled.

"I don't anticipate any problems."

The lady gave him one final look, and then nodded.

Ben started down the stairs, and then turned back. "You might hear some noises and scrapes. Please, whatever you do, don't come down after me; it will only make things more dangerous."

He turned and continued down into the basement, before she had a chance to change her mind. It got dark and cold remarkably quickly, and all of a sudden Ben could see his breath in front of his face. Though he walked softly, his breathing alone would have woken any suspects below. At the end of the stairs was a closed door. Ben drew his spellshooter and approached it cautiously. He took a deep breath. *Focus. Remember everything you have learnt. This is no ordinary kobold.*

Ben felt in his pocket for the reassuring collar and rope. Then, with a small intake of breath, he turned the handle, and pushed open the door.

The room was larger than he had expected, with a small, dingy light hanging from the ceiling. Ben absorbed everything as quickly as possible, looking for signs of life. The place was a storage area, and not a very good one. Boxes littered the floor, many half open, others packed to the brim with clothes and other peculiar objects particular to living life in the Unseen Kingdoms. Ben's curiosity was piqued by the old armour collecting dust in one corner and a large stack of hay in the other – for pets possibly? Above him the low-hanging ceiling was constructed of wooden beams, with plenty of dark spaces for hiding.

Dark spaces. The German kobold was drawn to dark spaces. Ben eyed the ceiling closely, but saw no sign of movement. With his spellshooter primed and ready, he methodically worked his way into a corner, and started poking round for a closer inspection. His nose twitched. The smell of ketchup was so strong here it was as if someone had started a factory in the basement. With heart-stopping certainty, Ben knew that the kobold was here, somewhere.

The problem was they were rather good at hiding, especially if they didn't want to be found. And if they did, you were normally the last to know about it. Ben used his spellshooter to move items aside to try to get a better look at things. He found nothing of interest, and his eyes were starting to sting, trying to see in the dark. It was time for his first spell. A flash of light ignited from his spellshooter, giving him better visibility instantly.

A scratching noise made Ben trip up on a box of clothes. Ben flung his arms out to try to catch himself, and looked up, heart hammering. There! In the ceiling, a shadow flickered. It disappeared before he could place it, certainly before he could target it.

Ben scrambled to his feet and tried to stop breathing, but it was no good. Whatever he had seen was no longer there. Or was it? The kobold could go practically invisible at the drop of a hat. For all he knew, it could be above his head right now, ready to launch itself at him.

Well, the sneak attack obviously wasn't going to work. That left only one other option.

Ben cleared his voice, and spoke in an authoritative tone. "I know you're up there. Come down and let's talk."

As far as opening salvoes, it wasn't the greatest, but Ben was rewarded with another scraping noise and a further flicker of movement. Now that he had spotted the kobold, Ben felt a little more confident, though the nerves soon started flaring again the moment it disappeared. Ben slowed his breathing once more to create silence, but the kobold was remarkably light on its feet, and it was only when he really strained that he could hear the creature walking across the wooden beams above. Ben tried to track the movement at ground level. He felt for the spells inside his orb – he had only a dozen, and he needed to choose wisely. *Shoot now or wait?*

"I'm going to give you one further warning," Ben said, raising his voice a little. "Come down and talk, or I will bring you down."

There was a soft cackle from above. "You come up, little boy!"

Ben caught the condescending tone in the kobold's voice, but he wasn't fazed. He pointed his spellshooter up at the rafters.

"Last chance, kobold," Ben said. "I'm going to blast the whole place down if I need to. You know I can."

Ben thought his threat sounded empty, so he was surprised when he heard a light thump hit the ground. Ben stepped backwards instinctively, and then cursed himself for the sign of weakness.

"Now what, little boy?" the kobold said.

To Ben's surprise, he found himself looking at a creature that didn't resemble a goblin at all – there was a confidence in those eyes, and intelligence. Physically too, they were different. The kobold had a long alligator jaw. He had scaly skin that was hidden by light leather armour, giving him a more primaeval appearance, compared to the street goblin Ben had faced in the previous exam. But there was nothing primaeval about the way he stood or talked. In his hand was a small spear, the tip of which glowed a dull red.

Ben knew immediately that any sort of diplomacy was going to be difficult, but he had to try.

"I am going to return you back to Germany," Ben said in a clear voice. "Whether you come peacefully or not is entirely up to you. However, any resistance to arrest will be met with the full force of the law."

"Germany?" The kobold twisted his head. "I travelled many miles to escape Germany. You think I would just return? You are crazy, little boy. Is that your only offer?"

"I can offer you protection in Germany, with our Institute arm over there," Ben said. He was now talking complete rubbish, but it was worth a go. "You will be safely lodged and given protection for a period of thirty days. After that time, you will be expected to fend for yourself."

Incredibly, the German kobold seemed to consider his offer. His green eyes narrowed, and his long tongue licked out. Ben kept a neutral face, trying desperately not to show how much he needed this deal. The fact was he was tired from fighting the Ferral Dog, and he wasn't sure he could tackle this kobold so soon after.

There was a moment's silence.

The kobold raised his spear, and shook his head. "I refuse your offer, little boy. I have decided to live here. The room is comfortable, it is warm, and I am content."

Ben thought about rationalising, but what was the point? He'd read how stubborn kobolds were.

"Your choice," Ben said.

The kobold was clearly expecting Ben to be flustered or at least momentarily taken aback. It caused the kobold to hesitate, just for a second. Ben had one opportunity, and he struck. No sooner had the words come out of his mouth, than he raised his spell-shooter and ripped a fireball right into the kobold's chest. The kobold flew back with a scream, crashing into the wall. He wasn't down for long, but Ben hadn't expected him to be. They were highly resistant to magic, and Ben couldn't afford to buy expensive spells with the budget he was given.

"That hurt," the kobold said with some surprise, rubbing his stomach, as he got up.

"That's the idea," Ben said.

The kobold flashed its white teeth, and brought forth its small spear. "Now it's my turn to hurt you, little boy."

Ben had read about the German kobold's competence with a spear, and he was ready. He fired a spell into his hand, producing a slender sword. The kobold registered the weapon. Ben had hoped for a reckless charge, but in another indication of the creature's intelligence, he advanced slowly. Ben was ready, or thought he was. The kobold attacked out of the blue, with blistering pace. Ben was immediately backpedalling, trying to shuffle his feet so that he didn't fall over the various debris lying on the basement floor. The kobold turned, and spun, the red-tipped spear cutting a stream of light through the air. Ben managed to cut and block several times before he felt the first painful sting, biting into his shoulder. He ducked and threw himself left, just about avoiding an impaling. But the kobold didn't let up – he turned immediately, chasing his prey, going for the kill.

Ben brought his spellshooter up, and fired. A flare of bright light filled the room, and the kobold screamed in pain. Ben launched forwards, and threw himself into the kobold's chest. They both went down in a heap, but the kobold recovered with remarkable speed and strength, and Ben was suddenly fighting not to have the creature all over him.

Ben was starting to tire. He tried kneeing the kobold, but couldn't summon the strength. The kobold's wiry hands squeezed down on his wrists, and his large jaw-like mouth closed in on his exposed neck. Ben kicked frantically, strength borne of panic, but to no avail.

No! He was not going to get eaten by a kobold. This couldn't be happening.

"Is everything okay down there?"

The lady's voice floated down the stairway, and into the room.

The kobold jolted upwards, and glanced towards the open door in surprise.

Ben struck, hard, taking advantage of the kobold's momentary weakened grip. He threw a fist at the kobold's exposed jaw. He adjusted his spell-shooter, and unloaded a flame spell right into the kobold's face. While the kobold was screaming in pain, Ben dived away and thrust his hand into his pocket, pulling out the silver collar and the rope. He looped it over the kobold's head, and pulled the rope, tightening it so it almost choked the kobold.

That did the trick.

The kobold's anger quickly turned to horror, and it scrabbled at the collar.

"Stop! Stop!"

Ben loosened the grip, but only a fraction. "Stop moving or I'll tighten it again."

The kobold obeyed immediately, and Ben realised then what a mistake he had made. Why hadn't he purchased more silver-based spells? They were so effective. It was too late for that now. Ben pulled the German kobold to his feet, none too gently. He wanted nothing more than to lean against the wall and attempt to recover, but now wasn't the time.

"We're going to the Dragonway," Ben said. "Any

funny moves and I'll choke you to death. Do I make myself clear?"

The kobold nodded, his sharp hands clawing at the collar, but to no avail.

Ben marched up the stairs, the kobold before him. There, in the hallway, was the lady, waiting for him the moment he appeared. Her eyes almost exploded from her sockets the moment she saw them.

"It's a bit messy down there," Ben said with an apologetic smile. "You might want to clear it up a bit when you have a moment."

The lady nodded silently. With a pale face, she muttered something that sounded like "thank you", and ushered them both outside onto the street. Ben heard the door lock twice behind him.

Now out in the open, the temptation was to relax, but Ben knew his work was far from over. The kobold was already starting to recover, and Ben saw him eyeing freedom with greedy eyes. It took several violent yanks to remove his obvious intent.

Ben walked, trying not to show how exhausted he was to the kobold, knowing one violent attack and the creature could probably escape. He got several stares as he marched the German kobold to the Dragonway, but the kobold got far more. They were not a common sight, even in Taecia, and the German variety was almost unheard of. Ben was thankful that most gave him plenty of room, for he lacked the energy to even bother telling people to get out of the way. He struggled up the Dragonway stairs, and up onto the bridge that ran over the platforms. Here he stopped. Number three declared an eventual passage to Düsseldorf, which was the only name Ben recognised as German. Düsseldorf it was, then. Ben tugged the kobold and was already heading down the platform when he realised what his next problem would be. Did he board the Dragonway with the kobold to ensure delivery? If so, he would never make it back in time. Or should he just dump the kobold on the Dragonway and hope he made it back safely? Somehow, Ben couldn't see that happening.

"Mr. Greenwood," a voice called from ahead.

Ben looked up, and to his great relief saw a man with three red diamonds over his shoulder walking right towards him.

"I'll take over from here," the man said, giving Ben an approving nod.

Ben was more than happy to hand over the collar to the Warden.

"You'd better get back – you have less than twenty minutes before the exam ends, and every second counts."

Ben watched as the Warden marched off with the kobold in tow, until they disappeared into the carriage.

Ben wanted to dash back. He knew he should,

and that the outcome of the exam could lie in how quickly he made it back to the Institute. But it was all he could do to drag his body out of the Dragonway and up the hill towards the Institute. He felt light-headed, and almost fell down on numerous occasions. He was vaguely aware that he was lacking blood. Ben glanced at his watch: 3:45pm. Fifteen minutes, and only five minutes away.

He would be fine. How had he done on each department? Ben couldn't even think each one through, let alone come up with an assessment of how he had performed.

As he approached the entrance, he was vaguely aware that Dagmar was standing by the door with a stopwatch in hand. Her eyes registered not even the slightest surprise at his condition, but Ben didn't care.

"3:48pm," Dagmar said. "You cut it tight, Ben Greenwood."

Ben couldn't summon up a reply. He walked to the marble stairs, and slumped down, unable to move anymore.

"Ah, you made it!"

Ben glanced up to see Aaron grinning down at him, along with the other apprentices. Only Charlie was missing.

"What did I tell you?" Aaron said. "Research and revision are the key to the exams. I got here at least an hour ago, and in far better shape, I might add. You look awful."

Ben was completely dead, devoid of energy, but somehow Aaron managed to summon something from within him. He stood up, with some difficulty, and gave Aaron a look that he hoped conveyed the revulsion that he felt.

Georgia, standing beside Aaron, certainly felt it, and she looked at him in shock. "What's that for?"

Ben blinked. Slowly – very slowly, he stepped forwards and launched a right hook at Aaron's face.

He missed by miles, and fell, unconscious on the marble floor.

CHAPTER 12

THE THIRD-GRADE

Ben woke to the pleasant feel of clean, crisp sheets and the wonderful absence of pain. His eyes shot open, and he found himself looking at an unfamiliar ceiling, in an unfamiliar room. He was lying in one of a row of empty beds.

"Morning!" Natalie said brightly.

Ben lifted his head, and saw Charlie and Natalie sitting on a couple of chairs that had clearly been pulled into what looked like a very clean hospital ward. There were no medical instruments, but several jugs of various breweries and a dish of fresh fruit were placed on top of a table. There were also vases of flowers all about, giving the room a sweet, fresh smell.

"What time is it?" Ben asked.

"Just gone eleven o'clock," Charlie said with a grin as wide as Natalie's.

"What? How's that possible?" Ben sat up, suddenly aware that he wasn't wearing very much. "What day is it?"

"The day after the exam," Natalie said. "By the way, those clothes at the end of the bed are yours. Charlie got them from your house this morning."

A quick change later, and Ben was sitting at the end of the bed, admiring his skin, which now showed only faint scratches and scars.

"Wren herself did the healing," Natalie said, sounding suitably impressed. "It was a combination of magic and herbs. Some of the cuts were pretty deep."

Her green eyes were full of curiosity, but it was obvious she was doing her best to resist asking what happened.

Charlie had no such restraints. "Why did you try to hit Aaron in the face? I'm sure he deserved it, but it has certainly got people talking, and not in a good way."

Ben frowned. "Who's talking? There were only a few people there at the time."

"True, but by the time Aaron had done a full stage reproduction, most of the apprentices probably think they were there too."

Ben clenched the mattress in frustration. "I

twitch, but resisted the urge to grab his one until instructed.

Dagmar inspected each of them, looking even more severe than usual.

"I don't know the results. As apprentices, it is always your right to see first. However, I will be at my desk for the next seven minutes, if you need to see me."

Without further ado, she left them alone with the envelopes.

Ben frowned. That seemed an odd statement for Dagmar to make, given that she knew nothing about the results. Did she suspect someone had failed? Ben glanced around, and saw six sets of nervous faces. Aaron was the first to grab his envelope, snatching it from the desk, and drawing it up to his face. Ben's eagerness to wallop the idiot was still strong, but there was a time and place for everything.

"Here goes nothing," Aaron said with a smile that somehow managed to look relaxed, despite the pressure.

Ben watched Aaron's expression as he tore open the envelope, and took out a small piece of card.

He burst into a grin. "As across the board!"

Amy and Georgia burst into applause, and Frederick gave him an envious smile. Charlie looked disappointed. Ben expected Aaron to stay and watch them open their results, but, to his surprise, he immediately left the room. Ben caught the merest flicker of annoyance on Aaron's face as he left. What was that about? He turned to Charlie, but he clearly hadn't noticed.

"No!"

Ben turned, and saw Georgia staring in horror at her results. Hand on mouth, she suddenly burst into tears and fled the room. Amy tried to console her, but Georgia was gone before she had the chance. With growing alarm, Amy and Frederick grabbed their own results. They both sighed with such relief the moment they scanned the results, but their smiles were less than they might have been, with Georgia still fresh in their minds.

"I passed," Amy said. "I can't believe Georgia failed. She was getting special guidance from Aaron. Do you guys mind if I go find her?"

Ben was more than happy to usher Frederick and Amy out of the room, leaving him alone with Charlie, and just the two remaining exam results.

"I don't know what you're worried about," Charlie said. He grabbed his envelope from the desk. "Time to put myself out of my misery."

Holding his breath, Charlie pulled open his results, and stared at the card, inches from his face.

He broke into a broad grin.

"Passed!" he said, flashing the card wildly. "I even

managed a B in the Department of Wardens. That's ridiculous!"

Ben enjoyed Charlie's elation, but at some point he had to confront his own results. He suddenly found his hands were sweaty and they stuck to the envelope when he picked it up. With a silent curse, he tore open the score card, and devoured its contents.

Name: Ben Greenwood

Exam: Second Grade

Department Results:

Diplomacy: B

Scholar: B

Spellsword: A

Trade: B

Warden: A

Overall: A (pass)

Ben's first thought was that someone had made a mistake. His second thought was drowned out by a feeling of sheer elation that ran from his head right down to his toes. He almost collapsed onto the floor with relief.

"I'm not even remotely surprised," Charlie said with a grin.

"I am," Ben said earnestly. "I thought I'd blown it with my stupid heroics. Come on, let's go tell Natalie."

They found her in the common room. The moment

they made eye contact, she squealed and practically leapt on them with delight. It took several minutes before they could disentangle and calm her down.

"That's a shame about Georgia," Natalie said, when she finally conceded to sitting back down. The common room was pleasantly empty, with most of the apprentices working on their handbooks.

"Yeah, it is," Ben said. "I quite liked her. What's weirder, though, was Aaron's reaction. I could have sworn he was angry about something, which doesn't make sense if he got straight As – unless he was lying."

"Which, knowing Aaron, is entirely possible," Charlie said, helping himself to a cup of tea.

They talked enthusiastically about the third grade. Ben kept on glancing at the three colourless diamonds now hovering over his shoulder, trying to get used to the increased number.

"They say the apprenticeship really starts in the third grade," Natalie said. "It's definitely harder, and there are a lot more practicals to do. Remember, this is the last grade where you have to do all departments. In the fourth grade, you can ditch two and focus on the three that most interest you."

"I know what I'll be dumping," Ben said. He regretted the words as soon as they came out of his mouth and turned to Charlie, who was looking at him silently. The obvious question went unspoken.

Were they going to focus on different departments? If so, they would surely see a lot less of each other.

"Oh, don't look so miserable," Natalie said, reading between the lines. "You'll both be fine, no matter what you choose."

Natalie's words cheered Ben a little, but as he glanced down at the Institute handbook on his lap, he found himself strangely reluctant to crack on. With such a big step finished, it was sometimes hard to start the next one. His mind was already turning to something even more important than the apprenticeship and, with the common room temporarily empty, now was a good time to bring it up.

"We need to focus on the next piece of Elizabeth's Armour," Ben said. He wasn't sure why he spoke so softly; there was nobody in the room, but it felt appropriate.

"Yes!" Natalie said, clapping her hands with unexpected exuberance. "I've been wondering when you would bring that up. What are we going to do about the dark elf symbol we found in that dwarf settlement? That's our only lead."

"We need to find someone who can tell us what it is," Charlie said. "And then, we have to hope that it somehow leads us to one of the pieces of armour."

"You don't sound that optimistic," Ben said.

Charlie looked unusually downbeat, given that mysteries like this one normally had him bubbling. "I still believe that the key Winkleforth gave us was meant to show us something different."

"Like what?" Ben asked. "We searched the whole place – there was nothing else there, except for the dwarf mage, who wasn't exactly forthcoming."

Charlie raised a finger in defence. "I know. Right now, the symbol is our only lead."

Ben couldn't help wondering if Charlie was trying to imply another possible solution, but what else was there? Natalie, however, was clearly more optimistic about the symbol than Charlie.

"So, how do we find out about the symbol? I'm open to suggestions," she asked.

"Plompton," Ben said immediately.

"You what?"

In all the hubbub of the apprenticeship and the War Room, Ben realised he hadn't told Charlie and Natalie about his discovery of the small West Sussex town with an unusually high population of registered dark elves. He quickly told them now.

"Wow, I didn't know they let so many dark elves into the Seen Kingdoms," Natalie said.

"I guess if they are properly registered like all the other Unseens, it shouldn't matter. Just as long as they're not running around causing chaos," Charlie said.

Ben took a bite of a bun he'd been holding out on. "The hard part is going to be finding them, as they will obviously be disguised as humans. I've already had a look at Plompton on the map. It's not big, but it's not exactly a village of five people."

"Well, we've always got spells, right? You can fire some serious ones now," Charlie said.

Ben gave him a look. "I can't just whip up a spell out of nowhere to track down a dark elf. In fact, dark elves are much harder to track than your average goblin or troll. I would need a very specific spell, and I would need to practise."

"I'll get you the spell," Natalie said with a look of determination. "I feel like I haven't done much recently, and you guys have been so busy."

"It won't be cheap," Ben said. "And I might need a few of them."

Natalie narrowed her eyes, taking up the challenge. "I'll get you the spell. Stop worrying."

"Good. So we have a plan. Now let's go have some more lunch. All this snacking is making me hungry again."

Their plan, like most plans, turned out to take longer in practice than they would have liked. The third grade threatened to take over their lives completely and, as Natalie pointed out, it was a huge step up from the second. Dagmar was quick to drive that into them the very next day at muster.

"The third grade can take anywhere from four to six months," Dagmar said. With Georgia gone, there were now just five of them listening to her lecture, the rest of the apprentices having been dismissed. "What I do not like to see is slow starters, apprentices who barely move on their checklist for the first few weeks, thinking they are on some sort of holiday. I want you to start hard and fast. I will be reviewing your progress weekly and getting updates from all departments. Do I make myself clear?"

If Ben thought Dagmar was making empty threats, he soon found out how wrong he was. For the next week, it felt like she was hovering over his shoulder every morning, whenever he had the Institute handbook open. To make matters worse, Natalie was just as busy and finding it difficult to get hold of the exact spell needed to track down the dark elves in Plompton. Ben, who had been so determined to start tracking Elizabeth's Armour, found himself treading water just to stay afloat. If that wasn't enough, they had to resume their studies at Barrington School, which ate up a few hours each day.

Their crushing schedule might have continued indefinitely, if not for the events that happened the following Monday morning, on the way to the Institute.

CHAPTER 13
THE DARK ELVES ADVANCE

Ben and Charlie entered the Institute headquarters in Croydon like they did every morning, and immediately ran into a crowd of Institute members huddled around the lifts. They were firmly shut.

"What's going on?" Ben asked, struggling to get a view of the lifts.

"The Dragonway station is shut," a Diplomat with three diamonds said. "Which can mean only one thing – a security threat."

Ben turned to Charlie in alarm, remembering the last time the lifts had been sabotaged – a dark elf had emerged, causing absolute mayhem.

"Should we come back later?" Charlie asked hesitantly.

"They told us to wait," the Diplomat said.

Ben wasn't a big fan of doing nothing, but there appeared little else to do. He put a light hand on his spellshooter for reassurance and waited along with everyone else.

The lifts made a humming noise less than twenty minutes later. Ben's heart gave a little lurch, and he saw several other people give a start. Clearly he wasn't the only one who remembered the dark elf. To everyone's relief, the lift doors opened, revealing nothing but empty seats. There was an audible sigh of relief, and the members started filing in.

It became obvious something was wrong the moment the lifts re-opened underground and they started walking through the tunnels. Security was double the norm, and they were stopped and searched at regular intervals. The security room and the all-seeing eye on the arch seemed to regard Ben far longer than usual, before he was allowed through to the station. Then their dragon was late. When it did arrive, Ben noticed with some alarm that it had a large gash along its scales.

Unsurprisingly, people were talking, the rumours were flying, and they all centred around one topic.

A dark elf strike.

Ben and Charlie spent the entire journey listening to conversations, but it was clear nobody really knew what had happened, and wouldn't until they arrived at the Institute.

Nearly everyone on their dragon disembarked at Taecia. The majority of them were members, and started a hurried walk up the hill to the Institute.

Normally Taecia was bustling with life in the morning, with the pubs and restaurants doing a roaring trade, capturing those who wanted to eat before work. But today, the shops and restaurants were shut, and it was eerily quiet. The citizens who were about were almost outnumbered by the Wardens and Spellswords Ben spotted, clearly on security duty and watching the citizens with a suspicious eye.

Ben's concern grew as he neared the Institute's front gates, which were manned by double the guards. Members hurried in, scrambling to find news.

"Guys, over here!" Natalie said.

Natalie was standing just inside the entrance, a little to the side, so as to avoid the members streaming in. Abigail was by her side, with an expression of innocent bemusement.

"What's going on?" Charlie asked.

Natalie had small bags under her eyes, which looked slightly red. Ben had never seen Natalie look anything but flawless before.

"Dark elf attack," Natalie said in a sombre voice, almost as if she was telling a secret that she didn't want anyone to know. "It's been mad here. My parents dragged me in at 5am and I've been helping the members trying to re-establish order."

"I've never seen it like this before," Abigail said with wide-eyed wonder. "Does this happen often?"

Charlie looked around furtively, as if expecting a dark elf to jump out of nowhere. "Where did they attack?"

Before she could answer, a deep voice called out from the Institute front entrance.

"Muster as usual for the departments and apprentices," a large Scholar said. "Do not be late."

"Come on," Natalie said. "I'm sure Dagmar will know more than I do. My parents would hardly tell me anything. Nobody else will either for that matter. They are either too busy or maybe they are under orders."

They had to squeeze their way up the busy marble staircase, before exiting on the first floor, and heading straight to muster. Many of the apprentices had already arrived, and there was a tension in the air. The younger apprentices were looking around in obvious confusion, but the older ones seemed to realise that something was clearly wrong.

Dagmar flew into the room just seconds before nine o'clock, like a woman on a mission. There were several restrained gasps the moment she turned to stand behind her desk and face them. There was a large gash running from her chin to her right ear. It had clearly been magically healed, but the skin looked raw. Any pain or anguish she might have felt was typically absent, and she looked every bit as calm as usual, her steely gaze scanning the stunned apprentices without a flicker of concern.

"Muster," Dagmar announced, as if it were just another day.

Names were rattled off a trifle quicker than usual. Once finished, there was an expectant silence – Ben wasn't the only one wondering what Dagmar was going to say.

Dagmar walked round to the front of her desk, baton in hand. "I have just spent the last half an hour being briefed by the executive council on what exactly you should know," Dagmar said. "However, I abhor anything that avoids the complete and total truth."

She stopped for a moment. Ben was torn between cheering her sentiment and wishing she'd keep talking. He wasn't the only one. He could see several of the older apprentices leaning forwards in anticipation.

"Last night, the dark elves declared war on the Unseen Kingdom of Olag," Dagmar said with typical understated simplicity. "It was conquered this morning. At the same time, the dark elves launched a sneak attack on a small town in southern England called Broomfield. That was also taken."

Despite Dagmar's reputation for strict discipline, the apprentices all started talking at once, until she raised a small hand, cutting them off.

"The attacks were made simultaneously to confuse us. Olag was a significant invasion, and we made them pay for taking the kingdom. Broomfield, however, was taken on the sly. There are still several thousand people completely unaware that their town has been conquered. They will know soon enough."

Questions erupted from the older apprentices, and it took Dagmar almost ten seconds to regain silence.

"You want to know why I'm telling you this. It is because, as apprentices, you live in a cocoon, unaware of what is happening in the outside world. I don't believe this is helpful. Even if there is little you can do at present, it will very much be your business if you gain your Institute membership."

Dagmar focused primarily on the front line of apprentices – the ones who might soon become members.

"The threat from the dark elves is real. It is very real. Slowly they are taking the smaller kingdoms, but they now have the strength to hit some of the bigger ones. If they do, we are looking at full-scale war, only this time, there is no Queen Elizabeth to save us."

Ben could have sworn Dagmar's gaze flickered to

him, but it happened so quickly that he couldn't be sure.

"I will allow three questions before dismissal," Dagmar said to everyone's surprise. Ben counted at least forty hands – including his own – that were suddenly thrust into the air.

"How is this going to affect us?" a burly grade five asked from the front row.

"As little as possible, for now," Dagmar said. "You will continue with your apprenticeship, though I will be encouraging some of you to move faster, especially those close to graduating. We need more members."

To replace the ones who were lost? Ben wondered.

"Security will be tighter all over the Unseen Kingdoms, but that shouldn't affect you. As long as you display your apprenticeship diamonds, you will be fine. Next question – yes, Ben Greenwood?"

Ben was so engrossed in Dagmar's reply, he had almost forgotten his hand was in the air. His throat suddenly felt dry. He hadn't even thought of what to say, and suddenly there were almost two hundred apprentices staring at him expectantly. Ben shook himself and asked the first question that came to his head, though certainly not the most important.

"Were you involved in combat yesterday?" Ben asked.

Ben thought she was going to say it was none of his business, but after a moment she gave a nod.

"I often join the Spellswords if resources are needed," Dagmar said. "I took a spell to the face. I was fortunate that Wren was by my side at the time or else I would not be standing with you now."

Ben knew he should probably be displaying some sort of empathy, or even sympathy, at her near-death experience. But something far more alarming was ricocheting through his head. Dagmar was a Guardian. Without her, and Elizabeth's Boots under her charge, they would never make it to Suktar. Ben tried in one intense gaze to convey that thought to Dagmar, but she had already moved on.

"Yes, Simon," Dagmar said, turning to Ben's ginger-haired spellstrike team member.

"What happens if we have a full-scale war? Will we get to fight?" Simon said with a manic grin. "We could do some serious damage."

"Let us hope it doesn't come to that," Dagmar said. "There has been no full-scale war that didn't cause misery, pain and much loss. I have witnessed several."

Ben frowned at Dagmar's last comment, and he saw several others do the same, but she dismissed the gathering before anyone could brave a further question.

They left muster and headed to the common

room, but it was rammed with apprentices busting out their books and chatting away like only teenagers could.

"Let's go outside," Ben said to Charlie and Natalie.

They looked at him inquisitively but didn't argue, and he led them down the grand staircase, and outside to the Institute gardens. Ben circled round the building until they were well out of sight of the main paths. He glanced around for any guards – saw none – and plonked himself on a bench. Natalie and Charlie joined him.

Ben slouched so far back that his neck rested on the back. He stared up at the blue sky, and took a deep breath. He could feel Charlie and Natalie looking at him, but neither spoke. Ben felt awful. Somehow, with the spellstrike game and then the apprenticeship, he had almost forgotten about the dark elves. Why hadn't they dedicated more time looking for Elizabeth's Armour? They could be that much closer to finding Suktar and stopping the destruction he was spreading.

"There's nothing you could have done," Natalie said, her voice gentle.

"Natalie's right. It's not like we could have gathered all the pieces and the Guardians, and defeated Suktar. We need more time."

Ben sat up, and ran a hand through his hair. "I

know. I just feel that we should have been working on it more."

"When?" Charlie said. "I've been with you the whole time. We've been working our backsides off these last few weeks."

"Was that the right move, though?" Ben said. He rarely experienced self-doubt, but he was feeling it now. "Could we have spent a little less time on the apprenticeship, and a bit more researching Elizabeth's Armour?"

"Possibly," Charlie said with a shrug. "But I believe we needed to do that work to pass the apprenticeship, to stay in the Institute, and have any chance of finding the armour."

"Anyway, what's done is done," Natalie said with finality. "We need to look forwards, not worry about the past."

Ben shook himself, and slapped his own cheek. "You're right. I don't know why I keep thinking about the past – I don't usually do that. I just can't help thinking there was something we could have done."

"There wasn't," Natalie said firmly. "So stop beating yourself up. Now, what's the plan? You're good at making plans."

Ben was still considering the question when he heard loud footsteps heading their way, accompanied by far softer ones. They looked up with varying degrees of alarm, and saw Dagmar and Abigail walking towards them.

Ben's first thought was that Dagmar had come to reprimand them – that they should be working on their apprenticeship, not bathing in the pleasant morning sun – but he discarded that notion the moment he saw Abigail.

Dagmar stopped in front of the bench, her stern face a stark contrast to Abigail's soft, honest expression.

"I assume you came out here for privacy," Dagmar said.

Ben was thrown by the question, but recovered quickly. "Yes, we needed to talk without people hearing."

Dagmar nodded. "Good. You cast a silencer spell, I assume?"

"Er, no."

Dagmar had her spellshooter out in a flash, and fired a spell into the air. A small, transparent dome formed around them, making the world outside shimmer. Abigail stared at the dome in speechless wonder.

"Never talk about sensitive matters without casting a silencer," Dagmar said, holstering her spell-shooter. "Now more than ever, security is needed. Just yesterday we found a colony of ant pixies roaming the Institute, spying for the dark elves."

"Ant pixies?" Abigail asked. "Those sound interesting. I've never read about them."

"You won't have," Dagmar said, flicking a glance at Abigail, before returning her attention to Ben. "Now, I don't have much time, so let's get to it. What is happening with your search?"

Even under the silencer spell, Dagmar talked cryptically. It took Ben a moment to realise what she was referring to.

"We are looking for the next piece," Ben said. He gave a subtle look around, double-checking that nobody was about, despite knowing it didn't matter whilst under the silencer spell.

"Do you have a lead?"

"Yes. In fact, we were just about to discuss when we should pursue it."

"Today," Dagmar said. It wasn't quite an order, though it sounded like one.

"Today sounds good," Ben said with a small smile. "However, there are a few things we need."

"Name them."

Ben saw Natalie's eyes light up beside him. "Dark elf tracking spells."

Dagmar glanced at Natalie and, for a moment, Ben thought she might question the request. Instead, she just nodded.

"You will have them by lunchtime. Anything else?"

Ben suddenly felt rushed. Here was the chance to get pretty much anything they wanted, but when put on the spot, he couldn't think of anything. Well, he could think of a few things, but nothing relevant. Fortunately, it was Natalie who came to the rescue. She gave Dagmar a small list, which Dagmar ran her eyes over and, once again, nodded without protest. Natalie, at least, had put some thought into the mission.

"Come to my office straight after lunch," Dagmar said. She looked ready to leave, but gave them one more look.

"Time is running out. Unless you gather the Guardians and their pieces of armour soon, Suktar will have already caused irreversible damage. I know the Institute is clueless, but it is we, and more importantly you, Ben, who hold the real key to defeating the dark elves. It is time to stop dallying."

She left the three of them dumbstruck, her footsteps clattering the pathway long after she had disappeared round the corner.

It was Charlie who broke the silence, but only when Dagmar was fully out of sight. "Thanks. No pressure, then."

Ben took a deep breath, and shook himself. It was then he noticed Abigail was staring at him, with a determined glint in her large, brown eyes.

"Dagmar said I should start learning more about the helm," she said.

"Did she?"

Abigail nodded. "I think she is right. I won't be much use if you're ready to go and I can't control its magic."

"That's true," Ben said, considering his words. "But are you ready? You remember what happened the last time you wore the helm?"

Abigail gave a nod. "The dark elf king looked into my mind. It was horrible." To Ben's surprise, Abigail bit her lip, and narrowed her eyes, until they were almost entirely covered by her long lashes. "But that was only because I got his attention in the first place. If I don't go near him, I don't think he'll notice me. I'm much too insignificant. And we don't have much time, do we? I need to learn, or else I'm not going to be much good."

Ben leant forwards on the bench, eyeing Abigail closely. He admired her bravery, though he wasn't surprised by it. She was a Guardian after all.

"I will speak to Dagmar," Ben said. "I'm sure we can come up with something."

Abigail gave a relieved smile, as if she had expected Ben to protest. "Oh, thank you. Dagmar seems really knowledgeable, though she can be a bit scary sometimes." She glanced down the path towards the Institute. "Would you mind if I go back to my studies? My friend Julia is waiting for me, and we have our first Spellsword practical."

They watched Abigail return to the Institute.

"Thinking about her making the journey to Suktar scares me," Natalie said.

"She's braver than you think," Ben said.

"Oh I know she's brave. But will she be ready? The helm is so powerful, and having that connection with Suktar – how can she possibly control that?"

Ben had no answer. "Let's hope Dagmar knows, because I haven't a clue. We'll worry about that later. Come on, if we're going to go to Plompton this afternoon, we should probably start getting ready."

CHAPTER 14

A VISIT TO PLOMPTON

They had a couple of hours until lunch. With Dagmar's permission to pursue the next piece of armour rather than work on their apprenticeship, Ben felt strangely liberated. There was a lingering guilt that he would start to fall behind on the apprenticeship, but he cast that from his mind. The apprenticeship wasn't important right now.

They hit the library first and went straight to the maps and guides section. It consisted of several great big shelves that were deep enough to stick a hand into and not feel wooden backing. It took almost twenty minutes to find a decent map of West Sussex County, where Plompton was located.

"It would have almost been quicker to go back home and load up Google maps," Charlie muttered, as they headed back to the reading area, map in hand. There they commandeered an entire table and spread the map out. Ben smiled the moment he saw the layout. It wasn't an ordinary map, but a magical one, rendered in 3D, so you could see and feel all the little buildings, cars and people walking around. The town was fairly typical of one in Sussex. It had the main centre and an old section dating back to the 14th century, where the architecture was similar to Taecia's. There were also affluent, exclusive areas, with large houses and expansive gardens. The three of them pored over the map, their faces inches above the little figures and zooming cars.

"Do you remember where you placed the dark elf flags on the map?" Charlie asked.

"Over there," Ben said, pointing at a private road just outside the centre of town.

"So they're wealthy," Natalie said. "Not surprising, I guess."

"Makes it harder, though, doesn't it," Charlie said, staring at a house with an outside pool – a real luxury in England. "Those places are going to have lots of security."

"We don't need to break in," Natalie said. "We only need to ask some questions and hopefully get some answers."

Ben glanced up. He hadn't even considered the fact that a dark elf might not know what the symbol meant, but Natalie was right – they might not immediately get the answers they needed.

"It's a good thing you asked for lots of dark elf tracking spells," Charlie said. He had a magnifying glass and was now looking at each individual house close up.

After studying the map, Charlie rather enthusiastically, bounded off to find out what else he could about Plompton. He returned swiftly with a small pile of books, and started reading. "Population: 24,952. Unseen population: 5,011. That means just over twenty percent are Unseens, which is way above the national average."

Ben stifled a yawn. "Fascinating. Anything else?"

"Dwarves are the most common; dark elves are listed at less than one percent. It does say they are an affluent group, though, so those big houses are starting to look like a good bet."

By the time twelve o'clock came round, Ben felt there was nothing more they could possibly learn about Plompton without actually going there. They ate a good lunch, which was peaceful enough until Aaron wandered over with a group of friends, talking and laughing good-naturedly. Ben hadn't forgotten Aaron's underhanded actions during the exam, but he had been so busy that he hadn't put any thought about how to gain revenge. A quick rugby tackle wouldn't go amiss. He was tempted, but warning glances from both Charlie and Natalie kept him in his chair.

"How are you guys doing on the third grade?" Aaron asked. "I know we just started, but I'm finding it a level up from the previous grade, which is good, because I felt like I wasn't being challenged before."

Ben had to admire Aaron's charisma; somehow he had distracted the entire table. Ben could feel several eyes on him, clearly awaiting his response, perhaps wondering if he might lash out. But it was Charlie who spoke up, dabbing his lips with a napkin.

"We've been a bit busy, so haven't made much progress. But thanks for the heads up."

"You've been busy?" Aaron said, eyebrows raised. Ben couldn't be sure if it was surprise or disbelief. "What could be more important than the apprenticeship, especially after everything Dagmar has been telling us, with the impending war?"

Again, it was Charlie who replied, with a casual shrug. "Don't know, don't care. Listen, before you leave, could you pass me the ketchup? We've run out over here."

There was some sniggering at the table, and Ben saw Aaron's lip give a small spasm. For a minute, he thought Charlie was going to get hit with one of Aaron's witty put-downs, but he merely gave a courteous smile and nodded to one of his followers, who passed Charlie the ketchup. Aaron departed without further ado.

"Nice one, Charlie," William said, who was sitting a couple of places down. "Though I have to admit, I was hoping he got angry enough to try to hit you. That would have given me the perfect excuse to clobber him."

"What have you got against Aaron?" a fourth-grader whose name Ben couldn't remember said. "He hasn't done anything wrong, and he has every right to be angry near Ben, after what he did."

"What did he do?"

"Assaulted him!" a young girl, one of Abigail's friends, said, clearly unable to contain herself.

"If by assaulting you mean didn't touch him, then yes, that's true," Charlie said.

"No, I mean punching him full in the face. Aaron even showed us the cut on his lip – it was nasty."

The noise at the table swiftly grew, as people threw opinions back and forth like exploding spells. The majority of the table were on Aaron's side, but what Ben's friends lacked in numbers, they made up in volume. Ben was dearly tempted to stay and fight his corner, but he didn't want to attract undue attention to himself, especially with their little mission this afternoon. He made eyes at Charlie and Natalie, gave a little salute to William, and then slipped out of the lunch room. The argument was now in full flow and nobody even seemed to notice him leave. Nevertheless, there was an air of discontent during afternoon muster. Ben searched out William, who gave him a little smile and a thumbs up. Ben was eager to find out what had happened after they left the lunch room, but thoughts of the argument passed aside as Dagmar entered.

It wasn't often that Dagmar repeated something – normally there was no need; her words were rarely forgotten. But after muster, she repeated, almost word for word, her warning about the dark elf attack, and even allowed the apprentices to ask a few more questions. This more than anything reinforced the magnitude of the dark elf attack.

"You think Dagmar has got everything for us?" Charlie asked softly, when muster was finished and the apprentices started filing out. "I saw Natalie's list; it was quite extensive."

"Let's find out," Ben said.

They headed straight to Dagmar's office and Ben, after only a moment's hesitation, gave three firm knocks.

"Come in," Dagmar said.

They found her sitting behind her desk. The place was tidy as always, but there was a remarkable amount of papers of different colours piled up in her baskets. Buried beneath the workload, Ben spotted a small spell pouch, which Dagmar grabbed and then beckoned them forwards.

"Normally I ask for an explanation of every spell used," Dagmar said. "But this time I will make an exception. Just make sure you find that dark elf and get the answers you need. It wasn't easy getting hold of the dark elf tracking spells – they are much in demand and we are running out of stock."

Ben thanked her and took the pouch. "We'll get the answers."

Dagmar nodded. "Due to an unusually high percentage of dark elves in Plompton, there are several Wardens in the area. Don't be afraid to use them if you need to. Even dark elves attempting to live peacefully in the Seen Kingdoms can be dangerous."

They left Dagmar's office and headed downstairs, towards the front entrance. It was still manically busy, and Ben had the uncomfortable feeling that they were escaping, especially when they passed a couple of senior members who glanced their way. For a moment, he thought they might be stopped and questioned. The urge to quicken his pace and get outside suddenly overwhelmed him, but he forced himself to walk calmly right out the door.

"That was strangely difficult," Charlie said, wiping his brow, as they entered the gardens. A moment later, they were past the front gate and walking down the hill.

Despite the severity of the mission, Ben had a spring in his step, and took a deep breath of the crisp autumn air. It felt good to finally be doing something about the dark elf symbol they had discovered.

"Do we have a plan?" Charlie asked, as they boarded the Dragonway. They were taking their familiar dragon back to Croydon, and from there they would take public transport down to Plompton.

"We have six dark elf tracking spells," Ben said, feeling his spellshooter. "They can detect dark elf activity within two hundred yards. I say we head straight for that private estate where most of the dark elves are located."

"But what do we do when we actually meet a dark elf?" Charlie asked. "How do we convince them to answer our questions? I can't imagine they'll be too helpful, with everything that's going on."

"I'll think of something," Ben said.

"You mean you'll wing it," Charlie said with a frustrated sigh.

Ben grinned. "More or less. Don't worry about it. Look, we're here."

They alighted at Croydon. With the heightened security threat, it took them a longer time to get through security, especially with their spellshooters.

"Be extra careful," the guard warned them.

"There have been quite a few Unseen sightings all over England, and it's getting harder to quell them all. There have been rumours on the internet, and even in some papers, about weird goings on. Don't give them a reason to write something else."

It was close to two o'clock by the time they took a bus from Croydon down to the town of Plompton. They got off by the supermarket, and Ben got his first look at the town he had spent so long looking at in the miniature.

"Looks almost the same as the map," Charlie commented. "Look, there's the church, and the graveyard. I feel like I've been here already."

The town was built on a steep hill, meaning they were either walking up- or downhill. They followed the main town road, and then veered off onto Haven Lane, which descended so steeply they had to hold themselves back from running.

"There it is," Natalie said.

Croft Hill was a small road that ran off Haven Lane, and the two could not have been more opposite. Whereas Haven Lane was in dire need of resurfacing, Croft Hill was paved with pristine stone slabs, and lined with perfectly manicured hedges and fluffy, round trees. A sign by its entrance said "*Private Road: Strictly Residents Only*".

"Should we be concerned about the sign?" Natalie asked.

"No," Ben said.

Natalie relaxed a little when she saw that even Charlie was unconcerned.

The constant noise of cars quickly receded as they started walking. Despite its proximity to the town centre, they felt like they had been transported to the countryside. Each house seemed to be competing in the design and size stakes, and they all had large double garages for their multiple luxurious cars.

"So, now what? Do you want to fire your first spell?" Charlie asked.

Ben had been thinking the same thing. The problem was that the houses were so far apart, the spell would at best catch only a handful of residents.

"Seems like here is as good as any other place," Ben said, drawing out his spellshooter.

Charlie and Natalie stepped back, giving him room. The detection spell was level three, which required some concentration, but Ben was now competent enough to fire them without too much effort. He pointed the spellshooter to the sky, and summoned the spell forth. A deep purple pellet shot up into the air. It exploded at peak height, and purple sparks rained down on the neighbourhood like a giant umbrella. Ben watched intently as the sparks hit the floor and disappeared. His body was rigid, waiting for a buzz in his body that would signify detection.

"Nothing," he said, letting his body relax after a moment. "That rules out these five houses surrounding us."

Charlie and Natalie were clearly disappointed.

"For some reason I was sure we'd find a dark elf first time," Natalie said.

"Well, we've still got five more attempts. Let's walk a little further and try again."

Ben hadn't been unduly concerned when the first spell produced nothing, but he frowned when the second one also yielded no results.

"Are you sure this is the right place?" Charlie asked.

"Yes," Ben said.

"Well, shouldn't it be swarming with dark elves?"

"I only flagged twelve, not twelve hundred. In the grand scheme of things, that's not very many," Ben said. "We just need to get lucky."

The third spell also produced nothing. As did the fourth, which they tried down a small cul-de-sac end that ran off the main road. Ben felt his orb, and gave a frustrated groan.

"Only two left," he said.

"What do we do if we run out and don't spot any dark elves?" Charlie asked.

"Let's not worry about that now."

"I disagree," Charlie said, clenching his fists. "We only have two spells left. It's time to start worrying."

Ben was about to respond, when he felt Natalie tap him on the shoulder.

"Guys, look," she said in a hushed voice.

A woman in a black tracksuit had just appeared and was coming down the street. She was speed-walking with headphones on and a water bottle in one hand. She looked European, with lush brown hair swept back in a ponytail.

"Do you think she could be a dark elf?" Natalie said softly, still clutching Ben's shoulder and staring at the lady, who hadn't yet noticed them.

"I have no idea," Ben said. If dark elves took on human forms that resembled their own figure, then it was possible. She even had slightly angular eyes, though her ears appeared normal enough. Her skin was pale, almost white – typical of a dark elf's.

"Do you want to fire another spell?" Natalie suggested.

Ben didn't like the idea. "I just fired one here – it would only be for that woman."

"I know, but I've got a feeling about her," Natalie said, her green eyes suddenly intense.

The woman continued towards them. She was on the other side of the road, admiring each front garden she passed, and still hadn't noticed them.

"I don't know," Charlie said. "Her disguise means she could look like anything – in fact, surely it would be in her interest to look less like a dark elf and more human, so she doesn't attract as much attention."

Ben fingered the trigger on his spellshooter. He couldn't make his mind up, which irritated him.

"We could ask her," Charlie said.

Ben looked at him with a raised eyebrow. "How?"

"The usual way – by using our vocal cords."

"Sure, good idea," Ben said, breaking into a smile. "Go for it. Natalie and I will watch from here."

"Oh, I didn't mean me," Charlie said, going slightly red. "I meant you, of course. You're the crazy one."

The woman was now almost across the street from them. Charlie was right – that was one solution. But if she wasn't a dark elf, he'd sound like a complete idiot.

"If you're going to do it, you need to do it now," Natalie whispered fiercely. "She'll be gone in a moment."

Ben stepped forwards just as the woman glanced their way. Ben froze, and gave an awkward smile. The woman returned it, and kept on walking. In the blink of an eye, she was past them, and walking down the street, around the corner and out of sight.

"Well, that didn't work," Charlie said. "Why did you freeze?"

"Because she looked at me," Ben said with exasperation. “Anyway, we’ve just wasted five minutes looking like plonkers. Let’s keep going.”

The road wound gently left, and opened up to a series of even larger houses, with magnificent trees and tended gardens.

“There’s the house with the swimming pool,” Charlie said, pointing. “I recognise the white walls and thatched roof.”

“Do dark elves like swimming?”

Charlie shrugged. “No idea. Can’t see why not – they have the body for it.”

Ben drew out his spellshooter again and stared at the orb. There were just two dark elf detection spells left; his hands suddenly felt sweaty and his stomach felt funny.

“Are you sure you want to do it here?” Natalie asked. “I was thinking, we might want to save at least one spell for the town, or a crowded area, where by sheer numbers, the chances are better.”

“Natalie has a good point,” Charlie said, tapping his cheeks thoughtfully. “Here you’re only going to hit two dozen people at most; whereas if we did it in the centre of town, we’d hit hundreds.”

The reasoning was sound, but Ben couldn’t take his eyes off the thatched house with the swimming pool. Something about it made his skin tingle, a certainty he couldn’t place or rationalise.

"I'll cast one more here. The last one we'll save for town," Ben said, raising his spellshooter.

Once more, Charlie and Natalie stepped back to give him room. Ben took several deep breaths, and focused more than usual. He fired, and the spell soared up into the air, exploding into an umbrella of sparks. Ben watched with bated breath, as slowly, the sparks hit the ground and disappeared.

His body jerked, as a small buzz pulsed through him.

"There!" Ben said, pointing.

From the corner of his eye, he saw one of the small sparks explode, forming its own mini shower. At the same time, a picture of the thatched house entered his mind.

"That's the one," Ben said, grinning.

Charlie let out a huge sigh. "Thank goodness for that." He paused. "Now what?"

CHAPTER 15
AN UNWELCOME VISIT

Ben, Charlie and Natalie stared at the large house. It stood out even among the luxurious homes, with its thatched roof and white walls. There was a small treehouse tucked up in one of the many trees that were spread throughout the front lawn.

"Let's knock on the door," Ben said.

"Should we show our diamonds?" Natalie asked. "It might make us look more authentic."

"What if the person who answers isn't an Unseen?" Charlie asked. "The floating diamonds would freak them out. Warden rule number one: don't freak out the Seens, remember?"

Ben weighed both options. "You're right, Charlie, but I think the pros outweigh the cons. Let's reveal them. It will save us a lot of explaining."

The front path was wide enough so they could walk side by side to the house, up a series of steps, until they reached the front door.

Ben rang the doorbell. "Let me do the talking."

"No argument there," Charlie said.

Ben heard footsteps. He checked his right shoulder, and saw the three colourless diamonds. He took a deep breath and composed himself. He didn't have an exact plan of what to say, but then he rarely did; spontaneity was his strong suit.

A woman opened the door. Ben was instantly reminded of the jogging lady who had passed just moments ago. She wore a dress that highlighted her figure. Her skin was pale and her hair full and wavy. It was her almond eyes, however, that Ben was focused on. They widened in shock the moment she saw the diamonds on their shoulders.

"Nigel – they're here!" she screamed in a frantic voice, and slammed the front door in their faces.

Ben, Charlie and Natalie stared at each other, open-mouthed.

"I hate to say it, but I think you were wrong about the diamond thing," Charlie said, scratching his nose.

Ben was about to ring the doorbell again, when he heard a noise from the other side – a deep, rumbling noise. Ben recognised it immediately, his heart exploding from his chest.

"Get off the steps!" he screamed.

Grabbing Charlie and Natalie, he leapt over the iron railing, and landed head-first on the flowerbed below. A whooshing sound came from behind and he turned around just in time to see the front door blasted off its hinges by a huge, purple fireball so bright Ben was almost blinded.

"What on earth is going on?" Charlie asked, covering his head.

Ben whipped his spellshooter out. He turned and pointed it at the front entrance. Slowly, he crept back towards the steps, stopping at the bottom. He could hear Charlie and Natalie next to him, their own ragged breathing mirroring his own.

"Now what?" Natalie whispered. "Should we go in?"

"Are you insane? There's a mad dark elf woman in there," Charlie said.

"We go in," Ben said, nodding. "Follow me."

Ignoring Charlie's groan, Ben tiptoed up the steps until he had a view of the inside of the house, minus the front door. The grand entrance appeared empty. Ben quickly entered the house, stopping just inside the doorway.

He saw them immediately, halfway up the stairs. The woman was now holding a baby, and there was a man, with the same pale skin and wavy, brown hair.

He was staring at them with a look of pure hatred. There was a large backpack strapped over his shoulder. Were they trying to escape?

"Back off!" the man ordered in a quite distinct French accent. He extended his arm, and purple fire started to form around his fist.

"Stop!" Ben ordered, raising his own hands in peace. "We're not here to harm you."

"Liar!" the man said, and threw the purple ball of fire right at them. Ben didn't need to bother firing his spellshooter – the magic connected to him from Elizabeth's Armour deflected the dark elf magic harmlessly away, leaving the man momentarily gaping in astonishment. He recovered quickly, though, and the hand soon started glowing again.

Ben stepped forwards. Something drastic had to be done – the man had a crazed look in his eyes; he was defending his family, and Ben knew the lengths he would go to.

"Stop!" Ben said again. With great ceremony, he slowly laid down his spellshooter and raised both hands. "We're not here to harm you. Can you please stop trying to kill us? We just want to talk."

The man's eyes narrowed, but Ben was relieved to see a flicker of sanity replace the rage.

"You lie. You are from the Institute. You have come to arrest us for illegally crossing borders."

Ben kept his hands raised in a conciliatory

manner. "No, we haven't. We just want to ask a couple of harmless questions; then we'll be out of here."

The fire lessened from the man's hand, though his eyes remained suspicious. "You know what we are, don't you? You wouldn't be here otherwise."

"Dark elves," Ben said, nodding. "I don't care about that – well, I do, but not for the reasons you expect."

The man glanced at his wife and the baby in her arms, and Ben felt his anger return, but the woman gave him a little nod.

"Questions?" the man said. The flame in his hand finally disappeared.

"Just one actually," Ben said with an encouraging smile. "Then we'll be gone, I promise."

The man clearly wasn't convinced, but he made his way slowly down the stairs, and approached them with caution.

"Ask your question," the man said.

Ben turned to Charlie, who stepped forwards, pulling a crumpled piece of paper from his trousers. The man flinched, clearly expecting a spell of some sort, but he relaxed when he saw the paper. Charlie unfolded it, revealing a drawing they had Abigail do of the symbol they had found.

"Can you tell us what this means?" Charlie asked.

The man took the drawing. Ben watched him

closely, looking for a sign of recognition as he studied the symbol. After a moment, he handed the drawing back to Charlie, and shook his head.

"It is not familiar to me," the man said.

Ben wanted to curse in frustration, but instead he bit his lip. "Are you sure? Nothing comes to mind?"

"Nothing."

Ben glanced at Natalie and Charlie, who looked as disappointed as he felt. It was a bust, and they had only one spell left to try to find another dark elf who might be able to help.

"What are you looking at?"

It was the wife, calling from the stairs.

Charlie lifted the drawing. "A symbol. Do you think you could take a look?"

To Ben's surprise, the wife nodded, and came down, baby in arms. She took – snatched – the paper from Charlie, and examined it. Ben held his breath and tried not to get his hopes up, even when she scrutinised it far longer than her husband. Was that a flicker of recognition in her eyes? After a good minute of looking, she handed it back to Charlie.

"I can't read it," she said.

Ben cursed, unable to help himself. Charlie did the same.

"No dark elf could."

"What?"

All three of them looked up.

The lady nodded, very sure of herself. "It is not our language. It looks like an old dwarf dialect. Some of our lineage parallels an old, now extinct race of dwarves."

She handed the paper back to Charlie, who stared at it in wonder, as if he could suddenly read the thing.

"Are you sure about that?" Ben asked.

"I am sure it is not our language. I am almost certain it is of dwarf origin."

"You mentioned a certain type of dwarf?" Natalie said.

"Yes, the arcane dwarves. As far as I know, they were wiped out several hundred years ago. Their language was similar to ours."

Ben did his best to calm his growing excitement. "Thank you, we really appreciate that."

"Is that all?" the man asked, clearly sceptical.

"Yes, that's everything. We are sorry to have disturbed you." Ben paused. There was something on his mind, and he knew it would bug him if he didn't ask it.

"Why did you panic so much when we arrived?"

The man gave them an even colder look, if that was possible. "Your Institute has already taken all our friends. We have been living in fear, expecting you to find us any day."

Ben was shocked, but he didn't show it, though

he could see Charlie and Natalie weren't concealing it quite as well.

"Why don't you leave, and go back home?"

"We can't," the man said, his jaw clenching. "We would get declared traitors and executed upon return."

"So why did you leave in the first place?"

It was the lady who responded. "Many of us don't like what King Suktar is doing to our nation and our people. Many have left; few will ever return, unless Suktar is overturned."

Ben was struck by the lady's honesty. They thanked her one final time, and finally left.

None of them spoke as they wound their way out of the private road, back towards the town centre.

"That was an eye-opener," Charlie said, breaking the ice.

Despite the importance of the dwarf symbol revelation, Ben knew Charlie was referring to the dark elf family.

"I don't know why, but I had this strange idea that all dark elves were evil," Natalie said, sounding a little guilty.

Ben had been thinking a similar thing. They had practically started a war, they were ruled by a nut case and they had his parents. But, he conceded, that didn't mean the entire population was evil. Were all humans evil because Hitler had started a war? The more he thought about it, the more he realised it was often just a small minority of those in power who caused the problems. Could that be the case with the dark elves? Were they innately good? Ben grappled with the concept, but came to no conclusion he was happy with. It left an unpleasant taste in his mouth.

CHAPTER 16

RESEARCH AND DISCOVERY

They met up in the library at ten o'clock the following morning. Natalie had a Diplomacy assignment she couldn't avoid, and as Ben and Charlie were unwilling to do anything without her, they spent an hour working on the third-grade checklist. Ben's initial reluctance to work on the Scholar Department was soon forgotten as he was tasked to study some of the great historic battles that would have been lost if not for the Institute. The pleasant silence and the calm, peaceful atmosphere in the library enabled Ben to lose himself in history. Natalie's voice, when it came, was almost an inconvenience. He would have to wait to find out how the Institute had foiled Napoleon.

"I'm sorry," she said, hurrying across to sit next to them.

It was busy this morning, but they had managed to acquire a small square table, and piled it with books, to discourage anyone from joining them.

"Diplomacy was a nightmare," she continued, fixing her hair, though Ben couldn't see a strand out of place. "Pretty much the entire royal court of Olag – the nation that was just defeated by the dark elves – have turned up on our doorstep. I know the Institute would rather just boot them out the door, but we can't, so they've turned them over to any Diplomat they can spare, which right now are the dregs."

"You're not dregs," Charlie muttered, looking up from his book. He blushed when she smiled at him, something Ben noted he hadn't done in a while.

"Thanks. I'm one of the few apprentices chosen, and the only third-grader, so I guess I should be flattered. But it's a real nightmare. They're not happy, and half my time is spent trying to assure them that everything will be okay, when I really haven't a clue what's going on."

"Ah, the white lie route – one that I've taken many a time," Ben said, smiling.

"Yeah, I guess so." Natalie gave a light rap on the table with her hands. "Anyway, let's move on to more pleasant things. What's our plan?"

It was obvious what she was referring to, but, perhaps wisely, she didn't mention it out loud.

"This is Charlie's arena," Ben said. "We're basically just going to do whatever he says."

"I've got no problem with that," Natalie said.

Charlie closed his book and stood up. "Right, follow me."

Ben never ceased to be amazed at how well Charlie knew the library. It was a mass of shelves and pathways – narrow; wide; zigzagging – and cross-referenced a dozen different ways, yet Charlie always seemed to know where to go. Ben was fairly certain Charlie knew the library better with his eyes closed than most did with their eyes open.

Ben watched the various sections go by – history; spells; Diplomacy; Unseens (categorised by size, danger and anatomy); as well as the more mundane areas, such as cooking, culture and social etiquette. Just when Ben felt he couldn't be more lost, they walked into a large, circular room, surrounded by curved shelving that fit the space perfectly. On top of each shelf was a title: *Battle Dwarves; Grey Dwarves; Street Dwarves; Trade Dwarves*. Each shelf had a title, and there must have been at least a dozen of them.

"I don't see arcane dwarves anywhere," Natalie said.

"They're not easy to find," Charlie said, sounding pleased about it, as he delved into one of the shelves. "The dark elf lady said they were extinct, remember?

They were probably always a small group. We just have to look. Let's start digging."

Ben couldn't believe how many different types of dwarves there were – living in mountains, forests, and even on boats in the ocean. Some of them got on with each other; others were mortal enemies. The sky dwarves sounded extremely cool, living up on giant airships, and he lost twenty minutes reading about them.

"Here's something," Natalie said.

Ben looked up, feeling a little guilty that he wasn't actively helping. Natalie was holding a battered, leather-bound book, whose pages looked ready to crumble.

"Listen to this," she said. "*The arcane dwarves were forced to retreat into the dense forests of Jimba after being overrun by the horse people. Several expeditions were made by Institute Scholars in the next decades, but no recorded sightings were ever witnessed.*"

"Is that it?" Ben asked, when Natalie stopped.

Natalie scanned the rest of the page. "Yeah, there's nothing else."

Charlie was smiling, a gleam in his eyes. "That's good! Something to work on. We have a location – Jimba Forest – and also a group who were close to them: the horse people. More things to research. Keep going."

It was another hour before anyone found

anything and, to Ben's great surprise, it was he who made the discovery. Buried behind several large books, he fished out a small, tattered diary by a man with the initials of A.B.R. Many of the pages were missing, but Ben was intrigued by the faint blood stains on the cover, and he always enjoyed diaries. He flicked through the remaining pages, and his stomach gave an immediate lurch.

"I think I have something," he said.

Charlie stopped trying to grab a book that was clearly out of reach. Natalie looked at him expectantly.

"There's no name on the diary except for the initials A.B.R. Looks like he's on some crazy mission. The first entry I can find is from 3rd November 1614.

"Arrived at the edge of Jimba Forest – it is both beautiful and at the same time a terrifying jungle. I hope the rumours aren't true, or else I may not last long. Fortunately, food and drink should not present a problem as there appears to be plenty of both. M.G., you would love the colours here – they make our forests at home look positively dull."

Ben stopped, though he continued to stare at the page.

"Is that it?" Natalie asked.

Ben nodded. He flicked through the next few pages, until he found one that was legible.

"14th November 1614. Saw the sun for the first time in

some duration. The trees are so dense, they do not permit much daylight. My knee still feels weak from the fight with the growl. They make tigers look like pussy cats. My spell supply is starting to run low, and I must hope I do not run into too many more enemies before my search is complete."

Ben cursed. "That's it for that one. Next one is a week later."

"22nd November 1614. Good news, M.G., I believe I have found my first sign of the arcane dwarves. It is not much, a faint footstep and a scrap of fabric, but, as we know, there are no other sentient beings here, so I must conclude it is them. I am hopeful that within the next few days I shall see more. I certainly hope so, as I am starting to get weary eating berries and insects."

Ben looked up to see the frustrated faces of Charlie and Natalie. "Sorry, page is ripped. Hold on."

Unfortunately, the next several entries were blurred and illegible, and he had to turn a few pages before he could find something more to read.

"30th November 1614. They are watching me, I am sure of it. I can feel eyes upon me, though they are extremely good at hiding, better even than the wood elves of Lithlorn. I fear they do not take well to strangers, but as I am just one old man, and clearly present no threat, I believe they are still deciding what to do. I have a plan, but it will require some diplomatic work, so I am hopeful

that I get a chance to talk and explain myself. I will know soon."

Ben looked up. He didn't know why, but his whole body felt cold and his breathing was laboured.

"Can you stop staring into space and find the next entry?" Charlie asked impatiently.

"Sorry. Let's see here.

"10th December 1614. As prisons go, this one isn't too bad. It may be small, but at least it doesn't smell, and I cannot see any faeces on the grass. I hope that means they will let me relieve myself elsewhere. The construction is some kind of wood I've never seen before, but it is incredibly strong. I have pleaded my case to their under-chief. He did listen, but I could not read his face, so I am in the dark. I know I ask a lot, but these arcane dwarves are, to my mind, the best hope we have. If we can just gain their cooperation, I will rest easy. If not, I fear you may have to come and rescue me, old friend."

"Please tell me that's not the end of the entry," Charlie said, pinching the bridge of his nose.

"Afraid so," Ben replied. He skipped ahead, his heart sinking. "And that's it – there's nothing else to read."

"How maddening!" Natalie said with feeling.

Charlie slid down his ladder and immediately started pacing the small, circular room. His eyes were alight, and his hands were placed behind his back in his typical thinking position.

"Fascinating. Absolutely fascinating," Charlie said. He muttered several more words to this end, until Natalie could take no more.

"What is fascinating?" she asked.

"Everything," Charlie said, thrusting a finger out, before the hand retreated behind his back again. "This fellow, A.B.R., is on a mission to find these arcane dwarves, in the hope of getting their help with something. Did you note the date?"

Ben flicked open the diary again. "Yeah, early seventeenth century."

"Right. The formative years of the Institute, not long after Queen Elizabeth would have passed away, leaving the original directors each with the task of guarding a piece of her armour."

"Interesting, but how is that relevant?"

"M.G.," Charlie said, pronouncing each letter with such emphasis his lips looked almost comical.

"You what?"

"In the diary, A.B.R. was talking to a person called M.G. Now, we know the timing fits – what if M.G. stands for Michael Greenwood – your great ancestor, first Spellsword Director, and Guardian of Elizabeth's Sword?"

Ben was speechless. Partly because of the revelation and partly because he couldn't believe he hadn't thought of that. He felt his lungs expand with sudden hope.

"That would be incredible," Natalie said. Ben couldn't help noticing her own excitement seemed in check, as if she wanted to believe, but wasn't quite ready. "But M.G. are common initials. It could be anyone; why do you think it's Michael Greenwood?"

Ben expected a backlash, but Charlie seemed to enjoy the challenge; his face was now positively glowing with energy.

"Good question. You're absolutely right: those are common initials, and I could be way off the mark. But as I said, the timing is right. Also, consider what was going on. A.B.R. was travelling to who knows where, hoping to find these arcane dwarves to help him with something. It sounds like a suicidal mission, doesn't it?"

"Yes, it does," Natalie said, clearly unsure where Charlie was heading.

"We know that the original directors were under orders to hide each piece of armour as best they could. That obscure forest sounds like as good a place as any – especially if he could get the arcane dwarves to help him guard it."

To this, Natalie had no response. Ben's heart was positively drumming now, and he felt like joining Charlie in his pacing. He thought of the helm, and how it was buried in a deep underground cavern, guarded by the forreck. Suddenly, Charlie's theory didn't seem so outrageous.

"I admit, it's a long shot," Charlie said, "but it gives us plenty to research. This A.B.R. bloke, for one. I'm sure we can find out if he was an original director easily enough."

"Let's say he is," Ben mused. "Then what? Do we go off to find these arcane dwarves, assuming they might still be protecting the piece of armour?"

"No," Charlie said, shaking his head vigorously. "For one, we don't even know if the arcane dwarves still exist. And if they do, they sound dangerous and would probably kill us as soon as help us. No, I think we need more information."

"About what?" Natalie asked.

Charlie pulled out the now crumpled drawing of the dwarf symbol. "We know this has something to do with the arcane dwarves, but we still don't know what. The dark elves were also interested in this symbol, and were probably trying to get the dwarf mage to tell them what it was."

Ben's head was starting to spin. "So the dark elves were interested – what does that mean?"

"Possibly nothing, potentially everything," Charlie said. "The dark elves are still after Elizabeth's Armour, remember? What if they were looking for the next piece, and this symbol was the clue they were following?"

Natalie put both her hands on her head. "I think I

need a drink of water. This is starting to make my head hurt."

Ben felt exactly the same, but he clung on to Charlie's theory. It sort of made sense, but there were a lot of assumptions. If A.B.R. was an original director trying to hide his piece of the armour with the arcane dwarves, then it was possible the dark elves were also trying to find those same dwarves, with the intention of retrieving said piece of armour. The only question was: what did that dwarf symbol represent? It was the missing piece of the puzzle.

"Let's take a break," Ben suggested. "I need some air, and my head is about to explode."

CHAPTER 17
DIRECTOR OF DIPLOMACY

It felt good to be outside after being in the hot, claustrophobic library for so long. After a sandwich and a cup of tea at a nearby café, they felt fully refreshed. They headed back into the library and dived in to continue their research.

It took Charlie less than five minutes to discover what they needed about A.B.R.

"Angus Bernhard Reed. He was the original Director of Diplomacy," Charlie said, stabbing an open page, with a huge grin. "I knew it!"

They were seated in a more comfortable, but little known reading area, full of squishy chairs and huge coffee table books. It looked a bit like a rustic version of the common room, minus the tea and coffee.

"So, where does that leave us?" Natalie asked. "We can still only assume that Angus was on his way to the dwarves to hide his piece of armour – we don't know it for a fact."

"And even if we did, we don't know if the arcane dwarves are even still alive."

"All true," Charlie said. "Like I said, I think we need to research this symbol more, and see if it reveals anything."

There was a moment's silence, which generally indicated agreement. But for Ben, a germ of an idea had started forming in his mind – one that he knew would get ripped to shreds the moment he voiced it. Yet the more he thought about his idea, the more convinced he became of its merit. It was dangerous – well, to be fair, it was far worse than dangerous; he wasn't even sure it was possible – but it had the potential to get them some real answers.

"Ben?"

Ben turned, unaware that both Charlie and Natalie had been looking at him.

"Are you okay?" Natalie asked. "You went all distant."

"I'm fine," Ben said, giving them both a hasty smile, and ignoring the suspicious glance Charlie threw his way.

"Let's split up," Charlie said. "I'll tackle the dwarf symbol. Ben, why don't you find out what you can about the Jimba Forest? Natalie, anything else you can discover about Angus would be great."

Charlie gave them directions to where they might find what they were looking for, and they set off. Charlie remained, whizzing back up a ladder to delve into a bookshelf.

Initially, Ben and Natalie's route kept them together, but Ben was too lost in his thoughts to talk. His mind drifted back to the idea that had formed in his head just minutes earlier. Yes, why not? After he was done with researching the Jimba Forest, he could do his own research. If he did break the idea to Charlie and Natalie, he'd need to be prepared.

"I'm this way," Natalie said, pointing at a sign. "*Important Historical Figures of the Institute.*"

"Oh, right." Ben hadn't realised it, but he had been following Natalie. She had been talking to him, but he couldn't recall a word she had said.

"Are you okay?" Natalie said, her green eyes narrowing. "You look distracted."

For a minute, Ben thought about revealing his idea – it would certainly be easier to do so without Charlie's laser-sharp reasoning and pessimism in the way.

"I'm fine," Ben said. "It's just a lot to take in. I feel like I need to sketch it all out."

Natalie smiled. "I think that's a really good idea. Well, I'll see you soon."

With the help of Charlie's directions, it took Ben less than five minutes to find the Unseen Geography section. There were hundreds of maps, packed tightly on shelves, as well as textbooks describing the geography of what must have been every possible land in the Unseen Kingdoms, from tiny islands to kingdoms as big as France.

Ben started running his finger along the shelf. Thankfully everything was alphabetised, making life easier, but due to the sheer number of books, it still took him a little while to find the right one.

"Gotcha!" Ben said, picking out a small fold-out map from a shelf that looked like it was about to collapse. There were no tables around, so Ben sat down where he was, and spread the map on the floor.

Jimba Forest, it turned out, was located on Jimba, a small island approximately the size of the United Kingdom, located off the east coast of Africa. Despite its remote location, Jimba was a lucrative source of silver, and had been conquered by the English during the height of the British Empire. The island used to be one huge forest, but, due to mining, it had been partially decimated. There was even a Dragonway station there, though Ben had no idea if it still worked. The island was hot, tropical, and sounded rather unpleasant. The population was split between humans and desert elves, with no mention of dwarves at all. Ben read the entire map, back and front, before slipping it into his pocket.

Assuming there was a functioning Dragonway,

that would at least give them access to Jimba. Otherwise they would have to commandeer a winged animal. The thought of flying all the way to Africa on a Pegasus did not appeal. The real question was – were there any arcane dwarves left in that forest? The fact that there had been no mention of them wasn't surprising, as they seemed a remarkably secretive race. But it would be useful if they could find out one way or the other before they travelled there.

Ben felt satisfied that he had done all he could with relation to Jimba. According to his watch, he still had thirty minutes left before they were due to meet up.

Perfect. That gave him just enough time to investigate his project. Thanks to his endless hours with Charlie in the library, Ben had some idea of where to start. After a few wrong turns and getting lost once or twice, he entered an older section of the library. The shelves creaked if he so much as looked at them, and some looked ready to disintegrate. The lighting here was dimmer too; not sinister, but secretive, as if the library knew you shouldn't be here and was helping you hide. The signs said things like "Undead", "Cosmology", "Superstition", and "The Underworld".

For the next twenty minutes, Ben lost himself in the books, with a diligence he rarely showed during his studies. Time flew by, and it was with some surprise that he realised he had less than five minutes to get back to the main library to meet up with Charlie and Natalie. He would have liked to stay, but knew his absence might worry them.

Ben reluctantly closed the book he was reading and headed back. As he returned to the main section, the library opened up and became once again a peaceful, harmonious space. Charlie and Natalie had already made it back, and had snagged a small table by themselves.

"I never thought you'd be in a library longer than me," Charlie commented, as Ben sat down.

The comment was innocent, but Ben felt his cheeks burn, and he coughed to distract them. "The library is growing on me. So, what have we got?"

"Nothing that exciting," Natalie said. "It wasn't hard to find out about Angus, given that he was an original director, but he certainly seemed to be the least interesting. He was a pacifist, a great orator, and single-handedly stopped over a dozen wars by peaceful means. He was also a big fan of eggs and bacon."

"How is that relevant?"

Natalie shrugged, a strand of hair falling over her eyes. "It's not, but it's probably the most interesting thing I could find."

"That's not true," Charlie said. "Tell him about London."

"That's true; there is London. When Queen Elizabeth I passed away, the new commander of the Institute was her son, Prince Henry – a madman by all accounts. He was obsessed with his mother's armour, and immediately tried to retrieve it. Most of the original directors left or went into hiding. Angus was the last to leave. He was liked by everyone, and not even the prince could just dismiss him out of hand. But eventually Angus disappeared, and was charged with treason by the prince."

"Where did he go?" Ben asked.

"Well, that's the interesting part. This happened just weeks before the diary you found took place. It could be that he realised the danger the armour was in and went to hide his piece."

Ben gave a low whistle. "That is interesting if it's true."

"We can't confirm it, but it does seem likely," Charlie said. "Anyway, it's a lot more than I found."

"What did you find?"

"Absolutely nothing," Charlie said. Ben wasn't sure if he was frustrated or delighted by the challenge. "Arcane dwarves are hard enough to find in the library, let alone a peculiar symbol from one of them. But I'm confident I'll find something; I just need time. What about you, Ben?"

Ben pulled out the map of Jimba and gave them a brief rundown of what he had found.

"Did you find out whether Jimba still has a Dragonway?" Charlie asked, as soon as Ben finished.

"No, but I will do, today," Ben said, feeling a little defensive. "I know that's important."

"Yes, it is," Charlie said, nodding. His eyes narrowed suddenly. "You were the last back, but that research couldn't have taken you a full hour, especially as I told you exactly where to go."

Ben was usually so good at keeping a calm head under pressure, but if there was anyone who could cut through his superficial nonchalance, it was Charlie.

"You told me how to get there, but getting back was a nightmare," Ben said in his most sincere voice.

The moment he uttered the lie, he knew it would fall on deaf ears. Even Natalie was now looking at him, with narrowed green eyes. Ben took a deep breath, and gave the table a small rap in defeat.

"Okay, you're right. I was doing something else. I had a hunch, and I was following it up."

Natalie punched the air. "I knew it! The last couple of hours, you've looked really distracted, which is really unlike you. What were you really doing?"

Ben grabbed hold of the table with both hands. This was going to be rough, but there was no backing out now.

"I've been thinking about the dark elves, and why they attacked the dwarves," Ben said, choosing his words carefully. "We believe they drew that symbol, right? Maybe they didn't know what it was either and were trying to get information from the dwarf mage."

"I agree," Charlie said.

So far, so good.

"The symbol was written in the language of the arcane dwarves, who we believe may be guarding the next piece of Elizabeth's Armour. What if the dark elves were also trying to find out about the symbol to get to the armour? And what if they thought the dwarf mage had the answers?"

Natalie nodded. "It makes sense, but we can't prove it, and Charlie can't find anything on that symbol to help us."

"That's true. But I know someone who will definitely know," Ben said.

Charlie's and Natalie's reactions were vastly different. Natalie was all surprise; whereas Charlie's eyes narrowed, as if he had already guessed the answer.

Ben took a deep breath. "The dwarf mage."

"I knew it!" Charlie said, slamming his fist on the table, and causing more than one annoyed reader to look round. Natalie jumped at Charlie's exclamation, unsure whether to look more surprised at Charlie or Ben.

"The mage?" Natalie said. "The dwarf mage?"

"Yes."

"The one who's stuck in the void?"

Ben nodded. "That's the one."

"Out of the question," Charlie said, swiping his hand across the air to emphasise the point. "Unless you want to die a swift, horrible death."

"Charlie is right. We know how dangerous that place is. You did the research when you discovered your parents were there, remember?"

"I remember," Ben said. How could he forget? "But they're still alive. It can be done."

"Your parents are special," Charlie said. "We've heard that time and again, from people like Wren. We are not your parents."

Ben had to bite down a retort. He needed to keep calm if he had any chance of making a case. "The dwarf mage is still alive – or was, last time we checked."

"He could be a dwarf of extreme power," Natalie said. "After all, just to get into the void isn't easy."

"Okay, fine. But listen, you can't argue that the dwarf mage is the best option we have to answer our questions."

"He's not an option," Charlie repeated stubbornly.

Ben massaged his temples. His temper was starting to flare, but he forced it down ruthlessly. "Aside from the risks, he is the one most likely to be able to answer our questions."

Charlie was about to give another biting reply, but Natalie put a hand on his arm and cut him short.

"Yes, you're right," she said. "Assuming we could reach the dwarf mage, he would be my first choice. The dark elves certainly think he knows something, and they're not normally wrong."

"Thank you," Ben said with a sigh. A concession, if a small one, and only from Natalie, but it was a start. Charlie was still looking at him with daggers in his eyes. Ben was surprised by the intensity in his friend's face, but he tried not to let it show.

"That's what you were researching, wasn't it?" Charlie asked. "More about the void?"

"Yes," Ben said. "I wanted to see if there was any feasible way to get in and out."

"There isn't," Charlie said immediately. "I've done the research myself. And even if we got in, we'd last two minutes in there. It's literally like hell in there. *Literally.*"

Ben found himself battling with his patience. Why was Charlie unwilling to even contemplate the idea? What had he read about the void that terrified him so much?

"I know it's dangerous; I don't think it's as bad as

the books make out. It can't hurt to do a bit more research, can it?"

For a moment, Charlie said nothing. His face was flushed, and Ben noticed his fists were balls on the table.

"This is about your parents, isn't it?" Charlie asked, his voice ominously soft.

"Charlie! That's not fair," Natalie said, shocked.

Ben didn't respond; he couldn't, not immediately. He was still trying to process Charlie's accusation. It was out of the blue and completely unfair, but, at the same time, not entirely false. It was impossible not to think of the void without his parents.

"Tell me I'm wrong," Charlie said, looking Ben in the eye.

"You're wrong," Ben said, raising his voice, and relishing the fact that Charlie gave a little jump. "Yes, I did think of my parents, and why shouldn't I? They're stuck there. But my intention is to go into the void to find the dwarf."

Charlie seemed to calm down, but only a little. "I can't believe the search for the dwarf mage wouldn't turn into one for your parents. I know you, Ben. It would just be too tempting."

Ben bit his lip, hard. All sorts of replies filled his head, many of them unpleasant. In the recesses of his mind, he was vaguely aware that frustration and anger were clouding his thoughts. He needed to get out of here before things got nasty. He got up and, ignoring Natalie's pleas to stop, quickly left the library, alone.

CHAPTER 18
A NEW PLAN

Ben left the Institute, ignoring the guards, who gave him a searching look, perhaps noticing the thunderous expression on his face. He let his feet do the walking, without caring too much where he went. He cursed Charlie every which way, sometimes silently, but mostly out loud, to the alarm of several passers-by. The plan to get into the void was their best option – Ben believed that more with every passing moment – and the fight with Charlie only enhanced it. They were never going to find out what that symbol was unless they could find that dwarf mage. Why was Charlie being so stubborn? Was he afraid? Yes, he probably was, but that wouldn't normally stop Charlie. Was there something else?

"Sorry, excuse me," a gruff, garbled voice said.

Ben looked up and almost ran into a large half-ogre, carrying a huge crate of fish on his broad shoulders. Without realising it, Ben had entered Taecia Square. Though not as bustling as usual, it still had a vibrant, lively ambience. The shops were busy, as were the restaurants, with much of the outside seating taken. Ben hadn't realised it, but he was hungry. He went into a small café, ordered a baguette, and sat outside, eating slowly. The food helped his mood, as did the fresh air and simply watching the world go by. He wasn't sure how long he sat there – he didn't care – but when he finally got up, he felt a good deal better. Dark thoughts still clouded his argument with Charlie, but he forced them aside. He didn't want to think about that now, and was relieved when neither Charlie nor Natalie was waiting for him back at the entrance of the Institute. Ben grabbed his handbook and for the rest of the afternoon threw himself into the third-grade checklist. He worked in every department, relishing the challenge. Every time he thought about Charlie, the void or Elizabeth's Armour, he would slap himself on the cheek, and re-double his work rate.

It was Natalie who found him in one of the Trading rooms, right in the middle of attempting to help a fellow apprentice get a better deal for some firecrackers from a cheeky-looking goblin.

"There you are!" Natalie said, tugging on Ben's

arm, and almost physically lifting him off the bench. "I've been looking for you all afternoon. Have you been avoiding me?"

"No," Ben said a little defensively. The truth was he had avoided the areas he thought they might look for him, like the Spellsword Department and even the library, where he had been tempted to continue his research.

"Come on, we have to go," Natalie said. She really was quite strong when she wanted to be, and Ben felt himself dragged out of the Trading room, into the hallway.

"Where are we going?"

Natalie gave him a look that indicated it should have been obvious. "To sort out your ridiculous argument with Charlie, of course. He's been moping about all afternoon."

"Has he?" Ben couldn't imagine Charlie moping. At the very least, he would have thought he'd simply bury his head in books.

"You can't just argue and then run off," Natalie said. Her eyes were flashing, and she kept giving him accusing looks.

"I needed a bit of time by myself. Is that allowed?"

"No," Natalie said firmly. "Not when you've had an argument with your closest friend – and me, I might add."

Ben stared at her. "Are you upset with me as well?"

"A bit, but mainly because you and Charlie are upset."

Ben would have much rather gone home, slept on it, and tackled it the next day. But Natalie led him unwaveringly to the apprentice floor, and then into a small exam room, which was now empty, except for the window and curtains at the back.

"You stay here," Natalie ordered, pointing a stern finger his way. "I'll be back in a minute."

Her voice brokered no argument, and Ben waited impatiently. Less than five minutes later, he heard Natalie's firm voice, along with Charlie's, which was protesting.

"I don't care!" Natalie said loudly. "You get in here, now."

The door opened moments later, and Natalie entered, physically dragging Charlie, as she had done with Ben.

Charlie looked a bit of a mess. His hair was slightly dishevelled, and his shirt, which Charlie normally ironed religiously, was creased and hanging out. He looked at Ben. Ben looked back. Neither of them said anything.

"Oh please," Natalie said. "One of you start talking. You're not babies."

They both started talking. They both stopped.

"Let me go first," Charlie said. "I may have overreacted slightly. I won't deny the void scares me after what I've read. As for your parents – well, if you can honestly tell me they never figured in your mind, then I'm sorry."

Ben felt something lift from his shoulders, hearing Charlie's apology of sorts. He gave an awkward smile and rubbed a hand through his hair.

"I did think about my parents," he said. The thought brought a strange lump to his throat. "And yes, I did think about trying to find them. I might not be able to rescue them, but it would be nice to see them again, face to face, you know?"

Charlie seemed to relax at this. "I can understand that. So – where does that leave us?"

"All made up, thank goodness," Natalie said. Her voice was cross, but Ben could see she was struggling to hold back a triumphant smile.

"I have an idea," Charlie said. "Give me three days to try to research this symbol a bit more. I have an idea where I might find something."

"Where?" Natalie asked.

"Old Bagdor Bones."

Ben frowned. "Who is he?"

"A dwarf librarian," Natalie said, "and one of the oldest dwarves still living – though I have to admit, I thought he had passed away."

Charlie scratched his nose. "Yes, the jury is out on

that. He has been proclaimed dead several times, and then turned up in the library weeks later. They call him the invisible librarian. If anyone will know about this symbol, he will. I just need to find him."

"And hope he's not dead," Ben added.

"I'm fairly sure he's not. Several times I thought I saw him, but he's really good at going unnoticed. He knows the library better than anyone, and all its secrets."

"Three days," Ben said. "That sounds like a plan. And in the meantime, I'm going to research the void more, and see if we have any chance of getting in, and more importantly getting out."

Charlie's sullen look returned, but he didn't protest.

It was going to be a busy three days.

CHAPTER 19
A MEETING WITH BAGDOR

Now that his plan was known, Ben wasted no time diving head-first into the subject of the void. Charlie preferred to do his research alone, so he teamed up with Natalie. It was a strangely new experience, hanging around with Natalie by himself, one that Ben enjoyed more than he expected.

"The first thing we should do is work out if we can even get in, right?" Natalie asked.

They were back in the older section of the library, containing the darker, less talked about subjects of magic.

"Good idea," Ben said. "Unless we can get in, the whole void thing is a bust."

The thought that they might not be able to get in played on Ben's mind, but he cast it aside. There was clearly a way in; they just needed to find out how it was done. It was both helpful and also frustrating, searching for such a specific topic. Knowing they were tight for time, Ben had to resist reading the wider subject of the void, and focus only on how to gain entry.

The first day produced nothing, despite hours of searching, and Ben and Natalie left the Institute that evening feeling both tired and slightly deflated. Charlie, too, had no joy in locating Bagdor Bones. He did find out that the old dwarf had not been classified as dead, though that didn't rule out the fact that he had simply passed away somewhere in the library and nobody had noticed.

The morning of the second day was little better. Charlie became convinced that Bagdor was purposefully hiding from him.

"I know it sounds ridiculous, but I can almost feel his presence sometimes. It's as if he's spying on me," Charlie said.

"Well, that's something," Natalie said. "Now if we could just convince Bagdor to stop playing hide and seek, we might get somewhere."

Far from being frustrated by his lack of progress, Charlie relished the search, and reported back regularly, somehow locating Ben and Natalie regardless of where they were in the library.

"I can smell him sometimes," Charlie said,

clenching a fist. "He is in dire need of a bath. A couple of times I turned and thought I saw a shadow, but then he was gone."

"Do you want me to help?" Ben asked. "Maybe there's a spell I could use."

Charlie shook his head. "No, that would just scare him away. He's curious now; I can feel it. I don't think anyone has shown this much interest in him before."

That afternoon, Charlie made his breakthrough. Ben and Natalie were busy poring over a book so small they had to read it with a magnifying glass, when they heard hurried footsteps. Ben looked up and knew immediately Charlie had found something. His face was flushed, his eyes alight.

"I think I have him!" he said, waving at them to follow. "Come on, we'll need to be quick."

Without waiting for a reply, he turned and headed back the way he had come. Ben and Natalie exchanged glances, and quickly followed.

"I saw him!" Charlie was saying with suppressed excitement. "He let me see him, of course. He was watching me, with obvious curiosity. For a moment, we locked eyes; then I blinked, and he was gone."

Ben frowned. "Then we've missed him?"

"I'm certain he'll reappear," Charlie said, rubbing his chin thoughtfully. "Curiosity has the better of him now. But I'm hoping you two don't scare him off. I was half-tempted to talk to him by myself, but I didn't want you to miss this – he's quite a character."

This section of the library was a complete maze. Passages kept sprouting left and right, others doubled back, and still others went nowhere. But Charlie walked unerringly, always seeming to know where to go, until he thrust a hand out suddenly and stopped.

"Here!" he said, turning to them and putting a finger on his lips. "I don't often say this, but can you let me do the talking?"

Ben and Natalie nodded vigorously.

Charlie started tiptoeing forwards, constantly looking at the shelves, as if the dwarf could somehow hide in them. Ben exchanged baffled looks with Natalie. How could the dwarf be hiding here? Charlie clearly thought he might be, the way he kept looking along shelves, even bending down to feel the floorboards.

"You're a persistent one, aren't you, boy?"

The voice came from behind. It was a gruff, old voice that left Ben in no doubt who had spoken.

Natalie jumped, but Charlie, who was normally so easily startled, spun with a knowing smile on his face.

Facing them was the oldest dwarf Ben had ever seen. His beard stroked the library floor, tied loosely with a band at the end. His face was so wrinkled there seemed to be too much skin. He had a walking stick in one hand and a long pipe in the other. He was stooped with age, but there was no sign of senility in those deep brown eyes.

"Mr. Bones," Charlie said. "Thank you for paying us a visit."

"Didn't have much choice, did I?" Bagdor said. "You wouldn't stop looking for me. You tire an old dwarf out."

"I'm sorry about that," Charlie said a little hastily.

Bagdor nodded, and Ben was pleased to see a hint of a smile on his old lips.

"Never mind that," Bagdor said. "You remind me of when I was a lad. The library was my second home. Now it's my only home. I live here, and I'll die here. Wouldn't have it any other way."

Bagdor puffed on his pipe, and Ben saw a small cloud of coloured smoke come out from the tip.

"So, you found me. Now what is it you want? You've got five minutes before I need to lie down and rest. So be quick."

Ben was glad it wasn't him speaking, because he hadn't a clue how best to question the old dwarf. Charlie, however, had no such issue.

"What can you tell us of the arcane dwarves?" he asked.

Bagdor rose a white, bushy eyebrow. "They are an

ancient, primitive race of dwarves. Most people think they are extinct, but that's rubbish. They just don't like to be seen. They are the most magically gifted of all dwarves, and share some of their heritage with the dark elves."

Ben felt a rush of adrenaline that electrified his body. Answers, at last. Charlie was clearly as excited by the response as Ben, though he wasn't concealing it quite as well. He thrust his hand into his pocket and pulled out the piece of paper with the symbol on it.

"We believe this was written in their language. Do you have any idea what it might say?"

Ben watched with bated breath as Bagdor took the drawing, and pulled out a pair of reading glasses. The surprise on Bagdor's face made Ben's stomach jump.

"Where did you get this?" he asked, looking up at them with squinted eyes. Ben couldn't tell if the old dwarf was suspicious or just curious.

"We stumbled upon it in an old dwarf chamber," Charlie said vaguely. "Is it important?"

Bagdor renewed his inspection of the symbol, and began tracing a wrinkled finger along the lines. "I didn't think I'd see this again," he said softly.

Ben tried to stay patient, as Bagdor spent what seemed like an eternity looking at the symbol, muttering to himself. When he finally looked up, Bagdor looked younger somehow.

"This is a family crest," Bagdor said. "And not just any family, but that of the Silver Dwarf."

Ben frowned, but Charlie's expression showed a flicker of recognition.

"I've heard of him," Charlie said. "Isn't he just a legend or a myth?"

"He is both," Bagdor said. "There has been much written about him, if you know where to look. I once spent a month trying to work out what was true, and came out none the wiser. What I do know is that he was an arcane dwarf of immense power. It is said that he single-handedly saved the race from extinction on multiple occasions. The arcane dwarves have a prophesy that one day he will return to lead them to glorious freedom. I would say that's unlikely, given that he died over a century ago. They even have a shrine built in his honour, housing the legendary armour he wore when in battle. They say he never lost while wearing that armour, and even now, the arcane dwarves wait for him to come and reclaim it."

Ben went very still, and was suddenly aware that he wasn't breathing. He had a strong urge to question Bagdor, but, with incredible restraint, he remembered his promise to Charlie.

"That is interesting," Charlie said, his voice

sounding a little choked. "Did the Silver Dwarf have any descendants?"

"Rumours only," Bagdor grunted. "Some say no; others say a dozen. The only creditable thing I ever read was that he had a son, who left Jimba as soon as his father died, and was never seen again. They say he was extremely gifted with magic, like his father, and left to continue his training."

Charlie was about to ask another question, when Bagdor raised a hand. "Time's up. I'm going to collapse unless I lie down. When you're my age, you have to listen to your body."

"Just one more—"

But in the blink of an eye, Bagdor disappeared. One moment he was there; the next, he was gone. It wasn't magic, Ben knew, but some incredible ability to not be seen.

Charlie gave a frustrated sigh. "I had more questions I wanted to ask. I'll try to catch him again later."

"You did great," Natalie said, gracing Charlie with a sweet smile, which helped ease Charlie's frustration.

Ben glanced around to make sure they were alone, before remembering few people probably even realised this section of the library existed. There was one question running round his head that drowned out all others.

"The Silver Dwarf. Do you think he was a Guardian?"

"It seems a real possibility," Charlie said, rubbing his hands together and re-gaining some of his enthusiasm.

"He must be," Natalie said. "And the armour that he wore that he never lost in – I bet one of the pieces was Elizabeth's."

It made perfect sense. Angus made it to the arcane dwarves, but did he convince them to help protect the armour or did they take it forcibly? Either way, it seemed the arcane dwarves had possession of it, and had given it to the Silver Dwarf. His prowess in battle could easily be explained by the armour's magic. It all made sense, except there was one rather large problem, which made Ben's stomach feel like a deflating balloon.

"The Silver Dwarf died a hundred years ago," he said, looking at Charlie and Natalie with sudden gravity.

Natalie gave a reluctant nod, but, to Ben's surprise, Charlie appeared unfazed, his enthusiasm undimmed.

"That's true, but, according to Bagdor, he may have had a son."

Natalie frowned. "Even if he did, where would we find him? He left Jimba when his father died a hundred years ago."

To Ben's amazement, Charlie actually smiled, and wagged a finger at them. "You're not connecting the dots. His son became the Guardian the moment he was born, right? Bagdor also said his son left Jimba to train in magic. If he is the Guardian and he's still alive, the dark elves would be hunting him down."

Realisation hit Ben so hard, he was almost knocked from his feet.

"The dwarf mage. You don't think...?"

Charlie was now grinning. "That he's the Silver Dwarf's son? Yes, that's exactly what I'm thinking."

"Oh my word," Natalie said. "That would explain why the dark elves were after him – maybe they were trying to get him to reveal where the piece of armour was."

Ben's mind was now running a mile a minute, and his heart was doing a good job of matching its pace. "Could it be possible?"

"I'd give it a seventy percent possibility," Charlie said.

Ben's elation at the discovery didn't last long, the moment he started to realise exactly what this meant. There was a Guardian stuck in the void. Without him, his piece of armour could not be utilised. Could they still defeat Suktar without all the Guardians?

"We need to go into the void and get him," Ben said, giving them both a serious look.

Natalie nodded and, after a moment, Charlie did too.

CHAPTER 20
SHOPPING AT GOBLIN AVENUE

Despite the time crunch, they left the library and decided to work on the apprenticeship for a couple of hours, simply to decompress. Even Ben was starting to feel the pressure of the last few hours; revelation after revelation was taking a toll on his healthy heart. It seemed strange, but the apprenticeship seemed like a bit of a break by comparison.

Ben went straight to the Spellsword Department, Natalie had work to do in Trade, and Charlie needed to catch up on Diplomacy. Ben managed to lose himself in the training and was able to switch off the constant thoughts about Elizabeth's Armour and the void for a full two hours.

"You're almost ready for the B3," James

McFadden said, watching Ben's monster-summoning spell form into a perfectly structured wolf.

Ben had a smile on his face as he left the spell-shooter room and headed back down to the library at their pre-arranged meet-up time of four o'clock.

"I don't know about you guys, but I made some good progress," Charlie said. "If we ever run into an elm dryad – highly unlikely as I'm pretty sure they exist only in South America – then I'm fairly sure I could negotiate safe passage through their forest."

Natalie smiled. "That's good to know. I also made progress; I finally managed to convince a real trader to sell a pound of liquid fire magic for less than five hundred pounds. I've been stuck on that step for ages."

Their apprenticeship chatter lasted until they reached the cramped, old section of the library, where the dark, claustrophobic air stifled their conversation.

"We haven't really covered these books here," Charlie said, pointing at a particularly dusty set of shelves.

They resumed their search, with a silent determination. Now that they knew they had to enter the void, time was against them, and they worked quickly, scanning each book and moving on if they saw nothing relevant.

An hour passed and they found little. Ben was starting to tire from the constant attention needed on the often tiny print, as well as the deflation of not finding anything. But each time he caught himself slowing, he rubbed his eyes and dived back into the books with renewed vigour.

Predictably, it was Charlie who made the breakthrough.

"I may have something," he said, his head buried in a book. Ben could just make out the title: *The Void: A Goblin's Domain.* "Listen to this: '*If there is one race suited to the void, it is the goblin. Their particular branch of magic is most harmonious with the nature of the void. They are the only race capable of transferring both their mind and body into the void, and there are several goblin clans known to have left the Unseen Kingdoms for the void. Its harsh, dry landscape suits the Arath Goblins the best.*'"

Charlie stopped reading, and started turning the pages quickly. "Okay, now it's gone off on a tangent. Hold on a second – ah, here we go. This is what I was looking for. '*Goblins, known for their willingness to buy and sell anything with no regard to ethics or morals, have set up a small but lucrative trade, offering spells into and out of the void, primarily aimed at those trying to escape the law. The Institute has tried shutting this operation down with some success, but there are still those who continue to trade.*'"

Ben felt like punching the air. “That’s it! That’s our way in and our way out.”

“It sounds promising,” Natalie said, nodding. “I wonder if there is a catch.”

Charlie shut the book and tucked it under his arm. “The catch will be the price, and the fact that we are dealing with goblins, who are about as trustworthy as convicted bankers.”

The mention of money quelled Ben’s optimism. “Do you think we could ask Dagmar to loan us something, on behalf of the Institute?”

Ben knew the idea was futile, and he wasn’t surprised when both Charlie and Natalie shook their heads.

“With the war with the dark elves, I’m sure they are already financially stretched,” Charlie said. “I think we’ll have to pool our money. Plus, I’m not sure we should tell Dagmar about the void.”

“Charlie is right,” Natalie said. “The Institute considers the void off limits, and it is illegal to even enter it.”

Ben frowned. “Why is it illegal? Surely it’s a person’s choice?”

“I’m not sure,” Natalie admitted. “It does seem a little over the top.”

“I think I know,” Charlie said, absently tapping a book. “The Institute doesn’t like the fact that they can’t control the void, especially as they know it contains so much evil. They made it illegal, in an attempt to stop people going."

Ben realised then that most of the books about the void he'd read were accounts from Institute members. "Do you think the Institute tried to scare people off by telling people how dangerous it was?"

"It's possible," Charlie said.

"I wonder if they made it sound worse than it is," Natalie said, chiming in.

Ben was glad it was Natalie and not he who voiced the idea. It may have accounted for Charlie's slightly milder response.

"I believe the void is very dangerous," Charlie said, "but yes, the Institute may have embellished things a little to try to scare people off." He frowned, and gave Ben a stern look. "But that certainly doesn't mean we should take it lightly."

"Of course not," Ben said with a reassuring shake of the head.

They left the library, and headed straight out the Institute, towards Taecia Square, where they took turns sucking their bank accounts dry. Ben felt horrible, not for drawing out his money, but because he could contribute so little.

"I'm sorry my savings are so pathetic," Ben said. "I do have some more at home, but I was hoping to use it to get Grandma's car fixed."

"Please, don't worry about it," Natalie said firmly.

"We have a thousand pounds – that should be plenty."

From Taecia Square, they headed east, towards Goblin Avenue. As they left the prosperous centre of Taecia and entered the East End, the streets started to narrow and become cramped. Slowly, the fine Tudor buildings were replaced by those in disrepair: some with broken windows; others missing doors. The pavement resembled a mud path and Ben was constantly watching out for large piles of pooh.

"Ah, yes, the smell," Charlie said, wafting a hand in front of his nose.

Strangely, the dark elf conflict seemed to affect the people here less than those nearer the Institute, perhaps because survival had always been tough here. Many gave Ben a curious glance, and he had the feeling they were eyeing up his clothes.

"Here we are," Natalie said, pointing to a colourful red sign that read "*Goblin Avenue*".

The contrast between the derelict East End and the vibrancy of Goblin Avenue was both stark and staggering. Even though he'd been here recently, the place never ceased to amaze him. Each house was painted in bright colours. In fact, it seemed to be a competition between houses, as to which could blind you most – some of them seemed to gleam magically. Ben spent several moments admiring the gravity-defying houses, and spotted several that looked like mushrooms, with huge upper levels built on small ground floors.

Much like the East End, the goblins were out in force, seemingly oblivious or more likely not caring about any outside turbulence going on in the Unseen Kingdoms.

"Where to?" Charlie asked, looking slightly lost.

"Let's walk down to the shops," Ben said. "Then I guess it's just a matter of going in and asking."

It didn't take long before the houses turned into shops – the only real difference was the appearance of signs. Just like the houses, there seemed to be an unspoken competition about who could create the loudest sign possible. They came in all colours and sizes – Ben even spotted one floating above a shop that must have been at least fifty feet wide. Most of them resorted to magic to get attention, with sounds, buzzing noises and sparks constantly flying from them.

"How about this place?" Natalie asked.

She was pointing to a wooden cabin that, by goblin standards, looked rather plain. The sign outside was flashing in rainbow colours and read "*Tonbell's Spells*".

"Sure, why not? We have to start somewhere."

Ben pushed open the door and entered a small,

but surprisingly neat spell shop. There were three shelves – two lining the walls and one that ran down the middle. On each were spells in colour-coded baskets, with labels and prices. Ben took a peek and recognised none of them, which only heightened his curiosity.

"The goblin at the back," Natalie whispered, giving Ben a little nudge.

Ben looked up and saw a small goblin – Tonbell, Ben assumed – sitting on a desk, which was also neatly arranged with pens, paper and a couple of stacked books.

"May I help?" Tonbell asked in a soft voice.

As far as goblins went, Tonbell wasn't exactly typical. He looked more like a gnome, small and scrawny, with large, floppy ears and intelligent eyes. In his hand was a quill, which kept writing, despite the fact he was looking right at them.

Ben approached, with a smile, and he heard Natalie and Charlie hang back. This was his area, and they knew it.

"You might be able to," Ben said. "I'm looking for some very specific spells, which I've heard goblins are famous for."

If Ben expected a reaction, he was disappointed. Tonbell didn't as much as bat an eye, and Ben knew immediately that he was dealing with a goblin of some experience in the bartering department.

"What spells are you interested in?" Tonbell asked.

Ben noticed he was subtly eyeing up their clothes and appearance, most likely judging how prosperous they were.

"We need to gain access to the void," Ben said.

Tonbell, who had been calm, but interested in their custom, suddenly became as solid as a brick, and immediately turned back to his writing.

"I am sorry, I don't deal in illegal spells," he said. "I do not want to get on the wrong side of the Institute – I am sure you understand."

Tonbell looked up then, meaningfully. Did he suspect they were apprentices? Ben suspected so. What now? Ben wasn't ready to give up without a fight.

"We need those spells," Ben said, attempting an honest, but sincere expression. "We're willing to pay well. If you won't sell them, can you tell me who will?"

"I'm afraid not," Tonbell said. "As I said, I take no part in anything related to illegal activity. I have a healthy relationship with the Institute, and I intend to keep it that way."

Ben got the distinct feeling Tonbell thought he was being inspected, and it was clear he wasn't going to budge. They had the misfortune of meeting arguably the only goblin with some sort of moral standards.

"Well, that could have gone better," Charlie said, as they left Tonbell's shop, and continued down the road.

"He was refreshingly honest, wasn't he," Natalie admitted. "I never thought I'd say this, but I hope our next goblin is slightly less scrupulous."

However, they soon learned that it wasn't ethics or scruples that were the problem – it was simply that they didn't want to get caught. It was clear the Institute came down hard on any goblins trading void spells of any nature. Other shops weren't as polite as Tonbell, but just as clear that they did not deal in illegal spells. Twenty minutes and five shops later, they were halfway down Goblin Avenue with nothing to show for it. Ben was getting increasingly frustrated.

"The Institute really doesn't want people going to the void, do they," Natalie said. "Maybe we should change our strategy. I could try talking. I know I'm not as good as you, Ben, but it's worth a go."

Ben was about to agree when he noticed a goblin child coming their way. There was something about him that caught Ben's eye. He was by himself, without any sign of parents, yet he didn't look awkward or alone. He wore a bright red shirt and his hands were buried deep in his jeans pockets. He was whistling cheerfully, and heading right towards them. The moment he locked eyes with Ben, he gave a knuckled salute.

"Afternoon, mister," the goblin said in a working-class London accent. "Fine day for walking, innit?"

"It is a nice day," Ben said.

The goblin stopped directly in front of Ben, making him stop. Ben was about to go round him, when the goblin gave a knowing smile and leaned forwards.

"Word on the street is that there are some humans looking for void spells."

Ben was careful not to react, and silently cursed Charlie for his sudden intake of breath.

"We might be. Do you know someone who might be interested in selling?"

"Course I do," the goblin said, slapping his chest. "I know everyone on Goblin Avenue. I know the exact goblin you need, and he'll give you the best price. I can vouch for him."

"And who might that be?"

The goblin grinned, showing some surprisingly white teeth. "My services aren't free, you know." He held out a hand. "My going rate is twenty pounds per piece of information. Five pound extra for a personal escort to your destination."

"That's outrageous," Charlie said, stepping up beside Ben, and looking down on the goblin like a scolding adult. "How do we know you're telling the truth?"

Ben, however, was smiling. He had taken an immediate liking to the young goblin. He dipped into his pocket and pulled out a few notes. "Deal. Here's twenty-five pounds. Lead on."

Charlie gave him an incredulous look. "Are you serious?"

"We haven't exactly been lucky so far. I don't want to spend all day trying every shop," Ben said. "Let's give the kid a chance."

The goblin tucked the money in his pocket with an impudent grin, and then waved at them to follow. He walked with a jaunty swing, clearly delighted with his recent acquisition. If he was trying to fool them, he was doing a good job of not caring about it.

"Where are your parents?" Natalie asked.

The goblin's jovial walk faltered, but only a little. "They are at work. I'm just bringing in some extra cash – pocket money, if you will."

Ben knew a lie when he heard one. Natalie also appeared to detect the falsehood, and she gave Ben a concerned look. Ben wouldn't have been surprised if the goblin had no parents, and possibly no home. But he looked like a survivor, and he certainly didn't seem to be doing too bad for himself. He wondered how many other young goblins were similarly hard up.

They walked to the very end of Goblin Avenue, before the goblin finally stopped, and pointed with a flourish and a bow at the shop at the end.

"Here we go," the goblin said. "Magical Mayhem Ltd. They'll sort you out, guaranteed. There's no finer shop in Goblin Avenue."

CHAPTER 21
MAGICAL MAYHEM LTD

The shop certainly looked impressive from the outside. It had large display windows that wouldn't have looked out of place in Oxford Street, with sale signs announcing ten percent off all air-based spells.

"What happens if they can't help us?" Charlie asked with an accusing glance at the little goblin. "Do we get our money back?"

"Absolutely," the goblin replied. "You know what? I'm going to wait here until you come out just to make sure you're happy. How does that sound?"

"It sounds like we won't see you again," Charlie muttered under his breath.

The goblin looked genuinely affronted.

Ben stepped in and extended his hand. "It's a deal. We'll see you soon."

Ben had a good feeling about Magical Mayhem the moment he stepped through the entrance. It was light and airy, and there was a variety of magic wares he'd not seen since his last visit to the "W" store. As well as spells, there was an array of weaponry and armour, plus various artefacts and trinkets of all kinds. Among the items that caught his eye were a necklace of enhanced vision and a spell-absorber vest.

"Eight hundred pounds," he noted, examining a label. "Slightly outside my five-pound budget."

"Should we look around or just ask to see someone?" Charlie asked.

The shop was busy, and Ben counted at least a dozen other customers perusing the shop, both human and goblin.

"Let's look around a bit first," Ben said. "Maybe we'll find something that can help us."

It was easy to get distracted, looking at all the magic on offer, but Ben concentrated on looking for spells or items that might be related to the void. They methodically worked their way through the shop, up and down the shelves. Though there were many strange and wonderful spells, none of them were in the same field of what they were looking for. Ben was starting to get that familiar sinking feeling, when Natalie gave an excited intake of breath.

"Look! That's got to be it," she said with suppressed excitement.

She was pointing to a black door at the back corner of the shop. On it, in white writing, were the words "*Dark Magic*". Ben couldn't believe they hadn't noticed it before. They had been so fixated on the shelves that they hadn't thought to check for any other rooms the shop might have to offer.

Ben approached the door cautiously, as if it might have some sort of in-built defensive magic, but it opened easily enough.

Ben had to squint the moment he entered the new room. It was dimly lit, and his eyes took a moment to adjust. The room reflected the nature of the magic. The walls were painted black, decorated with silver, Gothic-like symbols that seemed to pulse every time Ben looked at them. The magical wares on the shelves were all contained in small, silver boxes, under lock and key. Ben saw several of them humming, and a couple were vibrating.

"This room isn't for little children," a harsh, throaty voice said. "Leave before I call security."

The voice came from the back of the room. Sitting on a large, ornately decorated desk was a tall goblin, wearing a hooded green cloak the colour of his skin. His eyes were yellow, and his skin heavily pocked. There was a presence about the goblin that made Charlie and Natalie falter. He was a shaman, Ben realised. The bits of his body that were visible were tattooed, and he had a staff leaning against his desk.

"Go ahead," Ben said, stepping forwards with a nonchalant air. "This place is a disappointment. You came highly recommended, but it's clear that you don't have the spells we need. Is there a shop you can recommend that sells real dark magic?"

The reverse psychology trading tactic was favoured when dealing with goblins – they were quick to anger and easily baited, but Ben had never dealt with a shaman before. He knew he'd hit the mark the moment he saw those yellow eyes narrow.

"What are you looking for?" the goblin shaman asked, his croaky voice dangerously soft.

Ben locked eyes with the shaman. "I need a way in and a way out of the void."

The surprise in the shaman's face was obvious. "Who is it for?"

"Does it matter?" Ben asked.

The shaman sneered. "Of course, you idiot. Different body types require different spells. Choose a void spell designed for a dwarf and use it on a human, and he would explode into a thousand pieces."

Ben cursed inwardly. Why hadn't he thought of that?

"It's for us," he said.

To Ben's surprise, the shaman broke into a huge,

extremely unpleasant grin. "You? How ironic, the Institute's own apprentices violating their laws stopping people entering the void."

Ben was speechless. He glanced at his shoulder, but there was nothing there.

"Just because you can't see the diamonds, doesn't mean I can't," the shaman said.

Ben thought furiously. He decided to go for honesty.

"Yes, we are apprentices. But we are here on our own volition. The Institute don't know anything about this, nor will they."

"Unless you go missing and it gets traced back to me," the shaman said. "Which is quite likely, if you enter the void."

"So what?" Ben said. "If we go missing, they won't have a clue what happened, and certainly wouldn't think of looking in the void. The Institute shuns the void like the plague."

For the first time, Ben saw the shaman hesitate. Ben pushed home his advantage. He stepped forwards and pulled out a large wad of cash.

"What is the cost of getting in and out of the void?" he asked, waving the cash about. The shaman's yellow eyes followed the money back and forth.

"Two hundred pounds to get in; three hundred to get out," the shaman said.

Ben knew he was in no position to negotiate. He counted out the money and handed it over. The Shaman took one glance at it, and shook his head.

"That was per person, not total," he said.

Ben had performed many dramatic acts of outrage when trading before, but this time it was genuine. Both Charlie and Natalie chimed in with angry voices.

The shaman waited calmly for them to finish. "That's the price. Take it or leave it."

Ben choked back several choice retorts.

"You changed the price, didn't you?" he said, when he had finally composed himself. "It was going to be five hundred pounds."

The shaman gave a shrug. "It doesn't matter. That is my price."

"I can't take it," Ben said, crunching the bills in anger. "We only have a thousand pounds."

"That is unfortunate." The shaman seemed to be enjoying himself now. "It seems like only two of you can afford to go."

Ben wanted to tell the shaman to get lost, but he was caught between a rock and a hard place. This was their one chance to get into the void. He gave the shaman a withering look, and then turned away, calling Charlie and Natalie to him for a timeout.

"I hate to admit it, but we have a decision to

make," Ben said. "Only one of you can come with me."

Natalie was looking at Ben with a determined glint in her eye. "I'll go."

Ben turned to Charlie, who had a resigned expression on his face. He rubbed his forehead and gave a sigh, puffing his little belly out. "No, I should go."

To Ben's surprise, Natalie turned on Charlie with a flash of annoyance. "Why should you go? You were the one who protested violently about this whole thing in the first place."

Charlie was taken aback by the intensity of Natalie's reply."It wouldn't be right," he said, going slightly red.

"Why?" Natalie narrowed her eyes, and Charlie took a little shuffle backwards. "Is it because I'm a girl?"

"No," Charlie said, trying but failing to sound convincing. "Well, maybe. I don't know – it just seems wrong. I don't want you risking your life."

If Charlie was hoping that would mollify Natalie, he couldn't have been more wrong. Her eyes flashed, and she rammed a finger into his chest. "I can't risk my life, but you can risk yours? I'm the one who decides what I do, not you."

This was getting out of hand. Ben was about to step in, when the shaman intervened by clearing his throat. The three of them turned back to the shaman with contrasting emotions. Natalie was still furious, Ben annoyed, and Charlie clearly relieved.

"As enjoyable as it is watching you decide who gets to die in the void, I have business to attend to. So I'm going to have to ask you to pay up or leave."

Ben was almost glad for the shaman's intervention, as it silenced Charlie and Natalie. He paid the thousand pounds, slapping the money into the shaman's hand with more force than necessary. The shaman counted the money, and then slipped it into one of his desk drawers, under lock and key. Once he was satisfied the money was safe, he stood up and walked over to one of the shelves. He unlocked a couple of boxes, and returned with two spell pellets and a couple of silver brooches, engraved quite delicately with a goblin's head.

"These spells will get you in," the shaman said. "They are level-four spells, and you will have only one chance to cast them. I do not issue refunds if you fail."

"Fine. And how do we get out?"

The shaman held up the brooches. "These will travel with you to the void. If you cover them with a hand and focus on your body at home, you will return. But be warned, they only work for twenty-four hours. After that, you're on your own."

"Twenty-four hours? Is that it?"

"I could have given you ones that last a week," the shaman said with a smile. "But you were two thousand pounds short."

Ben had to resist the urge to throttle the shaman. He took a calming breath, and muttered quietly, "Twenty-four hours isn't enough time."

The shaman's ears were sharp. "Twenty-four hours is plenty in the void. I doubt you will last more than thirty minutes, so it's really not an issue."

The shaman laughed at his own joke. Ben decided now was a good time to leave the shop, before he lost his temper and did something he might regret.

It was a relief to get back outside and feel the wind on their skin, after the stuffy feel of the dark magic room.

"Well, did you get what you were after?"

To Ben's surprise, the young goblin was still waiting for them, as good as his word.

"Yes, thanks," Ben said with a smile.

The goblin gave a knuckled salute, and bounded off, looking for his next hustle. Ben watched him go, a smile on his face. It was only then that he realised Charlie and Natalie were staring at him expectantly.

"What is it?"

"The void," Natalie said. "We agreed that you should decide who goes with you. Which of us do you choose?"

Ben cursed silently. He thought it might come down to this, and he knew someone was going to get hurt. Ben was silent, and considered both friends carefully. Natalie's strong points were obvious – she was a glass half-full type of person; whereas Charlie was the opposite. She was determined, never gave up, smart and brave. She also had far more experience in the Unseen Kingdoms. But Ben had already decided who he should take the moment the shaman said only one of them could join him.

"Charlie will come with me," Ben said.

Charlie, wisely, showed no sign of elation. Natalie opened her mouth to protest, but emotion came over her. She nodded, and spun on her heel, stalking off down Goblin Avenue.

Charlie made to follow, but Ben grabbed him.

"Let her go," he said. "She needs to cool down."

Charlie watched her until she disappeared out of sight, and then turned glumly back to Ben. "I wish you hadn't chosen me, but I knew you would."

"Of course you knew. We started this together, and we'll finish it together."

CHAPTER 22
AN AWKWARD MAKE-UP

When they arrived back at the Institute, Natalie was nowhere to be found. They asked around, and discovered that William had seen her, but only briefly.

"She checked into the Spellsword Department," he said. He had cast a weight spell on his spellshooter and was using it to work out his biceps. "I think she was looking for someone. She didn't look too happy. Is everything okay with you guys?"

"Yeah, it's fine. If you see her again, can you tell her we're in the library?"

William gave a little smile. "You like that place, don't you? I never figured you for a bookworm."

Ben smiled. "It's not that – there are some great places to nap, if you know where to go."

William smiled. "Ah, I see. That makes more sense. Well, have a nice siesta."

Charlie gave Ben a disapproving look as they headed back down the grand staircase.

"Why did you lie to him? There's nothing wrong with being a bookworm."

Ben shrugged, feeling awkward. "I don't know. I'm just not used to people thinking of me like that."

Charlie didn't reply, but Ben could tell he wasn't happy. Ben didn't feel good about the lie either. Charlie was right – what was wrong with being a bookworm? He had never cared about his reputation at school – why should he now? Ben shook the thought from his head. He had more important things to worry about. Now that they had a way into the void, Ben was eager to get going. Time was critical, with the dwarf mage stuck in such a perilous place. But Charlie wasn't ready.

"I want to do more research," he explained, as they entered the library. Ben hadn't realised it, but he was starting to get a familiar, almost comforting feeling whenever he entered the library, with its spacious reading room, long tables and rows of books. What was going on with him?

"What further research is there to do?" Ben asked, trying to hold back his exasperation. "We don't have much time, especially if we want to find the dwarf mage alive."

"I'm more concerned about us staying alive. So far, my main research has been focused on how to get in and out of the void, but now we need to know how to survive in there – kind of important, as most people seem to think we'll be dead within an hour."

Ben conceded that point, and reluctantly joined Charlie in his search. They spent the remainder of the day looking, with Ben taking occasional breaks to pop out and search for Natalie, but without success. When they left the Institute that evening, Ben couldn't help noticing that Charlie was looking surprisingly upbeat, whereas he was still feeling guilty about Natalie.

"I never thought I'd see you this happy researching the void," Ben said, giving Charlie a sidelong look.

"I found some good stuff," Charlie said.

Ben perked up a little. "Like what?"

"I don't want to say too much. I want to finish the research first, and then commit it all to memory, as we're not going to be able to take anything with us," Charlie said.

Ben pressed him further, but Charlie wouldn't relent, and Ben went to bed that night wondering exactly what Charlie had found that had turned his mood around.

It wasn't until muster the following morning when Ben saw Natalie again. To his great relief, she made eye contact with him as they lined up, though the usual smile was absent. As soon as muster had finished and the apprentices started filing out, Ben made a beeline for her.

"Can we talk?" he asked, opting for the soft, contrite voice.

Natalie nodded. "Just you, though, not Charlie."

Ben frowned, but he didn't argue. They slipped into an empty exam room, and the noise from the busy apprentices receded, leaving the two of them alone. Ben suddenly felt strangely awkward and uncomfortable. His gaze threatened to drop to his feet, and he had to force himself to look her in the eye. Natalie had her arms folded and, likewise, seemed to be battling with some inner demon. She took a deep breath, to compose herself.

"I will go first. Don't interrupt me until I'm done," she said, breaking the silence.

Ben nodded, a little too vigorously.

"I know why you picked Charlie, even if I don't agree with it. You two are close friends, and you want those closest to you by your side when you're in a place like the void. What am I? We've known each other only a few months. I'm almost a stranger by comparison."

Ben made to intervene, but Natalie raised a finger.

"I'm not done. What I got upset about, and what

scares me, is that you are making a decision based on your heart, not your head. I love Charlie dearly, but the void is not a place for him. From what I've read, it's scary, harsh, and dangerous." She paused, and her voice became soft. "Ben, you might not come back, and I don't want it to be just because you picked Charlie over me. I don't want to lose you – or Charlie."

Ben frowned. Was there a pause there? Did she add Charlie as an afterthought, or was he imagining it? Natalie seemed to go a slight shade of red, but she kept talking.

"Remember, this is about Elizabeth's Armour, and ultimately taking down Suktar. If you don't make it, the Unseen Kingdoms, and possibly even the Seen Kingdoms, might fall to the dark elves." She gave a weak smile. "Okay, now I'm done."

Ben ran a hand through his ruffled hair, trying to compose the thoughts rattling around his head. She had said something about the dark elves that Ben knew was important, but the only thing he could really remember was the way she said she didn't want to lose him. Had she emphasised his name over Charlie's? He thought she had, but he couldn't be certain. Did she like him? Really like him? Ben wasn't sure what his feelings were. She was definitely the most attractive girl he knew, and he really enjoyed her company. She was funny, too. By all accounts, and under normal circumstances, he would have asked her out by now. But these were not normal circumstances; he wasn't living your ordinary teenage life. Normal had disappeared the moment he discovered the Royal Institute of Magic. Natalie was part elf, which shouldn't matter, but Ben had never really thought about going out with someone who wasn't entirely human before. Far more importantly, there was Charlie. He was almost certain Charlie had a crush on her, and so Ben had made a firm decision not to get involved, knowing how it might affect his best friend. But if she liked him, that changed matters. Did he have feelings for her? It was ridiculous to even be thinking of this on the eve of trying to enter the void.

Natalie cleared her throat, and Ben became aware that he was just staring at her without actually talking.

"Sorry," he said. *Focus on what's important right now.* "You're right: my decision to pick Charlie was largely based on my heart, not my head. I'm like that. We are lifelong friends and know each other inside out."

Natalie nodded, but was clearly unconvinced.

Ben raised a finger and smiled. "I'm not done. You are right – Charlie is not exactly suited to the void, but one thing you don't know is the way the void works. Remember, we are there in spirit, and though we display a physical manifestation of our bodies, Charlie explained to me that we are not limited to the normal physical universe limitations."

"What does that mean?" Natalie asked, frowning.

Ben scratched his head. "To be honest, I'm not quite sure. Charlie hasn't really explained it yet. But I get the idea that Charlie's disadvantage of being small, chubby and, let's face it, rather unfit may not be as much of an issue in the void."

This seemed to calm Natalie somewhat. The furrowed brow finally disappeared, and she relaxed a little. Ben knew he should have ended the conversation there, but he remembered her opening comment about friendship, and it bugged him, because it simply wasn't true.

"I know we've known each other only a few months, but we've hung out together pretty much every day. You are most definitely not a stranger. Quite the opposite actually."

Natalie gave him a dazzling smile that almost knocked him over. *Darn.* Had he overdone it? Was he leading her on? He cursed inwardly, quickly realising the possible implications of his statement. He tried fumbling for some clarifying words, but stopped in his tracks when she stepped forwards and gave him a hug. Ben returned it, trying desperately to work out if she was giving him a friend hug or something more. It felt different, but he couldn't be sure. She eventually stepped back, and they stared at each other in an awkward silence. She expected him to speak, but what was he supposed to say? Natalie gave an embarrassed smile, and fiddled with her hair.

"I should go and make up with Charlie," she said. "I said some nasty things that I regret."

"Good idea," Ben said far too enthusiastically.

"See you in the common room?"

Ben nodded, and she left, leaving him alone.

Ben smacked his head against the wall repeatedly, cursing his own stupidity.

CHAPTER 23
BACK TO THE CAVERN

When Ben caught up with Charlie, he was surprised to find a glowing smile on his face.

"Natalie will meet us in the library," he said, as they headed upstairs.

"Did she speak with you?"

There! The flush definitely reddened when he mentioned Natalie, but Charlie attempted a casual shrug.

"Yeah, we smoothed things over. How about you?"

Ben nodded. "Same."

For a second the two of them looked at each other, each trying to scope out what had happened with the other. Ben was tempted to ask, but Charlie purposefully changed the subject.

"I think we should enter the void tomorrow," he said. "I've done most of my research, and I don't think there's much left that I haven't read in the library."

The moment passed, and Ben realised it was best to let the matter drop, for now. With some difficulty, he turned his attention back to the void.

"How are we going to track down the dwarf?"

"We have to go back to the cave where we found him. If we enter the void there, we should be able to pick up his trail."

Ben's shoulders slumped. "So we are going to be lying in the cave while we do our search?"

"Unfortunately, yes."

The idea of his body lying on the cold stone floor did not appeal, and that was to say nothing of the danger – what if the dark elves came back? They'd be sitting ducks.

"Natalie will watch over us," Charlie said, when Ben voiced his concern. "Our bodies are safe while in the void, remember? But when we came out, we'd be in trouble, unless Natalie can somehow haul us to safety."

"Can't see that happening," Ben said.

"Nor can I. So we have to hope the dark elves don't come."

There was going to be a lot of hoping on this adventure, Ben realised.

"What about getting the dwarf out of the void?" Ben said. "We've got the brooches, but he doesn't have anything. Do you think we should have tried to buy something for him?"

Charlie shook his head. "No. He's been in there too long; an artefact like that wouldn't work. To be honest, I've got no idea how we'll get him out. I'm hoping that the dwarf mage will know that."

Ben frowned, but left the obvious question left unsaid. If the dwarf mage knew how to get out, why hadn't he done so?

They found Natalie sitting in the main reading area of the library. She stood up and waved as they entered. Ben instinctively turned to Charlie, but he didn't react. Research mode had taken over, casting aside the incident with Natalie.

They worked quietly but efficiently, searching for any last dregs they could find on the void in the most remote of bookshelves. A quiet tension had formed between the three of them. The magnitude of their journey was starting to dawn. It ended up taking less than an hour before Charlie declared himself satisfied he had learnt everything he could. They headed back to the reading area, and spent another hour planning.

By mid-afternoon, they were ready. They decided to enter the void the following morning. They attempted to do some apprenticeship work for the remainder of the day, but soon gave up, unable to take their minds off tomorrow. They left for home early, agreeing to meet at the Dragonway tomorrow at ten o'clock. Ben was eager to find out everything Charlie had learnt, but Charlie shook his head.

"If I tell you now, you won't get any sleep," Charlie said without humour. "And sleep is vital before entering the void."

Despite Charlie not divulging anything, Ben still had a hard time sleeping that night. He stared up at the ceiling, his mind in full flow. He kept trying to envision what the void would be like. Would it really be like hell? If thirty minutes really was the life expectancy of a "voider", then it must be close. But Ben had his doubts, especially as many of the dire warnings came from the Institute, and they clearly didn't like not having any control there. Was the dwarf mage still alive? Inevitably, no matter how hard he tried to avoid it, his attention turned to his parents. He might not go actively searching for them, but what if he stumbled upon their tracks? The thought made his whole body tingle with possibility, and it was some time before he found sleep.

~

DESPITE THE LATE START, Ben couldn't sleep past seven o'clock. He got up, made breakfast, and started packing everything he'd need, based on the list they had made yesterday. He ended up with a full backpack and a sleeping bag, and took them up to his room, where he spent an hour attempting to kill time by surfing the internet.

He met Charlie outside the house at ten o'clock, and immediately noticed the bags under his eyes. "Blimey, Charlie – did you even sleep?"

Charlie rubbed his forehead. "I think so, though I can't be sure. I kept going through my notes, making sure I had everything committed to memory. You never know what you might need."

"So, can you tell me about it?"

Because they left after rush hour, they were fortunate enough to find an empty carriage on the dragon, and Charlie spent the next hour going over the basic rules and laws of the void. Ben had thought he'd done his own extensive research, but he soon found out it was nothing compared to Charlie's. From climate to landscape, from cultures to creatures, Charlie had covered it all. Several times Ben wanted something repeated, thinking he had misheard. By the time they reached Alexia Bay station, he was no longer sure the Institute was exaggerating.

They met up with Natalie just outside the Dragonway and walked to the taxi station. Soon they were flying over Alexia Bay, towards the hill with the secret door. Ben was glad for the breeze; it helped shake away the slightly sick feeling Charlie's void briefing had brought about. None of them talked, but Ben was fairly certain by Charlie's and Natalie's increasingly haunted looks that they were all thinking the same thing. They were about to enter the void. Assuming they managed to get in within the hour, they could be dead before lunch. Ben felt like slapping himself for the negative thought, but his hands were tied up with bags. They would be fine. They would find the dwarf mage, and get out of there pronto. He kept repeating that mantra, but it had trouble sinking in.

Shortly, the taxi landed on the soft hillside and the driver gave them a polite smile before he left.

"Enjoy your camping trip," he said, as he took off again.

They all watched him, almost forlornly, as he disappeared over the hills. Finally, and very reluctantly, Ben turned to the hill with the concealed door. It took him a moment to spot the faint outline; the keyhole was entirely covered with grass. He took the key out of his pocket, and pried the grass out the way.

"You guys ready?" he asked. His voice was soft, lacking its normal vibrancy.

"Ready when you are," Natalie said, attempting a smile.

Ben pushed the door open and immediately got a whiff of the decaying bodies. He saw Charlie put a hand over his mouth to suppress a gag reflex. Ben pulled out his spellshooter and cast a lighting spell, causing the tip to flare. He started down the long, dark path. Their bags made for slow progress, especially when the path narrowed or rocks jutted out, forcing them to squeeze through. Ben could mark their progression by the smell, and it slowly went from bad to horrible. Ten minutes of silent walking passed before Ben spotted the dim light at the end of the tunnel. He slowed, his heart rate suddenly going up a notch. He turned back to Charlie and Natalie and put a finger over his lips. Ben dismissed the light spell from his spellshooter, so that he would be ready to use it, if necessary. The great cave had been devoid of life before, but was it still deserted? And, more importantly, was the dwarf mage still alive? These were the questions rolling round Ben's head as he approached the end of the tunnel. He held his breath as he took the last remaining steps out of the tunnel and into the cave, spellshooter at the ready.

Ben cast his eyes over the dimly lit battleground, ignoring the sick feeling in his stomach and searching quickly for any sign of danger. Nothing moved. He turned his attention to the very back of the cave, and sighed with relief. The dwarf mage was still there, protected by the transparent dome, which could mean just one thing: the void hadn't taken him just yet.

"He's still alive!" Natalie said, showing the first bit of optimism from any of them since they had arrived.

Ben led them down the stairs that connected the tunnel to the floor of the cave. He picked his way through the bodies, trying to ignore the lifeless faces of the dwarves and dark elves. He kept his eyes firmly fixed on his target: the dwarf mage. He was still sitting cross-legged, with the orb on his lap. Ben was pleased to see that it was still glowing, as if this might be a sign of his survival. There was a small cut on his lip. Had that been there before? The clotted blood on his torn trousers certainly hadn't.

"The injuries you suffer in the void are reflected on your body," Charlie said.

Natalie stared at the dwarf with something approaching admiration. "He must be strong to have survived this long."

That was true, Ben conceded. He was a strong one. Could he have inherited that from his father – the Silver Dwarf? Or was their whole theory a red herring?

They stared at the dwarf mage far longer than necessary. Even Ben was reluctant to take the next step, but eventually he forced the words out."We should get going, Charlie. Let's get set up."

Charlie closed his eyes, and nodded. "I guess there's no point drawing this out."

They put their bags down, and set out their sleeping gear next to the dwarf's dome. The rest of the bags' contents were for Natalie, who would need food and water for the next twenty-four hours. She moved them away from the predicted dome Ben and Charlie would create.

Charlie took his shoes off, but kept the rest of his clothes on, as he slipped into his sleeping bag. He pinned one of the brooches they had purchased from the goblin shaman onto his shirt. Ben clipped his own brooch on, but remained standing, and drew out his spellshooter. He had two spells: one for himself; one for Charlie – there was no margin for error.

"Take as long as you need," Natalie said in a soft, soothing voice.

"Yeah, I'm in no hurry," Charlie said.

For a full minute Ben did nothing but clear his head, and concentrate on breathing regularly, purging all distractions from his mind. It was a technique he had recently learnt during his third-grade studies in the Spellsword Department, and he found it extremely useful. When he finally felt ready, he turned to Natalie, and gave her a smile.

"We'll see you soon."

For an awkward moment, Ben thought Natalie was going to get emotional, but she just returned his smile.

"You guys will be fine. I know you will. Just

remember, you only have twenty-four hours before you have to use the brooches. Please don't forget that."

"We won't," Ben said.

He lifted his spellshooter, and pointed it at Charlie, who instinctively flinched. Ben had no more need to focus; he was in a perfectly peaceful place. He pictured the void as it had been described and focused on placing Charlie within it. The pellet started a slow descent down the orb, fighting Ben's will every step of the way. Even for a fourth-level spell, this one was difficult. A drip of sweat ran down his forehead, but Ben barely felt it. Slowly, painfully, the pellet reached the edge of the barrel. But instead of pulling the trigger, he let the spell hover there and dragged the second spell down so it lined up behind the first.

Ben pulled the trigger.

A black spell the size of a tennis ball cannoned into Charlie. Immediately Ben turned his spellshooter and fired the second spell into his own chest. It was like being punched – the impact made him grunt. He barely had time to recover, when he felt ice coursing through his veins, freezing his entire body. His stomach started groaning, and he started to feel sick and dizzy. Somehow he managed to stagger into his sleeping bag, where he rolled up, shivering, just about resisting the urge to vomit. He was dimly aware that Charlie was doing the same. The icy feel receded, but the dizziness got progressively worse, until he started seeing black spots. He blinked, and he found his vision starting to blur. Dimly, he was aware that he was losing consciousness. With a cry of pain and confusion, Ben slipped away.

CHAPTER 24
THE VOID

When Ben came to, he found himself lying on his back, staring up at a red canvas. For a terrifying thirty seconds, he struggled with his own identity. It was only when he sat up and saw the boy beside him that something clicked, and his memory came flooding back.

Charlie sat up a moment later with a similar blank expression, which also disappeared the moment he spotted Ben.

They had made it.

Realisation dawned on them quickly. They scrambled to their feet, and instinctively went back to back in a defensive position.

Ben half-expected something to jump out at them, and he immediately scanned the area for signs of danger. The sky was blood red and streaked with black. The landscape was dry, barren, and devoid of life. They found themselves on a narrow dirt path, which wound its way through the thin, wispy grass that surrounded them. The grass swayed gently, despite the lack of wind. Next to them was a leafless tree. Its trunk was scarred and much of the bark was gone.

"Roolers," Charlie said, pointing at the red sky. "I bet they're waiting for us."

Ben looked up and saw a couple of large birds circling at such altitude they were hard to make out except for their long, hooked beaks.

"They're like vultures, except they feed on the dying as well as the dead. They specialise in targeting the wounded."

Ben allowed himself to relax, just a fraction. Bar the roolers, they were alone. In fact, the place was so dead and barren, it felt like they were the only people alive.

"The dwarf mage must have done his research," Charlie said, who also seemed less on edge. "We are on the southern path – one of the least dangerous places in the void, simply because nobody bothers coming here. There are no resources, and the land is worthless. The trouble will come as soon as we start heading north."

Charlie stared down the path into the distance.

Ben knew they would have to get going soon, but questions were exploding inside his head like fireworks. "You look exactly like your body, down to the clothes you were wearing this morning. You've even got the brooch."

"The brooch physically transferred from home into the void," Charlie said. "As for the physical representation, that is something our minds mock up subconsciously."

"I'll take your word for that," Ben said, running a hand through his hair. It felt real enough. "So, now what? This is where the dwarf mage started, right? I don't see a trail anywhere."

Charlie was staring hard at the path. "It's there, somewhere."

The dirt path looked well walked, but Ben could see nothing to indicate the dwarf mage had been here. Charlie, however, got down on his hands and knees so that he was at eye level with the dirt.

"Aha! Got you," Charlie said.

As far as Ben could see, Charlie was pointing a finger at a random blade of dead grass.

Charlie waved at Ben, still staring avidly at the grass. "Come here and look. It's obvious when you see it properly."

Ben got down and joined Charlie. "What am I supposed to be looking at? That piece of grass looks like all the others."

"You're not looking hard enough. Remember, a lot of what happens here is to do with your mind. We're looking for a trail, and we know it's here. So tell the path to reveal it."

Had Ben not been so used to the way spell-shooters worked, he would have laughed. Instead, he did as Charlie suggested, and envisioned the trail created by the dwarf mage. Almost immediately the small blade of grass Charlie was staring at turned red. The moment it did so, the strand behind it also changed colour. In the blink of an eye, a thin line of grass followed suit, like a cascading set of domino pieces. Ben looked up and saw a slender red trail in the centre of the path, going off into the distance.

"Well, that's one problem solved," Ben said, smiling for the first time since they entered the void. "Let's get going."

Ben wanted to set a good pace, knowing they had only twenty-four hours, but Charlie seemed reluctant to match it. To make matters worse, they had no way to track the time. Ben had hoped there might be a sun or a point of reference to use. Charlie, however, didn't seem concerned.

"Look at your brooch," he said.

Ben did so. There was a small sliver of red at the bottom, as if someone had coloured in the metal with a very fine paintbrush.

"Eventually, the whole brooch will turn red.

When it does, the brooch will break, and we'll be stuck here," Charlie explained.

"How do you know that?" Ben asked. "I was with you when we bought them. The shaman never gave any instructions."

"Not surprising," Charlie said with a shrug. "I think he wants us to die here. It's something I read up on. A lot of artefacts work for only a set amount of time or have a limited number of uses."

It was the first of many times Ben counted himself lucky for choosing Charlie. He was used to his friend being a walking library, but for this trip he had taken it to a new level.

"So, I'm guessing there's a reason you're walking like a tortoise?" Ben asked.

Charlie nodded. "Yes, a good one. We need to take advantage of the fact that, right now, nobody is trying to kill us."

"Take advantage how?"

Charlie gave a sudden smile. "By practising. Let me show you."

Charlie suddenly ran forwards, jumped and performed an aerial forward somersault. He almost pulled it off but overcooked the landing.

Ben couldn't have been more surprised if Charlie had sprouted wings.

"That was insane! How did you do that?"

Charlie got up, and dusted his hands. "I've been

wanting to do that ever since I read about it in the library. Remember what I told you about the void? You are limited only by your mind, not your body."

A huge grin spread over Ben's face as Charlie's explanation sunk in. "You mean kind of like the Matrix?"

"Basically, yes. But you still have to have the knowledge for what you're doing. You can't automatically be a grand master of Kung Fu. You have to learn it first."

"Uh huh," Ben said, but he was barely listening. His attention had turned to the path in front of him, and he was rubbing his hands. "So, I should be able to do a somersault as well, right?"

"Absolutely," Charlie said. "But you can't just believe it or think it. You have to know it, with utter certainty. That's the tricky part."

Ben turned his attention back to the path, undeterred. "Right. So I need to get rid of the picture in my mind of me landing on my head."

"Yeah, that's not going to work."

Ben cleared his mind and envisioned a perfect forward somersault. But when he tried to jump, his natural survival instinct made him hesitate.

"You don't have that certainty," Charlie said, smiling with amusement.

"It's harder than I thought," Ben admitted. "How did you do it?"

"I've been training my mind for the last few days for these conditions. Plus, I read it in a book that I trusted."

Ben looked slightly affronted. "Why didn't you tell me?"

Charlie shrugged. "Because I know how quickly you'll adapt and how good you'll be, and frankly, I didn't want you flying round like superman while I tried to catch up."

Ben turned back to the path. "Okay, I can do this. What's the big deal? It's only a somersault. I've done them loads of times on trampolines and into swimming pools."

"Not exactly the same thing, but I'm listening," Charlie said.

"Are you trying to make this harder on purpose?"

Charlie was clearly enjoying himself. "Sorry. Keep encouraging yourself. I'll shut up."

Ben rocked back and forth, like a long-jumper attempting a super human leap. He ran and then jumped, throwing his head forwards. As soon as he saw the ground above his head, he knew he was in trouble, and promptly landed on his face. He got up, rubbing his forehead. The pain spurred him on, rather than acting as a deterrent. Three more times he tried and, with each attempt, his jump became a little bigger, the somersault a little more complete. On the fourth effort, he landed it cleanly.

Ben pumped the air. "Yeah!"

Charlie had also succeeded in a complete somersault, and they spent several minutes practising more complicated moves, until they both looked like professional gymnasts.

"What else can we do?" Ben asked.

"Technically, anything," Charlie replied. "But the harder the feat, the harder it will be to execute it, as your mind will naturally insist it can't be done."

Ben glanced around. The large birds – roolers – were still circling, but they posed no danger at present. A sweeping glance around the dead landscape revealed no other threat, but Ben was aware that could change any moment.

"What happens when we run into something that wants to kill us?" he asked. "Our athletic skills are cool, but we can't somersault someone to death."

Charlie nodded, suddenly becoming serious. "We need magic. That's the tricky part. Technically we should be master wizards – after all, there are no limitations to what we can do. But from what I read, it can take days to get anywhere."

Ben clenched his fist. "We don't have days. We have hours. So, can we just envision a fireball coming out of our behind, and it will happen?"

"Technically, yes, but it won't work."

Charlie was right, as usual. Ben tried to picture a small flame coming out of his backside, but the only thing that passed was a bit of wind. He tried something a bit more practical: opening his palm, and envisioning a small flame. Again, nothing.

"Am I missing something?" Ben asked, after a few minutes of staring at his hand.

"Your mind naturally rejects the idea of doing magic, because it's so unnatural. Even in the Unseen Kingdoms, you don't actually do magic; you use a spellshooter for that."

"Well, I can't summon a spellshooter, because that would take magic, which my mind isn't happy about," Ben said, getting slightly frustrated.

"No, but I think we have more chance of that over having a flame appear, because our mind is used to the concept of a spellshooter," Charlie said. "It's worth a go. If we are going to arm ourselves, we should do it now, before we encounter trouble."

Ben and Charlie dived into the challenge. For the next half an hour, they stood there, trying to clear their minds and summon spellshooters. In some ways, it was easier than the somersault, as there was no pain with failure. But it was one thing to make your body perform acrobatics; it was entirely another to summon a piece of matter from thin air.

"I'm exhausted," Charlie said, wiping his brow. "And we've barely moved a muscle."

Ben glanced at his brooch. Another sliver of red was now showing. How long had they been here? An hour? Probably more. He re-doubled his efforts, blasting aside doubts and irritating thoughts that kept crossing his mind. He knew it was possible – but possible wasn't enough. He had to know it with absolute certainty. *This isn't Earth*, he kept telling himself. *Stop thinking about its rules.*

"I saw something!" Charlie exclaimed, making Ben jump.

Charlie was staring intently at Ben's hand. There was nothing there.

"It was only there for a second, but I definitely saw a flicker of a spellshooter."

Knowing he had made something appear gave him the last bit of confidence he was missing. He glanced down at his hand, and willed the spellshooter to materialise. This time he saw it – a transparent flicker of something that looked like a gun. His heart leapt, and Charlie grinned.

"You're close. Keep going."

But he wasn't as close as he hoped. Time and again he tried, and though the spellshooter slowly started to become more solid with each attempt, it never stayed for more than a second or two. And as the frustration settled in, even that solidity started to fade.

"Take a breather," Charlie said.

They sat down on the dirt path. It was hot, Ben

realised – hot and dry – which just added to the general unpleasantness of the void.

The dust on the horizon appeared just as he was starting to relax. He squinted, making sure his eyes weren't playing a trick on him.

"Do you see that?" Ben asked.

Charlie's face was suddenly creased with worry. "I see it. I hope it's just the wind."

What wind? Ben wanted to say. Within a couple of minutes, Ben could make out the faint outline of a group heading their way, kicking dust up on the path as they went.

They were moving fast.

Ben and Charlie scrambled to their feet.

"No pressure, but now might be a good time to make that spellshooter appear," Charlie said, his voice shaking a little.

Ben tried again. Nothing happened, not even a flicker. He grit his teeth and tried again. Nothing.

"You're panicking," Charlie said.

"Can you blame me?"

"No, but somehow you need to relax, otherwise it's never going to happen," Charlie said in a voice that was anything but relaxed.

Ben glanced towards the dust in the distance and he cursed.

"Oh my," Charlie said, his voice a terrified whisper.

They were close enough to make out now: goblins, at least a dozen of them, running hard and heading their way. Ben calculated no more than a couple of minutes and they would cross paths.

"Should we run or hide?"

"Neither," Ben said, clenching his fists and snarling in a manner more suited to the creatures approaching them.

He took a deep breath, necessity giving him a sudden urgency. He flexed his right hand, and willed – demanded – the spellshooter to appear.

The handle materialised in the nook of his palm and he clamped down on it, solid contact making it real. He glanced down, and saw a perfect replica of his B2 in his hand, right down to the silver trimmings running down the barrel.

"Thank goodness for that," Charlie said, wiping his brow. "Now what?"

The goblins were now so close he could count them – fourteen in all. There was fear in their eyes. No, not fear, Ben realised, but terror.

The goblins weren't running towards them, but away from something else. Ben glanced behind the goblins, but he saw nothing.

One of the goblins screamed suddenly and went down, green blood flowing from a gaping wound. The other goblins cried out. They glanced at their fallen comrade, and ran all the harder.

Ben stared in shock. What had attacked the goblin? Ben had seen nothing, yet something had clearly taken a chunk out of the goblin's arm.

Suddenly, the idea of running didn't sound like such a bad one.

"Over here," Ben said.

He ran over to a dead tree on the side of the path, and they both hid behind the trunk. Ben raised his spellshooter. Charlie was right: having a spellshooter made casting spells a lot easier, simply because he was so used to it. He fired a couple of spells into his chest and at a flinching Charlie. The shield and shadow spells were strong, and Ben felt his body ripple as the spells took effect.

Charlie was peeking out from the tree, his hands shaking on the trunk. "Did you see that goblin go down? Something is out there. Something that—"

Charlie was still talking when another goblin went down in a bloodied heap, making them both jump. The goblins were less than fifty yards away; yet again, Ben saw nothing. Whatever was picking them off was either invisible or extremely good at killing. Probably both.

Ben quickly pulled back behind the tree as the goblins approached, their screams and pounding of feet reaching a crescendo. And then they were past, still running hard, without so much as a glance their way. Ben could see the terror in their eyes as they ran, and it made him shiver. He watched to see if any more would fall before they disappeared out of sight. None did.

They stayed behind the tree for a full minute, trying to regain some semblance of calm. Ben kept staring at the fallen goblin nearby, lying in his own blood. Occasionally he twitched and let out a weak groan. Ben had an overwhelming desire to help, even if it meant putting the goblin out of its misery.

The demon that materialised seemed to fade smoothly into existence like a video game animation. It must have been close to seven feet tall, with leather skin that was as red as the sky. There were small horns coming out of his forehead and a tail that looked as though it could double as a whip.

The demon was idly poking the squirming goblin with its clawed feet.

"Perfectly cooked," it said in a hissing voice, a snake-like tongue flicking out as it spoke.

The demon went down on its haunches, and began feeding. Thankfully the demon had its back to them, so Ben couldn't see the gory details. But that didn't make a difference to Charlie, who made a sudden retching noise. Ben clamped his hand over Charlie's mouth.

The demon stopped feeding, and raised its head. It stood up slowly, and turned, momentarily forgetting the poor goblin. Its red eyes were curious, and its tongue kept flicking out, as if it were tasting the air. Ben prayed the shadow spell would be strong enough.

It wasn't.

The demon locked eyes with Ben, who still had his head poking out from the tree.

"Oh, great," he whispered, whipping his head back.

Charlie looked as though he had gone into a state of shock. He was standing, back against the tree, muttering incoherently. It was only when Ben listened that he realised Charlie was saying the same thing over and over again.

"*Demon Underlord.*"

Ben didn't have time to ask what exactly this Demon Underlord was capable of. He could hear its languid footsteps heading right for them. Run or fight? The goblins tried running, and that clearly didn't work out very well.

Ben lifted his spellshooter. He took a deep breath and, ignoring Charlie's frantic shaking of his head, thrust himself away from the tree to face the demon.

CHAPTER 25

THE SOUTHERN PATH

The demon stopped and regarded him with a curious stare.

"A human child, and far from home," the demon said, licking his lips with his long tongue. "A delicacy I have not enjoyed in some time."

Ben kept his spellshooter trained on the demon, managing to keep the shaking to a minimum. "Stay back or I'll shoot."

His voice didn't sound quite as intimidating as he would have liked, and the demon cocked his head in amusement. "What if I choose not to? You will shoot me with your toy?"

Ben grit his teeth, his finger hovering over the trigger. What was the demon's weakness? Very little, if its confidence was anything to go by.

"Hit him with a snow storm."

Charlie materialised next to him. His face was ashen, but there was a fiery glint in his eye.

Ben pulled the trigger, and an explosion of ice and snow shot towards the demon with such force that the kickback almost made Ben lose balance. An icy wind tore into the demon, carrying with it icy snowballs and huge hailstones. The demon reared its head, and cried out, more in anger than pain, trying to waft away the mini storm.

"Hit him again!" Charlie said, watching the demon struggle with something approaching hope.

But the demon attacked before Ben had the chance. It moved with inhuman speed. Ben dived to his left, Charlie his right, and the demon's fist cannoned into the tree, punching a hole right through it. Ben rolled and fired, hitting the demon right in the chest with a six-foot spear of ice. This one left a mark, albeit a small one. This time the pain was evident on its gruesome face, but it didn't slow the demon. In one fluid motion, he removed his hand from the tree and leapt high in the air. Ben followed the demon's flight and fired another spear, but the demon batted it aside, and landed on top of Ben, flooring him. Ben stared up at the seven-foot monstrosity in horror. A red hand reached out and grabbed Ben's neck, lifting him off his feet.

"Dinner time," the demon said, his tongue flicking out to lick Ben's forehead.

Ben kicked and squirmed, but the demon's grip was like iron. The demon drew Ben close and opened its mouth. Ben screamed with defiance, then panic, and finally horror, as the demon's teeth closed in on him.

The demon paused just as he was about to take a chunk out of Ben's face. It frowned, and sniffed with its pig-like nose.

"You are Sparkstorm," the demon said. There was a sudden look of doubt in its blood red eyes, and for one glorious moment, Ben thought the demon was having second thoughts about eating him. But the lure of human flesh was stronger than whatever doubts crossed its mind. It licked its lips, and re-opened its jaws.

The ice spear hit the demon full in the back, and it lost its grip on Ben. The demon turned, just as another spear hit him in the chest.

Charlie had a spellshooter in his hand, and was firing for all he was worth. The demon approached its new adversary, but Charlie held his ground and continued to fire. The ice spears shrunk in size, as Charlie struggled to hold his nerve. Conversely, without the distraction of the demon, Ben was able to focus and call forth some huge spells. Dozens of arrows cast in ice struck the demon's back. It arched and tried to swipe them away, but the majority found their mark. Ben's spells were clearly stronger than

Charlie's, and the demon turned back to face him. The moment it did so, Charlie's spears grew in strength and size. The demon was being pounded from both sides. But despite the barrage, the demon stood up straight, and looked Ben right in the eye. For a moment, he thought the demon was about to strike, and he panicked – he was giving everything he had, and if that wasn't enough, then he was in trouble. But the demon didn't attack. Instead, it looked, gave him a nod, and then disappeared in a blur.

Ben collapsed onto the grass with exhaustion, massaging his neck, which the demon had strangled. Charlie staggered over and joined him. His hair was dishevelled, and there was a wild look in his eyes.

"I can't believe it," he said softly. "We took on a Demon Underlord and didn't get brutally eaten."

Ben managed a weak smile. "I was about to be, until you hit him with those ice spears. How did you summon the spellshooter?"

"I knew we were going to die unless I could get my hands on a spellshooter. I don't think I've ever exerted that much willpower before. I didn't know I was capable of it, to be honest."

It was tempting to sit there, in relative safety, but they knew time was short and they needed to get going. Once Ben's windpipe had recovered and he could breathe easily again, they got to their feet and continued following the thin, red trail.

For the first fifteen minutes, Ben and Charlie spent every second searching for any sign of danger. The demon had proven that creatures could appear from nowhere. But it was difficult to remain alert when the place was deserted; it felt like they were the only two people alive.

"The demon said I was 'Sparkstorm'. Do you know what that means?" Ben asked, turning to Charlie. He had been so focused on looking out for danger that he had forgotten all about the demon's words.

"Never heard of it," Charlie said.

Ben recalled the demon's expression. "It made the demon think twice about eating me, and I also think it helped persuade the demon to leave."

Charlie was intrigued. "The word never came up in any of my books. That is interesting."

Ben wasn't sure how long they walked for on the southern path, though he guessed at least a couple of hours. His legs started to tire, until he remembered that they weren't his real legs, just a spiritual representation, and he willed them to be strong. The pain went away immediately. He tried doing the same when he heard his stomach rumble, but it wasn't quite as effective.

"Eating and drinking are such critical parts of our body, the mind will not easily accept that you can just will yourself to being full. Food is also on the no summon list," Charlie said.

Ben sighed, and cast thoughts of Big Macs aside.

It was impossible not to think of his parents while they walked, especially as there was very little to occupy his attention. It was difficult to suppress the hope that they might somehow stumble across them. Whenever he found himself dreaming of such a scenario, he thrust it ruthlessly aside. That wasn't why they were here. But, inevitably, the thought would return.

It was another hour before the dreary, lifeless landscape started to change and, with it, came their first major obstacle.

"We've got a problem," Ben said, pointing ahead.

The land ended suddenly and quite dramatically. A mighty chasm barred their progress, splitting the land. It must have been at least a hundred feet across. Ben and Charlie walked to the edge, and looked down. It was black, an eternity of nothing. The void in its purest sense.

"This is the end of the southern path," Charlie said. "Over there is where the action starts."

CHAPTER 26
THE DEMON'S PRISON

"How do we get over there?" Ben asked.

The answer lay in the red trail they were following. It continued on serenely over the chasm, as if the dwarf had used some sort of invisible bridge.

"The dwarf walked," Charlie said.

"You mean he flew?"

"Basically, yes. Which is what we need to do, if we're going to follow him."

Ben stared at the chasm, a small smile playing over his lips. "I've always wanted to fly."

But they soon found that flying made summoning a spellshooter look like child's play. They managed some mighty leaps, but they simply couldn't levitate, even for a second.

"I can jump a good forty, maybe even forty-five feet," Ben said, eyeing up the chasm.

"Great. So you'll plummet to your death in the exact middle of the chasm."

"How did the dwarf mage do it?"

Charlie rubbed his cheeks. "Either his willpower is stronger than ours or he knows something we don't."

Ben walked up to the chasm's edge. "So we can't fly. But what if there was an invisible bridge we could walk across?"

"Yes, that would be handy. But there isn't."

Ben smiled, and tapped his nose. "Yes, there is. You just have to believe it."

"Ah, I see," Charlie said with an earnest nod. "Yes, there is definitely an invisible bridge there. You go first; I'll follow."

Ignoring the sarcasm, Ben concentrated on the first step he would have to take out into the open air. Technically he didn't have to mock up the entire bridge – a platform or a single stepping stone would do.

Ben pictured the type of stepping stone he wanted, envisioning every detail, down to its colour and shape. After a few minutes, he managed to get a small stone, barely big enough for a single foot, to materialise. It stayed there for less than a second and promptly disappeared again.

"Success!" Ben said, raising both arms in celebration.

Getting the stone the right size wasn't difficult, but it took a good hour of focusing to get the stepping stone to remain in place, floating in the air.

Ben stepped back to admire his work. "Now we have to test it."

"It looks rather transparent," Charlie said.

He was right – you could see right through the stepping stone. Ben spent a few minutes trying to solidify it, without a great deal of success.

"It will have to do," Ben said.

He approached the edge again, and peered down at the black abyss. It would take only a small step to get onto the stepping stone, but if it wasn't solid, he wouldn't have anything to jump back from to get to safety. He took his jumper off, held one sleeve, and gave the other to Charlie.

"Here, hold on to this," he instructed. "If I fall, you can catch me."

Charlie rubbed his chin thoughtfully. "That's not a good idea."

"Why not?"

"Having a safety net implies you don't truly believe the stepping stone is there, which means it will never hold your weight."

Ben put his hands on his hips. "So I have to step on it without any protection whatsoever?"

"I'm afraid so."

Ben turned back to the stone. It was real; it was solid. He just had to step on it. Of course it would take his weight. So what if it was floating in mid-air, defying the law of gravity? Ben shook that thought out of his head. The void wasn't a normal world; there were different rules. He took a deep breath, and focused, his heart rate moving up a gear.

"Okay, here goes," Ben said, rubbing his hands together.

He eyed up the stepping stone, willing it further into existence. It was definitely becoming more solid; Ben could barely see through it now.

He lifted a leg, and jumped onto the stepping stone. It held fast, as if it were lying on solid ground, not floating in mid-air. Ben let out a wild shout of joy.

"Success!"

He was still celebrating when he made the mistake of looking down, into the black chasm. His left foot sunk into the stone, and it was only with a lightning quick thought that he was able to lift his foot, and reassert the presence of the stone.

"Well done," Charlie said. "Now you just have to repeat the feat about fifty times, so that we have a bridge to the other side."

Now that he had done one, the rest came relatively easily, and he started hopping across. He turned back to Charlie, and found that he hadn't moved.

"What are you waiting for?" Ben asked. "I'm doing all the hard work, you just have to walk across."

"I still need the stones to take my weight," Charlie said, looking anxiously at them. "If I don't believe they can, they will disappear."

"You'll be fine," Ben said. "They're real. Come on, I want to get going."

Charlie inched forwards, until he reached the chasm's edge. He took a deep breath, closed his eyes and stepped onto the first stone. A mixture of relief and delight crossed his face when he realised the stone held strong.

Once Ben and Charlie were safely across, Ben allowed the stones to disappear, and turned to face the new landscape awaiting them. It was very different from the southern path. The land was rocky and constantly undulating, with patches of grass and shrubbery covering the ground. There were plants as well, some of them taller than Ben, coming out from the rocky undergrowth.

"We need to watch our step," Charlie said, eyeing the scenery warily. "Those tall plants are dangerous, but they're not as bad as the smaller ones hiding in the grass, which are extremely poisonous."

The red trail was still present, but it zigzagged

constantly; the dwarf mage clearly underwent the same task of picking a safe route.

Ben picked his path carefully, often jumping from rock to rock, to avoid the dangerous plantations on the ground. It was slow going and hard work. Danger lurked with every step, and not just from the plants. They spotted several animals watching them, some as small as rabbits, others as big as bears, and all interested in sizing them up for lunch. Ben concentrated on finding the path, while Charlie was responsible for scaring the animals off. Then there were the black streaks in the sky. They would slowly grow, and then, like a bursting cloud, unleash a bolt of electricity that would scar the ground. They almost got hit on more than one occasion.

An hour passed, then two. Ben began to tire. His eyes searched each rock mechanically now – he hadn't the energy to do anything else. He thought briefly of his parents, wondering if they were anywhere near them. Gradually the rocky terrain gave way to a more manageable landscape – the rocks became less frequent, and they found a rough path, which the plants and shrubs didn't encroach.

The brooch was now a third filled with red, meaning they had already been in the void for a full eight hours. The good news was that they were relatively intact, barring a few scrapes and bruises, but the red trail seemed to go on forever, and Ben started to get concerned that they wouldn't reach its end before the time was up.

"Look at that," Charlie said.

Ben, who had taken to staring at the ground as he walked, looked up. Charlie was pointing at a cluster of makeshift houses, surrounded by a wooden fence in the distance. The path split – left went to the settlement; right continued onwards.

"Goblins," Charlie said with distaste. "We need to watch out from now on. There will be other creatures, not just goblins, here."

Thankfully the red trail did not turn left, towards the village, but kept on going. The path was well worn here, and Ben knew it would be only a matter of time before they ran into someone or something. Sure enough, he soon spotted three goblins heading their way.

"Stay calm," Ben said, seeing Charlie shuffling uncomfortably.

"I'm really starting to dislike goblins," Charlie said with a sigh.

"At least they're not demons."

But that wasn't entirely true. The goblins that approached seemed to be a demon hybrid with red skin and small horns protruding from their foreheads.

The goblins had been talking amongst themselves, but they noticed the two boys and were now looking at them with interest. Ben thought he saw one of them lick his lips. The path was sufficiently wide that Ben had hoped they might just be able to pass by without incident, but when he subtly shifted his position to the side of the path, the goblins matched his movement. Ben was half-tempted to use his spellshooter and try to take them down from a distance, knowing goblins were better at close-quarter combat. But he couldn't bring himself to shoot without provocation.

Both groups stopped, facing each other, each sizing the other up. Ben was pleased to see the goblins eyeing up their spellshooters warily.

"Which clan are you?" the taller goblin in the middle asked in an accusing voice. "Only the Lartes are allowed here, and you're no Larte. They don't have no humans."

Ben exchanged confused looks with Charlie, who gave a helpless shrug. There wasn't much he could say; he didn't know the name of any clans, or else he would have used one of them.

"We don't belong to a clan," Ben said.

The goblin gave a snarl of surprise. "You are loners?"

"Well, there are two of us, so that's not technically true," Ben said. "But we don't belong to a clan, yet."

The goblins immediately started talking to each

other in a harsh language that Ben recognised but didn't understand, despite his basic goblin lessons. Eventually, the taller one turned back to them.

"My brothers want to take you in, but our clan has a temporary truce with loners, as long as you leave our land within the hour."

"We're leaving," Ben said a little too quickly. They had no intention of being here in an hour's time. The goblins gave them a nasty look as they passed, and Ben got the idea that they would much rather have taken them in.

"That wasn't too bad," Charlie said. "I was certain they would attack us, or at least capture us. But clan rules are pretty strict here, and I expect that held them in line."

Ben couldn't help thinking of the Institute. They made entry to the void illegal, citing the place as evil and without law or mercy. But that wasn't entirely true – there were laws, just not of the Institute's making.

The goblin villages, and indeed other settlements containing other races, became more frequent. Some were small, with no more than a dozen residences, but others resembled small towns. Each time they tried to skirt around them, but on a couple of occasions they found themselves fighting, or more frequently running from, the residents.

Eventually the urban district passed, and the towns ceased.

"I really hope we don't come across anything more," Charlie said. His face was scratched from a recent brawl with a nasty plant that he had stepped into when running at full pelt from a band of surprisingly quick trolls. Ben, too, was battered and bruised, and he could no longer put his full weight on his left leg. He tried healing himself by pure will, but he was tired, and it was no longer as effective as it was when they had first arrived.

Ben took to looking at his brooch every hour now; two-thirds of it was coloured in red, and somehow it seemed like it was speeding up. The only consolation was that the dwarf trail seemed to be getting stronger; the little red line was definitely becoming more substantial.

"I hope that means we're getting close," Ben said.

Charlie didn't answer. He was staring ahead; his tired eyes suddenly looked as though they were about to pop out of their sockets. Ben immediately saw why.

The landscape ahead of them was dramatically different to anything they'd seen so far. Life, which had been scarce before, was completely absent. The dry grass gave way to a peculiar, marble-like surface, with swirls of red and black. The landscape was flat and endless, devoid of scenery.

Except for one thing.

Dominating the horizon was a black castle, so large that the turrets seemed to touch the sky. Despite the distance, they could feel a peculiar, disturbing presence from the mighty structure that made both of them shiver.

"Demons," Charlie said. "I read about their castles, but I thought the author was exaggerating. Clearly not."

The red trail continued onwards, towards the castle, and it was with great reluctance that they continued to follow it.

"Why would the dwarf visit the demons?" Ben asked.

Charlie gave an uncomfortable shrug. "Maybe he thought only they would be strong enough to offer him a way out."

The castle became both more impressive and more daunting with each passing minute. It had a peculiar glaze that made the walls shine and added to its aura of invulnerability. The castle had the strange effect of making it feel like you were being watched. The feeling grew, and Ben soon realised it wasn't just a feeling.

"We're being watched," Ben said quietly.

Charlie wore a worried frown. "I can feel it too. We must be close enough to the castle to have attracted their attention."

When you are walking through such a bare landscape for so long, with nothing to look at bar the castle, anything that crops up on the horizon is interesting. And so it was with the forest. It materialised in the distance to their right, and ran parallel with them, towards and beyond the castle. Even from here, Ben could tell the trees were big. More significantly, they were green, and full of life.

Ben's neck started to hurt, as he gazed upon the forest, preferring to look at it rather than the daunting castle. But even if he had been staring dead ahead, he wouldn't have seen the barrier. Ben felt a sudden resistance, slowing his walk momentarily, before he passed through.

"What was that?" Ben asked, turning around and trying to see the barrier they had passed through.

Charlie started tapping frantically on his shoulder.

Ben turned back around and immediately realised the barrier they had passed through wasn't supposed to stop people. It was to prevent them from seeing what lay beyond.

It was prison hell. Hundreds of single cages floated twenty feet in the air, in neat rows and columns, creating a grid of prisoners. Many of the cells were occupied by goblins, but others were taken by humans, dwarves, trolls, even a few elves, and many more races Ben couldn't identify.

The noise was incredible, even from a distance. As soon as the prisoners spotted them, they started waving and calling, shaking their bars, and generally causing a cacophony.

"The demon's prison," Charlie said softly. "I read about it, but it's even worse in real life. They just leave them out here to die."

Ben was trying to see where the red trail went. At the beginning it had been no more than a slender piece of string; now it looked more like a rope, glowing bright and strong. The trail went right into the heart of the floating cages, but did it continue beyond, into the castle? Or was the dwarf trapped in one of the cages?

"Come on," Ben said. "We don't have much time."

The noise from the prisoners increased as they approached, and reached a crescendo when they entered the field of floating cages.

"Humans! Get me out of here!"

"Psst, over here, kids. I've got an offer for you."

"Please help me. I'm dying."

The desperate ones screamed and shouted at them. Others tried to coax them with riches or power; still others looked at them with curiosity but said nothing. The worst were those who had given up, and sat slumped in their cages, waiting, perhaps even hoping, for death. Ben was almost glad they were twenty feet in the air, as their outstretched arms (barring a few with ridiculously long limbs) couldn't reach them. Were the prisoners good or evil? Certainly the majority seemed the latter; the mere fact that they were inside the void reaffirmed that. But Ben spotted a few whom he wished he could have helped.

Ben forced himself to zone out the voices and focused on the trail, his heart accelerating. They were close. The dwarf was either in the prison field or in the castle. He didn't even want to think about the latter; the idea of breaching the castle was too daunting.

The red trail started to rise upwards, and Ben clenched his fist in hope. Soon it was as high as Ben, and it kept getting higher. The trail headed right for an ugly troll that barely fit into its cage. It swerved left, then right, and Ben followed it, now almost running.

Standing in his own cage, just behind the troll, the dwarf mage stared at them, clenching the bars, curiosity etched on his weather-worn face.

CHAPTER 27
HELLHOUNDS

There were a few subtle differences between the appearance of the dwarf here and the one lying in the cavern. He had the same prominent nose and thick, ginger beard, but his face had a worn expression Ben hadn't noticed before, and it looked thinner, almost gaunt. It was his eyes that really stood out; they had a haunted look about them, emphasised by the bags underneath them.

It occurred to Ben that he didn't even know the dwarf's name, nor had he given a moment's thought about what he was going to say; he always assumed it would come naturally, but natural was hard when you were surrounded by floating cages with prisoners screaming at you.

"My name is Elander Farseeker," the dwarf said

in a surprisingly deep voice. His manner wasn't unfriendly, but guarded. "I have been expecting you."

Ben gave the dwarf an incredulous look. "You have?"

Elander nodded. "I can sense your bodies resting near mine. I guessed you were looking for me."

Ben knew he should blast Elander out of the cage and get away from this horrible place as soon as possible, but he hesitated. Questions that he had been sitting on for some time suddenly started buzzing round his head, and he simply couldn't wait until they had made an escape before asking them.

"Yes, we've been looking for you," Ben said, carefully choosing his words. "We have been searching for anyone connected to a certain dwarf."

Elander appeared unsurprised. "The Silver Dwarf. My late father."

Ben managed to restrict his exultation to a subtly clenched fist. They had him. They had the Guardian.

A particularly loud cry came from a nearby cage, making him jolt. He turned and saw a troll shaking the cage bars with such force that it was a miracle they hadn't snapped. Ben knew they should get the dwarf out now and leave, but he couldn't resist asking one more question.

"Does Elizabeth's Armour mean anything to you?"

Elander's bushy, ginger eyebrows rose. He didn't

reply immediately, and Ben found himself waiting on tenterhooks, the screams and shouts from the other prisoners fading into a distant hum.

"I know about her armour. I know about its legacy," Elander said. "More than that I'm not willing to say until I am safe and know I can trust you."

Ben nodded, suppressing the euphoria that coursed through his body. He raised his spellshooter, but to his surprise, the dwarf raised both hands in warning.

"Wait. The moment you free me, or any of us, you will alert the guards."

Ben cursed. "Great. What sort of guards?"

"Hellhounds. Big ones."

Charlie groaned, and placed his hand over his face. "I read that they cannot be killed. Is that true?"

"You are well read," the dwarf said.

"A minor drawback," Ben said. "But it can't be helped. What's the best way to free you?" Ben nodded, suppressing the euphoria that coursed through his body.

"Use your spellshooter to cast an open-lock spell. The cage inhibits any magic from within, but it is vulnerable to external magic."

Ben raised his spellshooter, but Charlie immediately lowered it.

"Wait a second. I've read about these hellhounds. Like you said, they cannot be killed. I also read that they have three heads and relish pain. How are we supposed to stop them?"

"We don't," Elander said. "If we can make it to the forest, we will be safe. They fear the trees."

Charlie appeared caught off guard, as if he wasn't expecting a reasonable solution. Ben took the chance to step in.

"Has anyone ever managed a successful rescue?"

"Not during my time here," Elander said. "But that is only because few people attempt it. Agrath has a certain reputation that keeps people away."

"Agrath?"

The dwarf motioned behind him. "The castle."

Charlie turned to Ben, his face anxious. "Are we sure about this?"

"It doesn't matter now," Elander said, before Ben could reply.

"What do you mean?"

The dwarf tugged his thick, ginger beard. "They know you are here.. Can't you feel them? They won't let you leave."

If Elander was bluffing in order to convince them to set him free, it was convincing. Ben knew they were being watched; he had felt it before they had even come across the prison field.

"So, if we free you, what's the plan? Just run like mad?"

"Yes. Do you know how to use the void to run fast?"

Ben nodded. "Yeah, running and jumping we can do."

"Good. Don't look back, and don't stop. I may fall behind, as I am weak. Do not come for me; I can look after myself. Is that clear?"

"Crystal," Ben said. He lifted his spellshooter, and turned to Charlie. "You ready?"

"Can't wait."

Ben aimed his spellshooter at the small lock on the cage. An unlocking spell was a simple one, but he threw all his willpower and concentration behind it anyway. He pulled the trigger, and a tiny, peanut-sized pellet shot forth, right into the lock's keyhole.

There was a click, and the cage door opened with a creak. Elander shoved it the remainder of the way, and jumped down, landing lightly on his feet despite his bulk.

The roar that came from the castle was thunderous. The ground shook violently, and Ben was thrown from his feet. A stubby hand reached out, and Elander hauled Ben up.

"Run!" Elander said.

Ben leapt forwards, and saw Charlie and the dwarf do the same, taking giant leaps that would have been impossible at home. He flew across the plain; the captives in their floating cages became a blur, their voices slurred.

A chorus of roars came from behind. The hell-hounds had exited the castle. Against his better judgement, Ben glanced back, and immediately wished he hadn't. The hellhounds were at least five feet at the shoulder. They had three heads, and saliva flowed from their huge jaws. There was a manic look in their eyes – the look of a predator on the hunt. The other prisoners were watching, some urging him on, others shouting at the hellhounds, but most still crying to be set free.

Set free. Ben's eyes widened. There was an idea.

He slowed a fraction, drew his spellshooter, and started firing unlocking spells at the remaining cages. He didn't know how many hit the mark, but the thuds and exalted yelps indicated some had been freed.

Maybe they would distract the hellhounds.

In a heartbeat, Ben was out of the cage fields, and onto the open plain, hurtling his way towards the distant forest. He willed his legs to go faster, and felt a surge of excitement as he flew across the plain at speeds he'd only ever experienced in a car. Charlie led the way, but the dwarf was lagging a little, and it wasn't long before Ben had caught up with him.

The thundering footsteps came from nowhere. Ben glanced back in shock, and saw a hellhound right on his heels. Its paws left a trail of flames, and Ben noticed they weren't even touching the ground. The hellhound snarled, and Ben felt something sharp and wet scratch the back of his legs. He cried out in pain and almost fell. The left head of the hellhound was nearly upon him, snapping and snarling.

From somewhere deep inside, he summoned everything he had, and increased his pace so that he was practically flying. The hellhound fell behind for a moment, before responding with its own burst in pace.

A pained shout made Ben throw another look over his shoulder. One of the other hellhounds was chasing Elander, and had caught up to him, launching a series of lightning quick attacks with each of its heads. Elander had summoned a shield, which deflected some of the blows, but his arm was bloody, and the dwarf had noticeably slowed.

Ben was torn. They needed the dwarf, and it went against every fibre in his body to leave a comrade in danger, no matter how recently they had met. He glanced back again, and managed to make brief eye contact with the dwarf.

"Keep going!" Elander said with a furious wave. "Keep running, you fool!"

Ben felt a set of jaws snap right behind him, which was all the motivation he needed. The forest was close now, less than a hundred yards away. The trees were tall and imposing, standing in defiance of their evil neighbour. Ahead, he saw Charlie reach the tree line, and then turn, urging him on. Fifty feet. Twenty feet. Ten.

Ben didn't hear the hellhound jump, but he certainly felt it as the two-hundred-pound beast landed on his shoulders, its mighty claws digging into his flesh. Ben screamed in pain and fell, rolling and ending up on his back. When he looked up, the three heads were looming over him, saliva dripping all over his chest. There was an evil, frenzied look in their eyes. Ben used his knee to launch a kick into the hellhound's underbelly, but it was utterly ineffective. The hellhound sniffed and, in that instance, Ben knew he had seconds to live, before he was devoured.

Something white fizzed above him and smashed into the hellhound. For a fraction of a second the hellhound was distracted, and looked up, not in pain, but annoyance.

Ben scrambled from under the hellhound, and launched himself at the tree line. He heard the hellhound roar in anger, and felt something brush his leg. But his leap was true, and he landed just inside the forest, on the soft mossy floor. Ben lay there panting, staring up at the forest ceiling, pain and exhaustion coursing through his body.

"Ben!"

Charlie's cry cut through his agony and, with a

groan, he stumbled to his feet, and followed Charlie's horrified gaze out onto the plain.

The dwarf had been set on by two hellhounds. They ran by his side, launching their huge frames at him. The dwarf had a quarterstaff in his hands, and every time the hellhounds attacked, he whacked them on one of their many heads. The impact was monstrous, and enough to repel the hellhounds, if only for a moment. It was working, but the dwarf was slowing, and his defences were gradually become less effective.

Ben raised his spellshooter, and saw Charlie do the same. They sent spells that formed into giant rocks, hurtling at the hellhounds. It was probably little more than an irritating tickle, but it was enough. The attacks on the dwarf stopped just for a moment, while the hellhounds glanced their way. The burst of acceleration the dwarf made was astonishing, given his physical state. He flew across the plain, and leapt, as if gravity were a thing for lesser mortals, sailing over their heads, into the forest.

The hellhounds approached the very edge of the forest, snapping and snarling. But they didn't enter and, eventually, they turned, and headed back towards the castle.

Ben collapsed back on the forest floor, in pain and exhaustion. Charlie and Elander followed suit.

CHAPTER 28
ELANDER FARSEEKER'S STORY

Ben wanted to get up. There were questions burning inside his head and they had finally found the one person who could answer them. But his body wouldn't respond. His shoulders were agony where the hellhounds had dug their claws in, and his legs were scratched and bruised. His head was thumping, though he wasn't sure how that had come about. He lay on the forest floor trying to catch his breath and stem the pain that seemed to come from everywhere.

Something nudged his leg. Ben managed to raise his head, and saw Elander standing over him, his staff touching Ben.

"Brace yourself," the dwarf said.

An incredible surge of energy flowed through

every vein and cell in his body. Ben arched his back and gasped, as his body began a healing process a million times faster than the norm. It was all over in less than a minute, and left Ben gasping for breath. The pain, though, was gone, and when he glanced at his shoulders, he saw clean, unblemished skin.

"I'm sorry, that was the only effective way to heal such wounds," Elander said, stepping back.

Ben got to his feet, and saw Charlie beside him, looking haggard, but unharmed.

"I am in your debt," Elander said, extending a hand. "It will not be forgotten."

A tree rustled in the distance, and Elander whipped his quarterstaff out, his eyes darting this way and that. It was only after a full minute that the dwarf relaxed.

"Is it safe here?" Charlie asked anxiously.

"No," Elander replied.

It quickly dawned on Ben that there must be a good reason the hellhounds were scared of the forest. Ben glanced up at the trees; before they had seemed proud and noble, but now that they were beneath them, they felt threatening, suffocating almost. He had a strong desire to leave, even if it meant going back out onto the plain, at the mercy of the hellhounds.

"We do not have much time," Elander said. "It is

unwise to remain stationary here for more than a few minutes."

"Shouldn't we leave now, then?" Charlie asked.

"You will, soon," Elander said, glancing at Charlie's brooch with a flicker of envy. "I need to cross the forest."

For what? Ben wanted to ask, but the questions were going off on a tangent, especially if they didn't have much time. He cut straight to the point.

"You said you knew something about Elizabeth's Armour."

Elander tugged his beard, and eyed both of them carefully, before replying. "It is a closely guarded secret that ordinarily I would never reveal, but it is clear you are one of the few who know about it. Her armour is a legacy, entrusted to five Guardians whose task is to unite and use it to defeat Suktar."

Ben had expected the dwarf to know the truth, but hearing it from his lips still sent a shiver up his spine.

"Are you one of the Guardians?" Ben asked.

To Ben's surprise and dismay, a haunted look crossed Elander's face, and his eyes became distant. "If only that were true."

"What do you mean?"

"I was a Guardian, until my wife gave birth to our son, some forty years ago. That responsibility now lies with him."

Ben felt like collapsing on the floor. He put a hand over his eyes. They had been so certain this dwarf was the Guardian, they had never once considered he might have had a child. It was such a hammer blow, Ben felt physically sick.

"Does your son know?" Charlie asked.

Elander closed his eyes with a pained expression. "No. He doesn't know anything. He wasn't ready – he isn't ready, for such knowledge or responsibility. We kept waiting, hoping that in time he would mature."

"We?"

"My wife and I," Elander said. His face became dark. "She was killed in the dark elf attack. They tortured her, and I fear she may have talked. If so, it will not be long before they find my son." He slapped a fist into an open hand. "I must find him first."

"We need to find him, too," Ben said.

To his surprise, Elander gave him a dubious look. "He is not ready to be a Guardian."

Ben almost laughed. "Do you think I am? A few months ago I didn't even know the Unseen Kingdoms existed."

Elander shook his head. "You do not understand. Krobeg isn't like you. Even in the brief time we have been together, I can tell you have the qualities a Guardian needs. My son does not."

"He is a Guardian, whether you like it or not," Ben

said. "Wishing he was braver or whatever imagined standard you have isn't going to help."

Ben expected a backlash, but to his surprise Elander only turned away with a regretful look. "I should have raised him differently. I was too interested in my own studies. I was furious when he showed more interest in food and drink than following my path as a mage. I banished him from our household. It was a terrible mistake."

Ben nodded. He understood about parents' mistakes. "Where can we find your son?"

Elander paused again; Ben could only imagine the internal conflict going through the dwarf's mind. If he gave them the location of his son, he might end up fulfilling his role as a Guardian, which meant facing Suktar. But if he didn't, the dark elves would eventually find him. Ben waited impatiently, but forced himself to remain quiet. Finally, Elander gave a reluctant nod.

"We have not been in touch for many years, but as far as I'm aware, he still lives in Drinkmorr. That is where I will search upon my return."

Charlie's eyes lit up at the name. "I've always wanted to go there." He turned to Ben and glanced at his brooch. "We should get going. If the dark elves know about Krobeg, he's not safe, even if he does live in Drinkmorr."

Ben nodded, and turned back to Elander. "What will you do?"

Elander glanced into the depths of the forest. "There is a clan that might be able to help me get home. They are one of the few clans strong enough to resist even the strongest demons, and among their members are several goblin shamans, who are extremely skilled when it comes to getting in and out of the void."

Ben extended his hand. "I hope it works out for you."

Charlie, however, was staring strangely at Elander, his mouth half open. "What is the name of that clan?"

"They are called Sparkstorm."

Ben's eyes lit up. "That's what the demon called me!"

"You belong to the Sparkstorm clan?" Elander asked.

"No," Ben said. "It doesn't make sense. But the demon seemed to think I did, after giving me a good smell."

"Demons can identify people, especially humans, just by their odour," Elander said. "He may have mistaken your smell for someone like you."

Ben felt his stomach tighten. "My parents. They are here."

"What are their names?"

"Greg and Jane Greenwood."

Elander didn't reply, but his eyes betrayed his surprise.

"Have you heard something of them?" Ben asked, his voice suddenly urgent.

Elander nodded, looking at Ben in a new light. "Your parents are the clan leaders of Sparkstorm."

Ben was speechless, though from the look on Charlie's face, it seemed he had already connected the dots. Elander was looking for his parents' clan.

"Ben, focus," Charlie said with a sharp warning. He kept talking, but Ben zoned him out.

This dwarf was searching for his parents. Did he know where they were? He glanced at his brooch; the majority of it was now coloured red, and his heart sank. How much time did they have? Three hours? Less, probably. Still, what was to stop him going with Elander, and leaving just before the twenty-four-hour mark? That way he would at least have a chance to find his parents, and still have a way out.

"Don't even think about it," Charlie said, giving him a stern look.

"It's just three hours," Ben said. "What is there to lose? We might find my parents, and if we don't, we leave. It's that simple."

"We don't have three hours, Ben," Charlie said, raising his voice. "Every minute we waste here, the dark elves could be closing in on Elander's son. We need to leave, *now.*"

Ben clenched his fists, and bit his lip in frustration. He hated to admit it, but Charlie was right. The brief flare of hope that had burned brightly for a full minute was suddenly extinguished.

He turned back to Elander, who was looking at him closely. "Say hi to my parents for me."

Elander gave his first and only smile. "I will. And if you manage to find my son, tell him I am sorry, and that he was right about everything. Tell him that I will see him soon."

Ben turned to a relieved Charlie. "You ready?"

A peculiar, haunting cry drowned out Charlie's response. They turned and saw three tall, cloaked figures floating towards them, their feet never touching the ground. Within their hoods was nothing but a pair of soulless white dots.

"Go!" Elander said firmly. "I will deal with this."

Ben wanted to complain, but Elander was already walking purposefully towards the figures.

"Let's get out of here," Charlie said.

Ben cursed, and grabbed his brooch with both hands. He focused on home, and immediately the void seemed to shift. One of the ghostly figures gave another haunting cry and managed to skirt round Elander, heading right for them. The void solidified, as his concentration on his body at home wavered.

The demon ghost sailed towards them, and lifted a hand. In it he carried a scythe that looked far more real than the ghost itself. Against all reason and instinct, Ben closed his eyes, and focused again on his unconscious body – the feel of the sleeping bag; the pillow beneath his head; the cool air; and that awful smell.

Ben felt his eyes roll to the back of his head, and blackness consumed him.

CHAPTER 29
A NEW CHALLENGE

Ben rarely missed a day at the Institute, but the following morning he literally couldn't get out of bed. The battering his body had taken in the void transferred itself to his real body, and it was all he could do to stagger home with Natalie's help. Going to the Institute was out of the question, as his sorry state would surely have prompted unwanted questions. His desire to get back to the Unseen Kingdoms and find out how to get to Drinkmorr was temporarily dulled by the bliss of being able to lie in bed all day. It felt like they had been in the void for weeks, even though it had been less than twenty-four hours.

The cuts and bruises would take time to heal, but after twenty-four hours in bed, Ben felt well enough to return to the Institute. Charlie had also taken time off; his parents had been shocked but not overly surprised when he told them his injuries had been the result of bullies at school.

Autumn was well and truly on its way, and though central Taecia was primarily a city of stone, the trees in the Institute gardens were starting to decorate the grounds with golden leaves. A couple of first-grade apprentices fought a losing battle sweeping the leaves from the paths. Ben sucked in the cold, fresh air. It had been only a few days, but somehow the Royal Institute of Magic looked even grander than usual, with its leaded windows, black-timbered frames and multitude of gables, creating a mini mountain range. Ben spotted several Institute members standing on the many outside balconies, talking amongst themselves, some even enjoying the morning sun.

Ben's good mood was dulled slightly the moment he entered the Institute and felt the tension in the air. Despite the early hours, Institute members zipped to and fro, with a sense of gravity that clearly came from the dark elf situation. During a short briefing after morning muster, Ben learnt that the dark elves had not conquered any further land, but nor had the Institute reclaimed the areas in England they'd taken.

"I need to see the three of you in my office," Dagmar said, as they headed out of muster.

Dagmar's impassive face made it impossible for

Ben to determine if they were going to be scolded or praised.

"I wonder what she wants," Charlie muttered, as they walked over to stand outside her office.

Natalie was fiddling with the ends of her hair. "Maybe she wants an update."

Ben waited impatiently; he was eager to begin planning their trip to Drinkmorr, but part of him was also curious about what Dagmar had to say. She never spoke unless she had something meaningful to impart.

They didn't have to wait long. As usual, the heavy clomping of Dagmar's huge shoes preceded her appearance, and she marched right up to the door without even glancing at them. With a flick of her hand, she motioned them to follow her into her office.

"We have a problem," she said, matter-of-factly. "Draven has noticed that you are lagging behind in your third-grade apprenticeship, and he has started asking questions."

"What does he care?" Ben asked in surprise.

"Draven has taken an unusual interest in you, Ben, ever since you arrived. He asks me at least once a week how you are progressing."

"What do you tell him?"

"I normally tell him to mind his own business," Dagmar said. "However, he managed to get hold of your checklist and saw that you are behind in everything except Spellsword."

Ben ran a hand through his hair. "Great. What should we do?"

"Catch up," Dagmar replied without hesitation. "I had a look at the checklist myself, and it's not as bad as he makes out. If you put the hours in, you could catch up within a week."

Ben clenched his fist, trying to contain his growing frustration. "We don't have a week. We're trying to find the next Guardian, remember?"

If Dagmar sensed Ben's anger, she didn't show it, her hands remaining firmly clasped behind her back.

"What progress have you made?" she asked.

Charlie chimed in. "We know who we're looking for, and we are fairly certain he lives in Drinkmorr."

Dagmar gave an approving nod. "Good. That works perfectly. The foreigners' entrance to Drinkmorr is open only on Thursdays and Sundays. It's Monday now, which gives you three days to burn the midnight oil to catch up."

"Foreigners' entrance?"

Charlie nodded. "I'll explain later."

"In the meantime, if Draven does approach you, Ben, just refer him to me," Dagmar said.

She gave them a nod, and turned towards her desk, a sure indication that the meeting was over. But as they turned to leave, she spoke again.

"The dark elves are getting ever more dangerous, and we are running out of time. If you need any help with this Guardian, come and see me."

"No pressure, then," Charlie muttered, as they exited Dagmar's office.

It was just past nine o'clock, and they found the common room unusually busy, with the majority of the conversation focused on the dark elves. There were those who still seemed to think it all a game (such as Simon and his friends) and hoped they might be lucky enough to get drafted in as temporary Spellswords to fight. Then there were the more sensible ones, who talked about what a dark elf invasion might mean for the Institute, the Unseen Kingdoms, and even the wider world.

"We need to watch what we say here," Ben said, as they eventually found a few chairs in their favourite corner.

Natalie started cleaning up the coffee table, her eyes on Charlie. "So, what is this foreigners' entrance? I've heard of Drinkmorr obviously, but I haven't read much about it."

"I haven't heard of it at all," Ben said, kicking his legs up onto the table and earning a frown from Natalie. "What sort of town is it?"

"It's the only fully dwarf town in England," Charlie said. He managed to keep his tone soft, but Ben could sense Charlie's underlying excitement.

"Unlike Taecia, and much of the Unseen Kingdoms, it's completely untouched by our culture. From what I've read, it sounds like the sort of fantasy town you read about in books."

"And what is the foreigners' entrance?" Natalie asked again.

"Drinkmorr cannot be placed on an ordinary map. It can be accessed only by a portal. There are two – one for dwarves, which is always open, and the other for foreigners, which, as Dagmar said, is open only on certain days."

Ben removed his legs from the table and leaned forwards, elbows on knees. "Could we sneak in via the dwarf entrance? I really don't want to wait three days."

"I doubt it. It's well guarded, and even if we got through, security would be after us. Hardly ideal if we're trying to find someone."

"It's a pain," Natalie said. "But given that Draven seems to be obsessed with you and your progress, it might actually work out. We can all work on the apprenticeship; I'm also behind."

It took a bit of effort, but once they got rolling, the apprenticeship managed to divert most of their attention away from their trip to Drinkmorr. They worked every day from nine in the morning for twelve hours, taking only small breaks to eat. Ben upgraded to a B3 spellshooter; Charlie became the fastest person in the third grade to finish the Scholar checklist; Natalie caught the eye of several Diplomats interested in signing her up for the Department of Diplomacy.

Despite the crazy schedule, everything went smoothly, until Wednesday during morning muster, the day before they were due to travel to Drinkmorr.

"Third-graders, stay behind," Dagmar said, after calling muster. "The rest of you, dismissed."

Ben eyed the twenty-four apprentices who stayed, their curiosity matching his own. He knew most of them pretty well now, and counted many of them as friends, despite the time suck of being a Guardian.

"As some of you know, Roger Flintoff, your Chief Three, will be taking his third-grade exam shortly and hopefully moving into the fourth grade," Dagmar said, "which means you need to elect a new Chief Three."

Ben immediately saw heads turn to Aaron, who gave a modest smile.

"Why don't we just give the role to Aaron and spare everyone the bother?" Leslie said. She was a skinny, freckled girl with a mouth that often spoke before the brain had time to stop it. Her pale skin turned red the moment she realised who she had spoken to. Dagmar gave her a cold stare, and Leslie promptly lowered her eyes, mumbling an apology.

"For those unfamiliar with the rules, you must gain six votes within twenty-four hours to run for Chief. Those who succeed will then have a week to campaign before a vote is held. That is all."

There was an excited chatter as they left the muster room. Aaron was immediately accosted by several apprentices, and they were all talking about the same thing.

"...you're going to run, right?"

"...you're going to smoke it."

"...I bet no one else even gets six votes. You'll win by default!"

Aaron rose both hands in a calming gesture. "Let's not go overboard. I'm sure there will be several other nominations that I will have to overcome."

Aaron gave a meaningful glance at Ben, who returned it with a shrug. He had no intention of running, but he wasn't going to tell Aaron that. Thankfully, Aaron and his entourage continued towards the grand staircase, and Ben took a right, into the common room. He collapsed onto a couch, along with Charlie and Natalie.

"Is it just me or does anyone else find Aaron unbelievably arrogant?" Natalie asked, tugging her hair irritably.

"I just try to zone him out," Charlie replied. "It's hard, though; his voice has a way of penetrating your ear drums."

Ben slouched back on the couch. "I'll tell you one thing – unless this Chief gig comes with a bonus of a thousand pounds a week, I won't be running."

"What does a Chief Three do exactly?" Charlie asked.

"Quite a lot, actually," Natalie said. "I was Chief One during my first grade. You have all the obvious stuff, like helping and looking out for your fellow third-graders. You are also supposed to be the only person who can personally approach Dagmar, but we kind of make a mockery of that. Then there are the bonus points on your record, which helps when the Institute decides whether or not to take you on as a full member."

Ben gave an unimpressed shrug. "So, basically just more responsibility and work. Not really my thing."

"There are some perks," Natalie said. "But I'm not sure what they are for the Chief Three."

"Well, I'll pass," Ben said.

"I'm not sure that will be that easy," Charlie said.

"What do you mean?"

Charlie pointed at three apprentices coming their way, headed by Simon, with his mass of ginger hair and a gawking grin.

"Ben!" he said. "I've been looking for you. Good news, we've got your six votes already. You're in!"

Ben sat up sharply. "What are you talking about? I don't want to run for Chief Three."

"Oh, I know," Simon said, smiling. "That's why I got the votes behind your back."

To Ben's surprise, his own outrage was not matched by Charlie and Natalie, who were both smiling with amusement.

"I don't get it," Ben said, running a hand through his ruffled hair. "Why me? If you're into it, why don't you get votes for yourself?"

"Me?" Simon said, pointing a finger at himself. "Are you serious? I wouldn't have a chance against Aaron."

"Aaron? Is that what this is all about?"

"Yes. You are the only person who has a hope of beating him. And the third grade will become a nightmare if Aaron becomes Chief Three, especially for me."

"There has to be someone else," Ben said. "What about Will?"

"Already asked him. He's not allowed to run, as he's expected to progress to the fourth grade soon."

Ben struggled for words. He was flattered, yet his original sentiment towards running for Chief Three remained. "I don't have a chance against Aaron either. He's Mr. Popular."

"You will probably lose," Simon admitted with a shrug. "But it's not a certainty. We've done a survey.

Many of those who Aaron hasn't managed to capture with his massive ego are on the fence, and there are a few who hate him almost as much as we do."

Ben gave them a sincere smile. "Let me think about it."

"Okay, but you don't have long," Simon said. "Think about how much worse Aaron would be if he won. His head would be so big he wouldn't be able to get inside the Institute."

"Wouldn't that be a good thing?" Charlie asked.

"No. He would just call a committee and somehow convince them to widen the entrance."

Another apprentice caught Simon's eye, and he hurried after him. "Hey, John, wait a sec! You hate Aaron as well, right? I've got a great plan."

Ben watched as Simon and his friends chased John out the door, and then sunk back into the couch.

"I really don't want to run for Chief Three," Ben said. He turned to Charlie and Natalie for support. "Even if I did, I don't have enough time with everything that's going on. We're going to Drinkmorr tomorrow, remember?"

Charlie was surprisingly non-committal. "It's not a big deal. And Simon's right when he says you're the only one who has a chance against Aaron."

Natalie nodded. "It's worth a shot, right? You've got nothing to lose."

"Except losing itself," Ben said. "I don't like losing."

Nevertheless, Ben had trouble taking his mind off the Chief Three election while he worked on his apprenticeship that morning. His accuracy was below his impeccable standard when practising with his B3 during spellshooter practice. He didn't want to be Chief Three, of that he was certain, but there were two things that nagged at him. The first was that, like Simon, he couldn't stand the thought of Aaron taking the role and having some authority over him. The other factor was that he felt bad about the people rooting for him. He didn't like letting people down.

If he did fight Aaron for Chief Three, did he have any chance of winning? He was no closer to an answer when he headed down the grand staircase for lunch.

CHAPTER 30
AARON'S WARNING

"Ben Greenwood!"

Ben turned and saw a small girl bounding down the stairs, pigtails bouncing.

"Thank goodness I found you," she said, huffing and puffing, despite the fact that she had been going down, not up, the stairs. "Mr. D'Gayle needs to see you right away."

"Still his messenger boy, then, Sophie?" Ben said with a smile.

Sophie raised her chin. "Yep. Fended off three different candidates in the last month. I think he's really starting to trust me."

"That's great," Ben said, just about managing to keep the sarcasm from his voice. "Can this meeting wait till after lunch? I'm hungry."

Sophie was shaking her head before Ben had even finished speaking. “I’m afraid not. I’ve already spent almost half an hour searching for you. If you went for lunch, you’d be another hour. Aaron wouldn’t like that at all.”

Ben couldn’t care less what Aaron did or didn’t like, but he caught Sophie’s worried glance when she realised he might refuse. He bowed, and extended an arm.

“Lead on.”

Sophie immediately did an about-turn and bounded back up the stairs with Ben in tow. She didn’t stop until she reached the Diplomacy floor.

“Mr. D’Gayle negotiated with some big cheese in the Diplomacy Department to allow him to use one of the negotiating rooms for his meetings,” Sophie said.

She stopped at a room marked “Negotiating Room #3”.

“Wait here a moment,” she instructed, extending a hand to make sure he didn’t barge past her into the room.

She gave a timid knock.

“You may enter,” Aaron said from the other side of the door, his smooth voice somehow seeming to penetrate the wood.

Sophie waved to Ben, and he followed her inside.

In the middle of the room was a long, expensive-looking table, surrounded by luxurious leather chairs. On one of those chairs was Aaron, sitting with his legs crossed, smoking a Toogle. He blew out and sent a ring of coloured smoke to the ceiling. Ben managed to refrain from pinching his nose. He never liked the sweet smell of those cigarette-like objects. It was said that if you stared at the smoke too much, you could start craving them.

"Ah, Sophie, well done," Aaron said, gracing her with a dazzling smile. "I thought our target might have escaped to lunch, but you caught him just in time."

Sophie blushed with pride, and then stammered something unintelligible before excusing herself from the room.

"Please, take a seat, Ben," Aaron said, waving a hand expansively. "They are far nicer than the logs they give us in the common room."

"I'll stand, thanks. I'm sure this meeting won't take long, and I'm hungry."

"Fair enough," Aaron said. "Though I confess myself surprised at your willingness to eat the sewage they serve downstairs. Myself, I try to go home as often as possible, though one does have to show one's face now and again and eat with the masses. It's a small sacrifice compared to the good will generated."

Ben sighed. He didn't think it possible, but

somehow he managed to like Aaron less every time they spoke. "You wanted to see me?"

"Straight to the point, I see," Aaron said. He took another extensive puff of his Toogle. "I'm sure you know what I want to talk about."

Ben had a good idea, but he put on an air of disinterest. "Nope."

"Liar," Aaron said with another flash of his perfect teeth. "I've called you here to discuss the Chief Three election."

"What about it?"

"Well, I'm sure you're aware that you and I will be the only two apprentices with enough votes," Aaron said.

"Someone else might get enough."

Aaron shook his head. "I highly doubt it. Most of the apprentices will choose me, and those who don't will choose you."

"You seem confident," Ben said.

"Oh, I will win, and convincingly," Aaron said, as if the election had already been decided. "But, after much deliberation, I think it would look better if I win without a challenger. That will better reflect my dominance and, more importantly, look more impressive on my résumé. Nobody has ever won a Chief Three election outright before."

Ben frowned. "So, you want me to pull out?"

"Exactly. And in return, I will make you my official number two. That will annoy many of my supporters, but you know what, who cares?"

Aaron smiled at his own joke. Ben just stared, barely believing the words that were coming out of Aaron's mouth.

"You offered me such a position before," Ben said slowly. "I turned it down, remember?"

"I do," Aaron said. He re-crossed his legs. "However, much has changed. We were almost equals then, but my support now vastly outweighs yours. So, I would strongly advise you to re-consider my offer."

Ben almost laughed at Aaron's conceit, it was so absurd. It was as if he was completely oblivious to Ben's opinion of him. Did Aaron not remember the way he had acted on the second-grade exam? Ben still had half a mind to whack him one. But even as he considered the matter, he came up with a better idea. Up until thirty seconds ago, Ben had been leaning against running.

"You know what?" Ben said. "I think I'm going to run after all."

Aaron's lip twitched – just a fraction, before he re-composed himself with an oily smile. "It is your choice, of course, but I think you're making a mistake. The odds are heavily stacked against you."

Ben shrugged, starting to enjoy himself. "I've

never cared much about odds. I'm more of a gambler."

Aaron's eyes flashed with annoyance, but he managed to contain himself by taking a long drag of his Toogle and lifting his head upwards, watching the coloured smoke rise.

"You realise that I will crush you?" Aaron said, turning back to Ben with a sympathetic smile. "If I can't win by default, my next best option is to win by a landslide."

Ben shrugged. "Whatever."

Aaron put down his Toogle on the table and stood up. Ben always forgot how tall Aaron was, and well-built too. He might only be eighteen, but he could easily be modelling in a sports magazine.

The charming smile and easy-going manner vanished.

"This is your last warning," Aaron said in a soft, dangerous voice. "If you choose to fight me, I will undermine you at every turn. What is left of your reputation will be left in tatters."

The strength in Aaron's voice, coupled with his imposing stance, would have made most people back down. But not Ben. Aaron's warning achieved the exact opposite of its intention. Ben stepped forwards, until his forehead was almost touching Aaron's nose, and looked up into those cold eyes with enough fire to douse it.

"If I start to hear any lies about me, I am going to thrash you. Got it?"

Aaron looked uncomfortable with Ben's proximity, but he didn't back down. "You're in dreamland if you think you can take me on. Look at you – you're half my size."

"Really?" Ben said, and gave a little smile. "Shall we see, then? How about a fight, right now? No weapons, just fists."

The flash of fear in Aaron's eyes was unmistakable.

"What, now?" he stammered. "That's ridiculous. I've done nothing wrong."

Ben was sorely tempted to hit Aaron with an uppercut, but now wasn't the time. He stepped back, and gave Aaron one more meaningful stare, before leaving the room, and heading down to lunch. Charlie and Natalie had saved him a space, and he quickly filled them in on his meeting with Aaron.

"I wish you had hit him," Charlie said, when Ben had finished.

Natalie smiled. "So do I. That guy gets creepier by the day."

"He is quite something," Ben agreed, munching on his fish and chips. "So, now what?"

"The nominations get announced tomorrow morning. After that you have a week to get as many votes as possible."

"How am I supposed to do that? We're supposed to be doing something slightly more important."

"Your support team is supposed to do a lot of it," Natalie said. "Unfortunately, your support team consists of Simon and his two friends, who are probably more likely to lose you votes, rather than gain them."

"Great. Well, they'll have to do, as I don't have time to do it myself."

Natalie frowned, and pointed a fork at him. "You're going to have to do some work, Ben. Your only chance – and it's a small one – is if you get involved. I know you don't believe it, but some people in the third grade look up to you."

"Whatever for?" Ben asked with genuine surprise.

"Well, for some, I think it's because you're so good with a spellshooter, and I think that duel you had really impressed a few people. As for others, well, I guess some of them like you."

Ben was careful to ignore the fact that Natalie blushed, her face going a pretty shade of red.

"Okay, I'll do something once we get back from Drinkmorr tomorrow."

Ben spent the rest of the day feeling strangely torn. He was not looking forward to the whole Chief Three nomination process; the idea of having to go round to his fellow third-grade apprentices and try to win their votes did not appeal to him one bit. On the other hand, his heart gave an excited flutter every time he thought about going to Drinkmorr. They were on the cusp of finding the third Guardian. Time was running out, with the dark elves an ever increasing threat and his parents stuck in the void. If they drew a blank in Drinkmorr, they would be out of options. They couldn't fail. It was with those thoughts that Ben fell to sleep that night.

CHAPTER 31

JOURNEY TO DRINKMORR

Ben had trouble sitting still on the Dragonway the following morning. His eagerness and excitement to venture into Drinkmorr were only slightly dampened by the nomination process he would have to go through in the morning muster. To his surprise, Charlie also appeared unusually upbeat.

"Drinkmorr is supposed to be pretty cool," Charlie explained, when Ben enquired as to his cheery mood. "It has a lot of fascinating history."

Chief Three nominations replaced talk of Drinkmorr as they made their way up the hill to the Institute.

"Don't worry about it," Charlie said. "You don't have to do anything."

"I'm not worried," Ben said, slightly insulted.

Charlie kicked an idle pebble on the cobbled path. "Well, you should be. Per my calculations, you're going to get hammered, unless we pull off a miracle or Aaron somehow suddenly has a freak accident and can no longer run."

Charlie's words did nothing to help Ben's mood; the worst thing was, they were true: he was going to need a miracle. It was with that slightly depressing thought that he entered the muster room and Dagmar did roll call.

"All dismissed, except third-graders," Dagmar said.

Ben could feel an excited tension in the air, as they waited for the other apprentices to leave. As Ben looked around at the intense expressions of his fellow third-graders, he realised that this Chief Three gig really meant something.

Dagmar waited for total silence, and Ben strongly suspected several apprentices had stopped breathing.

"The results for the nominations for the Chief Three candidates are in," Dagmar said to a hushed audience. "There are just two candidates – Aaron D'Gayle and Ben Greenwood."

A cheer went up as the names were called. Ben gave a little smile to mask his disappointment. He had hoped that another candidate might have sneaked in to deflect the attention from himself and possibly take some votes from Aaron.

Dagmar's laser-like gaze went to Ben and Aaron. "Do you both accept your candidacy?"

Aaron nodded his head solemnly. All eyes suddenly turned to Ben, and he too gave a nod, though without the ceremony Aaron lent to it. To his surprise, Dagmar gave him the subtlest of frowns. It was barely noticeable, but for Dagmar it spoke volumes. Did she disapprove? Of course, she knew how important their quest to find Elizabeth's Armour was. Did she view this as an unnecessary distraction?

"Candidates, you have seven days to campaign. This time next week, I will announce the winner. Dismissed."

As soon as Dagmar left the room, many of the apprentices crowded round Aaron, wishing him good luck and clapping him on the back. Some even started chanting his name. It got worse when they turned on Ben, singing Aaron's name at him in a taunting melody.

Ben stood there, feeling awkward. He was already starting to regret not pulling out.

"Greenwood! Greenwood!"

Three obnoxiously loud voices started chanting. Simon and his friends stepped in front of Ben. What they lacked in numbers, they made up in volume. Aaron's group, at least a dozen of them, responded by stepping up to Simon. At the front was Jeff, an apprentice Ben strongly suspected was half-troll. He was at least six feet tall and almost as wide, with thick, curly hair and eyes that looked ready to pop out of their sockets.

Jeff pushed Simon, who immediately went sprawling. He gave a peculiar cackle and swiped a tree-trunk arm at one of Simon's friends. Ben cringed, but the blow never landed. William stepped in and caught the arm, muscle meeting chub. Jeff's anger quickly disappeared when he saw who had blocked his blow.

"Let's all calm down, shall we?" William said with an easy smile. "This is supposed to be a nomination, not a mass brawl."

There was an uneasy silence, but Aaron's group vastly outnumbered Ben's, and they knew it.

"Will is right," Aaron said, stepping forwards. "This is supposed to be a civilised affair." He turned to Simon, who had just got back to his feet and was still rubbing his backside. "Please accept my apologies. That was out of order and won't happen again."

Aaron turned and left, his supporters chanting his name and filing out the door and into the hallway after him.

"Thanks," Ben said, turning to William.

"No problem," William replied with a smile. "I'll be voting for you. Good luck."

Ben, Charlie and Natalie left and hurried down the staircase, heading for the exit before anyone else could grab Ben. Ben suddenly felt a little better about the election. Having William on his side was a major boost; he knew of several apprentices who would vote for him just because of William.

"You really need to win, Ben," Natalie said, as they left the Institute and started down the hill. "I don't think I could take it if Aaron became Chief Three."

"I'll do my best. Anyway, I can forget about that for now," Ben said. He turned to Charlie. "How do we get to Drinkmorr?"

"We need to go to London."

The foot traffic at this time of day was minimal, and it didn't take long for Ben, Charlie and Natalie to board an empty carriage on the Dragonway. Ben had been on the Dragonway to London only once before, when he had taken his first-grade exam. It felt strange not getting off at Croydon, but continuing north. After another fifteen minutes, the dragon arrived in London.

Despite having been here before, the station was still a sight to behold. The ceiling was impossibly high and had a faint curve, creating a dome-like effect. Thousands of twinkling lights shone down on a station that was both more modern and yet vastly older and grander than the Croydon one he was used to. Amid the smoke and roars from the dragons was the chatter of voices, hurried footsteps and the occasional whistle from the conductors. The majority of people were human, but there was a fair proportion of dwarves, elves and many smaller creatures whizzing about.

Ben, Charlie and Natalie followed the sign directing them to London Victoria Underground station. With the threat of the dark elves, security was tighter than usual, and it took them a good fifteen minutes to get through border control. As Institute apprentices, they were allowed to keep their spellshooters, though the guards checked their spells carefully, before letting them past. They followed a torch-lit passageway, which led them all the way to the lift. Unlike the one in Croydon, this lift contained no seats. They travelled up from what seemed like the Earth's core until the lift finally slowed and came to a gentle stop. With a ding, the doors opened, and everyone started filing out.

Ben couldn't help smiling. They were bang in the middle of the London Victoria Underground station, right near the escalators that went up to the main train station. Regular people passed the lift by without giving it a second glance.

"We need to go to Old Church Town, on the Circle & District line," Charlie said.

They travelled westbound, past South Kensington and Gloucester Road, before arriving at their destination. The air had that typical London smell, and the roads were buzzing with black taxis and red buses. They hopped on a bus and travelled several stops, past the town centre, and into a quieter district, full of big red buildings and odd boutique shops.

"This is us," Charlie said.

They hopped off the bus and started walking.

"Are you sure about this?" Ben asked.

Charlie was taking them through a series of narrow pathways that squeezed their way through large, red brick buildings, until the path ended at a bank that ran along a narrow river.

"Here we are," Charlie said, rubbing his hands.

Natalie glanced about. "I don't see anything resembling a portal."

"Well, you didn't expect it to be easy, did you?" Charlie said with a grin. "This is the fun part – we have to find it. I know it's around here somewhere, so don't go far."

They split up and started searching. Ben immediately went to the edge of the bank, but the river didn't hold any surprises. There were a couple of abandoned boats, and some fish in the murky water, but nothing else of interest. He turned his attention to the two buildings flanking them on either side. One was a fabrics factory. Ben poked his head inside and a receptionist looked up. He took a quick glance around, but saw nothing unusual. The other building looked more promising. It was an old abandoned warehouse. Ben managed to force open a creaky door, and all three of them searched it extensively, but their excitement upon entering soon dissipated when they found nothing. Eventually they returned outside, scratching their heads.

"Could you be wrong about the location?" Natalie asked.

"I could be," Charlie admitted. "But I was sure I had the right place."

"You're not normally wrong when it comes to directions," Ben said.

Natalie glanced down the lane. "I think we should extend our search a little, just to be sure. If we don't find anything, we'll come back."

They headed back the way they had come, walking slowly, eyeing every building they passed. The area was unusually quiet for London, and it seemed like an age before they crossed paths with anyone. A small, suited man with a briefcase hurried by, clearly in a rush. Ben gave him an absent smile and was surprised when he received a suspicious glance in return.

"Well, I'm flummoxed," Charlie said, rubbing his chin. He appeared quite pleased about it. "I know it's here, but those dwarves are obviously rather good at hiding things."

"Could we be overlooking something obvious?" Natalie asked.

Ben frowned. Natalie had a point: were they overlooking something obvious? For some peculiar reason, the man they had passed stuck in his head. Why had he looked at them suspiciously? Ben reimagined the man in his mind. He was small, stocky...

Ben stopped suddenly. "Dwarf!"

He turned and sprinted back down the alleyway. They hadn't walked far, and he whipped round a couple of bends, before coming back into view of the river and the bank. He made it just in time to see the dwarf disappearing into the side of the warehouse, right through the solid brick wall. Ben dashed to the wall, and started feeling and pushing.

"He went right through here," Ben said, hands still dancing around the wall as Charlie and Natalie arrived on the scene.

"Step back," Charlie said. "You won't find anything like that."

Reluctantly Ben stepped away, joining Charlie and Natalie as they stared at the side of the brick warehouse.

"Dwarves are exceptional craftsmen," Charlie said. "People often say their doors are magic, but they are just well concealed."

Natalie stepped forwards, and trailed her hand along the mortar that held the brick in place. "They must be really good, because I can't see a thing."

"It's there," Charlie insisted with that smile he often got when faced with a challenge.

They spent a good fifteen minutes inspecting the wall, beating it with frustration and going cross-eyed staring at it.

"There!" Natalie said with an excited yelp. She trailed her hand along the mortar, forming a peculiarly shaped door.

"Are you sure?" Ben asked doubtfully.

But even as he spoke, the outline of the door Natalie had spotted seemed to solidify and somehow form into an ordinary rectangular door, like some sort of magician's trick. Ben stared, concerned that if he looked away, the door would vanish.

Natalie's hand went to a perfectly camouflaged door handle. Ben held his breath as she eased the handle down. There was a soft click, and Natalie pushed the door open. Ben gave an excited grin as they stepped through, and entered Drinkmorr.

CHAPTER 32
GOOD FOOD AND HEATED MEETINGS

It felt as though they were stepping into a fairytale. In front of them was a cobbled street, coloured in every shade of blue. On either side were perfect, gingerbread-style houses, complete with arched roofs and smoking chimneys.

The silky smooth smell of chocolate filled the air, making inhaling an absolute pleasure. Every shop on the blue, cobbled street was a chocolatier. The shop windows were full of chocolate-shaped animals and figures of every kind, including a life-sized horse. They were carved with such intricacy and craftsmanship that Ben almost thought they were real. Unsurprisingly, there were a lot of children running about, staring at the shop windows and trying to force their parents into the stores. Though most of them were dwarves, there were plenty of humans and even some elf children about.

"You're both drooling," Natalie said.

"Can you blame us?" Ben said, wiping his chin.

"I've always wanted to come here since I first read about Drinkmorr," Charlie said. He pointed to a road sign which read "*Chocolate Street*". "Dwarves are famous for three things – armour, drink and chocolate."

They walked slowly, taking in the sights and smells. Ben almost stopped on several occasions to buy something, but he couldn't afford anything larger than a chocolate mouse. It was with some disappointment that they reached the end of the street, and found themselves at a crossroads. In each direction, the cobbled stones were a different colour. Each street was perfectly straight, creating a grid system Ben had previously seen only in parts of America.

"Which way?" Ben asked.

Charlie shrugged. "No idea."

"No idea? I thought you knew where we were going."

"What gave you that idea? Elander said his son lived in Drinkmorr, but he didn't know where."

Ben ran a hand through his hair in exasperation. "So what do we do? Wander round hoping that we stumble upon him?"

Natalie touched both their shoulders. "Let's both take deep breaths. There has to be a better solution than just walking around randomly trying to run into someone we don't even know."

"Yes, I was going to get to that, before Ben leapt at me," Charlie said, giving Ben the eye. "There are information booths. Dwarves love selling things, information included. I say we go round and see if any of them have heard of Krobeg."

"That sounds expensive," Ben said doubtfully.

"Not really, because you only pay if they have an answer." He gave Ben another pointed look. "If you have a better idea, I'd love to hear it."

And so they began their search for an information booth. Drinkmorr was not large, and Ben could just about make out the town walls surrounding it in the distance. Nevertheless, searching for an information booth was harder than they expected, simply because they were constantly distracted. Sometimes it was the shops; other times it was the architecture – there were statues that were so good Ben kept thinking they might come to life. Without meaning to, they veered towards the centre of the town, where the small cottage-like buildings turned into something a little grander, and the foot traffic became more substantial.

"There," Natalie said, pointing directly ahead. Ben tore his gaze away from a dazzling armoury.

Directly ahead of them was a small hexagonal building, which said "Drinkmorr Information Centre".

"That looks like a good place to start," Ben said.

He turned to Charlie, but he wasn't there.

Ben stopped, and turned.

Charlie was standing some ten paces back, staring at a building. Ben only had to look at the expression on Charlie's face to know it was important. It was a tavern, quite popular by the looks of it, with its doors constantly swinging open to let people in and out. Ben stared at the tavern sign and his stomach did a somersault.

The symbol next to the Royal Goose was an exact match of the Silver Dwarf's family crest.

"Oh my goodness," Natalie whispered. She had materialised next to Ben, hand over her mouth. "Do you think...?"

"That the owner could be Krobeg?" Ben finished. "Let's find out, shall we?"

Ben, Charlie and Natalie followed a couple of dwarves into the tavern. Ben's eyes adjusted to the dim light as they stepped inside. Other than the natural light coming in from the small windows, there was nothing but dozens of flickering candles to illuminate the place. To say it was busy was an understatement. The bar was packed, mainly with dwarves, and there wasn't a table in the eating area to be had. Servers danced expertly between the tables, holding platters filled with drinks and food. Ben caught a sniff of a passing roast pork, and immediately understood why the place was so busy. He wiped the saliva threatening to make its way down his chin and tapped a passing waitress on the shoulder.

"Excuse me, we're looking for a dwarf named Krobeg. Does he work here?"

The waitress gave him a slightly confused smile. "Of course, sir. He's the owner, but you won't be able to catch him until after lunch, as he's busy in the kitchen."

She dashed off, before Ben could ask anything more.

"Should we come back?" Natalie asked. She looked uncomfortable in the stuffy tavern, and being at such close quarters with so many boisterous dwarves.

"Why don't we get a bite to eat?" Charlie said, eyeing up a passing rack of ribs. "We might as well have lunch while we wait."

Natalie wasn't thrilled with the idea, but Charlie seemed oblivious to her sentiments, and as soon as an empty table became available, he darted towards it. The food, as it turned out, was as good as it looked, and in short order they were rubbing their stomachs contentedly. When the majority of the tables had cleared out, and the bar started to empty, they turned their attention to the kitchen door, where the waiters had constantly filed in and out.

"Do you think we'll recognise Krobeg?" Natalie asked.

Ben nodded. "We will if he's anything like his dad."

The first person to emerge was a skinny elf, who they immediately dismissed. The second and third were dwarves, but neither looked anything like the dwarf mage.

The fourth was right on the money.

A large dwarf with a neat, ginger beard emerged from the kitchen. Ben's eyes immediately went to his stomach – it was absolutely huge, as if someone had shoved a beach ball down his shirt. Somehow he still managed to fit an apron around it.

"Good takings, Mary?" the dwarf asked, wiping his hands on his apron. He had a friendly manner and sparkling, brown eyes.

"Really good, a record for a Thursday afternoon, in fact."

Ben watched the dwarf talk to the waitress. Other than the ginger hair, his whole demeanour was a world away from Elander's. He was jovial, jolly almost, compared to Elander's stern, serious character.

"Could that really be him?" Natalie whispered.

Charlie was also scrutinising the dwarf, though

not quite as inconspicuously as Ben and Natalie. "It makes sense. Remember what Elander said? Now we know why he didn't want to burden his son with the whole Guardian thing. He's not exactly Guardian material."

Ben was still pondering the matter when the serving lady pointed them out to Krobeg, and he ambled over to them.

"Good afternoon, lads and lady," the dwarf said with a friendly smile. He was holding a large mug filled with ale. "Mary says you wanted to speak to me?" He gave a friendly wink. "I warn you, my recipes are off limits. They are top secret – I've worked for years refining them. Did you try the braised lamb by the way?"

"I did," Charlie said, connecting a finger with his thumb to make an "O" shape. "It was superb."

Ben wasn't often thrown off guard, but this was one of those rare occasions. He had prepared for a multitude of eventualities, but having the Guardian be a fat, soft-looking chef wasn't one of them.

"Are you the Krobeg Farseeker everyone talks about?" Ben asked. After all, he wasn't one hundred percent sure they had the right dwarf.

If the question was an odd one, the dwarf didn't show it, simply smiling with appreciation. "I am indeed. I hadn't noticed how far my reputation went. You're not from the Unseen Kingdoms, are you."

"How can you tell?" Charlie asked.

Krobeg shrugged, and took a substantial sip of his ale. "It's the little things – the way you walk, the way you dress, that foreign air about you."

Ben glanced casually around the room. There were still a few punters about, though the tavern was far emptier than before.

"We have something we would like to talk to you about," Ben said, putting on a serious face. "However, it's of a sensitive nature. Could we go somewhere private?"

"Of course," Krobeg said, looking surprised, and just a little wary. "Come with me, we'll go to the staff meeting room."

They followed Krobeg through a door marked "private", and into a small hallway, lined with several doors. Krobeg opened one and bid the three of them enter, before following in behind. The room was small, with a well-worn table surrounded by several chairs.

"Please, take a seat," Krobeg said. He had to pull his own chair out a considerable way to sit down himself. "Now, how can I help you? The Institute is not in trouble, is it? I know it's under a lot of pressure at the moment."

"How did you know we were from the Institute?"

Krobeg smiled. "It wasn't hard. You're not Unseens, and you're not adults. Apprentices, I presume? Third or fourth grade would be my guess, as they wouldn't let anyone with less experience come out here."

Ben nodded, quickly reassessing Krobeg. He might be a large, teddy-bear-shaped chef, but he was clearly as sharp as one of his kitchen knives. The fact that Krobeg knew they were from the Institute might help them – it would certainly lend some authenticity to their plight. But how much should he reveal to Krobeg? He had been confident he would know once he'd established what sort of character Krobeg was. But the dwarf, he sensed, was a complicated individual. Outside, he seemed jovial and friendly, but underneath, Ben suspected a different Krobeg, hidden from view. Having just met the dwarf, he knew it was nothing more than a gut feeling, but it was a strong one.

Ben felt Krobeg watching him and became aware that an awkward silence had fallen. Charlie and Natalie were looking at him expectantly.

Ben made a snap decision. If Krobeg was the Guardian, which they were now certain was the case, then they had no option but to trust him.

"What's your history like?" Ben asked.

"So so," Krobeg said, shaking a hand back and forth.

Ben considered his words. He instinctively wanted to leave out the more sensitive bits, so ingrained had he become in keeping Elizabeth's Legacy secret. Ben cast that thought aside; as a Guardian, Krobeg had the right to know the whole story. And so he gave a succinct, but accurate retelling of Queen Elizabeth's role in the Institute and her battle with Suktar. He introduced the armour and its role in defeating Suktar when he returned. Krobeg listened without interrupting, his face unreadable. It was only at the end when Ben noticed that Krobeg's natural joviality was looking slightly strained.

"A fascinating story," Krobeg said. "Though I am at a loss as to why you came all this way to tell it to me."

"I'm getting there," Ben said.

Ben then told the story of Angus, the original director, and his journey to safeguard his piece of Elizabeth's Armour by venturing into Jimba Forest, his meeting with the arcane dwarves and how the armour was inherited by the Silver Dwarf.

"Have you heard of the Silver Dwarf?" Ben asked, when he was finished.

"Tales only," Krobeg said with a shrug. "Myths, legends, and kids stories."Krobeg glanced at the door, and wrapped his knuckles on the table. "Well, I am grateful for the history lesson – whether fact or fiction – but time is getting on. You're welcome to stay here as long as you wish."

Krobeg started to haul his massive frame off the chair. Ben reached out and put a restraining hand on his shoulder.

"Don't you want to know why we came here to tell you this story?" Ben asked, his voice quiet, his eyes intense.

"Not really," Krobeg said, his voice curt. "I can't see what any of it has to do with me."

Ben knew Krobeg was lying by the way he kept turning to the door.

"It has everything to do with you," Ben said. "The Silver Dwarf was a Guardian, charged with protecting a piece of Elizabeth's Armour. When he passed away, that role was inherited by his son – your father. The moment you were born, that responsibility was handed to you."

Ben watched Krobeg closely as he went very still, his eyes becoming distant. He shook his head, even managing a good-natured smile.

"Is this some sort of joke? Did someone put you up to this?" Krobeg pointed a sausage finger at Ben. "It was Limbek, wasn't it? That scallywag is always conjuring up new ways to give me a heart attack."

"It's no joke," Ben said.

Krobeg didn't appear to hear him, and rattled off several other possible suspects responsible for the prank. Ben waited patiently for him to finish, before calmly repeating himself.

Krobeg frowned, appearing genuinely confused. "It's not a joke? Then what on earth is it?"

"The truth," Ben said. "You are a Guardian, just like me."

Krobeg stood up, his massive stomach hitting the table. He stared at Ben, and then Charlie and Natalie. And then he laughed – a loud, booming thing that made Charlie cover his ears.

"You really expect me to believe that? Three kids turn up and tell me that the Silver Dwarf is real, I am his grandson, and a Guardian of Elizabeth's Armour? Come on, you'll need to do better than that."

Krobeg waved an arm at them, chuckling to himself, and started towards the door.

From the corner of Ben's eye, he could see Natalie's and Charlie's panicked looks, but their protestations aimed at Krobeg did nothing to slow him down. He put his hand on the doorknob, and was about to exit, when Ben played his last card. He hated bringing the dad into the equation, but he was out of options.

"Your father said you weren't ready," Ben said, his voice soft, but carrying just that bit of accusation in it.

Krobeg stopped, his hand still on the doorknob. Slowly, he turned, his face stern.

"What are you talking about?" he asked with narrowed eyes. "How do you know my father?"

"We met him in the void," Ben said, keeping his voice level. "He still lives, though he has been in the void so long now it is difficult for him to return."

Doubt flashed across Krobeg's face, before he shook himself.

"Impossible. I don't believe you."

This time, Ben was prepared. "Your father's name is Elander Farseeker. He is a dwarf mage of great renown. Do you want me to describe him for you?"

Krobeg's eyes widened for just a second, before he clenched his fists. "You need to leave, now."

Ben shook his head. "Not without you. We need your help."

Krobeg took a meaningful step forwards. Ben suddenly became aware that the soft, chubby chef didn't look very soft anymore. There was a hardness in his thin lips that reminded Ben of Elander, and his fists were balled like boxing gloves.

"I don't know what nonsense my father told you, and I don't care. I learnt never to trust my father." Krobeg lifted a fisted hand. "Now get out, before I throw you out."

Ben stood up, his hand going to his spellshooter. But Natalie put a restraining hand on his arm.

"Not now, Ben," she said.

"But we need him."

"Natalie is right. Let's go," Charlie said.

Ben wanted to protest, but one look at the iron-faced Krobeg and he knew it would be pointless. Instead, he looked Krobeg deep in the eye as he passed him by, and said, "Like it not, you're a Guardian. Without you, Suktar will not be stopped, and the Unseen Kingdoms will fall."

Krobeg didn't even blink, let alone acknowledge Ben's statement, and they left the tavern without the Guardian.

CHAPTER 33

VOTERS AND DARK ELVES

"We shouldn't have left," Ben said, shooting a backward glance at the tavern.

"We had to," Natalie said. "You and Krobeg were about to start fighting. That dwarf is like a sumo wrestler; he could have crushed you."

Ben clenched his fists. "We need him. The whole quest to find Elizabeth's Armour is pointless if he doesn't join us."

"We weren't going to convince him," Charlie said. "You could see that in his face. And you know what, I don't blame him – it's not like we have a mountain of evidence."

"I disagree," Ben argued. "He knew we were telling the truth, at least part of it. He was hiding something from us. I think he's in denial."

"Maybe. But the way he was acting, I don't think he would have joined us even if we reincarnated Queen Elizabeth and brought her along to try to convince him," Charlie said.

"So what do we do now?" Natalie said. "Obviously we're not giving up, but we need another plan."

None of them had a solution. The only idea Ben could come up with was so outrageous and desperate that he didn't even bother voicing it. Krobeg might hate his father, but he might still listen to him. If they could just get them to meet up. Of course, that would mean getting Elander out of the void or convincing Krobeg to go into it. Both options bordered on madness, but as they left Drinkmorr and headed back to the Institute, Ben couldn't help thinking it might be their only hope.

THE LAST THING Ben felt like doing was campaigning for the Chief Three position. His mind was still on Krobeg, and his normally cool, composed persona that he would need to corral votes was missing. He alternated between frustration, despair, and apathy. They were so close to the next Guardian, yet it seemed just out of reach.

"You need to stop sulking and start talking to the

third-graders, if you don't want to get hammered by Aaron," Natalie said.

It was lunchtime, and the three of them were sitting outside in the Institute gardens. It was brisk, and the cool air went some way to knocking Ben out of his apathetic slumber.

"I know," Ben said. He had his elbows resting on his knees and was staring at the grass. "I just don't care. I'm regretting getting involved in the stupid thing in the first place."

"You'll care once Aaron is Chief Three," Charlie said. "You've got to snap out of it and start campaigning, else you might as well just concede right now."

Ben sat up, feeling slightly irritated. "Don't either of you care? Unless we can get Krobeg on our side, we're screwed."

"Of course we care," Natalie said. "I spend so much time thinking about it that I can hardly sleep. But I know we will work out a solution. We have to."

"I've got one or two ideas," Charlie said. "But I need a bit more time to research them."

Ben perked up a little. Why was he taking the setback with Krobeg so much harder than Charlie and Natalie? He was normally the relaxed one. Was it because he was more closely attached to the quest? Charlie and Natalie were helping every step of the way, but, at the end of the day, they were not

Guardians, and they could not possibly feel the same weight of responsibility. It wasn't they who would eventually be facing the dark elf king. Yes, he might be overreacting a little, but he had good reason. The thought had the peculiar effect of making him feel considerably better.

"You're right: I'm being an idiot," Ben said.

Natalie smiled. "I wouldn't go that far."

"I would," Charlie said.

The sun felt a little brighter than it had a moment ago, and Ben looked around the gardens, scanning the Institute members and apprentices. Bingo. A slender, somewhat goofy-looking boy was passing by. He had his head down, most likely trying to avoid unwanted attention. John was known to be terrible in the presence of pretty girls, and could barely string a coherent sentence together when Natalie was around. But he was a third-grade apprentice, which was all that mattered right now.

"John!"

Ben called with such intention that John's head flung up, as if someone had just screamed in his ear.

Ben leapt off the bench and walked briskly over to him. "Can I have a quick word with you? It's about the Chief Three election."

"Uh, sure," John said in an uncertain voice.

"Great," Ben said, giving him a smile and joining him on a slow walk towards the Institute. "Listen, I don't want to take up your time, so I'll be brief. I'm appealing to those who – to put it mildly – aren't part of Aaron's fan club."

Ben was about to rattle off a completely off-the-cuff speech, but before he could begin, John said, "I'm in."

"Great," Ben said with a surprised smile, and gave John a friendly clap on the shoulder. "I hope everyone's as easy to persuade as you are."

"Try Arnold," John said. "Last I saw, he was on the verge of being talked into voting for Aaron, despite the fact that he hates him as much as I do."

And so it began. Ben, never one to do things by half measures, flew into the campaign with vigour. The apprenticeship took a backseat, and Ben spent every moment at the Institute, talking, debating, and occasionally arguing with third-graders about all things apprentice-related. It was exhausting, especially when Ben had to learn many of the issues on the fly.

At the end of each day, his team, including Simon and William, as well as Charlie and Natalie, would meet and discuss numbers. There were thirty third-grade apprentices, which meant they needed sixteen or more votes. On Thursday evening, they had seven. By Monday they had ten, and Ben felt good. But on Tuesday they garnered only one more, and by Wednesday evening, they found themselves sitting round the meeting table, looking slightly glum.

"We appear to be stuck on twelve," Ben said. He stood at the end of the table, while the rest were seated. "Which means we need just four more. Any bright ideas?"

"I reckon I can persuade Lilly," Will said. He was looking at a piece of paper with names on it. "She wants a date in exchange, which I'd rather not do, but if she ends up being the decider, I'll have to reconsider."

"Good man," Ben said, giving him a thumbs-up. "That would take us to thirteen. Who else has a possibility?"

Simon was doodling idly on his own piece of paper. "Andy's still an option, if you ever change your mind about the money bribe. Personally I think a couple hundred quid is worth it, if it stops Aaron."

Ben scratched his nose. "It's not about the money, Simon."

"What's the problem, then?" Simon asked, looking confused.

Natalie gave Simon a disgusted look. "If you can't figure it out, then you need to take a long hard look at yourself."

Simon grinned. "I look at myself every day."

"Moving on," Ben said. He scanned the room.

"Guys, we can't lose by a couple of votes – that would just be annoying."

Natalie got out a small notebook and started reading from it. "Aaron has thirteen third-graders who would practically walk through fire for him. We have twelve. Of the five remaining, three are leaning towards Aaron. The other two are Andy and Lilly, who we've just talked about."

Ben drummed the table. He knew the three who were undecided because he'd already spoken to them.

"Okay, Will and I will tackle them again. Maybe the two of us together can make a difference."

William didn't complain, but, barring Natalie, the lack of optimism in the room was palpable. Ben didn't blame them. He scanned the room, gearing himself up for yet another morale-boosting speech, when he noticed someone was missing.

"Where's Charlie?"

Ben had been so involved with the meeting that he hadn't even noticed Charlie's absence. Nor, it seemed, had anyone else, as they looked around with mild confusion. Ben directed his gaze at Natalie, but she just gave a shrug.

That was odd. Charlie was often silent, but never absent, unless he had a good reason. Ben finished up the meeting with one final rallying speech, and they started filing out.

Charlie came bursting through the door, just as everyone was leaving. He ran headlong into William and rebounded as if he'd hit a brick wall.

Charlie shook his head, muttered an apology at a mildly confused William, and then darted past, pulling Ben and Natalie back into the meeting room. As soon as the door shut, Charlie started hopping on either foot, looking as though he was ready to burst.

"This had better be good," Ben said. "Have you managed to use your charms to claim a couple more votes?"

"Shadowseekers," Charlie said, sounding breathless. "Six of them broke into Drinkmorr, via the main entrance. Two were killed; the others are still at large."

All thoughts of the election vanished.

"What? Where did you hear this?" Ben asked sharply.

"Overheard a couple of Spellswords talking about it," Charlie said. "They weren't trying very hard to conceal the news, and I bet half the Institute knows by now."

Ben felt his insides go cold. Four Shadowseekers inside Drinkmorr. He had first-hand experience knowing just how deadly Shadowseekers were. They were an elite dark elf assassin unit, commanded directly by the royal family. If they had broken into Drinkmorr, it could mean only one thing.

"How long do you reckon Krobeg has?" Ben asked.

"Depends if they know where he is or not. Drinkmorr isn't a big place, but it could still take a while to find one dwarf."

Natalie gave a little squeak, and she put her hand over her lips. "The sign on the tavern!"

Charlie cursed. "I'd completely forgotten about that."

A nasty feeling started working its way deep into the pit of Ben's stomach. If the Shadowseekers recognised the symbol on the tavern as the Silver Dwarf's family crest, it wouldn't take them long at all. Days? Hours?

Ben slammed a hand on the table. "We need to go back, now."

"We can't," Charlie said. "The guest entrance doesn't open until tomorrow."

"What about the main entrance? The Shadowseekers got through."

"Even if we knew where it was, the dwarves would never let us through. Two of the Shadowseekers died trying."

"Is there no other way in?" Natalie asked.

Charlie shook his head. "No. We have to wait, and hope the Shadowseekers don't find Krobeg."

With the election due tomorrow, Ben knew he should be using the final few hours to throw himself into garnering votes, but the momentum he had gathered was no longer there. He continued to talk to people, but the energy, wit and humour he had used to gain votes were conspicuous in their absence.

"This isn't going to work."

Ben turned, and found William frowning at him. The two of them had spent the last hour campaigning together, though it had passed in a blur.

"What's going on? You weren't like this a few hours ago," William said. "You're not paying attention. Do you even remember who we just spoke to?"

Ben blinked – he could just make out the backs of a couple of third-graders whom he was fairly certain he'd just made a speech to.

"Frank and Henry, wasn't it?" Ben said, trying his luck.

"Wrong." William crossed his arms, and gave him a stern look. "Do you want to win this thing or not? Because I've got better things to do with my time if you're not interested."

William was possibly the only friend Ben would ever consider revealing his whole Guardian story to, and a small part of him wanted to tell William why he had suddenly lost interest in the election.

"Sorry, you're right," Ben said. "I've just got a few things on my mind."

"Anything you want to share?"

"No," Ben said with a smile. "Okay, where were we? How many people have I lost by acting like an idiot?"

"Only a few," William said. "But we're about to run into Christine, and she's one of the ones who's on the fence. She's smart, so you need to be prepared to answer some tricky questions."

Ben rubbed his hands together, trying to generate genuine enthusiasm and at the same time dismiss thoughts of Krobeg from his mind.

Through sheer force of will, Ben managed to focus on the election the rest of the afternoon, even managing to come up with a few thoughtful responses to Christine's laser-sharp questions. He went round with William, talking to anyone they could find, even those who were die-hard Aaron fans, on the off-chance they could jolt some sense into them. By the time five o'clock rolled round, he was exhausted.

"Well, I think you've got a chance," William said. "Not a big one, though."

"Thanks, Will," Ben said, clapping his friend on his sizeable biceps. They were standing by the Institute entrance and, from the corner of his eye, Ben could just make out Charlie and Natalie standing outside waiting for him. But he refused to be rushed, after all the effort William had put in.

"How does tomorrow work?"

"We have the morning to make our last push. Votes must be in by lunchtime. The announcement will be made at three o'clock."

Ben felt like a traitor when he looked into Will's eyes and said, "Sounds like a plan."

The truth was, he had no intention of being at the Institute tomorrow morning, but he wasn't going to tell Will that, and they left, with the plan to meet up right after tomorrow morning's muster.

"I feel awful," Ben said, as he joined Charlie and Natalie walking down the hill, towards the Dragonway. "Will and the team have been working so hard, and I'm going to completely betray them."

"Yeah, there's no getting round that. They're going to hate you," Charlie said with a shrug.

"That makes me feel better, thanks," Ben said.

"They'll forgive you, eventually," Natalie said, giving Charlie a pointed stare. "You just have to come up with a really convincing excuse as to why you weren't able to make it."

"A family death might do it," Charlie mused.

Ben wasn't sure how he felt about such a lie, but the fact that he might be able to come up with something to mitigate tomorrow's absence brightened him a little. He was finally able to take his mind off the election, and on to their journey to Drinkmorr tomorrow, which brought a whole new range of problems. Would the Shadowseekers have found Krobeg? If so, was he even still alive? They would find out tomorrow.

CHAPTER 34
SHADOWSEEKERS

Ben met Charlie and Natalie the following morning at London Victoria station. It had only just gone seven o'clock, but the station was still busy with commuters heading to work, oblivious to the world around them.

Charlie was munching on a McMuffin as they headed towards the Underground.

"Ugh, how can you eat that this early?" Natalie asked.

"I'm always hungry in the morning."

"Aren't you anxious about today?"

Charlie gave Natalie a confused look. "Of course I am; what's that got to do with anything?"

"I can't eat when I'm anxious."

Charlie tucked the remainder of the McMuffin

into his mouth. "Oh, it's the opposite with me. I eat more when I'm anxious."

"Moving on from the subject of McMuffins, have either of you thought about a plan?" Ben asked.

Ben knew they were unlikely to be overheard while walking through the Underground, as most people were lost in their music or on their mobiles.

"You're the plan person," Charlie said. "Don't we always just end up doing what you say?"

Ben dodged a business woman who was so intent on her phone that she wasn't looking where she was going. "Probably, but I want to hear what you guys think about Krobeg. We didn't exactly leave on good terms."

"Haven't a clue," Charlie said. "It's not like we're going there with fresh evidence. Why would he suddenly believe us now?"

"The dark elves," Natalie said. "We warned him that they might come."

"But will he believe that they are after him?" Charlie said.

Their conversation stopped as they entered the Underground train, and didn't start again until they arrived at Old Church Town, where once again they made their way through the small lanes, surrounded by the red brick buildings.

"Natalie's right: the Shadowseekers are our best hope," Ben said. "Plus, I still think that Krobeg is hiding something and that some of what I said hit home. Plus, he's had time to think things over, and possibly change his mind."

They soon reached the bank by the river, and Ben turned his attention to the building with the secret door. Despite knowing its location, it still took them a good fifteen minutes to find the door handle. Ben took a quick look around, to make sure nobody was watching, and then pulled the door open.

The smell of chocolate hit him, but this time he barely noticed it. He was too busy staring at the axe pointing inches from his chest. A line of stern-faced, armoured dwarves blocked the street.

"State your business," said the dwarf with the axe at Ben's chest.

Ben cursed inwardly for not expecting the road block and allowing the surprise to startle him. He thought fast. The tourist plea was his initial response, but the moment the dwarf spotted their spellshooters, he knew that wasn't going to work. Instead, he revealed the Institute diamonds floating above his shoulder.

"Institute business," Ben said, trying to mimic Dagmar's imperious authority.

"You are just apprentices," the dwarf said, lowering his axe.

Ben raised an eyebrow. "So what? We're still on official business. If you have a problem with that, you can take it up with Dagmar Borovich, Master of Apprentices."

That did the trick, as Ben hoped it would. The mention of Dagmar's name made the dwarf take a step back, and the guards parted.

"I have to inform you that, as foreigners, you are not our responsibility. You are aware of the Shadowseekers presently at large?"

"Yes, we are," Ben said.

The dwarf nodded. "Very well. Move along."

Chocolate Street was almost deserted. Only a few brave children with their parents were about, and even they ran from shop to shop. The smell was still remarkable, but not quite as strong as before, and Ben spotted more than one shop closed. That theme continued beyond Chocolate Street, and into the main centre of Drinkmorr. Those who ventured out did so in twos and threes, and there were many a furtive glance. Ben spotted several groups of Drinkmorr guards, but even their stern faces were etched with anxiety. Ben could well understand why. The Shadowseekers were deadly, and could appear from nowhere.

Ben's own anxiety was not for himself, but for Krobeg. If the Shadowseekers spotted his tavern, and the sign, he would be as good as dead. The thought made him quicken his pace, and place a reassuring hand on his spellshooter.

Ben half-expected a scene of destruction when he spotted the tavern, and let out a sigh of relief when they found it untouched. Unlike several taverns he'd passed, Krobeg's was still open and, amazingly, still doing business. Was that down to Krobeg's bravery, stubbornness, or simply a belief that the Shadowseekers would have no reason to pay him a visit? Ben sincerely hoped it wasn't the last option, as it would make their job of convincing him even harder.

"Look at the sign!" Natalie said, pointing up at the tavern's signage.

The lettering "Royal Goose" was there, just as before, but the symbol representing the Silver Dwarf had vanished.

"He's taken it down," Charlie said, staring up at the sign.

Ben smiled with unexpected hope. "You know what that means? He listened to our warning."

Natalie gave an excited clap, but Charlie wasn't convinced, and continued to stare at the signage thoughtfully. Ben wasn't in the mood for whatever pessimistic thought was going through Charlie's head. He entered the tavern, and nearly ran right into a couple of patrons leaving. When his eyes adjusted to the dim light, he saw that it was almost as busy as before. The bar had a few empty seats, but the restaurant was jammed, and the smell of bacon and sausages filled the air, stimulating Ben's taste buds.

"Do we have time for another breakfast?" Charlie asked.

"No," Natalie said firmly.

Ben eyed up the kitchen door. "I bet he's cooking."

Charlie nodded. "I agree. We should probably wait until he's done. Might as well get a quick bite to eat while we wait, no?"

"No," Ben said. He eyed up a passing waitress and quickly moved forwards, tapping her on the shoulder. "Excuse me, we need to speak to Krobeg."

The lady gave him a surprised look. "Krobeg? I'm sorry, sir, he's busy in the kitchen, and cannot be disturbed until breakfast has finished."

"It's urgent," Ben said, giving the waitress a serious look. "I'm sorry, we cannot wait. Tell him it's about the dark elves."

Ben clearly said the right thing, for the waitress gave a hurried nod, and dashed off into the kitchen.

Ben, Charlie and Natalie watched the kitchen door intently, waiting for Krobeg to emerge.

"What are we going to say?" Charlie asked.

"I've got an idea," Ben said. "Whatever happens this time, we cannot leave without him."

"Don't be too rough, Ben," Natalie said, giving Ben an anxious look. "And please don't mention his father, as he clearly has issues with him."

Ben didn't have time to reply, for Krobeg, all two

hundred pounds of him, came through the door, his eyes searching the tavern. He frowned the moment he spotted them, but Ben took heart in the fact that Krobeg's face didn't go red and explode.

"I had a feeling I'd be seeing you again," Krobeg said.

"You know why we're here."

Krobeg glanced at the dining room – a habit perhaps, making sure everything was okay – before turning back to them.

"Come with me," he said, giving them a wave.

Krobeg led them back into the small private staff room where they had their explosive meeting just a few days ago. This time they remained standing. Krobeg stroked his short, ginger beard, his eyes momentarily distant. While he was considering what to say, Ben decided to jump in.

"You took down the symbol," he said.

"What? Oh yes. A precaution, just in case."

Ben pressed on, sensing an opportunity. "Which means you must have believed at least some of what we said."

"I'm not an idiot," Krobeg said. His voice was stern, but without malice. "You come and say the dark elves are looking for me, and then Shadowseekers break in to Drinkmorr. They may have nothing to do with me, but if there was any truth in your story, it made sense to take the sign down, for now."

"So, where does this leave us?" Ben asked, keeping his voice soft, making sure there was no unnecessary accusation.

Krobeg gave a subtle, disbelieving shake of his head. "I have spent many hours thinking about your story. I admit that some of it rings true. I know my father originally came from Jimba, and many of the stories of the Silver Dwarf state he also lived there. I never knew my grandfather; my father rarely spoke of him. I got the feeling that he and my father had a falling out." Krobeg gave a rueful smile. "It must run in the family."

Krobeg paused, clearly considering his words. Ben made no move to hurry him.

"As much as I dislike my father, there is no doubting that he is a great mage. If the Silver Dwarf really did exist, I can imagine my father being the sort of person who might have been his son."

Krobeg stopped, and Ben had to resist the urge to do a fist pump. Instead, he stayed calm, and asked, "So what's the problem?"

"The problem is me," Krobeg said with a sudden ironic laugh, patting his enormous stomach. "Look at me. I'm just a chef, not a Guardian. The idea that I might be responsible for defeating Suktar is utterly ridiculous."

"I thought the same thing," Ben said with a faint smile. "Your credential is simple – you are the son of your father. That's how it works. I know it's crazy, but it's true. We have found other Guardians and their pieces of armour. We have never been wrong."

Krobeg rubbed his stomach absentmindedly, and Ben could almost see the cogs turning inside his head. He might be a slow thinker, but he wasn't stupid – far from it.

"What proof do you have?" Krobeg said eventually. "Your stories are well told, but they are just that: stories – unless you can back them up with evidence."

"How about the Shadowseekers?" Natalie said, her voice soft. "They are here for you."

"You don't know that for sure," Krobeg said.

Proof. It wasn't the first time they had been asked that question, and Ben wished they had something more tangible. A piece of the armour would do, but it was far too risky parading Elizabeth's Armour in public. If only he had the sword; he was sure that would do the trick. But he didn't, and he wasn't even sure where it was.

"You're going to have to trust us," Ben said. He put all his reason and intention behind his voice. "Why would we travel all this way to tell you some nonsense story? Why would we risk coming back into Drinkmorr with Shadowseekers present? If you come with us back to the Institute, we can prove our story, but not here."

Ben watched Krobeg closely. He was fighting with the idea, but Ben had the horrible feeling it was a losing battle. The words of Krobeg's father rang again in his ears. *Krobeg isn't like you. Even in the brief time we have been together, I can tell you have the qualities a Guardian needs. My son does not.* Ben could see where Krobeg's father was coming from, but Ben suspected a hidden strength within Krobeg – if only it would come out. After all, he was the grandson of the Silver Dwarf, one of the greatest legends in dwarf history.

Krobeg shook his head slowly. "I'm sorry, I just can't—"

His words were cut off by a scream – multiple screams – making them all jump. Krobeg reacted first, turning and almost yanking the door off its hinges. Ben dashed after him, Natalie and Charlie right behind. Krobeg flew down the corridor, like a bowling ball out of control, crashing into the walls, and knocking off a couple of frames.

Ben followed Krobeg back into the bar, and entered a scene of chaos. Dozens of patrons were flooding out the door. A few of the hardier ones remained with weapons drawn. Many of the staff were looking anxiously out the window. Krobeg grabbed a meat cleaver and thundered through the front door. Ben, Charlie and Natalie followed right behind.

Dwarves, humans, and several other races were fleeing down the street, many taking frightened backward glances. A dozen Drinkmorr guards had formed a blockade, axes drawn.

Krobeg marched up to the guard in the middle, who was clearly the leader. "What's going on?"

The guard turned, his stern expression relaxing a fraction when he saw the giant chef. "Shadowseekers spotted, at least two, heading this way. No place for a cleaver, Krobeg. Get back into your tavern and lock the doors or get out of here. Unless you want to get your axe and help us? We could use it."

Ben was taken aback by the hopeful expression on the guard's face. Krobeg, however, turned towards Ben, his face intense.

"I need answers, and I need them now," Krobeg said, sticking a huge sausage finger at Ben. "Is everything you say true? Because if there is even a doubt of uncertainty, I'm staying here and joining the guards."

"It's all true," Ben said, looking Krobeg right in the eye. Krobeg glanced at his tavern, then at the line of guards, and clenched his sizeable fists. He took a deep breath, his massive stomach heaving. "I hope I don't regret this. Follow me."

Before Ben could ask where they were going, Krobeg headed back into the tavern. Ben followed, exchanging confused glances with Charlie and Natalie. They passed the main bar, and headed through another private door, which led to a narrow set of stairs that Krobeg could only just squeeze up. At the top was a small hallway with another series of doors. Krobeg went to the end door, took a large key out, and entered, beckoning them in, before locking the door behind them.

They found themselves in Krobeg's living quarters, consisting of three rooms, including a predictably large kitchen, a small living space, and a bedroom, with a bed Ben assumed was designed for a giant or a troll. Krobeg, still moving like a kid who has had too much sugar, snatched a long, wooden pole from the corner of the room, and poked the ceiling. A wooden panel swung down, giving access to the loft above. The pole had a small hook at the end, and Krobeg used it to grab and pull down a series of steps.

"Wait here," Krobeg ordered. "I'll be right back."

Krobeg disappeared into the loft. Ben heard a rustling noise, drowning out the faint screams from outside.

"Are you both as confused as I am?" Charlie asked, as he stared up at the loft.

"He obviously needs something from up there before we leave," Natalie said.

Sure enough, Krobeg emerged from the loft

holding an incredible battle axe in one hand. The handle was wrought with intricate engravings, and the head gleamed silver.

"What's that?" Charlie asked.

It took Ben a moment to realise that Charlie wasn't referring to the axe, but an item in Krobeg's other hand.

"This," Krobeg said, upon reaching the floor, and closing up the loft, "is a map, given to me by my father."

It was an old folded parchment that looked so delicate it appeared ready to crumble.

"I looked at it once, many years ago, but it made no sense," Krobeg explained. "And given the relationship with my father wasn't exactly great, I really wasn't that interested. Frankly, I haven't thought about it in years, until you came by a few days ago."

Ben's heart leapt up a gear, and he saw Charlie rubbing his hands with excitement, as Krobeg gently laid the map on the floor, and started unfolding it.

"My, it is old," Natalie said, kneeling down to get a better look.

"Yes, don't touch it, or it may crumble."

The map was frayed at the edges, but the colours were still vivid, full of blues, greens and yellows. There was an "X" marked in the upper left corner.

"I don't recognise any of these places," Ben said, frowning. He immediately looked up at Charlie, who was staring so intently at the map, Ben feared his gaze might tear a hole through it.

"That's exactly what I thought," Krobeg said. "And even now, many years later, I still don't recognise anything."

"It's got to be somewhere in the Unseen Kingdoms," Charlie said. "This name here 'Trilthorp' sounds familiar. I just need a moment to think."

Krobeg gave an enquiring look at Ben.

"Charlie's our encyclopaedia man," Ben explained.

But time was something they didn't have. A crashing noise came from downstairs, followed by screams, shouts, and clashes of steel.

"Uh oh," Ben said.

Krobeg stood up.

"Wait!" Charlie said, trailing his finger lightly over the map. "I'm close – I know I am. Just give me a minute."

Krobeg hesitated, grappling with his axe, his eyes darting towards the door. He was itching to go, and Ben prepared himself to block the big dwarf.

"You can't help," Ben said. "I've seen the Shadowseekers fight. The axe is not the right weapon, believe me."

Ben thought his line of reasoning was sound, but it had the exact opposite effect. Krobeg gave Ben a grim smile.

"Not the right weapon, eh? We'll see about that."

Ben heard the soft sound of footsteps coming up the stairs – light and nimble. Shadowseeker footsteps.

"They're coming!" Natalie cried.

"Good," Krobeg said.

"No!" Charlie said, as Krobeg stepped forwards, his heavy boots crumpling the frail map.

But Krobeg's legs didn't destroy the map. They stepped into and through it, like a black hole. With a mighty yell of surprise, Krobeg disappeared into the map, leaving nothing but the tattered parchment remaining.

Ben, Charlie and Natalie gave a chorus of screams.

"A portal!" Charlie said, finding his voice.

Ben glanced up. The Shadowseekers had climbed the stairs and he could hear them approaching the door.

"Go!" Ben said.

Natalie didn't hesitate. She stepped right onto the map, and vanished, just like Krobeg had.

A slender sword sliced right through the thick bedroom door, and started methodically sawing out the lock.

"Oh dear," Charlie said.

"Get a move on!" Ben said.

Charlie looked at the map, and hesitated – only

for a moment, but enough for Ben to give him an impatient shove, sending a screaming Charlie into the map. Ben took one more look at the door, which was now being shoulder-charged by the Shadowseekers. Huge cracks lined the door, and Ben could make out a dash of purple beyond.

With a quick check on his spellshooter to make sure it was secure, Ben leapt into the map with a cry of exhilaration.

CHAPTER 35
ARCANE DWARVES

Ben landed softly on thick undergrowth. He afforded himself the brief glance around the forest, before rolling and pointing his spell-shooter up, aiming at the point he had fallen through. There was nothing there, except for a huge tree – no sign of any portal. But Ben kept his spell-shooter trained on the spot, holding his breath, heart pounding, waiting for the Shadowseekers to come leaping through.

They never came, and eventually Ben relaxed. He turned and saw Natalie, Charlie and Krobeg do the same.

"Either they didn't think to step into the map or else they can't get through," Charlie said.

"My tavern," Krobeg said, anguish in his voice. "I need to get back before they destroy it."

"Your tavern is safe," Ben said, sitting down on a large trunk that had been felled. "They were after you, not the tavern. Now that you're not there, they won't hang around. They will try to find where you went."

"Where are we?" Natalie asked, looking up. "This place is unlike anything I've ever seen."

Ben knew what she meant, and yet the place seemed strangely familiar. The trees were huge, bigger than anything he'd seen in England. They weren't all green either; some of them were shades of purple or red, creating a thick, leafy roof, hundreds of feet up. The forest floor wasn't a simple bed of grass, like home, but a dense undergrowth, full of life – Ben saw bugs, both big and small, and instinctively shook his legs.

"Jimba Forest," Charlie said, his voice full of wonder.

"Jimba?" Natalie frowned. "That's from the diary, right?"

Charlie nodded. "Angus, the original director, came here to find a place for the piece of armour he was entrusted with. He met the arcane dwarves and eventually the armour found its way to the Silver Dwarf."

They all turned to Krobeg, who stood silently, his mouth wide open, staring up at the mighty trees. Ben could almost see the realisation and, with it, acceptance, slowly dawning on the dwarf's face.

"I can't believe it," he said softly. "All this time, I had that map in my loft and I never knew its significance." He shook his head slowly. "Why, though? Why would my father want to send me here?"

"The arcane dwarves," Ben said. "We're now in their domain. I'm willing to bet all the money I don't have that they are the custodians of the piece of Elizabeth's Armour."

Krobeg gave Ben a long, searching look, which he met without flinching.

"You think my father intended me to come here to retrieve the piece of armour, don't you," Krobeg said.

"I know that's what he intended," Ben said with a small smile.

A brief silence followed, and Ben could see Krobeg slowly processing the magnitude of events. He might be slow, but he wasn't stupid, and Ben was fairly certain he was starting to believe.

"The question is – are the arcane dwarves still here?" Natalie asked. "Could they still be guarding the armour after all this time?"

"Yes," Charlie said without hesitation. "Remember the prophesy? The Silver Dwarf shall return and lead them out. I think they're still waiting for him."

"Intelligence can't be one of their key attributes, then. Why don't they just leave?" Natalie asked.

"Haven't you read fantasy stories? Prophesies are important things – you don't treat them lightly, and they always come true."

"This isn't a book, though," Natalie said.

Ben glanced around at the huge trees and dense undergrowth. "If the arcane dwarves are guarding the armour, where can we find them?"

"We need to travel east – that's what it said in the diary. I'm sure it can't be far," Charlie said. "It would be silly for the map to drop us off days away. I bet we're just outside the arcane dwarf boundary zone."

"Well, let's get cracking," Ben said. He glanced up again at the portal they had come through, checking for dark elves one more time, but saw nothing.

The going was slow, as the undergrowth was so thick. Charlie, with his in-built orientation skills, ensured they were always heading east, but it was rare that they managed to do so in a straight line. There were creatures, both big and small, that they tried to avoid. Even the plants watched them, and Charlie nearly got bitten several times by some of the larger ones.

"What is that?" Ben said, stopping suddenly, with a sharp intake of breath.

A huge, black cat with sparkling yellow eyes was watching them, less than fifty feet away. It must have been at least twice the size of a lion, and it stood right on the path they had mapped out.

"I don't know, but I think it's hungry," Charlie said, taking an instinctive step back. "I've seen that look before; I get it every time I'm about to devour my egg and bacon sandwich."

"You're right, I've seen it too, among many of my patrons," Krobeg said.

"It's a growl," Natalie said. "I remember now, from the diary."

"Do you remember if the diary said anything about how to kill it?"

"I don't want to kill it," said Natalie, looking shocked. "It's not evil, just hungry."

The growl started towards them, its footsteps surprisingly soft, given its size.

"It's going to rush us, any second," Charlie said. He had his spellshooter out, but his hand was shaking.

Ben considered their options, fast. It was too late to turn away, and if they ran, he was fairly certain the growl would catch them. He whipped his own spell-shooter out.

"Stun it," Ben said, looking towards Charlie and Natalie. "You've both got stunning spells, right?"

They nodded, though not with the sort of conviction Ben was hoping for.

"Natalie, you go first. If that doesn't do the job, Charlie, you fire. I'll go last."

Ben had barely finished speaking, when the growl launched forwards with frightening speed, powering through the undergrowth as if it was no more than a bed of tulips.

"Fire!"

Natalie shot a small, silver spell at the growl. It hit him right on the nose, and created a small shockwave on impact, but the growl didn't break its stride.

"Charlie!"

Charlie's spell hit the growl less than twenty paces away. The shockwave was greater, and the growl slowed noticeably, but the dazed look on its face lasted only a moment, and it continued its advance, suddenly lengthening its final few strides.

Ben fired. It was impossible to miss at such a range. The shockwave was greater still, and Ben saw the growl's yellow eyes roll back, but its sheer momentum carried it on. Too late did Ben realise he wasn't going to get out the way in time.

A mighty arm swatted him aside. Krobeg stepped forwards and charged into the growl with the force of a raging bull. There was a mighty impact, and they collapsed onto the ground. Krobeg shook his head and got straight back up, but the growl was out cold.

The four of them stared at the mighty animal.

"Well, we didn't kill it," Charlie said after a moment.

Ben glanced at Krobeg, appraising him yet again. "That was incredible."

Krobeg shrugged, looking a little uncomfortable. "I did some wrestling when I was younger. Shall we keep going?"

They went a little slower now, eyes peeled for the larger animals, both on the ground level and above. The growl was big, but Ben was fairly sure there were bigger, more dangerous animals about, and he didn't want to run into them.

The incident with the growl left them on their toes, silent and alert, and it was at least twenty minutes without incident before they started to relax.

"I wish I had packed a lunch bag," Krobeg said.

"You sound like Charlie," Natalie said, stepping delicately over a small log that she knew from experience was actually a living animal.

"I don't normally go more than a couple of hours without having a drink – and I'm not talking about water," Krobeg said.

"He doesn't sound like me," Charlie said. "Unless you're talking about a cup of tea? Because I find I need a caffeine dose every couple of hours."

"I wonder if these arcane dwarves will have

anything worthy to eat or drink," Krobeg said, his eyes twinkling.

Ben was pleased to see some of Krobeg's old joviality returning. Had he finally accepted his role as a Guardian? Ben liked to think so, but it was too early to tell.

"I'm sure they'll have something," Natalie said. "Speaking of which, how are we going to convince them to hand over the piece of Elizabeth's Armour, assuming they do have it? Aren't they keeping it safe for the Silver Dwarf?"

"Yes," Ben said. "I'm still working on that part."

The truth was, Ben hadn't a clue, but he wasn't going to tell them that. He was hoping that the arcane dwarves would recognise Krobeg as a descendant, and possibly even make the connection to the Silver Dwarf. But it was a forlorn hope, especially as Krobeg, with his ginger beard and large stomach, looked nothing like the Silver Dwarf. The other option was acquiring the piece of armour by brute force, which seemed highly unlikely; after all, the armour was here in the first place because it was so hard to get. Ben's head kept going round in circles, searching for an idea. He was so intent on coming up with a plan that he didn't hear Charlie shout, and reacted with some surprise when Krobeg grabbed his shirt and hauled him back.

"What is it?" Ben said.

"Look."

They were pointing to a series of trees ahead of them that ran across their path. Each tree was painted with a red circle. Underneath, was a peculiar symbol, and underneath that, written in plain English, were the words "DO NOT ENTER".

"Well, we're on the right track," Ben said.

His humour was lost on the others, who eyed the trees warily. Krobeg loosened his axe from his belt, and both Charlie and Natalie drew their spellshooters.Ben did the same.

After some misgivings from Charlie, they continued on, four sets of eyes constantly scanning the forest for signs of life. Ben remembered exactly what Angus said about the arcane dwarves. "*They are extremely good at hiding, better even than the wood elves of Lithlorn.*" Were they being watched right now? Ben felt the hairs on the back of his neck rise, but every time he thought he saw a flicker of movement, it was gone before he could spot anything.

"They're watching us," Krobeg said. "I can feel it."

"I think you're right," Natalie replied. "Let's not make any threatening movements. Do you think we should put our weapons away?"

"I don't think it will matter," Ben said. He might not be able to see the dwarves, but he felt better holding his spellshooter.

Despite knowing they were being watched, they

still stepped quietly, as if this would somehow assist them. Ben could hear their breathing, louder even than the rustling trees.

None of them spotted the arcane dwarf who fired the arrow.

The first Ben heard of it was the soft whistling through the air, and then a *thunk*, as it embedded itself into a tree just in front of them.

Ben gave a start, and he heard Charlie curse and fall to the floor. Ben hurried up to the arrow and pried it from the tree. The head, shaft and tail were all red.

"A warning," Charlie said, rubbing his backside. "Exactly the same thing happened to Angus, remember?"

Ben followed the flight path of the arrow, but wasn't surprised to see nobody there.

"Should we keep going?" Krobeg asked. He didn't look scared, only doubtful.

"Yes," Ben replied emphatically. "We're going the right way. It won't be much longer now."

"I hope you're right about this," Krobeg said.

"And if I'm not?"

Krobeg looked at him, his eyes serious. "If you're not, and we somehow get out of this alive, then you're all banned from my tavern for life."

Charlie gave a moan. "That's just cruel."

"What if I'm right, and we get out alive?" Ben said.

Krobeg gave a hint of a smile. "If you're right, then it's free meals all round."

"Wow," Natalie said. "So there's a lot riding on this; it's not just about saving the world from the dark elves."

The light-hearted moment was brief, and silence soon resumed. They continued on, apprehensive of where the next arrow might come from. Would they get another warning or would they be the next targets? Occasionally Ben would glance over to Krobeg, looking for signs that he might be cracking. After all, this was a lot for him to take in. Just a few days ago, he had been a successful chef, and now he was a Guardian and descendant of the Silver Dwarf. But though he saw the occasional flicker of concern, there was no sign of fear. From everything Ben had seen of Krobeg these last few hours, he was starting to think Elander's assessment of his son was completely off the mark.

Ben's thoughts were interrupted by a sudden movement ahead, and a warning shout from Natalie, who flung her arms out.

Out from the trees stepped a dwarf. He was slender, almost man-like, in appearance. His skin was pale, perhaps from the lack of sunlight, and his long beard was neatly split into three bunches. Ben was relieved to see that he was unarmed, and approached them in a relaxed, almost serene manner.

"Greetings, strangers," the dwarf said. His voice was neither friendly, nor unkind. His gaze took them all in, but settled on Krobeg the longest.

"Greetings," Ben said, placing himself firmly in the front, so that the dwarf looked his way.

"I come with a message from my chief," the dwarf said. "You have ignored our signs and our arrow. I am here to give you one last warning. Turn back now, and no harm will come to you. Continue on, and you will not leave our forest alive."

Ben still hadn't worked out any sort of plan as to how they would actually get the armour, so he did what he did best – improvised.

"We need to speak to your chief. It is a matter of utmost importance."

"My chief has nothing to say to you," the dwarf replied calmly.

"No, but we have something to say to him." Ben took a deep breath. He could see the dwarf was ready to leave. He needed to take a gamble. "We have come to take back the armour that was placed under your guardianship by the Royal Institute of Magic."

Perhaps the dwarf had been trained to maintain a straight face, for he gave only the briefest flicker of surprise. "The armour is not intended for you. It waits for another. I shall say no more on the matter.

This is your last warning. Turn back now or face the consequences. That includes you, cousin."

The dwarf nodded towards Krobeg, and then left, unhurriedly, disappearing into the trees.

"Now what?" Charlie asked. "What's your plan, Ben?"

"We don't have a choice – we have to keep going," Ben said. "If we keep going, we die," Krobeg said. His voice was calm, matter-of-fact.

"I don't think so, not straight away, anyway," Ben said. "I think they will capture us first."

"Oh good," Charlie said. "So they'll capture us, *then* kill us. How is that any better?"

"Because we'll get another chance to talk to them," Ben said. "That's what happened to Angus, remember? He was captured, but he managed to talk his way out."

"That was a long time ago," Charlie said.

"Doesn't matter," Ben said. "These arcane dwarves aren't evil; they're just uneducated. Our one chance is to talk to the chief, and convince him that Krobeg, not his grandfather, is the one the armour is intended for."

"You're a good talker, Ben," Natalie said. "But I think even you will have trouble convincing him of that. They seem very fixed on their prophesy that the Silver Dwarf will return."

"Natalie is right," Krobeg said. He was idly

fiddling with his battle axe. "Let's face it, even if I am the Silver Dwarf's grandson, what evidence do we have? It's not like we can do DNA tests, like you do at home."

"I'll think of something," Ben said.

Krobeg wasn't convinced.

"I know it sounds like an empty promise," Charlie said, giving Krobeg a tap on his shoulder. "But believe it or not, he's said that many times before, and somehow he nearly always comes through."

Upon resuming their walk, it became obvious that they had now entered arcane dwarf territory. They passed various well-trodden paths, criss-crossing their own, and they even spotted a few empty cabins in small clearings. The dwarves no longer bothered concealing their presence, and Ben spotted several as they progressed. They kept their distance, and watched, but Ben could feel their discomfort. They clearly didn't get many visitors, but at least it seemed that they had been ordered not to engage... yet.

"I see something," Natalie said, her keen eyes squinting in the distance. She gave a sharp intake of breath. "Oh my, look at that."

It took Ben a minute before he could see what Natalie was referring to. A flicker of gold between the trees – a building in the distance. Ben had to resist increasing his pace, as the building began to reveal itself. They arrived on the edge of a large, circular clearing that had been meticulously cleared of trees and undergrowth, leaving only a carpet of grass, lined with small, colourful flowers that any English garden would be proud of. In the middle of the clearing was a magnificent, golden shrine. The rectangular building gleamed in the sunlight and had a textured, arched roof. The golden door in the front of the building looked more secure than a bank vault.

"Now what?" Charlie asked, his voice tense. He was no longer looking at the building, but at the edge of the clearing, which was full of arcane dwarves. There must have been at least two dozen of them. They were armed, and they were watching them.

"Why are they just standing there?" Natalie asked.

Another look at the shrine door, and Ben had his answer.

"They aren't in any rush," Ben said. "They think we won't be able to get inside, and will just grab us in their own good time. That was their plan all along. That's the only reason we've been able to get this far. They must have been waiting to see what we were up to."

"That door looks pretty solid," Krobeg said, feeling his axe. "I doubt I could make much of a dent."

“No. It’s going to take something special to open that thing,” Ben mused.

“Do you have something special?” Natalie asked, glancing at Ben’s spellshooter.

Ben wrapped his hand around the spellshooter handle, and focused on the orb, searching for spells. He had a couple of open-lock spells, but they were intended for ordinary doors, not something like this. That left blasting spells. He had just one candidate – a concentrated air blast, fourth level. Would it be enough? He would have to cast it perfectly, and throw every ounce of intention he had behind it to knock off a door that strong.

“I’ve got one possibility,” Ben said.

“What do we do if that doesn’t work?” Charlie asked. “We’re not going to take on two dozen arcane dwarves, are we?”

“No,” Ben said. “Not unless they attack us. Otherwise we surrender, and go for the talking option.”

“Shall we do this, then? I want to see what’s inside,” Krobeg said.

Ben was surprised, and reassured, to see the look of curiosity and determination on the dwarf’s face.

“Walk just behind me,” Ben said. I don’t want you in my peripheral vision, as I need to concentrate. If the arcane dwarves rush us, let me know. Otherwise all my attention will be focused on the spell. Are you guys ready?”

"No," Charlie said. "But then, I never am."

Ben stepped into the clearing. He couldn't help taking a glance at the arcane dwarves. They were all watching, but thankfully, none of them made a move to follow. Ben was confident he'd made the right call – they were waiting for them to fail to open the door.

That wasn't going to happen. Ben cast aside thoughts of failure, of the arcane dwarves, of the pressure. He focused on the gold door he was walking towards. Hand on the spellshooter, he commanded the spell forth, and felt the little pellet move serenely to the bottom of the orb, ready for firing. But Ben didn't pull the trigger. Instead, he envisioned in perfect three-dimensional colour the door being blown off its hinges. Still he didn't fire, until he felt he had every ounce of intention and willpower behind the thought. He was able to see the delicate engravings within the door, less than ten paces away, when he finally felt ready. He lifted the spellshooter, aimed at the middle of the door, and pulled the trigger.

The kickback almost knocked the spellshooter into his face, such was the force of the white pellet that fired from the barrel. It grew quickly, until it was a football-sized mass of compressed air, swirling with vigour. It smashed into the door. The impact was colossal and the explosion of compressed air bounced back with such force that Ben was almost thrown from his feet. For a moment, the door was covered in white mist. When it cleared, there was a large dent in the middle of the door.

But the door was still there, still on its hinges, and still functioning as a door.

Ben couldn't believe it. That spell would have knocked a house down, yet the door had survived. He ran to the door, and grabbed the handle. It didn't budge. He turned, and saw Charlie, Natalie and Krobeg looking at him with alarm.

"We're in trouble," Ben said with false calm.

They turned, backs to the shrine, to face the oncoming arcane dwarves. The dwarves had formed a semicircle, designed to prevent any form of escape, but appeared to be in no rush. Their casual nonchalance almost made it worse; their confidence was unnerving.

"If we charged, I bet we could break through," Krobeg said. His eyes had narrowed, and he had his axe drawn. Ben was starting to think Krobeg was suffering from a case of overconfidence.

"Even if we made it through, then what? With all due respect, I don't think we could outrun them," Natalie said.

The arcane dwarves continued to approach, the semicircle gradually getting smaller, until there was barely room to swing a sword between each dwarf.

"Put your weapons away," Ben said softly. It went

against every instinct, but he holstered his spell-shooter, and watched as the others reluctantly did the same.

Ben focused on the dwarf in the middle, raised his hands, and spoke in a clear voice. "We need to talk."

The dwarf didn't respond, but continued with a dead-eyed stare at Ben. A couple of the dwarves on the fringes drew their weapons, upon hearing Ben's voice.

"Not good," Charlie said, his voice bordering on panic. "Do we draw our weapons again?"

"No," Ben said firmly. The dwarves were less than two dozen paces away now, and Ben could make out the stubble on their beards, the buttons on their leather jackets, and the intelligent gleam in their almond-shaped eyes.

Yes, there was intelligence there. So why weren't they listening?

"We need to talk," Ben said, throwing every ounce of intention behind his voice. "It is about your prophesy regarding the Silver Dwarf. It concerns your very future."

This time, a few of them hesitated, but the ones in the centre appeared either deaf or unwilling to listen.

Just a dozen paces separated them now. Ben was fairly sure that they would simply capture them and wouldn't use violence unless it was used upon them first. Fairly sure, but not certain, especially when he looked at a few of the dwarves on the fringes, who were armed with arrows.

"Er, Ben?" Natalie said, her voice rising an octave. "Are they going to take us in peacefully?"

"That one looks like he wants to rip my head off," Charlie said, pointing with a trembling finger to a dwarf who was testing the string on his bow.

Ben had been in tighter spots before, but he was struggling to remember when. He could feel his spell-shooter calling his name, but knew any motion towards his weapon could be construed as aggression and be fatal. Instead, he raised both arms, preparing for a final impassioned plea, knowing full well their lives depended on it.

Click.

Ben turned, and found the door ajar, Krobeg's hand still on the handle. His face was stunned, as if he hadn't quite realised what had happened.

"I opened the door," he said stupidly.

"Get in!" Charlie said, pushing Krobeg inside.

The arcane dwarves were close – a quick dash and they would catch them. But they froze in shock, their mouths opening in unison. It was only a second, but it was enough. Natalie darted inside, and Ben followed, slamming the door shut behind them. Seconds later he heard the sound of footsteps, and then the rattling of the door handle. It remained shut.

"They can't get in," Natalie said, clapping her hands in delight.

"Good," Charlie said, wiping his brow. "But how do we get out?"

"We'll worry about that later," Ben said. Though temporarily safe, his heart rate barely slowed, as he turned to inspect the grand shrine.

CHAPTER 36
ELIZABETH'S BREASTPLATE

It was like nothing Ben had ever seen before. The arched roof cast a soft golden glow upon the wooden floor, supplying enough light to make up for the lack of windows. Lining both sides of the shrine were huge statues of dwarves standing to attention. They were clearly done by a master craftsman, as the detail was extraordinary, right down to the individual hairs of their beards. But as incredible as they were, Ben's attention drifted to something else – something he had rarely stopped thinking about these past few weeks. There was a pedestal at the back of the shrine. On it was a mannequin of a dwarf, and on that was Elizabeth's Breastplate. The sheer quality of the piece left Ben in no doubt of its heritage. Just like the helm and the boots, it was a simple piece, cast in silver, and gleaming as if someone polished it on a daily basis. Simple, but oozing craftsmanship and radiating an intangible magic that Ben could almost feel on his skin.

"There it is," Natalie said, her voice a whisper.

Krobeg stared, open-mouthed. "I can't believe it. The Silver Dwarf's armour."

"Your armour," Ben corrected.

The armour was less than fifty paces away, but none of them moved. Ben knew from experience it was never this easy, and his eyes went to the floor, looking for any sign of traps.

"Do we just go up and get it?" Natalie asked. She made to lift a foot, but Charlie grabbed her.

"No." He turned to Ben. "Well?"

"I don't see anything," Ben said. "What about you, Krobeg?"

"Like a trap or something? It does seem a bit straightforward."

"Too straightforward," Ben said. Even as he spoke, he knew he was right, and the hairs on the back of his neck confirmed the thought.

"Well, we're not going to get anywhere just standing here, are we," Natalie said.

"No, but— wait!"

Charlie's shout was no good. Natalie took a step forwards.

Nothing happened.

Natalie turned, and gave them a smile. "See?

Would you all stop worrying so much? It's not always hard work."

Ben exchanged a shrug with Krobeg and Charlie, and they moved forwards, joining Natalie.

Six fully armed arcane dwarves slipped out from behind the statues.

The four of them stopped dead.

Charlie muttered something aimed – Ben was sure – at Natalie, but he didn't catch it. He was too busy staring at the dwarves. They were not like the ones outside, who wore little more than leather. These ones were dressed in what looked like ceremonial armour, with gold- and silver-plated armour, complete with a feathered helm. They each held a short sword in their right hand. Their faces were lined with age, their beards were grey, but they moved with surprising grace.The dwarf in the middle, the only one with a red feather on his helmet, stepped in front of the others.

"Welcome," the dwarf said in a surprisingly soft voice. "My name is Lidbank. I am the protector of the Silver Dwarf's armour." He paused, and gave each of them an appraising and almost curious look, with Krobeg receiving the most attention.

"How were you able to enter?" Lidbank asked.

"There's a door," Ben said, pointing behind him.

"The door would not let you in."

Ben frowned. "It did. That is how we got in."

Lidbank gave his head a soft shake. "I am sorry, that is not possible."

"How did we get in, then?" Natalie asked.

"I do not know," Lidbank said. "That is why we are having this conversation and you are not already dead. I am curious."

Ben resisted the urge to touch his spellshooter. This might be the one chance they had to talk. There was no point in holding back now; they were so close.

"Look, that's how we got in. Krobeg opened the door. I don't know how, but it might have something to do with the fact that he is the Silver Dwarf's grandson. We have come to collect the breastplate, which rightfully belongs to him."

Lidbank gave Krobeg another searching look and, for a moment, he thought the arcane dwarf was considering the possibility that Ben might be telling the truth. But decades, perhaps even centuries, of waiting for the Silver Dwarf seemed to kick in, and Lidbank's face clouded.

"The breastplate belongs to the Silver Dwarf," Lidbank said, sounding strangely robotic. "We wait for his return."

Ben clenched his fists, and worked hard to keep his cool. "The Silver Dwarf departed a long time ago. This is his grandson, who by blood right inherits the breastplate."

To Ben's surprise, his words impinged, if only a

fraction, and only for a moment, before Lidbank shook his head again, almost sadly. Ben cursed inwardly. It didn't help that Krobeg looked nothing like the Silver Dwarf, with his ginger hair and his barrel-like belly.

"Only the Silver Dwarf may claim his armour," Lidbank said with an almost sad finality. "This is your last warning. Leave now or don't leave at all."

The arcane dwarves raised their weapons as one, with frightening synchronicity.

Ben cursed. It was obvious these dwarves were stuck with a rigid belief in their prophesy. How long had they been guarding the armour for? Hundreds of years most likely. One quick conversation wasn't going to change their minds, after centuries of believing they were waiting for the Silver Dwarf.

That left two options: run or fight. He took one glance behind the dwarves, to the armour beyond, and knew the answer.

"Spread out," Ben said softly. "One shot, then arm yourselves. Don't shoot until they attack."

Ben expected Charlie, and possibly even Natalie, to protest, but they sidestepped silently to the right, while Krobeg went left. His hands suddenly felt sweaty, and he could feel the adrenaline coursing through his blood, fuelling his body with energy.

The arcane dwarves held their weapons well, but

they looked old, even for dwarves, and Ben couldn't imagine they could leap into action swiftly.

He was wrong.

There was no chorus of attack, just a sudden movement that caught Ben by surprise. They came forwards as one, with a speed Ben couldn't have believed possible at such an age.

Ben fired a dual-stunning spell, and a single pellet split in two, going for the two dwarves coming at him. They lifted a hand, and Ben watched in amazement as the spells swerved out of harm's way.

Magic. Of course, the arcane dwarves were capable of magic. He cursed inwardly for not expecting such a move.

Ben aimed a spell into his palm, and fired. A sword, tinted red, formed into his hand. Immediately, he felt the room slow, as the magic imbued in the sword enhanced his reflexes and reaction time. He was vaguely aware of Charlie and Natalie forming their own weapons and meeting their opponents with a clash. On his other side, he heard Krobeg give a wild cry and launch into battle. But any further attention to his friends was cut off, as Lidbank and the other dwarf cut at him. Even with his enhanced reflexes, Ben only just fended off the attacks. He aimed a quick riposte and caught the nameless dwarf just below the collarbone, and he cried out and went down. In response, Lidbank spun his sword and launched a flurry of cuts and thrusts, which had Ben backpedalling like mad. He was afraid he would hit the back wall, until he finally spotted an opening, and managed to launch a counter attack, halting his retreat. Summoning every ounce of strength and speed, he slowly pushed the dwarf back. They clashed swords and held their positions, leaning into each other. Ben looked into Lidbank's eyes – there was no fear there, but Ben could see sweat running down the dwarf's face. Yet, despite the exertion, the dwarf gave a hint of a smile and, with incredible strength, pushed Ben back.

"You are worthy," Lidbank said with a respectful nod. "I will take no pleasure in killing you."

"Nor I you," Ben said, returning the smile.

Ben used the brief break to steal a glance left and right. Krobeg had downed one dwarf, and was deep in combat with another. He could fight. Really fight. Despite everything, Ben couldn't help but be surprised. He turned the other way and saw Charlie and Natalie had also taken down one dwarf, but were struggling against the other. Charlie was bleeding, and Natalie looked dazed. But any chance of help was cut off when Ben saw a sword coming for his face. Ben brought his own sword up, and the battle resumed.

It seemed like an eternity of attacking and blocking, cutting and thrusting, but Ben was dimly aware that they had been fighting only minutes. A couple of times, Ben breached Lidbank's defences, but the arcane dwarf would throw up a magical shield or disappear for a split second. It became increasingly obvious that, with Lidbank's magic, they were evenly matched, and it would come down to a question of stamina.

Another cry came from his right, and Ben risked another glance. Natalie was down, clutching her head.

Ben cursed, and tried to make a move towards her, but Lidbank cut him off. Panic started to creep in. Charlie wouldn't survive long by himself. He had to do something, yet he was breathing hard, and had no energy left to launch a surprise attack.

"Krobeg!" he shouted.

"Busy," Krobeg grunted, momentarily throwing his opponent back.

Ben wiped his brow, surprised to find a mixture of sweat and blood on his hand. His sword felt heavy, but he summoned the last vestiges of his energy, awaiting the dwarf's next attack.

It never happened. The dwarf raised a clenched fist.

"Enough!" he said in a commanding voice. Immediately, the two remaining dwarves stepped back. Charlie was just about still standing. Krobeg looked better off, but his massive stomach was heaving with exertion.

"There has been enough blood shed," Lidbank said. "You have fought well, and because of that, I offer you one last chance. Your lives are not worth wasting. If you leave now, I can offer you safe passage home. That I promise you."

Ben admired Lidbank's integrity, and used the much needed break to gather his breath, and think. He desperately wanted to accept the dwarf's offer.

"We need the breastplate," Ben said, leaning on his sword. "We cannot leave without it."

"That is the one thing you cannot have," Lidbank said, almost sadly. "We have spent decades protecting it, waiting for the Silver Dwarf."

As exhausted as Ben was, he could tell the three remaining dwarves were hardly better off, on top of which, they were old, far older than he. Charlie could barely stand, but Krobeg looked in decent nick. Could he and Krobeg finish the three remaining dwarves? One look at the over-sized chef, twirling his axe, and Ben could tell Krobeg was thinking the same thing.

"That won't happen, I'm afraid," Lidbank said, as if reading Ben's thoughts.

Ben immediately spotted movement by the back statues, next to the pedestal holding the armour. Six more fully armoured arcane dwarves slipped out from behind the statues, and lined up behind Lidbank.

"Oh, darn," Ben said.

Any lingering thoughts about how they could grab the breastplate vanished. Ben's shoulders slumped, as he stared at the six fresh arcane dwarves. He focused on his spellshooter, but knew without looking he had no spell big enough to distract everyone long enough to pinch the armour. Even then, how would they escape?

Charlie, who had dragged a semi-conscious Natalie over to the side and out the way, stumbled over to his side.

"What now?" Charlie said, his voice almost delirious with exhaustion. "Personally, I'm rather tired. Not sure I can go on much longer."

"I could take out a few of them," Krobeg said. "Maybe you could make a dash for the armour?"

Ben glanced at Krobeg, and couldn't help smiling. "I can't believe you're saying that."

Krobeg shrugged. "We've come this far; I don't want to fail now."

Ben thought about Krobeg's idea, but was forced to discard it. It was too risky, even for him. They'd never make it out alive. There was only one way they could get out now, and that was without the breastplate.

"Lower your weapons," Ben said with a heavy heart.

Ben was just about to extinguish his sword, when another movement caught his eye. At first, it looked like a flicker of light; then a shadow caught his eye.

Three of the arcane dwarves suddenly screamed, as their helms were ripped off, and their throats cut. They fell to the floor, in a pool of blood.

Standing over them, barely visible even in the open, were three Shadowseekers. The sight of them was unmistakable: bald heads, gold piercings everywhere, and black cloaks that seemed to reflect light.

"Back!" Lidbank commanded.

The new arcane dwarves spun, and quickly backpedalled, but not before another one suffered a lightning quick thrust into the stomach, and went down. The remaining two arcane dwarves lined up beside the surviving three. Ben, Charlie and Krobeg joined them.

The three Shadowseekers advanced, sword drawn in one hand, purple ball of energy in the other. Ben stepped forwards, his own spellshooter drawn, and fired, just as the Shadowseekers did the same. Two of the purple balls were absorbed by Ben's white spinning disc, but one made it past. Ben dived towards it, and his natural dark elf defence deflected the purple ball away, sending it crashing harmlessly into the wall.

The instant Ben picked himself up, the Shadowseekers were upon them. The arcane dwarves were excellent fighters, but they were old, and three of them were already tired. The Shadowseekers were ruthless, and inhumanly fast. It was only the dwarf magic that kept them alive, magically deflecting or avoiding the Shadowseekers' blades.

Ben, along with Krobeg and Lidbank, stepped in, and the battle began again. From the corner of his eye, Ben was pleased to see Charlie step back, and attempt to pepper the Shadowseekers with spells.

Ben and Krobeg fought as a team against a Shadowseeker; somehow the dwarf managed to wield his battle axe with such dexterity that he was able to hold his own, while Ben sought the killer blow. He launched a quick stab to the chest, and pierced the elf right between the shoulder blades. The Shadowseeker went down, but not before swinging a return cut deep into Ben's shoulder. Ben cried out, but before the Shadowseeker could bury the sword further, Krobeg ended his life.

Ben's shoulder was in such agony he was forced to extinguish his sword, so he could clasp his hand on the injury to try to dull the pain.

There were just two Shadowseekers left, but, to Ben's despair, only three dwarves were still standing, including Lidbank. Krobeg stepped in to help, but Ben saw blood spilling from numerous cuts, slowing him down. Ben wanted to move, but the pain was so excruciating that his head started to spin. Beneath the pain, he was vaguely aware that their situation was desperate, and unless he did something now, they would be cut down.

It was Krobeg who acted. With a roar of defiance, he managed to barge past one of the Shadowseekers, and all of a sudden, he was sprinting towards the back of the shrine, towards the breastplate.

The Shadowseekers immediately turned and gave chase. Krobeg was quick, and he had the advantage of surprise, but he was no match for the Shadowseekers. Ben somehow managed to raise his spellshooter, and started firing, calling forth whatever spell he could latch on to. By some miracle, one of his spells hit the trailing Shadowseeker on the leg, tripping him up. Lidbank was on him before he could recover, and finished him off. Ben focused his spellshooter on the remaining Shadowseeker chasing Krobeg, but he knew he was too late.

Time seemed to slow, as Ben watched Krobeg reach the mannequin, and pull the breastplate off. In one smooth motion, he pulled it over his body. The breastplate had only just slipped over Krobeg's stomach, when the Shadowseeker's sword clattered into it, snapping in half on contact. The armour, just like the helm and the boots, moulded perfectly onto its

Guardian's body, and Krobeg went from a chef to something far more deadly in a matter of seconds.

Krobeg's eyes expanded, even as the armour did the same, and a sense of wonderment, of realisation, filled Krobeg's face, looking about the shrine as if he was seeing it for the first time.

The Shadowseeker, seeing Krobeg's distraction, pulled a knife from his cloak and leapt a full twenty feet, aiming for Krobeg's face. Ben screamed, and launched a series of spells in desperation, but Krobeg appeared not to notice, and was staring at the ceiling as the Shadowseeker's deadly knife sailed towards his face in a blur.

An arm extended, almost casually, blocking the knife and slamming into the Shadowseeker's face in one smooth, effortless motion. It took Krobeg a moment to realise what he'd done, looking down upon the motionless Shadowseeker.

There was a stunned silence. In a flash, the Shadowseekers were down, Krobeg wore the armour, and all eyes were on the chef. It took Ben a moment to realise why. His beard was no longer ginger. It had turned silver.

CHAPTER 37
THE SILVER DWARF

Ben's exhaustion and pain were momentarily forgotten as he stared at Krobeg. The breastplate fit him perfectly, making him look slightly slimmer somehow, but it was the face that made Ben's jaw drop. His hair and beard were an illustrious silver. They hadn't changed length, yet they looked thicker and fuller.

Krobeg was shaking his head slowly, and whispering, "It's not possible."

A series of sudden thuds made Ben turn and, to his astonishment, he saw the three remaining arcane dwarves bent down on one knee, heads bowed.

The Silver Dwarf. Krobeg. Could it be possible?

Krobeg slowly made his way towards them, still shaking his head. "This isn't right. Please, stand up. I'm not the Silver Dwarf."

The three dwarves rose. Lidbank was battered and bruised, his wrinkled face covered with blood, but he wore a tired smile.

"You are not the Silver Dwarf that was. But you are the Silver Dwarf. The prophesy has been fulfilled, though not in the manner we expected."

Krobeg looked at Ben with alarm. "Prophesy?"

"Long story," Ben said with a wave. He turned to Charlie and Natalie, who were both lying on the floor. Lidbank gave a sharp nod to his two colleagues.

"Help them."

Ben watched anxiously as the arcane dwarves hurried over to Charlie, Natalie and the others who had fallen. To his immense relief, Charlie started groaning almost as soon as the dwarves lay their hands upon him. Natalie took a while longer, but eventually she came to, rubbing her head and looking as though she'd just been hit by a truck. Two of the other dwarves also recovered, and the rest were carefully laid aside. Something ice cold touched his shoulder and the intense pain receded to a dull throb.

Ben felt like collapsing on the floor. They had done it. They had the Guardian, and they had his piece of armour. But one look at Krobeg and he knew his work wasn't done. The dwarf was still struggling to take everything in, occasionally glancing down at his breastplate – and his beard – to make sure it was real. Ben watched him carefully. This was the big test.

Was Krobeg ready? Was the chef ready to become a Guardian? Not only that, but a leader for the arcane dwarves, according to the prophesy? Ben could well understand the stunned expression on Krobeg's face.

"He reminds me of myself when I first discovered that goblins and stuff were real," Charlie said, hobbling over to Ben. "What do we do now? The arcane dwarves will be expecting him to lead them to glory, won't they? That's what the prophesy says."

"No."

Lidbank's voice was surprisingly strong. "You have, I fear, not read the prophesy, but some shortened version of it. Am I correct?"

"Probably," Charlie said with an embarrassed shrug.

"So what does it say?" Natalie asked, walking gingerly over to join them.

All eyes turned to Lidbank, who in turn focused on Krobeg, and recited. "The Silver Dwarf shall lead his tribe out of the blackness that envelopes this world, into the glory of light."

Charlie frowned. "How is that any different to what I said?"

"It's very different," the dwarf said.

Ben was surprised to see that Krobeg looked thoughtful, rather than horrified, at the dwarf's recital of the prophesy.

"I need to think," Krobeg said.

"I understand. We have waited centuries; we can wait a little longer."

Ben felt a little uneasy. Could Krobeg possibly be considering prioritising the prophesy over his role as a Guardian? He resisted the urge to ask; now was not the time.

The sound of Charlie and Natalie chatting among themselves made him turn.

"Well, we did it," Natalie said, as Ben joined them. She had a nasty welt on her head, but her elation and cheerfulness somehow shone through her battered body.

"Yeah. Now we have just the sword and shield left to find."

"And the sword is yours," Charlie said. "Which means we only have one Guardian left." His face soured a little. "Unfortunately, we've got no leads, not even a flying key or a faded photo."

"Let's worry about that later," Ben said. The last thing he wanted to do right now was think about the next piece of the armour. What he really needed was a bed.

"How do we get home?" Natalie asked. "Do you think those arcane dwarves are waiting for us outside? I hope they're not too mad."

"I don't think it matters if they were bloodthirsty. We've got the Silver Dwarf," Ben said.

Getting out happened to be easy, but getting home was another matter. The portal they had come through was no longer there, which meant they had to find another way back. Thankfully, the arcane dwarves escorted them back through Jimba Forest, and knew exactly where to go. The forest, such a dangerous place on the way in, seemed no scarier than the ones he was used to at home now that they were under the protection of the dwarves. Ben's thoughts drifted to the Shadowseekers. Their arrival had wreaked havoc, but had they not come, Krobeg may never have been desperate enough to grab the armour. But how had they got there in the first place?

"I wondered the same thing," Charlie said, when Ben voiced the question. "Jimba is too far away from home for them to have travelled here so quickly. They must have gone through the map, like we did."

"But how did they get into the shrine?" Natalie asked. "All those other arcane dwarves couldn't get in."

"Couldn't they? I'm not so sure whether they couldn't or if they felt they weren't allowed. Either way, the Shadowseekers got in the same way as the guards did. You didn't think they were just standing there endlessly waiting for us, did you?"

"I hadn't given it much thought. I was too busy getting stabbed," Natalie said.

"Those statues inside the shrine were hollow. They are connected to underground passages. That is how the Shadowseekers got in. Remember how good they are at getting into places? We found that out at the Institute."

With the Shadowseeker mystery resolved, Ben couldn't help turning his attention back to Krobeg. The dwarf chef had been remarkably quiet as they trudged through the forest, clearly deep in thought. Ben desperately wanted to find out what was going through Krobeg's mind, but knew better than to ask. Instead he resorted to glancing over at the dwarf every so often, in the hope of attracting his attention. Krobeg still had Elizabeth's Breastplate on, and Ben couldn't help wondering what ability it had imparted on the dwarf. He vividly remembered the way he had blocked the Shadowseeker's attack. Was it simply an improved ability in combat or something more?

It took a full two hours of walking before Krobeg gave any indication that he had come to a decision. The forest was starting to thin, allowing the evening sun to shine through. The walk was taking its toll on Ben's injured body, and it was all he could do to concentrate on placing one foot in front of the other. But the moment he saw Krobeg looking at him, the pain was forgotten.

"I've figured out what I need to do," Krobeg said. His voice was soft, but certain.

Ben attempted in vain to feign nonchalance. "Oh yeah?"

Krobeg nodded. "The prophesy says I will lead the arcane dwarves out of the darkness into the light. But it doesn't say how. That, I believe, is key. There is only one way I can lead the arcane dwarves into a world that isn't full of darkness."

"And what way is that?" Ben asked, trying not to hold his breath.

Krobeg gave a grim smile. "By defeating the one thing that is threatening the Unseen Kingdoms. The dark elves. King Suktar."

Ben wanted to raise his arm and cheer in exultation. Instead, he settled for a highly suppressed smile. "I couldn't agree more."

Krobeg gave a little glance around, noting that other than Charlie and Natalie, who were listening avidly, the rest of the arcane dwarves had their attention on the forest.

"So, tell me, what's the plan? I hear you're the man for plans."

Ben wasn't sure how long he and Krobeg spoke, but his conversation was so involved that he barely noticed when the forest cleared, revealing an old, seldom-used Dragonway station by the beach. He only vaguely remembered boarding the train or the journey home.

"Give me a week," Krobeg said, as he stepped out

of the carriage upon arriving at the London Dragonway. "There are some things I need to work out with the tavern."

Ben gave him a smile. "Oh, I think we'll need more than a week. We still have to find two more pieces of armour, remember?"

CHAPTER 38
A LITTLE REVENGE

Ben's alarm had never sounded so cruel at seven-thirty the following morning, and his initial reaction was to throw the thing onto the floor, with the hope of permanent damage. But something stayed his hand, a vague thought at the back of his head, telling him that he needed to get up.

Guardian? Check, job done. Breastplate? Done.

So why wasn't he going back to sleep? One late morning wouldn't kill him at the Institute. Dagmar, of all people, would understand.

Ben's eyes shot open, his heart attempting to jump out of bed without him.

The Chief Three election.

Ben sat up, suddenly wide awake. The result would have been announced yesterday afternoon. He was supposed to have spent yesterday morning garnering the last few votes. Not only had he missed that, but he'd missed the entire announcement.

Ben flew out of bed, and was out the door in five minutes flat, ringing Charlie on his way to the Dragonway.

"I only needed three more votes," Ben said, as they boarded the carriage to Taecia.

"I know," Charlie said. His face was glum, and he held on to the protective bars a little too tightly. "But you weren't there yesterday morning, which was probably the most important time. I can only imagine how Aaron would have taken advantage of that."

It was almost too horrible to think about. Aaron would have had open rein on any number of insults and lies as to why Ben hadn't turned up that morning, and there was nothing his team could have said in response.

But, despite all logic, Ben refused to believe the election had been a forgone conclusion. Those three votes could have gone either way; anything could have happened. William was a very persuasive character – perhaps he had pulled off something incredible.

As he and Charlie climbed the hill to the Institute, Ben realised he needed to come up with a semi-plausible excuse for yesterday's absence. The best he could think of was illness, but how would that explain Charlie and Natalie's disappearance? Some freak contagious bug? Ben sighed. It was so pathetic he wasn't even sure he could bring himself to say it. Part of him wished he could just hide in a hole for a week, until the whole thing blew over. No, that was wrong. He needed to deal with this head on, even if it meant getting pounded for a day or two.

Ben grit his teeth, and kept an eye out for a third-grader. It didn't matter who; he just needed to find out what happened so he could prepare himself.

They made it all the way to the entrance, before Ben spotted someone who would know the results.

"Uh oh," Charlie said. "Should we find someone else?"

"No," Ben said, and increased his pace.

The moment Simon turned and scowled at him, Ben knew that the outcome wasn't good.

"Oh, you decided to turn up," Simon said. Ben had never thought he would care about Simon's opinion, but the disgust in Simon's voice hurt.

"Yes, I did. I'm so sorry, Simon," Ben said. "What happened?"

Simon gave a scornful laugh. "What do you think happened? Without you, we had no chance. We were supposed to be electing you, remember? Bit pointless if you're not even there."

Ben suddenly felt light-headed, and his voice came out a whisper. "How much did we lose by?"

"Five votes." Simon shook his head, and even managed a weird laugh. "Aaron is the new Chief Three. And I'll tell you what, he hates me, but he hates you more, so good luck with that."

Simon turned and headed up the stairs, before Ben could think of a suitable reply. He turned to a grim-faced Charlie, who was at a loss for words for once.

"Ben!"

Natalie came darting through the entrance. Ben was vaguely aware that somehow she looked close to perfect again, the nasty bruise on her forehead almost gone. But her hair swung wildly, and her gasping breath made it clear she had been running.

"I just heard as I was coming off the Dragonway," she said. "I can't believe I had completely forgotten about the election. That bump to the head must have affected me worse than I thought."

Natalie's energy was a stark contrast to the dull apathy Ben was feeling. "You heard the result, then?"

"Yes, I heard," Natalie said. She frowned at him. "You can't beat yourself up over it. There was nothing you could have done."

"I could have turned up yesterday," Ben said, feeling slightly sour. "I think I could have made a difference."

"Don't be ridiculous," Natalie said angrily. The three of them started a slow ascent up the stairs, to the apprentice floor. "We made the right decision. The election was less important, you know that. It was just unfortunate the timing was so horrible."

Ben knew Natalie was right, but right now it didn't help much. He could feel the eyes of every third-grader on him as they entered the muster room. He felt like staring at the floor, but he forced himself to meet their gazes, as much as it hurt. He managed to keep his composure, though he almost lost it when Aaron strode into the room, moments before nine o'clock. Ben could see now that one of Aaron's colourless diamonds had a small glow round it, indicating his new position as Chief Three. Ben wished then that Aaron would give him some provocation he could react to, but Aaron glided serenely to his position as head of the third-graders in the line-up, with nothing more than a faint smile. Ben ground his teeth but kept his cool, though it was probably a good thing that Dagmar came in just moments later.

Ben was eager to get out of muster as soon as possible. He could feel the attention on him, and it wasn't pleasant. He just wanted to throw himself back into the apprenticeship, and put the painful incident of the Chief Three election behind him. But to his frustration, Dagmar had other ideas.

"Third-graders, remain. The rest of you, dismissed," Dagmar said, as soon as muster had finished.

Ben cringed. What could Dagmar possibly want to say? Surely it had nothing to do with the Chief Three election? Was she going to publicly dress him down? Ben cursed silently. Surely he had suffered enough – couldn't they just move on?

Dagmar surveyed the third-graders, tapping her baton on her open hand. Ben managed to catch her eye, but she didn't respond. Perhaps this had nothing to do with the Chief Three elections after all.

"I want to talk to you about yesterday's elections," Dagmar said.

Ben cursed silently, and felt several apprentices glance his way.

"The result, as you know, was a victory by five votes for Aaron," Dagmar said. "That, of course, stands. However, I do wish to bring up a minor point, which I think you should consider."

She paused, and Ben became aware that he was holding his breath. He could just about make out Aaron's polite, quizzical expression in front of him.

"Yesterday morning, Ben Greenwood was called upon by the Spellsword Department for an urgent assignment. This assignment was confidential, and Ben Greenwood was forced away from the Institute for the whole of yesterday. I would like to note that he completed this task successfully, and the Spellsword Department wishes to convey their appreciation."

Ben was vaguely aware that his mouth was hanging open, and he shut it, before people realised how surprised he was. Dagmar was flat out lying. It was unheard of, but it certainly had the desired effect. He received several forgiving looks, especially from his team. Simon even had the good grace to blush, and William gave an approving nod. Ben felt a tightness around his shoulders disappear, and it felt wonderful. He had to resist the urge to beam gleefully, and instead calmly acknowledged the looks he got. But best of all was Aaron's expression – it looked as though he'd just swallowed a lemon.

"Apprentices, dismissed," Dagmar said.

Ben received several claps on the shoulder and more than one apology from an apprentice who had doubted him. The majority of Aaron's team left in double-quick time; few looked him in the eye as they passed.

"I wish Dagmar would let us re-do the election," Simon said. He still looked disgruntled, but the anger that had been directed at Ben was now clearly aimed elsewhere.

"So do I," Ben said. "It was just bad timing."

Simon gave a shrug and muttered something that Ben suspected was an apology.

"I knew it would all work out," Natalie said with a smile, as they made their way to the common room.

"How'd you figure that?" Charlie asked.

"Oh, you know, karma," Natalie said with a shrug.

"Karma?"

Ben left the two of them bickering as he popped upstairs to pick up his spellshooter. He still couldn't believe Dagmar had lied for him. What if she got caught out? He wondered if she had somehow collaborated with Wren, though he couldn't see how that was possible, without giving away what they'd been doing.

Spellshooter in hand, Ben headed back down to the common room. Most apprentices had already left to study and the corridors were empty. A shadow caught his eye just as he was about to enter the common room.

"Ah, Ben. Just the person I was hoping to meet."

Ben looked up, and saw Aaron walking towards him. Ben couldn't help glancing again at Aaron's diamonds.

"Nice, isn't it?" Aaron said, looking at his shoulder. "Not flashy, but just enough to remind people that I stand above the other third-graders, including yourself."

"Very nice," Ben said. The last person he felt like talking to was Aaron, especially as he had been in such a good mood. But Aaron raised a hand as Ben was about to enter the common room.

"Just a second, if you please," Aaron said.

Ben paused, as Aaron approached. Despite his perfect poise and perfect dress, Ben couldn't help thinking Aaron resembled a snake, slithering his way forwards.

"Remember my promise?" Aaron said. His voice was soft, and there was a glint in his eye. "If I won the election, you would suffer. Do you remember that?"

"Vaguely," Ben admitted. "To be honest, I don't pay much attention to most of the drivel that comes out of your mouth."

Aaron gave a little laugh. "A nice riposte, very good." The laughter faded, replaced by something rather more serious. "I wasn't joking, Ben. From now on, your time in the third grade is going to be rather less pleasant. I have seen to that. There will be unpleasant chores, lots of them. They all need doing, of course, so you will be putting in valuable work, though perhaps not of your own choosing."

Aaron chuckled at his own joke, and Ben felt a shiver run down his spine. What sort of jobs was Aaron referring to? He recalled his first-grade days, when he was forced to shovel animal pooh.

"You'll find out this afternoon," Aaron said, correctly guessing what was going through Ben's head. He started walking away, shaking his head and chuckling to himself. But after just a few steps, he turned around. "Oh, and Ben – don't expect to see too much of Natalie or Charlie. I've taken great pains to make sure you three aren't together all the time."

Ben had somehow managed to keep a rein on his temper, but the tide finally broke, and he lost it. He raised his spellshooter, took aim, and fired. A swirling, spinning boomerang shot towards Aaron, and pinned him against the wall by the neck, lifting him from his feet. Aaron's hands scrabbled with the boomerang, his legs kicking. Ben walked up to him, and pointed his spellshooter so that the tip of the barrel was touching Aaron's nose.

"Listen to me," Ben said, his voice surprisingly calm. "I don't care about the chores you give me, but if you try to stop me from seeing my friends, we are going to have a problem. Do I make myself clear?"

Aaron somehow managed to shake his rapidly reddening face. The satisfaction on seeing Aaron struggling was extremely gratifying, and he let the moment linger.

It lingered just that bit too long.

The sound of quick, heavy footsteps sounded, and Ben barely had time to look up, when Dagmar appeared from round the corner. She took in the scene in one smooth glance, and stopped right in front of Ben. She glanced at the struggling Aaron, and then back at Ben. Her impassive expression didn't change one jot.

"Did you get what you were looking for yesterday?" Dagmar asked.

The question was possibly the last thing Ben expected, and it took him a moment to realise what she was talking about.

"Yes, we got it. Just two left now."

Dagmar nodded. "Very good." She gave another appraising look at Aaron. "You may want to release him; I think he's about to lose consciousness."

Before Ben could comply, Dagmar marched off, without so much as a backward glance. Ben released the spell, and Aaron gasped for breath, clutching his neck. He tried to speak, but his normally perfect vocal cords wouldn't comply. He glanced at the direction Dagmar had disappeared to, and promptly decided to head the other way.

Ben grinned, as Aaron skulked off.

Perhaps having Aaron as Chief Three wasn't going to be as bad as he thought. He headed into the common room, searching out Charlie and Natalie, feeling better than he had in a long time.

NEXT IN THE ROYAL INSTITUTE OF MAGIC SERIES

COMING SOON...

Vinci-books.com/thelastguardian

With the final two pieces of the Armour still missing and the last Guardian yet to be found, Ben must navigate a treacherous path. His only lead comes from a dangerous and unreliable source, forcing him to question everything he knows.

Turn the page for a free preview...

THE LAST GUARDIAN: CHAPTER ONE

UNLIKELY ALLIES

Date: *3rd January 1603*

Michael Greenwood glanced up at the extravagant house, and knew there was going to be trouble. Rumour had it that this was the most expensive residence in London – a rumour, no doubt spread by its owner, Lord Samuel, Guardian of Elizabeth's Shield.

Michael gave a firm rap of the iron-wrought handle, and waited. He wasn't armed, as he knew Samuel would never let him inside with a sword or spellshooter. He shouldn't have any need for weapons, but with Lord Samuel, you never knew.

Michael heard the sound of footsteps from within and composed himself. Lord Samuel had requested the meeting, and though he hadn't said what it was about, Michael had a good idea.

Queen Elizabeth's Armour.

The specifics of the conversation were a little harder to guess, as the queen's instructions had been very clear. Those entrusted as Guardians were to safeguard their designated piece of armour until the dark elf king, Suktar, returned.

Michael was still pondering the matter when the door swung open. Samuel's butler was dressed in an immaculate, tailored black suit, which was probably more expensive than anything Michael owned.

"Mr. Greenwood," the butler said with a slight bow. "Do come in. Lord Samuel has been waiting."

Michael stepped inside to a grand hall that was almost as big as his entire house. A lavish staircase ran up the middle, and split two ways to an open gallery. There were large portraits lining the walls, most of them of Samuel, though a few were of his family.

"This way, please, Mr. Greenwood," the butler said, directing him with a pristine, white-gloved hand.

Michael followed the butler through several drawing rooms, each lavishly decorated by Lady Samuel, until they reached a set of double doors, which the butler pushed open and walked through, Michael following just behind.

As magnificent as the previous rooms were, this one rivalled the queen's palace. Perhaps that was the idea, Michael thought. A huge, glistening chandelier hung from the ceiling, casting a soft light on thick carpet and lavish furniture. The room was so large, it was divided into sections. There was a reading area and a section for music, complete with a grand piano. Small tables, decorated with flowers, vases and antiques, were dotted everywhere.

"Greenwood. You decided to turn up, I see," a deep, overbearing voice said.

Lord Samuel sat, legs crossed, on a black leather couch, holding a drink. It had been only a week since they had last met, but Samuel seemed to have managed to gain a few pounds, mainly around the chin. His hair, too, somehow seemed thinner, but he compensated that with a thick, perfectly groomed moustache.

He didn't get up, nor did he offer Michael a drink. The couch Samuel sat on was large, but the big man somehow seemed to consume most of it, so Michael chose a small chair nearby. He noted the spellshooter strapped to Samuel's waist, but was careful not to show any concern.

"I shan't waste both our time with social pleasantries," Lord Samuel said. Michael had to resist the urge to put a finger in his ear to partially mute Samuel's booming voice. "You must know why you're here."

"Not really," Michael said with a shrug. "I'm

assuming it's something to do with Elizabeth's Armour."

"Of course it is," Samuel said, tapping his glass impatiently. "But more than that, it's about the mistake our queen made, most likely due to her poor health."

"What mistake is that?" Michael asked.

"You know very well," Samuel said. His face looked a little red, but Michael couldn't tell if it was from the drink or his simmering anger. "I'm referring to the fact that she put you in charge. She made *you* the Head Guardian."

Michael couldn't help noticing the contemptuous way in which Lord Samuel said "you".

"It was her choice," Michael said, keeping his voice light.

"Impossible," Lord Samuel said. His moustache twitched as he shook his head. "Her decision was clearly clouded by her ill health. Have you seen her recently? She won't last much longer."

Michael couldn't argue that point. The queen was now confined to bed and, with a heavy heart, he knew it wouldn't be long before they had a new commander at the Institute.

"I saw her recently and was sorry to see that she was so poorly," Michael said with a nod.

Samuel seemed to relax a little at this. "Then you

agree that her decision was not made with a clear mind?"

"No," Michael said firmly. "I remember well when she summoned us and told us about her armour. She was as lucid as you or me."

"Absolute nonsense!" Lord Samuel said, slapping a great big thigh. He gave Michael a sneer, his perfectly groomed moustache rising up to his nose. "Do you really think she would choose you, a baker's boy, over me on such an important mission? It defies all logic and reason."

Michael could always tell when Samuel was getting worked up by his large nostrils, which would start flaring. They were doing so now, reminding Michael of a pig sniffing for food.

"I believe she had a reason for her choice," Michael said, keeping his voice calm. "I think we should trust her."

Lord Samuel hauled himself up with surprising ease, and starting trooping round the couch.

"I don't believe it," Lord Samuel said. "I can't believe it. Do you realise what sort of responsibility she has entrusted you with? Suktar will return one day, and your bloodline will be responsible for finding the Guardians and gathering Elizabeth's Armour to stand against him."

"I'm aware of that."

"I don't think you are," Lord Samuel said, shaking his head. "No, it's madness. I cannot accept it."

Michael had to quell his own frustration. "What do you suggest?"

Lord Samuel turned to him, and placed both hands on his chest. "Let me take on the burden. I have the resources. My family is large, rich, and powerful. We have the ability to track the Guardians over the centuries, if need be."

Michael saw a sincerity in Samuel's small, brown eyes that wasn't born of selfishness, but genuine concern.

"I'm sorry, Samuel," Michael said. "Queen Elizabeth chose me for a reason. I truly believe that. I will not betray her on this. Those are my final words."

Michael decided against mentioning the real reason he felt the queen chose him – it would only infuriate Samuel further.

"Stubborn boy!" Lord Samuel said, slapping a hand on his thigh. "You risk jeopardising this entire mission with your stupidity."

Michael stood up, his eyes narrowing. "We are done here, I think. Is there anything else you wanted to go over?"

Lord Samuel's hand hovered over his spellshooter, and Michael's heart lurched, but he pretended not to notice. Samuel stood very still, staring hard at Michael.

"I will not," Lord Samuel said stiffly. "I cannot allow my family to be led by the family of a baker's boy. It is demeaning, insufferable and it will not be endured."

Michael stared right into Lord Samuel's brown eyes. They looked slightly bloodshot, whether from the drink or simply from his blood boiling, Michael didn't know. What he did know was that Lord Samuel was on the verge of one of his famous outbursts. Michael could remember only too well when Samuel last lost his temper – little of the Diplomacy meeting room was left undamaged.

Eight feet, Michael estimated. Eight feet between them. Could he leap that far and reach Samuel before he drew his spellshooter? Despite his bulk, the man was no slouch, especially with a spellshooter.

Michael inched forwards, pointing his finger at Lord Samuel. "This isn't a game, Samuel. The future of our nation, of the world, is at stake," Michael said. He kept his anger in check, mostly. "I don't want your sense of self-importance getting in the way. You are responsible for the shield. Remember what the queen said? The Guardian of Elizabeth's Shield will be responsible for blocking Suktar's deadly blows, so that the Guardian of Elizabeth's Sword can strike the killer thrust. That means your family and mine are going to be working together. It might not happen in our lifetimes, it might not happen for centuries, but it *will* happen."

Lord Samuel stared at him, his hand inching closer to his spellshooter. Michael eased forwards a little more, and continued talking.

"When it does happen, your descendant had better be a little more accommodating to mine. Do I make myself clear?"

The moment he spoke, he knew he'd gone too far.

Lord Samuel drew his spellshooter so quickly that Michael barely had time to move.

"You've made yourself abundantly clear," Lord Samuel said. "Now, get out of my house."

Michael resisted the urge to duck for cover and held his ground. "Hide the shield well, Samuel."

Samuel's finger twitched on the trigger. "Get out, *now*."

Michael knew he was in danger, but he bit his lip and remained where he was. He was the Head Guardian; he had a responsibility, no matter what Samuel thought.

"The shield," Michael said again, his voice soft. "I need to know that you have a well-thought-out plan for keeping it safe."

To Michael's surprise, Lord Samuel gave a little smirk. "The shield will be well hidden. It will make finding your sword look hopelessly simplistic."

Michael knew he wasn't going to get any more

from Lord Samuel without risking getting his head blown off.

"We'll be in touch," Michael said with a little salute.

Michael left, expecting at any moment to feel the soaring heat of a spell smash into his back. To his great relief, it was only curses, not spells, that Lord Samuel let fly as he departed.

THE LAST GUARDIAN: CHAPTER TWO

DANGER IN THE SKY

Present Day

"Can you stop that thing from spitting acid?" Charlie shouted, as he darted left to avoid a spurt of green liquid. "I happen to value my life."

"Working on it," Ben grunted. He was straddled on the wyvern's neck, and had a huge acid-resistant toothbrush with which he was attempting to brush the wyvern's teeth. "Come on, Thomas, do we have to go through this every single time?"

There was laughter coming from around the paddock. From the corner of his eye, Ben could just make out a dozen apprentices, Aaron amongst them, watching on as he, Charlie, Natalie and Abigail attempted to clean the most ill-tempered wyvern in the Institute.

Despite the fact that apprentices were supposed to rotate cleaning duty, to better understand each beast, they had landed the task of cleaning Thomas every single week for the last month. Of course, it didn't take a genius to work out why – Aaron was the one responsible for the rota.

“Got it!” Ben said triumphantly, as he cleaned the last bit of rot from the wyvern's front teeth.

“Oh, well done,” Abigail said. She was standing just out of harm’s way, but still inside the wyvern's paddock. In her hands was a clipboard that she was looking at intently. “Next are the ears. Are you ready, Ben?”

She bent down and produced a soapy sponge from a bucket next to her. With a throw of considerable accuracy, she launched it up to Ben, who reached out a hand and snagged it, while still holding on to the wyvern's neck. He went to work on the back of the ears, trying to ignore the smell of pus. He took a quick glance down and saw Charlie working on the wyvern's body, and Natalie the tail. They had tried several different cleaning combinations, but this one worked the best.

“Don't forget inside the ears! Remember what happened last time?” a voice said, laughing.

Ben would have liked to identify the voice, so he

could clobber him round the ear when he'd finished, but he was too busy hanging on for dear life. His left hand slipped a little and he almost lost his grip on the wyvern, resulting in more laughter.

"Done with the body," Charlie said, wiping a hand over his brow. He looked up at Ben, who was slowly losing his grip. Wyverns didn't like having their ears touched, and Thomas was especially sensitive. "You almost done, Ben? I'm getting hungry."

"Getting there," Ben said, snaking his way back up the wyvern. He dropped the sponge, and Abigail immediately threw up a Q-Tip that must have been at least a foot long. Ben caught it expertly. He took a deep breath, and made sure he had a firm grip on the wyvern. This was always the worst part. Cringing slightly, he shoved the Q-Tip into the wyvern's giant ear, and turned it. There was a squelching noise that always made Ben's stomach heave. The wyvern cried out and reared its head, shooting acid skywards. Some of it fell back down on Ben, but his protective jacket stopped the acid from reaching his skin. He pulled the Q-Tip out and applied it to the other ear, receiving the same treatment from the wyvern.

"Done!" he said, leaping off the wyvern, and landing next to Abigail. He quickly threw the Q-Tip in the bucket and the four of them moved out of harm's way. The wyvern gave Ben a baleful look, before waddling away, back to the centre of the paddock.

"Twenty-seven seconds slower than last week," Aaron said, tapping his expensive-looking watch. "I'm a little disappointed. You will keep cleaning Thomas until you can get the job done in under ten minutes."

Ben checked his anger. He was too exhausted to come up with a retort, though Natalie and Charlie gave Aaron hateful stares, which Aaron seemed to enjoy and responded to with a pleasant smile. Ben couldn't help noticing that while most of the apprentices were caked with sweat and dirt, Aaron looked as though he'd just bathed and dressed. There was not a hair out of place. However, few people seemed to care that he'd done no actual work. Indeed, many of the female apprentices probably hadn't even noticed, being too busy staring at that strong jaw and dark, smouldering eyes.

"Let's get going," Aaron said. "Thanks to your less than impressive time cleaning old Thomas, you've made the rest of us late for lunch. I've half a mind to make you clean the dishes to make up for the damage."

Tiredness suddenly forgotten, Ben was about to tell him what he thought about that idea.

He never got the chance.

A high-pitched screeching noise made them all jump. As one, they turned their heads skywards, and immediately saw the perpetrator. It flew at an altitude similar to a small plane, but Ben could still make out its massive bat-like wings on its long, slender body.

"Get inside, now," Aaron said, humour forgotten.

Even as they moved towards the rooftop door, Ben saw a couple of Spellswords burst out and run to a pair of giant eagles. Within moments they were airborne, and gaining altitude, fast. But as swift as the eagles soared, Ben knew they were unlikely to catch their target.

Ben followed the rest of the apprentices inside, and they headed down the main staircase. Stomachs were rumbling, but lunch was the last thing on their minds.

"That's the fifth ptryad this week," Charlie said. "They're getting braver to be able to scout Taecia so easily for the dark elves."

"Our Spellswords will catch them," Ben said, trying to sound convincing.

"I doubt it. As well as being the ultimate spying beast, they can also fly at a great pace. With their insanely keen eyesight, they'll spot the eagles and be halfway home before the Spellswords can get that high."

"You're full of optimism this morning," Natalie said, giving Charlie a poke in the back. She and Abigail were a step behind Charlie and Ben as they headed down.

"Sorry, I can't help it. At this rate, they'll know Taecia inside out before the end of the month."

"Does that matter, though?" Natalie asked. "They'd never dare invade Taecia."

"No, but I've read about those ptryads. They can hear a bee buzzing from a mile high. The Institute has already had to cast spells to make sure they're not eavesdropping on us."

"They might be nasty, but they look cool," Abigail said with a distant smile. "They are so graceful, the way they fly."

Charlie scratched his nose. "Yes, I think you might be missing the point here."

Ben leapt down the last steps, and headed towards lunch, his stomach rumbling. "You guys haven't forgotten about Dagmar, have you?"

"The meeting? No," Natalie said. "I wonder what she wants to talk about."

"I think I can guess," Charlie said, though he didn't elaborate with apprentices everywhere. "Did you see how serious she was? Even more so than usual. I think it's important."

"I saw," Ben said. "Come on, let's grab some lunch, and worry about that later."

THE LAST GUARDIAN: CHAPTER THREE

THE CRIMSON TOWER

"I have several announcements to make," Dagmar said.

Ben and the rest of the apprentices stood to attention, ears perked. Despite the increasing turmoil from the dark elves, Dagmar remained as unflustered as ever. He sometimes forgot that she was so small, such was her presence. She held her baton and stood so straight Ben long suspected that there might be another baton thrust down her back. Her only concession to extravagance was a pair of green shoes that would have been too big for most people double her size.

"For those of you able to cast level-four spells, we will be supplying long-range tracking spells, which you are to fire at any ptryads you see. Needless to say, if you are in the Seen Kingdoms, make sure you do it discreetly."

There weren't many apprentices who could cast level-four spells, but Ben was one of them.

"Secondly, for those who took exams at Barrington's, your results have come in."

Dagmar pointed to her desk, on which were several white envelopes. There were a few intakes of breath, though Ben barely reacted. He had taken the bare minimum of subjects and wasn't overly optimistic about his results. The exams were mandatory and were ordinarily an important part of the education system, but with Ben's plans firmly set on becoming an Institute member, he really wasn't that bothered and was glad to be done with school. Charlie, on the other hand, was shifting from foot to foot, clearly desperate to find out what his results were. He was one of the few people who would continue to study at Barrington's, taking advanced levels.

"Thirdly, the executive council has asked me to brief you on the latest situation with the dark elves."

There was an inevitable murmur of voices, which Dagmar quickly silenced with a raised hand.

"As apprentices, there is much I cannot tell you, but at the same time, your position gives you the right to know more than those outside the Institute."

She paused, scanning faces. There was an expectant, almost deathly silence. Ben was just as eager for information as the rest of them. It had been a month since they had found the Guardian Krobeg and Elizabeth's Breastplate, and it didn't take a genius to notice that the dark elves had since made rapid, almost frightening progress in their quest to conquer the Unseen Kingdoms. To make things more frustrating, Ben, Charlie and Natalie had made little progress in searching for the final two pieces of Elizabeth's Armour, as well as the missing Guardian.

"The dark elves have now conquered seven Unseen Kingdoms, and another seventeen are in lock-down mode, only accessible if you have a special pass, issued by the Diplomacy Department. We are helping those kingdoms as best we can with resources and Spellswords, though we are stretched. However, that is not the most pressing matter at the moment."

Ben wasn't sure if she paused for dramatic effect, but it certainly worked, as he could see some of the apprentices physically craning their necks forwards, willing her to speak.

"It has probably not escaped your notice that we are beginning to fortify the south coast of England. We have established small outposts, and are working on stationing larger defensive units there."

"Why are we doing that? Surely the dark elves are focusing on the Unseen Kingdoms?" a new voice asked, clearly unused to Dagmar's policy of silence.

Thankfully, she accepted the question without reprimand.

"It seems as though the dark elves' ultimate goal might end up being not the Unseen Kingdoms, but the Seen ones," Dagmar said.

Ben had strongly suspected that might be the case, but it still shocked him to hear Dagmar say it with such frankness. Several more voices piped up, but Dagmar's fleeting generous mood had disappeared.

"We do not know this for sure, but we cannot rule it out, for the consequences would be great," Dagmar said. "For now, the executive council does not wish to reveal any more information on this."

There was a groan from the apprentices, but nobody dared venture any further questions. Nevertheless, Dagmar waited for complete silence before continuing.

"I have one final announcement, and it is by no means the least important. Just because the dark elves are causing mischief, that is no reason to start slacking on your studies. There will be times where you will be expected to help the Institute, but that simply means when you are studying, I expect you to work harder. You all have deadlines to make, and several of you will soon be graduating to Institute members. Do I make myself clear?"

There was a military-like chorus of agreement,

though Ben couldn't help noticing one or two disgruntled looks.

"Good. Dismissed," Dagmar said, and she promptly clomped out of the room.

Charlie and Natalie darted towards Dagmar's desk and, amongst a multitude of arms, grabbed their exam result letters. Ben did the same, with considerably less enthusiasm. He ripped it open, his heart giving a little flutter as he took out the small slip of paper. As soon as he saw the results, his concern turned to relief.

"An A and three Bs," Ben said, smiling. "Not bad, given that I barely did anything."

"Six As!" Natalie said with a squeal of delight, flinging her arms round Ben's neck.

Charlie, however, was looking at his card with genuine confusion. "That can't be right. They've only given me an A for Geography."

"Only an A?" Ben said. "What were your other results?"

"Eleven A*s." Charlie shook his head, looking genuinely put out. "My parents aren't going to be happy. They were expecting A*s across the board."

"They'll be fine," Ben said, wrapping an arm around Charlie's shoulder. "Now, we should get going. Dagmar is expecting us, remember?"

A meeting with Dagmar was normally enough to focus them, but as they left the room and walked down the corridor, Charlie was clearly still thinking about the exam results, right up to the point when Ben rapped on Dagmar's door.

"Come in," Dagmar said.

Ben led them into the office, which was neat as always, though lately he had noticed a sizeable number of files on her desk. Dagmar remained seated, but she stopped writing and looked up as they entered. Ben, Charlie and Natalie approached the desk with their customary deference.

Dagmar pulled out a rustic red key and placed it on her desk. "That's your key to get in."

Ben frowned. "Sorry, key to what?"

Dagmar returned to her writing for a moment, before looking up again. "You didn't think we were going to have a meeting here, did you?"

"What's wrong with here?" Charlie asked.

Dagmar finished her writing with a flourish and put her pen down with a sharp snap. "Too risky, with the dark elves."

Ben couldn't hide his surprise. "You think the dark elves have got in here? I thought the Institute was the most secure place there was."

"Yes, it's secure from a direct attack," Dagmar said. "But the dark elves are masters of infiltration, and the executive council is concerned that their reeters might have sneaked in."

"Reeters?"

"They are tiny lizards. They can get into almost anywhere, and are nearly impossible to detect as they are masters of camouflage."

"So we're being listened to?" Charlie asked, looking around furtively.

"Unlikely," Dagmar said. "The Institute has sophisticated magical defences, so even the smallest bug shouldn't be able to get in. But it's better to be safe, especially given what we will be talking about."

"Makes sense," Ben said, pocketing the key.

"Your destination is the Crimson Tower," Dagmar said.

"Ooh!" Natalie exclaimed, before she could help herself. "Sorry – I've heard a lot about the tower from my parents, and I've always wanted to go there, though they never let me."

"It is only used for very specific purposes – confidential meetings being one of them. I trust you know where to go?"

"Oh yes," Natalie said.

"Good. I will be there within the hour. I will meet you there," Dagmar said.

She picked up her pen and began writing again, signalling the end of the meeting. But as they were about to exit the door, Dagmar cleared her throat, making them turn.

"Make sure you shake off your tail," Dagmar said, looking pointedly at Ben.

"My tail?"

"Aaron's lackeys," Dagmar said. There was rarely a hint of emotion in her voice, but Ben was sure he detected a modicum of disdain when voicing Aaron's name. "He'll have a couple following you. I'll leave you to deal with them, but they absolutely cannot know we are going to the Crimson Tower."

Vinci-books.com/thelastguardian

About the Author

Victor Kloss was born in 1980 and lived his first five years in London, before moving to a small town in West Sussex. By day he built websites, by night he wrote (or tried to).

His love for Children's Fantasy stemmed from Enid Blyton, Tolkien, and recently, J.K. Rowling. His hobbies included football, golf, reading and taking walks with his wife and daughter.

Victor passed away on 5 November 2016 after fighting a losing battle against an aggressive form of lymphoma.

www.ingramcontent.com/pod-product-compliance
Lightning Source LLC
LaVergne TN
LVHW030914080826
845145LV00013B/2895